Lucy's Launderette

BETSY BURKE

was born in London, England, and grew up on the West Coast of Canada. She has a Bachelor of Music from the University of Victoria. Among the many jobs on her résumé, she includes opera singer, dishwasher, guitar teacher, nurse's assistant, charwoman, mural painter, salesclerk, puppeteer, English teacher and, most recently, freelance translator. She currently lives in Italy. Her interests include art, music, books, rejection-slip origami, turning the planet into a garden rather than a toxic waste dump and trying to convince her four-year-old daughter that chocolate is not a breakfast food. She is also the author of a murder-mystery set in Florence.

First edition September 2003

LUCY'S LAUNDERETTE

A Red Dress Ink novel

ISBN 0-373-25034-7

© 2003 by Elizabeth Burke.

Visit Red Dress Ink at www.reddressink.com

Printed in Canada

Lucy's Launderette

BETSY BURKE

**RED
DRESS
INK**
™

Many thanks to Liz Jennings, Jean Fanelli Grundy,
Salva, Sara, Mom, Kato, Yule Heibel,
Margaret O'Neill Marbury and Kathryn Lye.

For David Burke

"Your prince could show up anytime, anywhere." My mother's words. Words not to be discounted, I'd decided. It hadn't exactly been a bumper year in the man department. Winter had come with a vengeance and I spent a lot of time shivering under my duvet, finding true love and sensual thrills in hot paperbacks and the occasional Belgian chocolate hedgehog, emphasis on hog.

To make things worse, Anna the Viking, legs that never quit, mind that never started, had moved in the month before. Ours was one of those West End Vancouver apartments just off Davie Street, post-war Bauhaus sterile, nice hardwood floors, but with walls made of meringue. It became pretty clear after a couple of weeks that Anna was going to be the star of an ongoing Bonkfest that I would have to endure through the connecting wall of our bedrooms.

Anna was from Sweden and had men…and more men,

and I don't think conversation ever blighted her relationships. But none of them were THE ONE, because she would have stuck with him for more than a night. Let's face it; it takes energy to find THE ONE, and I mean the kind of man who can walk, talk, dress himself and doesn't have his finger up his nose while sitting alone in his car waiting for the light to change.

I was running on empty that winter. Too long out of university to consider myself a student, I was determined not to run with my tail between my legs to my parents' mind-numbingly tranquil suburb of Cedar Narrows. What would I do in Cedar Narrows anyway? It had all the vestiges of a self-sufficient town: shopping malls, cinemas, brand-new homes for families of ten, churches, schools, more shopping malls; it had everything but a soul of its own. For me it had always been like one huge waiting room in a train station. The last stop before the real city.

So I'd given in to financial pressure and let Anna move in. With her ThighMaster, her mini-trampoline and her G-string. I tried turning the heat right down but she still paraded mostly naked around the living room.

For the Viking's share of the rent, I'd packed up what had been my studio into cardboard boxes and toted it all downstairs to the storage rooms. It was like locking my children away. Okay, ugly and deformed children, but my children nonetheless. Besides, how could I call myself an artist when I wasn't even making art?

Not only was I a non-artist, but it had been so long since I'd had a decent relationship that I was considering the possibilities of romance on distant shores. I was still worth a couple of camels, at least.

There had been Frank, the "writer," the year before, but he didn't qualify as a decent boyfriend. He hadn't even been a diamond in the rough. He was a zircon, emphasis on con, and it was because of him that I was forced to rent the spare room to Anna.

Frank had all the requirements of a writer, the B.A. in English, the promising first half of a first novel rewritten a hundred times then abandoned for the first half of another promising first novel. He had the permanent three-day growth of beard, the scruffy corduroy jacket, the scotch and Gauloise halitosis, not to mention the scumbag buddies who always seemed to be flopping on my couch for the night. And could he talk! But lately, he confided in me, he was suffering from some kind of burnout or writer's block. He just couldn't seem to commit all those fine words to paper, just couldn't push past it. That would have required hard work and hard work, as I found out too late, wasn't really Frank's line. My bank account and I were relieved to be rid of him.

My only source of income was my job at Rogues' Gallery in Gastown. Over the four years I'd worked there, it had lost its glamorous sheen. I was still getting minimum wage and still being called the assistant manager, a term that meant glorified gopher. Being a gopher for my boss, the oh-so-miraculously thin Nadine Thorpe, meant an exaggerated number of trips to all the delicatessens and pastry shops in the neighborhood. But more about that later.

My situation was so tragic that winter that I even flirted with the idea of exploiting what little suppleness remained in my bod, a plumpish but pleasant twenty-nine-year-old bod, to find some rich old codger who would set me up as his bit of naughty. At least then I'd have a studio. But I just didn't have it in me. My parents, in spite of all the odds against it, had brought me up with moral fiber, as well as plenty of the other kind.

And it snowed a lot that year, something that doesn't happen often on the West Coast. The sky loomed steely gray then dumped far more than was needed to make the scene quaint. Heavy snowfalls would have been okay if it had been my dream life, the one where me and some gorgeous hetero-sexual man are walking through the white wonderland dis-cussing post-post-modernism, then returning home to drink brandy in front of the fireplace that my apartment didn't have. Instead, it went on and on. The dark days of work at Rogues' Gallery, mounting dreary exhibits by gay friends of Nadine's, the works all heavily concentrated on the male member, Na-dine drawling at me in her phony English accent to get the phalluses erected, then ordering me out to slip and slide through the slush to the bakery to get her daily ration of a couple dozen pastries; then the dark nights of insomnia, the Viking and her conquests sloshing and moaning in the wa-terbed next door, and me, with the pillow over my head try-ing not to listen.

And then one morning, I looked out my window, and the sun was shining. Not that brittle, illusive midwinter sun, but the sun you can feel when you've turned the corner into spring, the warming hardworking sun. I made myself a cap-puccino and sat down to enjoy it at the kitchen table, think-ing, good, now the snow is melting, the ground is showing through, the winter is finally over. And then the phone rang.

"Lucy." It was my father.

"Hi, Dad. How're things?"

"It's Jeremy." Jeremy was my father's father. My favorite grandfather.

"What about Jeremy?"

"He's dead." My father's tone was odd, like Jeremy de-served what he got.

I couldn't speak and when enough silence had gone by, my father said, "They tell me he was doing at least a hundred on his Harley. He went into a ravine up the coast. The funeral's the day after tomorrow."

"Will you be there?" I asked.

"I haven't decided yet."

"Your prince could show up anytime, anywhere." In which case it was going to be a beautiful day for a funeral. Going on the principle that our mothers can be right from time to time, I decided that if my prince was going to be there, I was going to make sure he didn't miss me. I look good in black, and thanks to my old university friend, Sky Robertson, I had the clothes.

Sky manages the Retro Metro Boutique for the owner, Max Kinghorn. Max lives in Seattle and is hardly ever there, so Sky has a free hand.

She and I share the same tastes in a lot of things, especially clothing. We have other worlds in our heads. One of them is black-and-white, with sleek women in well-tailored suits or dresses cut on the bias, men in tuxedos looking as though they were born in them and not jerking and straining as if they were dressed in straitjackets. In our fantasy world, everyone gets to smoke, sip martinis and live in gleamingly smooth Art Deco high-rise apartments with views of bustling but not yet ruined cities glittering below. In our dreams.

Sky really pushes the Metro chic, the tough but sexy businesswoman. I think she pushes it too far. She doesn't want to be like her mother. Sky's mother went to Woodstock and spent the rest of her life paying for it. Both Sky and her name are souvenirs from those three days of music and muck.

Sky saves nice pieces that she knows will fit me, like the clothes I wore that day to the funeral. It was a little fifties number, maybe worn once by its original owner, a black wool crepe suit, jacket with three-quarter sleeves and velvet collar and cuffs, tightish skirt with a little kick pleat at the back. Jeremy would have approved of the black fishnet stockings and stiletto heels.

The day of the funeral, I got dressed, then went into the bathroom to work on my hair. Every day is a bad hair day for me because my hair is red, and curly, and if I'm not careful with it, it ends up looking like a bush. I keep it pruned to shoulder length and with enough gel and mousse and whatnot, I can make it cooperate.

Anyway, the bathroom door was open and the Viking strode in and out, amused by me, a sneering little smile creeping into one corner of her mouth. There are women who undress to make a good impression and women who cover up every inch of themselves to make a good impression. I considered myself to be in the second category, believing that if I were five foot eleven with mile-long gleaming sinewy bronze limbs I, too, would stride around the house naked, planning my next bone-crunching assault on the male population.

Anna depressed me. She reminded me of how much dieting, depilation and general suffering I had to go through to make myself desirable. I consoled myself with the fact that she still couldn't put together a proper English sentence, although she'd been in Canada for over two years. She had something to do with sports development in the physical education department at the university, but she'd never specified which sport, or how it was being developed. I had a few ideas though.

When I was ready, I called a cab. It was an extravagance, and I knew it, but I was going to remember Jeremy in style. I was going to take a little break from my miserable, penny-pinching daily life. When I got there, I paid the cabby, stood up straight, saying to myself, I am beautiful, I am beautiful, and walked through the cemetery gates. I must have looked quite chic until I hit the patch of snowy grass and my stiletto heels sank deep into the wet earth. I had to creep on tiptoes the rest of the way. By then, Jeremy's death had become a reality and any attempt at being beautiful and finding the prince my mother was always yattering about, was going to be marred by the mascara streaming down my face. I missed the old scoundrel and couldn't stop blubbering like a baby when the moment of truth came.

At the graveside, there were quite a few people to see him off on his last big ride, so to speak. A number of women, all different types and ages, old girlfriends. A few older men in very natty suits standing at a distance. His real pals clustered close around the hole to watch the glittering heap of wrecked metal be lowered into the ground.

His friends had names tattooed on their fat, hairy, leather-bound arms, names like Spike, Snake, Muncher and Brew-belly. Instead of tossing flowers, they guzzled beer from tins, crushed and tossed the empties onto the corpse of the Harley, and belched with a lot of commitment and respect. A biker's ten-gun salute.

Jeremy's remains, on the other hand, had already been cremated. As far as I knew, there was no will, but his buddies knew how he wanted it all to be done. They were paying for the funeral.

My parents were there, too, my father being his only child, or at least the only legally recognized child. But they had no intention of coming nearer or joining the boozy group. They lurked behind some poplar trees, pretending to be part of someone else's interment a few yards away. From time to time, they sneaked distressed peeks in the direction of our group of geriatric rabble-rousers, then looked away before anyone could catch them at it.

My father is terminally conservative. He's the principal of

Cedar Narrows Senior Secondary School, wears sock sus-
penders, and has spent most of his life in a state of mortifi-
cation and denial over his biker dad. If he'd been born later,
he would have been one of those kids that tries to get a di-
vorce from their parents. I gather his mother, my grandmother, was a biker babe. She abandoned them, found a
bigger, badder man with a bigger, badder machine and ran
off, leaving Jeremy to look after a newborn baby.

Jeremy was pretty amazing. He managed to raise my father and make a life for himself. He had a little income from
his Laundromat business and so could devote himself exclu-
sively to his son, and the gang on weekends and summer holidays.

And my father actually did okay until he hit thirteen and
decided he didn't want to be who he was anymore. He
started hanging out with the leaky-pen crowd at school, got
religion, one of the noisier ones that involves near-drown-
ing in a baptismal font the size of an Olympic pool, and became mortally tedious.

He met my mother at a church social. The joke was on
him though. My mother, a resourceful woman at heart, was
there under false pretenses, just trying things out, trolling different waters looking for a man. Over the years, she's been
able to mess my father up a bit, making him a little less respectable. But she never really took to Jeremy, who kept
making passes and lewd propositions.

My parents live in the 'burbs. My mother's idea of an or-
gasm is making Rice Krispie squares, vacuuming the beige
wall-to-wall carpet and securing the plastic covers on the living room furniture. My father's is finding all his pens and pencils lying exactly the way he left them. He's a control freak.
He goes to Mars if anybody moves his pens and pencils.

It wasn't that my father hated Jeremy. He just didn't know

what to do with him. I adored Jeremy because he had taught me how life could be exciting in unexpected ways. He was always ready to see the funny side of things and never too interested in control. And when I started going to university, before I had an apartment of my own, he let me hold parties in his big old house.

I had trouble with Connie, though, Jeremy's last live-in.

Connie was at the funeral, too, standing a little apart from everyone, but still close to the grave. I just couldn't like her. Maybe it was because she was only four years older than me. Jeremy was over seventy when he died. I thought Connie was a gold digger. A gold digger who'd made a mistake because Jeremy wasn't rich. Her hair was big and platinum and when Jeremy wasn't looking at her, her face became haggard and hard. Her fashion sense was Las Vegas pro. That day she was wearing a red leather pantsuit, and frankly, she shouldn't have been because those tight pants made her look fat. She'd been with Jeremy for the last six years but she was rarely around when I got together with him. I guess he sensed my discomfort, as well as hers.

It would probably all go to Connie, whatever Jeremy had left. The big ramshackle Victorian house near Commercial Drive, his other bikes and the launderette. The building the launderette was in had five apartments. The rents from four of them would go to Connie. But there'd be no rent from the ground-floor apartment. And if Jeremy had arranged things the way he'd intended, she wouldn't be able to sell the launderette. Not in Bob's lifetime.

Bob was the tenant in the ground-floor apartment. He'd lost the use of his legs in a motorcycle accident and Jeremy had given him a lifelong rent-free lease. Bob managed the launderette and overhauled the washers and dryers when

they needed it. I'd heard Jeremy promise Bob that the launderette would always be there for him.

When the funeral was over, the gang invited me to join
them for a farewell brew to Jeremy at the Eldorado Hotel, a
charming place where the cockroaches have running tabs.
But I declined. I had to get back to work. Snake, the gang's
leader, gave me a bear hug that nearly crushed my ribs and
said, "Luce, he wanted you to have this." He thrust a paper
bag into my hand. The thing inside was about the size and
shape of a soup tin.

I thanked Snake and walked toward the cemetery gates.
There were a few cabs idling nearby. I waved brightly to my
parents and got into one, clutching the paper bag tightly.
Once we were moving, I opened the bag. Inside, there was
a small brass container with tape sealing the lid. I knew what
it contained, but to be sure, I peeked, then closed the top
quickly. Jeremy's ashes. I put the urn back in the bag.

When I got to the gallery, nobody was around but there
were men's and women's voices coming from Nadine's office. A man was saying something and the women were
laughing uproariously. I hung up my coat, took the urn out
of the bag and set it on my desk, then entered Nadine's office. I couldn't believe it. My mother was right about princes
showing up. There he was.

2

It was my idol from university days. The man who was making them all laugh. Paul Bleeker, THE Paul Bleeker, the British-born artist who worked in all sorts of different mediums. I'd read about the clamorous success of his show at New York's Hard Edge Gallery. It was called The Breadwinners and featured figures in business suits, the bodies sculpted in shellacked loaves of bread; rye, whole-wheat, raisin, seven-grain, sourdough. In another show, he'd used the wax from votive candles stolen from churches all over North America and Europe to sculpt figures of famous martyrs, each martyr with huge chemically-treated wicks sticking out of all their orifices. On the last night of the show the wicks were lit and the sculptures went off like fireworks, eventually melting to the floor. Nothing remained but waxy puddles and the photos documenting the event. He'd also done some very interesting things with other foodstuffs: nuts, dried pasta, legumes, squashes.

A few years back, he'd come to the art department as a guest lecturer for the 400 seminar and everybody fought for his attention, and I mean *everybody,* including the large contingent of girls with steel-toed boots and buzz cuts. I have a particularly glowing memory of Paul Bleeker cornering me at a party and asking me all about myself in a tone that suggested delicious things for later. I started to tell him, concentrating on the exciting and rebellious moments of my life, and banishing the Cedar Narrows parts to amnesiac oblivion. But then he was whisked away by the hostess (married, but canoodling him just the same) and I was spared having to embellish any further. Since then I've spent years imagining the end to that evening in all its lascivious detail.

And here he was—white teeth and black leather jacket, satanic beard and tousled hair, fitted jeans displaying his endowments. And there were Nadine and her cronies. Nadine's best friend was Felicity, a hefty blonde who filled her days getting manicures, pedicures, facials, massages, electrolysis and meeting others for lunch. I'd nicknamed her Mae West. She toted pounds of jewelry and wore suede and silk under her chinchilla coat even for minor occasions. The man who accompanied her was not her husband but an expensive ornament who looked frequently at his platinum Rolex with an air of smug boredom. Among the others in this odd social circle, there was a man I called Onassis, a short fat Greek fast-food tycoon who wore heavy gold knuckle-dusting rings and always had a wet nub of unlit cigar in his mouth. Then there was the critic for one of the local newspapers—a tall, soap-white cadaverous type always ready to pronounce a DOA verdict for any exhibition. I called him the Mortician. The other women were limp clones of Nadine and Felicity.

Usually, the gallery was deserted during the day except for

a few tourists. Normal people showed up for evening openings when they could scarf free food and drink.

Here was this little crowd of society men and women with nothing better to do on a winter's afternoon than coo and fawn over Paul Bleeker. Somebody had brought a case of champagne and they were all drinking it out of plastic cups. Nadine pretended not to notice me for a while and then, when she decided to, she sidled over and hissed, "Lucy, where the hell have you been?"

"You knew. I told you. A funeral."

She huffed impatiently and jingled an armful of eighteen-karat gold bracelets at me. "You have to go to the deli and get something for people to nibble on. And don't stint." Nadine liked to nibble. Her tastes sometimes extended to the human species. By the way she was eyeballing Paul Bleeker, I figured he was going to be dinner.

"What are we celebrating?" I asked.

"Paul's upcoming show."

"Where?"

"Well, here of course, you little idiot."

I didn't let it get to me.

Nadine was another of those towering women, but then I'm only five foot two, so a lot of women tower over me. And she was disgustingly thin, with Cleopatra hair and black almond-shaped eyes. And an attitude. And that terrible accent. A recent infusion of royal blood in a Swiss clinic? As far as Nadine was concerned, there was no one smarter, more beautiful or as important as she. I was almost certain she'd shelled out a fortune for face-lifts and tummy tucks. Too bad they can't invent the ego tuck. I did the only thing I could in that moment and whispered, "You've got something black stuck between your front teeth."

As I headed out into the cold to buy lox, she was furtively

trying to catch her reflection in the glass of one of the exhibits.

When I got back to the gallery, everyone was getting a little sloppy. They'd finished four bottles of champagne and were starting in on another. I set the food trays down on a table in the main part of the gallery. They moved toward the trays with all the grace of a pack of jackals. Paul Bleeker looked over at me several times between mouthfuls of cream cheese and caviar, a queasy expression on his face, as though he had an ulcer that had just started acting up. No light of recognition dawned though, and he turned back to his little claque, munching canapés and beaming hundred-watt smiles. He didn't remember me.

I poured myself a large glass of bubbly. Nadine would never notice. She had just draped herself all over Paul, as close to being a human overcoat as anyone ever got. I watched him extract himself delicately from her grip, reach into his pocket and pull out a small square black box. He was still smoking those silly Sobranies. But I forgave him when he lit up. I wanted to *be* that cigarette, stroked by those eloquent fingers, moistened by those sensuous lips, thrust in and out of his mouth…and then he looked around, spied Jeremy's urn, removed the lid and flicked his ashes into it.

I was there in a second to snatch it away. "That's not an ashtray," I splurted.

"Hey…it's full of ashes." He must have realized what it was because he banged his hand against his forehead.

"A friend of yours?"

I nodded, hugging the urn.

"Really sorry. And you are?" He squashed the *R* like a true North American. His accent had temporarily lost all its Britishness.

"Lucy Madison. Assistant manager here."

"How're ya doing. Sorry about your friend."

"Me, too."

And then I did the unthinkable. I gave in to grief in front of my idol. Tears rollicked down my face. Paul Bleeker took my elbow and guided me into the washrooms. He parked me near the ladies' mirror then went into a cubicle and came back with a huge wad of toilet paper. It was cheap, scratchy toilet paper. Nadine liked to cut corners with those little things.

He handed it to me and I mopped my face. Kindness always makes it worse for me and my tears turned to those jerky hiccuppy sobs.

I felt an arm pull me into a leather-clad shoulder and a hand stroked my hair.

When I'd calmed down a little, I said, "Actually, it was my grandfather." I stared at the urn.

Paul Bleeker just nodded as if he understood absolutely everything, everything from my feelings of loss to super-strings theory…and then a strange light came into his eyes. You have to be careful when famous artists get strange lights in their eyes and you happen to be holding a dead person's ashes in your hands. For one thing, the famous person usually has enough money to finance his eerier inspirations.

I pulled back a little. Paul had already changed tack though. He took my chin in his hands and began turning my head from side to side. "Have you ever modeled?" he asked.

"For an artist?"

"No, for a mechanic. Well? Have you?"

"Informally." I recalled an old boyfriend from university days who had once used me as a model. His basement suite had been glacial, its decor, early dirty gym sock, late pizza box and cigarette butt in beer bottle. He fancied himself to be the next Francis Bacon. When he finally let me glimpse his work, I looked like a fat mutant baby after a nuclear meltdown.

"Only head modeling," I said primly. The world was not going to get the chance to laugh at any of my naked body parts even if the artist was as famous as Paul Bleeker.

"Pity," he said. "You have a somewhat classical look."

If he had gone on to say "Rubenesque" I would have been forced to deck him. But he said, "Give me your phone number anyway. You never know when I might need a head." It was a ploy, of course, but I quickly rattled off my number and the gallery's e-mail address. I could hear the natives getting restless beyond the bathrooms, and the irritated staccato of Nadine's size ten Ferragamo heels clacking toward us. Paul Bleeker scribbled fast in his little black book and pocketed it as Nadine came through the doorway.

She just avoided snarling at me. "Lucy, you better get out there and start cleaning up. It's a hell of a mess." She turned to Paul and said so sweetly it made my teeth hurt, "Umberto's all right for you?" He nodded, then shrugged at me, a poor helpless creature caught up in the tide of his adoring fans.

They were all gone by the time I came out of the bathroom. I put Billie Holiday on the CD player and cleaned up. It was nearly eleven when I trudged back out into the cold. I was freezing by the time I got on the bus. As it jostled through the slushy dark streets, I pictured the lucky group, stuffing themselves at Umberto's Ristorante, funghi porcini, risotto di mare, tiramisù. Nadine taking second and third helpings.

Then I thought about what I would do if Paul Bleeker actually phoned me. Would I dare to tell him that I was a sometimes painter?

Would we be able to talk about…art? It's a word I usually have to whisper because it's all become so tricky.

When I first started making big paintings, I figured that with people hanging animal carcasses in galleries or cutting off their own body parts, bleeding to death and calling it artistic expression, I had a lot of leeway. My work is ultra-conservative in comparison to just about everybody else's. I like decorative, and I like functional. I like something I can hang on my own wall. And for that I usually get into trouble. I was harassed at university for the "prettiness" of some of my paintings. But I couldn't help it. I had started depicting my night dreams, in a kind of quasi-naïf, colorful, surreal way. They were so much more vivid and promising than anything that was happening in my waking life. They were full of wild things and creatures: tigers, snakes, bluebirds; orchids, roses, turquoise oceans and murky-green ponds. Sky jokingly christened my work "Frida Kahlo without the mustache." In my night dreams, I once wore a shawl of white silk embroidered with brightly colored vines, birds and flowers, over a gorgeous tight-fitting red silk dress with matching shoes. Of course, my nighttime body is beautiful. But I think that's good, don't you? It means that whatever I really look like in the daytime or consciously think of myself, my deepest, barest mind thinks I'm okay.

At class exhibitions, my work was always put in the out-of-the-way poorly lit back rooms. It didn't bother me. Somebody always found their way back there. And I don't know why, but when the exhibitions were dismounted, pieces of mine always went missing. I don't want to use the word *stolen*. I prefer to call it art appreciation.

If there's one thing you have to do in your art, it's be true to yourself. And you can take that further, into your life. It's the same. You're filling up your personal canvas, adding the daily strokes. You want it to be good and right, you don't want to have to take the white and cover it all up quickly before anybody sees the amateur mess you've made. But messes *do* get made.

I stepped off the bus and gingerly walked the last frozen block. When I got home, I called out the Viking's name. There was no answer, so I relaxed. There was a letter for me on the hall table. I realized it wasn't a bill, and suddenly my heart was pounding. I tore it open and unfolded the one page. The signature at the bottom was such an unexpected surprise that my hands started to tremble.

The letter read:

Sorry Lucy Honey. I had to do it this way. No half measures for us, right? I won't go into the gory details. It was one of the members of that nasty big C family and the future didn't look too rosy. I could just about feel one good ride left in me so I took it. Must have done it if you're reading this letter.

One last very important thing. I beg you to go and see Connie. I'm begging you on bended knee Lucy honey. When you talk to her you'll know why. She can be a little stubborn, so if she tries to slam the door in your face or anything like that, you jam your foot in there. Don't go away till she talks to you. Tell her I sent you.

I'm signing off now. You're a great kid and I love ya.

Jeremy

The tears were rolling again but this time I just let them come. I went to the fridge looking for some wine to cry into, but there was none left. However, there was a half bottle of some strange Swedish liqueur that Anna called Glug. So I glugged and cried until I was too exhausted to think anymore.

★ ★ ★

The next morning I put on my power suit in an attempt to dress up for business and hide my hangover. Knee-length, gray wool, very stern. But with just a hint of lace peeping from under the jacket. Just in case Paul Bleeker happened to come in, he was going to see what a no-nonsense woman I was, and not the wet-faced ninny of the day before.

I had my own set of keys and was the first to open up the gallery each morning. This suited me fine. It meant that the dragon lady could simmer in her lair a little longer before fuming into action. She needed a lot of time to put on her makeup and, oh yes…consume a couple of breakfasts.

It was just after nine-thirty. I sat at my desk in the Rogues' Gallery and yawned. I took small sips from my caffe latte forcing myself to make it last. I checked my e-mail. The usual load of forwarded jokes were there from Sky. When the postman came, I tried flirting with him but he didn't even flinch. If he thought I was cute, he wasn't letting on. I was definitely out of practice.

I yawned some more and opened the envelopes addressed to the gallery. There were a lot of bills, from transporters, caterers, insurance companies and a cheque from a customer. Surprisingly, we were selling pieces that season. Nadine had taken a big risk on exhibiting all those phalluses, but she'd succeeded. The platoon of pizzles actually had buyers.

After four months, though, the subjects were getting to me. I hadn't seen a live one in ages. Another month of staring at them, and they would have started talking to me, their little singsong voices taunting me, "We're having more fun than you-oo, nah nah nah nee nah nah."

I stifled another yawn and let my mind slide into reveries about Paul Bleeker. Then I remembered Jeremy's letter.

"Damn." I said it loud enough that my voice ricocheted through the empty gallery. Connie. There was no avoiding her. If Jeremy said I had to go and see her, then I had to go and see her. But the thought of it was like a freezing-cold bath. It was like Sunday night when you had school the next day and hadn't done your homework. As the prospect of visiting Connie loomed over me like a big black cloud, disaster struck.

3

Disaster, dressed in a Superman costume, lolloped, cape a-flutter, past the huge plate-glass window of the gallery and vanished from view. I ducked down behind my desk and peeped out from under it. The superhero stepped back into view, examined his reflection, flexed his limp biceps in a superhero-like way, and whizzed out of sight.

It was happening again. Just like a really bad déjà vu. And once more, it wasn't happening in Cedar Narrows, where the damage could be contained, but in downtown Vancouver, where the repercussions could travel a lot farther.

I immediately called my mother.

"He's here," I wailed. "I thought you said he was in Hawaii."

"He's…? Oh. Well, he was in Hawaii for a while. And he's there, is he? I see. Well." My mother's voice was so calm I wanted to scream.

"Well?" I whined.

"Don't be melodramatic."

"Numbers. I need the phone numbers, Mom. The Vancouver ones. Mine are all at home. Quickly."

"Calm down," said my mother.

"I am calm. Under the circumstances."

My mother hummed under her breath as she searched. Her casualness unnerved me. "Yes, here they are. But I don't know how useful they're going to be. They're a couple of years old."

"Just give them to me. Quickly."

"Don't be rude, Lucille."

"I'm sorry. I can't help it. This whole business affects me that way."

I could hear my mother sigh just before she began to read off the numbers. I scrawled them down and hung up.

I tried the first number on the list and got an answering machine. With panic in my voice, I left a very long message and hung up to wait. I was too edgy to do anything practical, so I got out a flannel rag and began to dust. Moving nervously around the empty gallery, I buffed frames, glass cases, pieces on pedestals, in short, the entire phalanx of phalluses. As I was rubbing away at an all-too-lifelike marble sculpture of one, a voice from behind me made me leap out of my skin.

"You do that with a practiced hand."

"Paul…"

"In the flesh," he grinned. He was looking very sharp in black jeans, black sweater, black leather jacket.

Oh God, I thought, don't let Dirk come back this way dressed as Superman, not while he's here.

"What can I do for you?" I asked.

"You can come and have a drink with me sometime."

My heart did a double-flip. I didn't want to seem too eager. "Just let me check my agenda," I said, very smoothly.

I didn't have an agenda. I didn't need one. My life wasn't so hectic that I needed to write things down to remember them. I found an old address book in the bottom of my purse and flicked through it with an efficient air.

He said, "How about tonight? The Rain Room? Eight o'clock?"

For years I'd dreamt of someone asking me out to the Rain Room. No one ever had. Unfortunately, I had to take care of Dirk first and that could take time. "I can't tonight. How about tomorrow. We'll have to make it nine. I have another engagement tonight."

"Fine. Tomorrow, then." Tomorrow was Wednesday and I was free. He grinned again and was gone.

I sank into my chair. It had all happened so fast. I had a date for a drink, a real drink with the real Paul Bleeker. My next thought was, I have nothing to wear. My mental shopping spree was interrupted by the phone.

"Lucy Madison, please," said a man's voice. It was a deep voice, frayed with exhaustion.

"Speaking."

"Sam Trelawny here. You left a message on my answering machine?"

"Hello, Mr. Trelawny. You must be new."

"Why do you say that?" Sam Trelawny sounded harassed.

"Because I know everybody else. Or at least I used to."

"I was transferred from North Van into the downtown area a few months ago."

I said, "I'll have to fill you in, I guess."

"I have Dirk's file in front of me."

"He's been away."

"So I gather from the paperwork," he said.

"Yeah. He was in Hawaii for a while."

"Uh-huh? For how long?"

"About a year."

"How did he manage that?"

I said, "I gather a lot of people there are in the same boat. Long-term tourists without green cards."

"I see."

"He was in California for a while before that."

"Yes?"

"Yeah. He was hanging around on a street corner and some Moonies picked him up. They drove him back to their plantation or their ashram or whatever they call it. I guess after one evening with him, they didn't want him anymore. They delivered him back to the street corner as quickly as possible. He got a free meal out of it, though. I imagine that was his idea all along. He can manage on shoestrings and ear-wax if he's forced to."

I heard a guffaw at the other end of the line, then silence.

"Are you still there, Mr. Trelawny?"

"Yeah. Some papers fell on the floor. Too smart for his own good, right?"

"That's more or less the way it is. Are you going to see him?"

"It's unfortunate, but there's not a lot we can do at the moment, Miss Madison. You probably know how it goes. We have to wait for something to happen."

"Just before he went to California, he started wearing a Burmese Wot on his head, this kind of colorful knit hat with a little peak, fluorescent colors actually. He took a suite at the Hotel Vancouver and enticed a seagull into the room. He said he was teaching it to walk in a straight line. He said he was sure the seagull was capable of learning but lazy and not committed to the goal. Needless to say, Dirk left without paying his bill."

"And this was before he went to California and then Hawaii?"

"Just before. He must have skipped town the same day. Payday. You know, the government check?"

"Do I ever. It's always a busy week."

"Mr. Trelawny?"

"Yes, Miss Madison...I'm assuming it's Miss?"

"Why would you? You have a fifty percent chance of being mistaken." I was curious.

"Your voice just sounds...I don't know, peppy, lively...like you don't have six kids and half an alcoholic husband dragging you down."

"Thanks," I laughed. "It is Miss. Mr. Trelawny?"

"Yes?"

"Something serious is going to happen very soon. Probably in the next day or so."

"How can you be so sure?"

"He was wearing a Superman costume and moving fast. He's on a roll."

"Well, any signs that he might harm himself or others around him..."

"Can't we just have him picked up?"

"Look. Take down these numbers. They're emergency numbers. Not in the book. He makes an appearance, you keep him there, call the police, and we'll have the assessment team arrive and do a follow-up."

He gave me the numbers and I wrote them out carefully. Gratitude toward the faceless Mr. Trelawny oozed from my every pore.

He said, "Good luck. We'll be in touch. I'm afraid I've gotta go. Got an emergency call on another line. Bye, Miss Madison."

"Bye, Mr. Trelawny."

My hand was shaking as I put the receiver down. On another occasion when my brother Dirk had decided his life wasn't interesting enough, before California and Hawaii, he had boarded a downtown bus with a toy pistol. It had been snowing then as well and everyone was getting sick of the cold and slush. He had held the pistol to the driver's head and ordered the poor man to take him to Cuba...where it was *warm*.

Dirk was a one-man raid on sanity. And he was six feet, four inches tall. So people usually took his threats seriously.

On the subject of Dirk, my mother took a classic position, the ostrich position, with her head well-buried in sand. Whereas my father pleaded the fifth amendment and arranged to be out or busy whenever his only male heir was around. As far as my mother was concerned, Dirk had nothing that a good meal, his family's love and a few lithium cocktails couldn't cure. She was always going on about how talented he was.

Dirk had trained as an actor at the National Theatre School. As far as I was concerned, he was still acting, but with a rotten script. He had once confessed to me, when we were both teenagers, that he would never work at a normal job, that he wouldn't have to, because he was such a mind-boggling genius. I concur with the mind-boggling part.

I was on the lookout for the Superman costume all day but it never showed. Probably slowed down by a lump of kryptonite.

The next morning I took the bus down to the East End of the city and the Italian neighborhood. Jeremy and Connie had shared a big old Victorian house, a ruin with a vague whiff of damp rot about it. For years, the dilapidated four-story mansion had hosted big parties, biker friends and whoever happened to need a place to crash. And then Jeremy had taken that trip to the States six years before and come back with Connie. The doors that had always been open were suddenly closed. Jeremy took Connie very seriously. There were still parties, but never at the house.

After that, I always met him at one greasy spoon or another—some place where we could get cheap bacon and eggs and talk for a while. He'd intimated that Connie reminded him of someone he'd been crazy about. But there was more to it than that. There was a sense of mission. He was like a schoolteacher guiding a favorite pupil and this had never made much sense to me.

There I was on the rickety doorstep peering through the beveled glass door into the interior. Connie was the last person in the world I wanted to talk to. I always had the feeling that she was sneering behind my back, probably thinking how tough and world-wise she was and how bourgeois and artsy-fartsy I was. It was the expression on her face whenever she saw me, a blunt skepticism, and it completely unnerved me.

But Jeremy's wish was my command. I rang the bell and waited. A few minutes passed and no one came. I lifted my hand to ring again when I saw a dark shape at the end of the corridor. It was her. She moved slowly and when she got to the door and opened it, she didn't look pleased to see me.

To say she looked like she'd been scraped off the bottom of someone's shoe would be putting it nicely. She had a cigarette hanging off her lower lip. Her face was puffy with a greenish tinge. Her hair was greasy and limp, and the housecoat she was wearing looked like it was hosting miniature colonies of thriving alien life.

"Hi, Connie." The sound of my own voice made me shrink. It was too chirpy, like a cheerleader's. Connie just nodded.

I qualified myself. "Jeremy asked me to come and see you. I have no idea why. He thought I should."

"I guess you better come in." The sound of her voice scared me. It was a low-pitched monotone at the best of times, which made it impossible to read her emotions, but now there was something else lurking there.

She slouched toward the living room and I followed her. The air in the house was close and fuggy and the curtains were drawn. She slumped into an armchair, narrowed her eyes at me and blew a smoke ring. "So Jeremy wanted you to see me, eh?"

"He sent me a letter. He must have sent it just before he…uh."

"Bit the big one?"

"Yes. Did you know he was going to do what he did?"

"Not exactly. But I had a feeling it was coming. He was sick. They didn't give him much more than a few months. He was feeling really bad."

"Why didn't you tell us he was sick? Why didn't *he* tell us?"

"He said he didn't want to see that look in people's eyes. He didn't want anybody feeling sorry for him."

I wanted to be able to blame her. I wanted to hear that Connie had talked him into it, that she was somehow responsible, but I could see that it wasn't the case. Still, I was mad, and when the "Jesus" came out of my mouth she was quick to answer.

She said, "You don't like me, do you? None of your family does. You all think I'm trash."

My mouth opened like a fish's and then shut again. I didn't know what to say.

She went on, "I didn't choose Jeremy. He chose me. If he hadn't, I'd have been dead in a ditch a long time ago, I can tell you." She squinted at me again. There was a long silence and then her voice was so low, she was nearly whispering. "Jeremy got me off junk, you know. He got me off the street, got me out of the life I was leading. I don't know why he picked me, why he thought I had anything special. But I can tell you, after a few months with him, I thought I was worth saving, too. Now I'm not so sure." She started to look even greener than before. She muttered, "Oh, Christ," shot up out of the chair and ran down the hall. I heard a groan and the sound of a toilet flushing. Connie came shuffling back down the hallway and just as it was dawning on me as to why she looked so chunky, she plopped herself back in the chair and said, "Damn him. He wouldn't let me get rid of it and now it's too late."

I was early for my date at the Rain Room. Mostly because I wanted to see if Paul Bleeker was serious and had booked ahead. The Rain Room was the kind of place where you practically had to have reservations just to look inside. It was on the top floor of a very tall high-rise overlooking the harbor. It had a central courtyard full of trees and the walls were of molded glass. On the outside, rivulets and cascades flowed down the contours. It was like being under a waterfall or at the center of a rainstorm. At night it was lit with thousands of tiny white lights and the whole place glittered. The background music was watery, too. I recognized Saint-Saens's "Aquarium."

Sure enough, Paul Bleeker had booked a table for two. I lingered in the doorway for a minute. I had decided to go in and sit down when I saw it. Across the Rain Room, outside in the courtyard, Dirk, still dressed as Superman, stood completely still, looking important. He then took one step forward and pressed his face against the glass. Water splashed onto his head and flowed down his body but he was oblivious to it. I bolted.

As the elevator descended with me in it, I wondered what Paul Bleeker would think of the way I'd stood him up. In that moment, I didn't care. Until my brother had been dealt with, I wanted to crawl under a rock. I hailed a cab, got in and looked over my shoulder the whole way home. No one was following me. I paid the driver with the last of my spare change, raced through my front door and double locked it once I was inside.

I went into the bedroom and took off my all-purpose little black cocktail dress. I could hear the Viking in the other room. Without knocking, she opened my door and handed me an envelope. "This for you," she told me.

"Who left it?" I asked. There was no stamp on it. She just shook her head in linguistic bewilderment and walked away.

I ripped it open. Scrawled on a tattered piece of paper were the words "I'M SENDING YOU TO THE PHANTOM ZONE."

I ran to the phone and dialed the first number on my list. I was expecting another answering machine but a real voice said, "Sam Trelawny here."

"It's Lucy Madison. Am I glad to get you," I said, "I think I just got a threat." I told him about Dirk's note.

"The guy moves fast," he said. "Listen, just hang on. Don't panic. I know, easy to say when you're not there. There've been more reports. It seems Dirk is making his presence felt all over town. He was hanging around eating people's leftovers at a restaurant in the West End this afternoon. We're going to have him picked up as soon as we can locate him. You hear anything more from him, call me straightaway. Here, I'll give you my private cell-phone number. And, Lucy?"

"Yes?"

"Don't worry. We'll have him looking and behaving like Clark Kent at his desk in the Daily Planet in no time."

I began to wonder what kind of face went with Sam Trelawny's plummy reassuring voice.

4

The next morning, I left for work at six-thirty, hoping the semidarkness would give me cover. I snuck out of my apartment dressed like an escapee from a black-and-white British movie. One of those dowdy sixties flicks. *Georgy Girl*. The *Carry On* gang. My hair was squashed under the kind of head scarf that you tie under your chin, a silk souvenir covered with sketches of the Eiffel Tower and Parisian urchin children. I wore a huge wooly coat with sloping shoulders, a pair of black gumboots and dark glasses. I had hoped to look a little like Jackie Kennedy sneaking past the paparazzi incognito, but in fact I looked more like Jackie Kennedy's cleaning lady. Taking these precautions was exhausting, but I counted on the fact that Dirk could sometimes be thrown by small things.

Along with the Superman disguise, Dirk had a few other personas in his manic closet. One was a tatty spy. During one endless spring, Dirk had introduced himself as "Bond, James Bond," then waved the plastic pistol in everyone's face and told them he was off to squash Goldfinger. For this Bond personality, Dirk had a very grotty white tuxedo, a garment he'd acquired from a bum in California, who'd claimed he'd got it from Our Man in Havana. The suit was several inches too short in the pants and jacket cuffs, covered with stains whose origins I preferred not to think about, and so creased you knew he and a dozen other people had slept in it.

He also had several sporting personas. Sometimes he pretended he was Tiger Woods, roaming around with an old golfing iron, swinging dangerously in all directions. I'd mistakenly tried to reason with Dirk, telling him that he was the wrong color to start with, would always be the wrong color, and how he lacked the discipline to be a golfing champion. This enraged him. I still hadn't learned that you can't reason with a man who's down on his lithium. I always hoped that I'd get through that thick, sick hide of his, get through to that other Dirk who had to be in there somewhere.

Maybe I was overestimating him. After all, Dirk had been no great shakes as a child either. He'd terrorized me when I was small by opening up *The Wizard of Oz* to the Wicked Witch of the West illustration. Her green face and clawlike hands had made my whole being curdle. Dirk used to chase me from room to room holding up the scary page and forcing me to look.

He'd drawn swastikas in indelible ink on the foreheads of every one of my dolls and hung them from the curtain rod in my bedroom.

He'd tormented me from the day I made my entrance into this life.

Was it any wonder I couldn't get through to him?

★ ★ ★

I clumped to work through the gloomy streets, dodging in doorways and scaring myself every few minutes with my own reflection. My first stop was at La Tazza, the little café next to the gallery. Lunging through the entrance, I was hit with the rich, dense aroma of ten different kinds of coffee. Ah, caffeine, my drug of choice. Behind the counter, a plump purple-hued girl moved lazily, taking glass jars down from shelves and pouring coffee beans into cellophane bags, folding the tops, and smoothing on the little gold labels as if it were a kind of meditation.

"Hi, Nelly." She looked miffed for a second. "It's me, Lucy."

Behind her back, we called her Nelly the Grape. She wore only the color purple, in every variation. Today, her skirt was a deep periwinkle shade, her blouse lilac—while her hair, angelized, glinted like garnets when it caught the light. Her nails, eyelids and lips were a similar wine shade.

"I didn't recognize you. How's it going? I don't know how you can sit there all day in a gallery full of penises. I'd get worked up...you know...being reminded...thinking about it."

"I'm dead from the neck down. Numb from disillusionment." I shrugged. "But at least this way, I don't forget what they look like."

"Crappy love life, eh?"

"Nonexistent. Put one of those big gooey slices in a bag for me, will you, Nelly? What are they anyway?"

"It's a Black Forest slice, double fudge and cream, cherry filling, layers of chocolate, whipped cream and cherry along the top as well."

"That ought to make up for two love lives."

Nelly prepared my double latte and put the huge sweet gooey slice of empty calories in the bag. "Here you are.

Enjoy." She unconsciously ran her tongue around her lips, like a big fluffy cat enjoying the cream.

I was ready to climb into the trenches. The enemy incursion would be hard to predict. It was silly to take chances.

I unlocked the gallery door, darted inside, locked it again, and got down to the serious business awaiting me.

I had to track down Paul Bleeker's number and let him know why I hadn't been at the Rain Room to meet him. Let him know that I hadn't meant to ditch him. That I was interested. That I still existed. But his number wasn't listed. I tried calling new listings, found nothing, gave up and opened the e-mails.

I got a jolt when I double-clicked on the incoming mail and there was a message from pbleeker@coastnet.ca— "Sorry, I couldn't make it last night, Lucy Luv"—I lingered over the "Luv" for a bit—"Something came up. Cheers. P.B."

The reptile! He hadn't shown up after all. Well, it was a two-way dumping ground. I typed a new message. "Sorry I didn't show yesterday. Unavoidable business. Perhaps another evening? Lucy Madison."

He was supposed to believe that I hadn't seen his message, that I didn't even know he'd sent one? All he had to do was look at the time on my message.

What I really needed to know was why? Why had he stood me up in the Rain Room? But then I'd stood him up, too, thanks to Dirk. Whatever Paul Bleeker's excuse was, if he even bothered with one, I'm sure that Nadine was to blame. She would have to add him to her list of scalps. It was impossible for her not to try. It came to her more easily than breathing. See desired object. Take desired object. It was as simple as that. And I knew from past experience that very few men could resist her allure. Translation: resist her money.

I stifled my disappointment with some of the gooey sweet slice.

The morning crawled. No superheroes or spies materialized. The only interruption was a middle-aged Japanese couple, tourists without a word of English. They tittered and chattered over some etchings for a good half hour and then made their choice. You would have thought they were buying a Van Gogh, they were so pleased with themselves. They picked out a monster member in lurid pinks and purples, then with much bowing and smiling, they put it on their VISA and took it away. One less willy in my life.

I surfed the net for a while then e-mailed Sky, "Help, I'm a prisoner in a Gastown weenie factory."

She e-mailed back, "Aye, there's the rub."

We agreed to meet for lunch at our usual place.

It was ten minutes to one when Nadine finally arrived. She wore dark glasses and when I said "Good morning" too brightly, she let out a grunt of disgust and retreated into her office. I was surprised that she didn't send me out to get her something to eat.

"I'm going for lunch," I yelled in the direction of the door. When there was no answer, I put on my coat and headed off to meet Sky.

Evvie's Midnight Diner was one of those Naugahyde-booth, dusty plastic aspidistra, twirly-stool-at-the-long-steel-counter kind of places near East Hastings. A hungry part of town. Evvie was actually a huge ugly-beautiful Lebanese man. His name was unpronounceable so everyone just called him Evvie. He had bought the place from the real Evvie back in Jeremy's day, sold it in the eighties, gone home to Lebanon, seen what a Swiss cheese had been made of his home country, hightailed it back to Canada, bought his old diner back, and restored it to exactly what it had been in the seventies, right down to the liverish color of the booths.

Evvie's Midnight Diner had been a well-kept secret for decades, a haunt for vanilla drunks, Korea crazies, fresh air inspectors and actors waiting up to read their reviews in the morning papers. Now it was becoming fashionable again simply because it was so unfashionable. The real thing. Sky and I had given up being virtuous and eating at those health food places with the nut rissole burgers and grass cutting teas. Evvie's served cheap old-fashioned unhealthy food and piles of it.

Sure, there were salads on the menu at Evvie's, too, but it would have been frivolous for a person in my financial position to bypass the mountainous, double-cheese, bacon and mushroom burgers with the side of fries for a sagging lettuce leaf and an anemic tomato slice. Or the platter of battered and deep-fried halibut and prawn with loads of tartar sauce. It was good dollar value.

Let's be frank here. Only the rich can afford to starve.

And there was another problem. The food I left in the fridge at home disappeared mysteriously before I could get to it. I thought I was being clever, eating out, keeping my food out of the Viking's mouth. She'd denied touching any of it, just as I'd denied touching her Glug. I asked her if maybe her conquests didn't get hungry and thirsty in the night, and perhaps didn't make a raid on the provisions, but her eyes and mouth narrowed into a sneering expression and she said, "You jealous."

Sky was sitting in our booth at the end of the diner. She was not alone. With her, was a man whose hair was just a little too blond. His trimmed mustache lurked on his upper lip like a small yellow rodent. His face was buffed to an unnatural shine. He wore a lavender-colored Lacoste T-shirt, a preppy gray knit sweater knotted around his shoulders, and a pair of jeans that were so tight I wouldn't have been surprised if he squeaked when he talked. He was fit though, and very neat. Nice and tidy right down to his fingernails. He must have been edging on forty—perhaps he was older—but he gave the impression of eternal forced youth.

He was running his hand up and down Sky's arm and if he kept at it much longer, he was going to leave her with no skin. There was no doubt about it. He had taken possession of her. And Sky seemed pretty happy to be possessed. She had a slightly goofy expression on her face and a bruised, trampled look about her. When I sat down at the table, she held out her hand, palm up, in a Ta-da gesture and said, "Lucy Madison, Max Kinghorn."

So this was the guy who had hired Sky to manage the store, the famous boss from Seattle. I peered rudely.

Max didn't bother to stand up on my arrival as I might have expected from such a tidy polite-looking person. He must have sensed my hostility. He laughed a nervous, whiny, slightly nasal laugh and went back to the arm stroking as if his life depended on it.

I stretched out my hand to shake his, and to stop him from doing all that damned stroking.

"Sky's told me all about you," I said, forcing myself to smile.

He whinnied again.

She had told me all about him. She'd gone into quite a lot of gory detail.

Max Kinghorn was the owner of the Retro Metro Boutique, but he lived in Seattle where he had other vintage boutiques. He was a strange bird. A vulture, to be precise. He stocked his stores by reading obituaries published up and down the West Coast, from California to B.C. He was always ready to swoop down on the defunct's family and offer to take the horrid burden of dusty antiquated clothing, furniture and knickknacks off their hands. As vintage vultures go, I gathered he was the best in his trade. But Sky, I wanted to scream, Oh Sky, what about that little thing you told me about Max, that one, really important detail?

Max shifted, gave a few last frenzied strokes, then pecked Sky demurely on the cheek. "Well, I'm sure you ladies have a lot to talk about. I'll get going. I have business in Port Townsend." Then he whispered to Sky, "Ciao, liebchen, I'll call you."

I could picture it already, Max hovering and slavering as he waited to pick over the corpse down in Port Townsend, offering condolences to the bereaved family along with his certified cheque.

I watched him leave then glared at Sky across the table. "That's Max, Sky? The infamous Max?"

She glared back at me. "Don't get worked up about it. I told you I thought he was interesting."

"I didn't realize you thought he was that interesting."

"Just what do you mean by that?"

I held the menu high in front of my face. "I really shouldn't be having all this fried stuff but I just can't help myself. It's all so yummy and tempting."

"Don't try to change the subject, Madison. Just spit it out."

Sky looked fierce. She was already a dark, scrawny, pointy little person with spiky techno-punk black hair, and when she became fierce, she was like a Jack Russell terrier, hanging on to the object of her passion until she had ragged it to death.

"I love you, Sky. You're my best friend in the world, but if Max handcuffed you to the bed, beat you with rubber hoses, then drove over you with his car and left tire tracks, you'd still look better than you do now. He's been staying at your place these last few days, hasn't he?"

Sky blushed, and she's not a blusher.

"He's so…so…"

"Gay?"

"That's one facet of Max's personality. Besides, he's celibately gay. For the last few years anyway."

"That's a good one. Celibately gay. Except for the fact that he had sex with you. Or am I presuming too much? Did you have sex with him, too? It was sex he had with you last night, wasn't it?" I stared at a bruised area on her neck and raised my eyebrows.

Sky looked even fiercer. "Don't get worked up about it, Madison. In case you haven't noticed, men aren't exactly leaping out of the woodwork these days. Men I have something in common with, I mean. I'm as surprised as you are that he's good in the sack. But it's not just the sex either. It's a business relationship, too. He's looking at other boutiques around Vancouver. We might be…you know…expanding and consolidating."

"I think I need to start worrying about you."

"You don't get it. I don't really count. I'm unofficial," said Sky.

"Ooo, ouch. Let me think on that one for a minute. YOU DON'T REALLY COUNT. It's time you started listening to your mother, Sky. All those talks of hers about self-esteem and so on."

"You're not listening to me, Luce. Shut up for a minute. What I mean is, I'm something new for him. I'm exotic. By comparison, I mean. You know, by comparison to being with men."

"Sure you are, dear," I said in the voice my mother used on me when I was eight.

"And Christ, Lucy, you should see the way he looks in a suit."

I wanted to see the way he looked in a suit. A suit of armor. Dropped into the ocean, with him in it.

Sky always had been a sucker for a nice garment. Her degree is in theatrical costume design. We met when the university theater department roped me into doing a little set painting for a production of *Peer Gynt*. During that particular show, she was fighting with the director, who'd slept with her then refused to acknowledge her. She took revenge by using weak seams in strategic places. A few belly dancers accidentally bared their nipples during the dance sequence and some trolls had codpiece problems while trogging around in the Hall of the Mountain King. We giggled like idiots from backstage. Apart from that, it was an uneventful production.

Sky had had a lot of boyfriends back in the university days, but none of them had left her with the day-after evidence that Max had.

"I can't resist him." She shook her head, then grimaced and stuck out her tongue at me.

"When are you seeing him again?"

"I don't know."

"You don't know?"

"Of course I don't know. Why would I know? He's a busy man. So stop asking me trick questions."

I didn't remind Sky of that drunken evening just after I'd gotten rid of Frank. The one where Sky and I started out delicately sipping white wine and ended up falling headfirst into gallons of tequila sunrise, sloppily guzzling and making a lot of drunken Never Again promises. Never Again would we go out with men who were lechers, men who were leeches, men who were misogynists, men who were polygamists—our list was quite long and we pretty much eliminated half the human race.

After all the Never Agains, and since Mr. Perfect still hadn't shown up, it was just a question of choosing one of the guys off the Never Again list.

I said, "Let's forget about him for a minute. Let's not let men ruin our lunch."

"Good thinking." Sky suddenly looked like her old self again.

I launched into all my news. Jeremy's funeral, Paul Bleeker's big show and small advances, Connie. When she heard the Connie part, Sky said, "I think you need to talk to Reebee on this one. You might need a shot of voodoo."

Reebee Robertson is Sky's mother and my creativity expert. In her forty-seven years of life, Reebee has been Rolfed, Reike-ed, Shiatsu-ed, acupunctured, transactionally analyzed, regressionally analyzed, re-birthed, de-birthed, Jung-ed, Freuded, Adlered, Kleined and Winnicotted. These days she offered up her own kind of psychological hodge-podge. Her techniques may not have been highly regarded by the head-shrinking intelligentsia but they worked for me.

For a small painting, she would leave me thinking how wonderful I was and get me unstuck when I was blocked and unable to paint. Of course, I had to put up with Sky snickering on the sidelines at what she called all that New Age drivel.

Reebee had turned a life's worth of experiments and hapless wandering into a psychology degree. Then she had added a whole lot of other elements—myth and superstition—to her treatment. In her New Age way, she had renovated and furnished her Kitsilano house with favors.

She traded her way through life, something that Sky couldn't tolerate. "Give me the delicious feel of cool hard cash any day," Sky was prone to saying, punctuated with, "I'm a material girl." Sky lusted after clean sheets and her own pristine space. It was hard to blame her really. Reebee had dragged the protesting toddler from a Salt Spring Island commune to Victoria group house to a California Hari Krishna plantation to a hammock on a Maui beach, before finally dumping her with the grandparents back in Vancouver when she decided to go back to university.

The waitress brought our orders and just before Sky threw herself on the club sandwich, she said, "Really terrible about Jeremy. Easter's going to be awful without him, isn't it? God, I can still remember that year when we all went out to Cedar Narrows for the big meal. I nearly peed myself laughing, Jeremy making all those Jesus jokes, and your dad turning scarlet with rage."

"That was Jeremy all over. A terrible tease."

"Where are you spending it this year?"

"Don't know. My parents' place in Cedar Narrows as usual, I guess."

"You could spend it with us. Reebee will probably be doing something obscene with tofu but there'll be lots of good wine." Sky became emphatic. "She really wants to see you. I've been keeping her up-to-date, but she wants to see you in person."

"I don't know about Easter."

"Call her."

"I will."

"Promise you'll call her today, when you get back to work."

"I promise. But I've got to do something about the Dirk situation. I've got to see my parents and get this thing sorted out. He might show up. I should go out to Cedar Narrows and act as a decoy. Big holidays always bring out the worst in him. If only he'd just come out and behave badly and we could have him arrested. And there's one other thing about going to Cedar Narrows for Easter."

"What's that?"

"Having to show up alone and unmarried when that walking hormone of my cousin and her perfect husband will be there. You know Cherry. She'll be front and center with Michael and her entire demon spawn and probably pregnant with triplets if I know her."

Sky nodded and then a wicked smile crept across her face. "You could ask Paul Bleeker to Easter at your parents'. I'm sure he'd appreciate your mother's collection. All that marvelous sculpture."

I swatted her with the menu.

I took my time getting back to the gallery that afternoon. Max was far from perfect but at least Sky had someone to stroke all the skin off her arm. All I had was a vague possibility that Paul Bleeker might, if he happened to remember, ask me out again. And even at that, there was no guarantee that he'd show up.

When I got back to the gallery, Nadine's office door was open and she was moaning into the phone. "So did I, darling, so did I...so are you, darling, so are you...it was, darling, it really was...it was so...what, *Night Porter?*...no, I rather think *Last Tango in Paris.*"

I confess I haven't seen these movies but the word-of-mouth rehashes of the important bits have a wide circulation.

Nadine stuck her head out of the office, glared at me, and continued talking. "Do let's do it again. I'll supply the champers and the toys. You supply the...yes, that. Yes, of course I will."

I don't know about you, but when I really want a man, I choose to ignore his past, even if it's a very recent past, like a just-a-minute-ago-on-the-other-end-of-a-telephone past, just as long as it really is past and doesn't creep into the present or the future. I couldn't be sure who was on the other end of the line, but I wanted to be prepared for any eventuality. I mean, a man that came with no past, what kind of a man could he be? On the other hand, a man that sleeps with Nadine Thorpe? Nadine Thorpe was one big walking appetite. And Nadine looked flattened and mussed-up today. She had definitely had sex last night. Everybody—Nadine, Sky, Max, that middle-aged Japanese couple, possibly even my parents (repellent thought)—was having sex but me. It was time to take action. It was time to get therapy. I phoned Reebee and got myself invited for dinner that Friday night.

It took some courage. I hadn't seen her in a long time. After the Frank episode, I was afraid to see her, afraid of what she'd tell me because I'd avoided her the whole time I'd been involved with him. I was like a Catholic who hadn't been to confession in a really long time, and all my sins had piled up so that I was going to Hell for certain and no priest could save me.

I rang the doorbell and waited. Reebee opened up and stood there nodding and smiling smugly. She was tiny, even smaller than Sky. Her long silvery-dark hair was pulled into a braid, and she wore an antique Chinese silk dress that hung to her feet. Her earrings were coin yen with ivory gambling sticks dangling from them. Although it was March, and still cold, she wore thongs on her feet. There was a strange musty odor to her, like closed rooms and incense.

Her first words to me were, "Your aura, Lucy. It's very strange. Come inside and we'll fix it."

"Sure," I said, "get out your aura repair kit. Why, what's wrong with it?"

"It's full of anger and jealousy, with a little sadness thrown in." She put an arm across my shoulders and said, "I'm sorry about Jeremy. But then it's clear to see that it was his time. He had to move on. But I wouldn't worry. His karma was good. He'll be moving onto a higher plane. Do you want some tea before we start?" she asked.

"Uh…dunno," I muttered. Reebee called it tea but the stuff she served was mulch in my opinion. "You wouldn't have any real tea, would you, something with a punch to it like Twinings English Breakfast or Lapsang souchong?"

"Ah, Lapsang souchong. What memories. A remnant of another life."

Reebee and her lives.

"Yes?"

"It seems I was a Chinese courtesan as well." She said this proudly. It explained her new get-up.

"No kidding. When did you discover this?"

"Last week. I was having a session and this came up."

"Go on."

"It's not too clear. I just have the end, which is usually the way it goes with these sessions. The death scene. I think I must have been a wealthy man's concubine, because my clothes were gorgeous. And I had these tiny feet. I was trying to get away, to run, but I could barely walk with these terrible feet the size of children's fists. I'm sure it was the other wives and concubines who murdered me because the last image I have is of lying on the ground and looking up and there are all these other women standing over me with knives. I was pregnant, too."

"Oh my God, Reebee, that's awful."

"It's passed. I've moved on."

"Yeah, I guess you have."

And that was how it went with her. She was always discovering new past lives, and for a while she'd drift around in the costume of the person she'd been until the next life or this life took her over. She'd been a friend of Archimedes, helping him on the construction of the great lighthouse at Alexandria. She'd been a general of Genghis Khan's, in the end slicing off heads all along the Khan's funeral route until her own head was sliced off. She'd been at the courts of Catherine the Great and Elizabeth the First. I envied her. She really got around.

Reebee said again, "So how about this tea?"

"Lapsang souchong?"

She shook her head as if I were a lost cause and sighed heavily, "Hibiscus tea. That's what I'm going to give you. Your aura is demanding it."

She disappeared into the kitchen and I sat down on her couch. Reebee's house had a view of the ocean from its glassed-in sunporch. I could see freighter lights glittering in the dark distant bay. The whole house shivered and shimmered with bells and wind chimes, Ojibwa dream catchers, wall hangings, mobiles. It was full of color and clutter in contrast to Sky's high-rise apartment with its clean sparse lines and neutral colors.

Reebee's house always made me feel as if there were great and infinite possibilities, that my life could work out the way I wanted if I just applied myself somehow.

She came back a few minutes later and set a tray with two mugs down on the coffee table. Without a word she grabbed both of my hands, scrutinized them, then frowned. "You haven't been painting."

I told her about the Viking invasion.

"So the Swedish woman is supposed to help balance the budget."

I nodded.

"And all this deficit is because of Frank the Writer?" asked Reebee.

I nodded again. "The so-called writer. You're welcome to say I told you so."

"I would never say I told you so. Tell me how it ended."

The ending. It was funny because I had been thinking about the end of Frank just before Jeremy died. A few months back, Sky and I had had the bright idea of going for a drink at the Sylvia Hotel. Of course, I should have realized what a stupid choice the Sylvia was. As soon as I was through the door, I saw Frank. And god, it was like being in a time warp. He gave the impression of having been born in that spot, of never having moved, of having stagnated in that corner forever. The girl sitting across from him even looked a little like me. I felt sorry for her and hoped she didn't have a lot of money in her bank account.

I knew exactly what he was talking about, because his voice rose above the others, but also because I had endured his rant a million times. It was his party piece, his hobbyhorse. If only I'd known back then what it would all amount to. Back then, I'd thought he was very clever and intellectual.

Frank was going on and on about the play *Waiting for Godot*.

He'd dragged me to see it shortly after we first met. I'd been up for the whole of the previous night helping to mount an exhibit and was tired when I got to the theater.

The play is about these two characters, Vladimir and Estragon, or Didi and Gogo, who are waiting for this guy

Godot. I kept nodding off and waking up and whispering to Frank, "Has he arrived yet? Wake me when Godot arrives." And Frank just looked at me with an expression that said, "What a pathetic ignoramus!" How was I to know Godot never shows up? The second time Frank dragged me to a different production of it, I found the play sort of funny in places and I actually stayed awake.

As for the third and fourth productions, well, I'd rather not talk about it. Let's just say I probably won't sit through two showings when they make the movie.

Afterward, the first time, we went for a drink at the Sylvia Hotel and Frank sat in his spot and lectured. Are Vladimir and Estragon—Didi and Gogo—a sort of everyman, a representation of all mankind? I argued (he didn't expect it) that it was a thin representation of mankind, and extinct by now, because there weren't any women on that stage unless it was a futuristic play about cloning, then it was okay. Frank launched in… You've missed it entirely, Lucy, the biblical allusions, *God* in the word *Godot,* the prayerlike elation in the hope that Godot will come and the certainty that he will not, blah, blah, blah.

Standing in the doorway to the Sylvia's lounge with Sky, I knew exactly what Frank was saying to that plumpish girl with the red hair, the girl sitting exactly where I used to sit. Frank was even wearing the same old rancid corduroy jacket he'd always worn, the same expression of superiority animating his face. The only difference was that his hair was shorter. Well, it would have to be, wouldn't it? After what I did to it.

I turned around and dragged Sky away with me to some more respectable drinking establishment. I hate flogging dead horses.

The day I put an end to me and Frank, the day I discovered the overdraft at my bank and the fact that he'd forged my signature on a cheque, I'd planned on a lot of revenge, mostly cliché scenarios. I seethed and plotted all the way home. I thought of the woman who had cut off one sleeve of each of her husband's suits and shirts, but that only works if the man has a vast, expensive wardrobe. I thought of feeding Frank one meal so full of chili pepper that it would put him in hospital.

When I got home, Frank wasn't there.

His daily routine consisted of getting up after I'd left for work, then spending the day "writing his novel," which was a project that required intense study of nearly all the shows on daytime television, and involved a lot of overflowing ashtrays and scrunched-up cheeseball bags. After that, he was off to the Sylvia Hotel for a few beers in his usual corner before I got home, giving me plenty of time to clean up his mess and prepare dinner. Then he'd saunter in around seven, full of the local lager and himself, ready for his meal.

The night of the forged cheque, I didn't prepare anything. Food was the furthest thing from my mind. When I saw that he hadn't come home yet, I went out again and sat in the cinema at the end of the street. It was running a Fellini festival, so for a while I slouched in the seat and watched large lazy women and small horny men cavort relentlessly. I decided to go home when the subtitles started to blur before my eyes.

I approached my building by the back way. The two homeless men who often slept in the Dumpster—I'd privately nicknamed them Didi and Gogo—were there with their shopping carts and plastic bags full of junk, or rather, their worldly goods. They were ready to settle in for the night. It was September and just starting to get chilly.

I waved. They waved back.

Inside, I found Frank sprawled out on the double bed, facedown and snoring. He was wearing nothing but his dingy boxer shorts. The sight of him made me furious. Tears began streaming down my face, which rage had turned the color of a ripe tomato. I went into the living room and screamed into the sofa cushions. If I had been a Fellini character, I might have had the nerve to wake him up and smack him around directly. But I was just Lucy, about to be Frankless, and that meant some act of quiet treachery.

I was careful not to make any noise, which wasn't easy because I was sobbing and hiccupping. I went around the apartment and gathered up all of Frank's stuff, his clothes and books and general rubbish, and heaped them into a pile by the bedroom window. The window faced the back with the Dumpster and Didi and Gogo. As I was building the pile, Frank snorted and gnashed his teeth a couple of times in his sleep but didn't wake up.

I left the mound by the window and went to get the scissors from my sewing box. While Frank slept, I sheared a chunk of hair out of the middle of the back of his head, as short as I could get it without rousing him. His hair was shoulder-length at the time and he was quite vain about it. I opened the bedroom window and let the lock of hair waft down to the street below. Didi and Gogo saw me. I waved to them, still silently blubbering, and began to drop Frank's things out the bedroom window. They hurried over and gathered up as much of his stuff as they could carry or cram into their shopping carts. When I'd finished, I yelled so that the whole neighborhood could hear, "Godot has arrived."

Frank woke up with a start and said, "Wuzza?"

I threatened him with my aerosol-pump can of pepper spray, told him to put on his disgusting corduroy jacket and leave. He staggered out of the apartment in a stupor, wearing nothing but that jacket and his boxer shorts, and the last I saw of him, he was playing tug-of-war for his possessions with Didi and Gogo at the back of the building.

"That was a bit naughty of you," said Reebee. "You realize you had to go through it. Being with Frank had its purpose although it's usually a while before we know what that purpose is. Did you press charges?"

"No. I was too embarrassed. I didn't want anybody to know how stupid I'd been by putting up with such a lout. I thought I was supporting the next Michael Ondaatje."

Reebee smiled. "I grew up in the sixties and seventies, Lucy sweetheart. You and Sky, you girls, your generation is miles ahead of mine. I fell for men just because they had nice threads and longer, nicer hair than mine. Now tell me about your dreams."

Reebee always asked about my dreams. When I first started taking my problems to her, I was always asking whether or not I was going crazy. It was my private terror, that the genetic pool would try to drown me, that I'd become like Dirk, put on a Supergirl costume and start wandering around town harassing people, and not even realize I was doing it. According to Reebee, my dreams could gauge my mental state. In fact, it was Reebee who first encouraged me to start painting them all those years ago.

So I told her about the one I'd had the night before.

Mother was having a big house party. My father was nowhere around, in fact I didn't even know he existed. It was sort of like our house in Cedar Narrows but it was better. There were more rooms and conservatories and rolling lawns. Drunken guests were sprawling everywhere and having a good time and I was aware that they'd been there all night, that it was light out and morning was coming. I went into the dining room and there was my mother and her new husband sitting at a very elegant table, just the two of them, about to have breakfast, like the king and queen of some land where people did nothing but party. The table was set with white linen and silverware, croissants and orange juice and caffe latte.

My mother's new husband was Ugo Tognazzi, the actor who was in *La Cage aux Folles,* the macho one living with the transvestite performer.

In the dream, I was quite pleased with my mother's choice of husband. When I came up to the table, Ugo Tognazzi told me that he had decided to give me a present for my high school graduation. He was holding a Victoria's Secret catalogue and pointing at pictures of fancy black lace underwear. I told him that I'd graduated from high school years ago. So then he said, "University graduation then, you did graduate from university, didn't you?" And in the dream I honestly couldn't remember if I had or not. I had the sensation that there was a lot of unfinished business left over from university days.

Ugo Tognazzi said, "Look, this is what I'm going to give you." It was the same shawl that keeps showing up in my other dreams: the white silk and lace one embroidered with flowers and vines and birds. I was touched by his gesture because it was beautiful. The perfect gift.

Reebee was nodding and smiling.

"What do you think it means?" I asked her.

"Hell if I know," she said. "You're the one who's got to figure it out. But there is one interesting point in there."

"What's that?"

"Ugo Tognazzi. You like your mother's choice of husband, a gay man in the movie, but in actual fact, straight in real life. The actor I mean."

Then she left the room and came back with a large pad and oil pastels. "Draw the shawl," she said. "Show me what it looks like." I hesitated. It was like a smack in the face. It should have been so simple to just pick up the pastel and draw, but I realized that with all that had been going on in my life, it had been at least six months since I'd actually drawn a single line. Reebee looked at me knowingly and nodded as if to say, go on, you can do it.

"While you're sketching, tell me about Jeremy's girlfriend. Sky mentioned that there was some problem but I want to hear it from you."

"Connie."

I couldn't say her name without feeling a twinge in the pit of my stomach.

"Jeremy wanted me to keep an eye out for Connie. A request from Jeremy was something you didn't ignore when he was alive. And I know if I ignore this one now that he's dead, he'll come back to haunt me in my dreams. Connie's pregnant. The thing is, she told me she used to use heroin. Jeremy met her in Las Vegas but I don't know where she's from before that. She looks like an old showgirl. One that never quite made it. Not sunny enough, if you know what I mean."

Reebee's expression was deadpan.

"Reebee, I can't explain it. When I'm around Connie I feel like I'm going to be sucked into a black hole. She's one of the scariest people I've ever met and I can't even say why. But it's Jeremy's baby she's having. That's if everything goes okay. She was smoking her head off last time I saw her and who knows what else she might be doing while we're not watching. She looked terrible when I saw her."

"Go and see her again, Lucy. It was what Jeremy wanted. He wanted someone to watch out for her and the someone he chose is you. That's a responsibility."

"Don't remind me."

"Well, you could ignore your responsibility and just not bother, but can you imagine how you'd feel?"

I nodded.

"Watch out for her. You have to do it. Okay?"

"Okay."

I left Reebee's after eleven. We'd had one of her meatless dinners of pumpkin soup, blue corn bread and a green salad, and I was starving again. I got off the bus and hurried through the windy streets toward my own refrigerator hoping the Viking might have left me a few measly scraps of something Swedish—some rye crispbread, some pickled herring.

As I turned up my street, I could hear footsteps behind me. I walked a little faster. The footsteps were coming closer. I crossed over to the other side and heard the footsteps cross over with me. I shoved my hand into my bag and groped my little spray-pump bottle full of lemon juice and chili pepper. The footsteps were right behind me. I reeled around to face my attacker, but he had grabbed the bottle before I could squeeze.

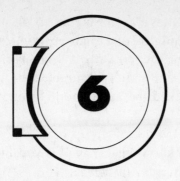

6

"Lucy!"

I screamed, "What are you trying to do scaring me to death like that?"

Paul Bleeker said, "I was in the neighborhood and thought I'd call on you."

"It's nearly midnight."

"I was passing through the area and thought I'd look you up. I've been thinking about you."

"Really?"

"Yes. I've been thinking a lot about you. I was asking myself tonight, 'Where is that sumptuous redhead when I need her? I'll go and find her.'"

"At eleven-fifty at night?"

"My best ideas come at night."

We were nearly at my building. He stopped, grabbed me by both shoulders, moved me over to a cement wall, grinned and leaned in to kiss me, pressing me up against the Virginia creeper. I was too surprised to say anything.

"You live here," he reminded me, taking me by the hand and leading me up the steps. I fumbled the keys out of my purse and unlocked the main door. His breath was hot on my neck.

Because I was well brought up, I said, "Would you like to come in? I don't know what I can offer you. I'm afraid I don't have anything. A glass of water?"

"Get what you need. I want you to come out with me."

"You want me to? …Uh…sure."

"I want to drop in on some friends first. That all right with you?"

I nodded.

"They're artists. Very interesting people." He gave me an intense look, and added, "Will you model for me? The show only needs a couple more pieces. You would round the whole thing out very nicely."

Little did I know at the time how literal his words would be.

"And I work very quickly once I have my concept," he said. "Would you do it for me?"

"What? When? Tonight?" I had planned to go on a diet first. I had planned to lose about a thousand pounds before taking my clothes off in front of him. There was the question of that little roll of midriff lard.

"That all right with you, Lucy?"

In my head, I'd played my encounter with him over and over, the clothes, the moves, the snappy retorts. All I could do now was mumble, "Okay."

As I unlocked the door to my apartment, his hand slithered around my waist. We moved, crablike, into the hallway. Anna was in the front room doing yoga. Her chest was on the floor and her legs arched backward over her head so that the tips of her toes nearly touched her nose. She straightened out, rolled over, put her feet over her head and her perfect buns in the air.

"My roommate Anna," I said.

Paul said, "Hallo."

"Hallo," came a voice from somewhere under her butt.

He whispered in my ear, "Get your stuff. I'll wait here."

I dashed like a fast-forward video clip, collecting things from the bathroom and bedroom and shoving them into a large purse. Everything that deodorizes went into that bag, as well as some new peach lace underwear I'd been saving for a special occasion.

Paul hustled me out of the building and down to where his black Ford van was parked at the end of the street. I thought it was gallant of him to open the door on the passenger side. I climbed in. The van smelled vaguely of gerbil's cage, and the back was full of black garbage bags. Art supplies, I imagined.

"You know, Lucy," he said. "I've met you before, but I just can't remember where."

The light was dawning. I wasn't such a zilch after all. "Art 400 seminar. About seven years ago. University."

"Was it there?" He looked worried.

I had the opening. I should have said, "I'm an artist, too," but it just wouldn't come out. It seemed like a ridiculous thing to say to Paul Bleeker, one-time Bad Boy of British Underground Art and now Star of the International Art Scene. He was too famous. I'd never sold a single painting. People had stolen my paintings, or traded something for them, but never actually paid real money.

"I got my degree in Fine Arts," I said to my feet.

He shook his head and sort of half laughed, half snorted.

"One of the Ivory Tower lot, are you, duckie? Thought you would be safe in the cocoon of academia? No one's safe." His British accent was back. He laughed again. This time, it was a weird, quiet snicker-snacking sound.

There'd been a lot written about Paul. About how he'd run away from home at the age of thirteen because his father had wanted him to go into the corner-store grocery business with him. How his mother had died when he was ten. How he'd lived hand-to-mouth with a group of derelict artists that eventually became known as the East Sheen Group. And then how the East Sheen Group picked over refuse heaps looking for usable materials for their works.

I'd read all about Paul Bleeker's breaking out of the Group with a one-man show of his own, all crafted in found bits of rusting metal. He had been involved in big conceptual projects, too, like the one that got him three days of jail—the giant game of Cat's Cradle over Stonehenge, using bungee cords and professional rock climbers.

As for his personal life, he had stated in the interviews, "I like women if that's what you nosy lot want to know." There was a lot of speculation about who his women were in those days, but nothing concrete was reported.

I remembered this and sighed to myself. He was gorgeous. He reminded me of the singer from Wet, Wet, Wet.

Okay. Yes, I confess, I've always been a bit of a Wettie. Paul Bleeker's resemblance to Marti Pellow was strong enough in certain moments that I half expected him to croon all those lyrics about wanting to get close to me, right into my ear in the same languid sexy tones. If he could sing like that, I would willingly be his slave.

I snuck glances at Paul as he drove. He certainly had a profile like Marti Pellow's. He had those same dark, sexy looks. But I could see there wasn't going to be any serenade. Paul was a busy man, a true artist with true art to make. What I hadn't realized before was that a working artist had to make sacrifices. He had no time to be crooning or sitting around in places like the Rain Room drinking big sloppy drinks with little umbrellas in them.

We drove in the direction of the university. I was encouraged. It was an area of big comfortable wooden houses with large yards and beautiful gardens. I could picture us already, standing around in a plush living room with a bunch of savvy people discussing art with a capital *A* and drinking a decent chilled Italian white wine, while we waited to help ourselves to the buffet, which the considerate hosts had prepared. I was starving.

Paul stopped the van in front of a brown house with peeling paint and a garden that featured, above all, waist-high thistles, dandelions and morning glory. Paul reached across the gear shift and touched my cheek. "You're an artist. You'll like these guys, luv. Old-fashioned Bohemians."

An artist! A famous artist had just called me an artist. How did he know? He hadn't even seen my work. Maybe someone had told him about it. Nadine perhaps. It didn't matter. I climbed out of the van and followed him into the darkness. He was pushing his way through the overgrowth that blocked the path leading around the side of the house to the back. I stayed close, getting whipped in the face by the branches as they left his hand and snapped backward.

A dim bulb lit the stairs leading up to the back door and revealed a yard full of junk. Most of it was rusting scrap metal. There was even part of a smashed-up Cadillac, its massive snout crinkled up long ago in some nightmarish impact.

I followed Paul closely. The steps weren't safe. There were more rotten boards in the staircase than good ones. Paul seemed to know his way because he bounded fearlessly up all the right ones while I picked my way as if through a field of land mines trying to ignore the dangerous splintering noises under my feet. Paul didn't bother knocking. He just walked right in.

The kitchen was in darkness but I could make out the sink full of unwashed dishes, the take-out Chinese food and frozen TV dinner boxes piled on the kitchen table and counters. And I couldn't help but notice the paraphernalia. Paul caught me staring and said, "The lads like to do a little spliffing-up from time to time." There was a contraption in the corner that was straight out of Alice in Wonderland. All it needed was a caterpillar.

"Spliffing-up? That hookah's bigger than me," I said too loudly.

He smiled. "C'mon," he said, taking my hand and pulling me toward the living room.

His four friends, "the real Bohemians," were slouched around the dimly lit space and seemed intent on creating a thicker, smokier fug in the room. They all rolled their own from pouches of Drum tobacco. Two of them were seated on the floor, another on a sofa whose stuffing was popping out in several places, and the fourth was stretched full-length in the middle of the floor staring at the ceiling, fascinated. I heard the one on the sofa say to no one in particular, "Yeah, oi fink it's super ven, really, fabulous, absolutely staggering, yeah, amazing ven, innit?"

One of the floor sitters, a guy with black hair growing on every available part of his face, noticed Paul and leapt to his feet. "Corrr, Bleeker you ol' git, where'ya been?" His beady black eyes did a quick tour of my body. "Corrr, ooo's the bi'a crumpet?"

I tried not to let it get to me. Nobody was calling me anything edible these days so I tried to take crumpet as a compliment.

"Bloody good crack, it is, seein' you, you ol' wanka," said the man on the sofa. He was a superannuated hippy, fiftyish, thin droopy features and long reddish-gray hair, much like an Irish setter's. He got up, came over and gave Paul one of those self-conscious cool-guy hugs.

At that point, the others all followed suit, including the prone ceiling-gazer. I had to listen to a lot of corr and blimey and fooching roights and poxy thises and thats before I realized that these guys were part of Paul's old East Sheen group. It accounted for the garbage dump out the back. Since I had so much trouble following their accents—one was from Liverpool, another from Edinburgh, and the remaining two from "Souf' London"—I sat back and pretended to drink from the bottle of Guinness that was offered to me.

I think the conversation turned to art, but I can't be sure. There was a long argument that seemed to be about belly-button lint as a medium, and then the topic turned to jelly. Jellied everything. As an art form. Using enormous life-size moulds. Beef broth jellied into the shape of a cow, for example.

At the jelly part, I was finally able to cut through the accents and follow the drift. I saw my chance and leapt in with "aspic?" Unfortunately, it was misinterpreted, and there were a lot of lewd comments and guffaws, so I shrank back into my corner of the floor and kept my mouth shut for the rest of the evening. Who would have thought that suffering for one's art could take such an unusual direction?

It was Paul's success that rescued us. As I've mentioned, he was a very busy man. He suddenly looked at his watch, said quick goodbyes all round and hustled me out of the house, this time through the front door.

When we were in his van, he said, "Amazing blokes, eh, luv?"

"Amazing," I said flatly. My backside was numb from sitting on the cold floorboards, my stomach churning from the smoke and the sickly taste of the beer.

"Listen, Lucy luv, just a word. These chaps are not exactly living here legally so it might be best not to mention your meeting them."

"Oh, okay. I see. I'm curious though. How do they keep body and soul together?"

As if I didn't know.

"Oh, they do a little of this, a little of that." He stared straight ahead and drove faster.

Paul's loft was in Gastown not far from Rogues' Gallery, in a huge, old brick building. He all but pushed me up the four flights of stairs. As we climbed, he said, "This building was once a brothel." He opened the door and flicked on a light.

"Interesting," I mumbled. There was nothing brothel-like about it now, and it was too bad, because the place could have used a little frou-frou. His warehouse space was done in black: shiny black floor, brick walls painted over with dull black, black leather sofa and armchairs in one corner, black glass coffee table and big black bed (!!!) in another corner. The only relief was the computer, and the studio area comprising a curving white ultra-modern psychiatrist's couch and a white sheet draped on the wall behind it. Along another wall was a row of huge stainless steel walk-in refrigerators, which kept his art supplies, I imagined.

"It's very…er…black," I said.

"Absence of light. I need it for my work. The influence of color can be a dangerous thing for an artist."

"I see." But I didn't see at all.

He threw a big switch and the corner with the white sheet became a glare of spotlights. He pointed to the wall near the white zone.

"Over here," he said. "You can hang your clothes on that hook."

Just like that. No preliminaries. No coyly helping me ease my way out of my clothes. No stroking all the skin off my arm or other parts of my body. Just straight to the total nudity. He rummaged around and began to prepare his drawing materials. I stood frozen to the spot.

"Well, hurry up."

I didn't move.

He laughed that snicker-snack laugh again then came over and put his arms around me. "What a sod I am, asking you to strip just like that. A drink?" He was already headed toward the refrigerators. He opened and closed one of them so quickly I couldn't see inside, then he came over with a bottle of vodka and two chilled glasses. He poured two huge slugs and handed one to me. "Nasdrovya. You have to knock it back fast." He finished his in a gulp.

I sipped politely.

"You do want to be my inspiration, don't you, Lucy luv? My muse?"

I shrugged.

"Well, do you?"

"Errr…"

"Drink up then. It'll help you relax."

I downed it. I told myself, what the hell, Paul Bleeker the famous artist wants you to model for him and you stand there like a moron.

He held up both hands. "Okay, okay, just a minute." He disappeared through a door in the bed area and came back with a black bathrobe. "You can put this on until you're warmed up. Another drink?"

"Yesh, pleashe."

I was warming up nicely. After a few more minutes, my clothes seemed to have taken themselves off and I lounged on the shrink's couch wondering what all the fuss had been about. With the vodka firing through my veins, it became clear that I was born to pose nude, a natural artist's model, my creamy-skinned gorgeous body poised for immortality...

"Bloody hell, your knees and elbows are blushing. Too sloppy, that pose. Straighten up. Tits front, girl. Arse we'll do later."

It was a very long night. Paul Bleeker sketched for hours. He went through reams of paper. I held walking, running and dancing poses. I sat. I stood tall. I bent to the left, willowed to the right. Crouched. Sprawled. Rolled myself into a ball. Stretched out like a corpse. It was exhausting.

Sometime around daybreak, Paul put down his stub of charcoal and came over to me. I was kneeling on the floor. It wasn't by chance that I was on my knees. I was praying the modelling part of the session would be over soon.

He took me by the elbows and pulled me to my feet, then started kissing me. It was hungry-aggressive kissing. One of his hands gripped me around the waist while he unbuckled and unzipped himself with the other. We stagger-hobbled in the direction of the bed and somewhere just short of it, he pulled me down to the floor. There were a few books lying around and one of the thicker tomes got me in the center of my back. My head was to one side and I could see dust-balls the size of tumbleweeds scudding around underneath the bed. Paul had the condom on in three of the deftest seconds I've ever witnessed, and within another twenty seconds, it was all over and he was flopped to one side puffing on a Sobranie and flicking ash onto the floor. I extracted a complete anthology of Henry Miller from between my shoulder blades.

Let's face it. First times never live up to their promise. It would improve. It would have to. We just needed time to get used to each other.

He fell asleep like that, with the burning cigarette dangling between his fingers. I removed it and stubbed it out. Paul was comatose. I could barely see his breathing.

I grabbed the black robe, pulled it tight around me and stretched out on his bed. I sank into sleep and dreamt I was in a field of wildflowers: poppies, daisies, dandelions, blue cornflowers, borage and lavender, dog roses, nasturtium and burning bush, crocuses, tansy, marigolds. Every season of flower had been rolled into one and dazzled my eyes with their brilliance.

I was aware that there were women standing in the field, each one with a different petal's color and fragility. A bird like a crow or raven flew overhead, blocking the sun, and in its wake a huge black cloud stopped over the field. It began to rain soot. The petal women melted into the mucky dark ground. I started to run, trying to escape the black rain, but it was like moving in molasses. The rain was coming harder and faster and now there was such loud thunder that I started awake and wondered where the storm was.

It was my stomach rumbling.

Paul was still asleep on the floor and I was famished. I got up, dressed myself and went over to his fridges. There were five of them, and somewhere inside one of them, there had to be a tiny little snack. I grabbed the handle and was about to open the door when a voice barked, "Get away from there." Paul was sitting up and looking mean.

"Sorry, I didn't realize you kept your victims' bodies in the fridge."

He didn't look amused. "You are never, ever to open any of those. Do you understand?"

"I didn't realize…"

"Do? You? Understand?" he enunciated, as if I were a child.

"I said I was sorry."

"Just as long as you understand."

My lower lip trembled and my eyes began to water.

I know they say crying is healthy, cathartic, that it's a bad idea to bottle it all up. But tell that to someone like me, a natural crier, whose tear ducts open up and produce white-water rapids over the slightest provocation. Just once in my life, I longed to be less transparent.

His evil expression softened. He came over and gave me a hug. "Lucy, Christ, I'm a wretched sod. No tears now. It's where I keep the tools of my trade. Top secret. If you knew what was in there, you'd be susceptible. Some clever bugger of a journalist would find out you've been up here and make you spill the surprise. Surprise is a lot in my kind of art. So the less you know the better."

This was different from the other artists I'd known. The others were usually clubbing journalists over the head with their work, rough or finished.

He coughed and looked at his watch. "You better hurry or you'll be late for work." As he hustled me out the door all I could think was, What, no breakfast? No white linen table-cloth? No croissants? No caffe latte?

Chivalry was dead and buried.

Before I started down the stairs, he pulled me back and gave me a proper kiss. "I'm only four blocks away from Rogues' Gallery. Keep that in mind for your lunch break,

won't you? I'm usually here at that hour. Run along now."
He grinned and shut the door.

I hurried down the street. It was a rotten windy day, candy
wrappers, scrap paper and leaves gusting around me. I stopped
at La Tazza and had Nelly the Grape make me my usual double caffe latte. I bought a huge fattening pastry as well. I de-
served two pastries but I held back, thinking of all the
nakedness that might still take place.

The door to the gallery was unlocked which meant that
Nadine was already there. Her office door was closed and I
could hear her voice but not make out the words. I took off
my coat, put my bag on my desk and sat down. The little brass
urn full of Jeremy's ashes was still sitting on my desk. It was
comforting to have it there in front of me during my long
boring gallery days.

"Hi, Jeremy," I said to it. "I had quite a night. I'll tell you
about it sometime when I figure it all out. I hope you're okay,
wherever you are. I hope you're watching. I hope you're
going to find a way to help me from the other world, you
know, look after me a little, put in a good word with the
powers that be. I wish you would. I don't need to tell you
how much I miss you. I went to see Connie. I just don't get
you, Jeremy. I'm sorry but I just can't see what you saw in
her. She looks like a real mess. And I just don't know how
much help I can be in all of this…"

A loud "Heh-hem" interrupted my murmuring. Nadine
was standing in her office doorway looking superior. "If
you're finished communing with the dead, Lucy."

"Isn't it in my contract that you have to respect my reli-
gious beliefs?"

Nadine shook her head. "It's in your contract that if you

screw up, you're out the door. In fine-print legalese." She peered at me more closely. "Whatever have you been doing?"

"What do you mean?"

"Your face is all smutty. Go and look at yourself."

I went into the bathroom and stared into the mirror. I looked like a chimney sweep. Paul Bleeker's charcoaly fingerprints were on my face. I probably had smudges all over the rest of my body as well. I scrubbed myself with wet paper towels, brushed my hair and put on a little lipstick. A nice dark shade.

When I'd finished cleaning up and was back at my desk, Nadine said, "I've got an IT expert here. Jacques needs to examine your computer. He's going to be putting in some new software."

"Jacques? Jacques who?" My heart skipped a beat. A computer whizz would be able to see where I'd been on the Net, see all the hours I'd frittered away checking out eBay, Big Brother sites and Lonely Hearts Web pages.

"I'm upgrading," said Nadine. "Jacques, this is my assistant, Lucy Madison."

Jacques came into view and I laughed.

"Hey, Luce, how're ya doing?"

"Jacques. What are you doing here?"

Jacques came over, picked me up and whirled me around. I only came up to his chest. Next to him I was a sylph.

He put me down and glanced over at Nadine's raised eyebrows. He said, "Miss Thorpe wants to buy the farm, add a few more gigabytes. And some fancy stuff for showing off artists' work to full advantage. That right, Miss Thorpe?" I could tell by the way Nadine was looking at him that she wanted a few of Jacques's private bits and bytes as well. It was understandable. Jacques was six feet four inches of broad-shouldered barrel-chested male sweetness. Because he didn't have to impress anyone, he always wore the same uniform: jeans, lumberjack shirts and long straight black hair that went past his shoulders. He had a hint of local native blood and an easy smiling expression. Like Geronimo on tranquilizers.

He was a computer genius. He'd been finishing his studies when I first met him. In university days, he'd been lost in love with Madeline from the art department. Madeline was his only defect. He would come looking for her, his dark eyes puppy-dogging along all the routes Madeline might have taken, checking out all the places where Madeline might be. We made friends during his long waits for her. What Jacques didn't know back then was that Madeline was a very busy girl, very popular, with a lot of extra-curricular men, and she loved having Jacques as a personal six-foot-four doormat.

"So what are you doing these days, Jacques?" I asked.

"Working at the university, rescuing departmental techno-dummies all over the campus whenever they melt down. Hey, you still painting, Luce?"

"Mmmm-hmmm." It was neither a yes nor a no. I hate lying to friends. "How's Madeline? She still making…"

"Heart art. Yeah. She's doing some really great stuff." He sounded slightly panicky, the way the less-loved partner in a relationship sounds when they are afraid of losing the other. "She's selling quite well in New York." He sighed. "She's there right now. Gonna be there for a couple more weeks." He sighed again.

These words crushed me like a ten-ton block. Back then, Madeline had been into this mock-sixties pop art stuff using a lot of pink and hearts and doe-eyed Twiggy-like female figures. The worst part was that there were professors who thought she was the great promise of the art department.

Hearts.

She still had Jacques's heart after all these years, and it looked like she was still reducing it to pulp.

I reached for my caffe latte and knocked my bag off the desk. Its contents, including my virgin peach lace underwear, spilled all over the floor.

Jacques smiled and raised his eyebrows quizzically. Nadine looked peeved. I would like to have told them that it had been a great night, a masterpiece of lovemaking, but the fact was, the Maestro had barely dipped his brush.

7

Jacques was there all morning fiddling with the computers. Nadine sent me out on errands three times. First it was to the post office to mail some packages, then the department store to buy cleaning supplies and finally to the bakery for cinnamon buns because she was feeling a little peckish. Around one o'clock she said, "I have a yen for some Dim Sum today. Shall we all go to lunch? My treat?" She smiled her porcelain smile at both of us. I rarely refuse a free lunch and I was happy to have the chance to hang out with Jacques again after such a long time. We drove to Chinatown in his Porsche. Nadine raced to get into the front seat next to him. I had to sit in the back.

In the restaurant, Nadine gleefully chose something off every trolley that came around: shrimp dumplings, steam buns with sweet bean filling, sausage wrapped in grape leaf, ducks' feet, spring rolls, it all just kept coming. Nadine had a sneaky way of eating that made it look as though she were just picking at her food, but she was really putting it away. During the hour and a half lunch, she got up three times to go to the bathroom.

"Miss Thorpe must have an awfully weak bladder," said Jacques.

"Acute observation."

The thought of elaborating on Nadine's bladder depressed me, so I didn't bother.

Jacques spent the rest of the afternoon working on the computers. Around six o'clock Nadine tried her "me and a few friends are meeting for drinks. Would you care to join us?" routine on Jacques.

"Sorry, Miss Thorpe, I'm going for beers with Lucy," he said. His voice was blunt. It seemed to say, "Shame on you for asking."

I was flattered. I pulled on my coat, grabbed my bag and left the gallery with Jacques. He took me to the Four Seasons. They let him in, dressed in blue jeans. When we had our beers in front of us he said, "It's great to see you again, Lucy Madison."

I knew what was coming.

He launched into his favorite subject: Madeline.

Madeline and her affair with her New York gallery manager, Madeline and the wealthy businessman she met on a plane and oh it was just one of those things that happened—it doesn't mean anything. I kept wanting to pipe up, Madeline and the postman, Madeline and the plumber, Madeline and the paperboy, Madeline and anything in pants that breathes.

Poor Jacques. He needed to talk to someone and I let him talk. He was finally growing up a little. But knowing about all her betrayals didn't seem to help him. If anything, they made her more desirable in his eyes. I couldn't understand it. I resisted saying what I'd always wanted to say, that he should dump her cold, forget about her forever because she was bad news.

He would never leave her, and even if he did, she would always stay with him, metaphorically, occasionally popping out of a huge, messy emotional scar to say "Cuckoo." Any smart woman would sense Madeline's ghost.

It was about nine when we left the Four Seasons. Jacques abandoned his car in town and we both took a taxi. In the back seat, he held my hand and I thought for a minute things might get interesting. But he just went on holding my hand, the way an old friend or a brother might. The decent brother I wished I had. Then I said, "Hey, Jacques, what are you doing for Easter?"

"Nothing, I guess. Madeline will still be in New York."

"Come with me to my parents' for the big meal."

He brightened a little. "Sure." He wrote his phone number on my hand, and we promised to be in touch to organize Easter Sunday.

When I got home, there was a number scrawled on a piece of paper with the word *irget* next to it. Anna's handwriting.

"Anna? Are you home?"

"In bathroom," came her voice.

"This message. Who's Irget?"

"It is very very important…uh…you know…irget."

"Urgent?"

"Ya."

I picked up the phone and called the number. A man's voice answered.

"This is Lucy Madison," I said.

"Oh, hi, Lucy. I've been trying to reach you for a while. It's Sam. Sam Trelawny."

"Hi, Sam. Sorry to get back to you so late."

"That's okay."

"You said it was urgent?"

"Yeah. It seems there've been a few more sightings of our slippery guy in the Superman costume."

"Oh God."

Sam laughed. "We haven't been able to grab him yet, but he's really getting around. According to the reports, he's added a few more touches to his outfit."

"Oh damn."

Sam was still laughing. "…gold stars hand-painted on gumboots, a T-shirt with a crude rainbow hand-painted over the front, and an old suitcase, the kind women used as cosmetic cases in the fifties, painted with gold stars."

"Double damn."

"He's been stopping women in the streets and telling them he's a big producer and that if they don't star in his film, he'll have his men break their boyfriends' or husbands' legs. We're starting to wade into deeper water here with these threats, but we still don't have anything concrete. Whenever the police get to the scene of the complaint, he's gone and his victims think it's too silly to prosecute. It seems he also had one of those rubber chickens and was threatening some guy with that, too. But I don't know. A rubber chicken. It doesn't really constitute a significant threat."

I was silent.

"Lucy, are you there?"

"I'm here. You're laughing."

"Believe me if I tell you, you're not the only one."

I was slightly shocked. "You don't have relatives like this, do you, Sam?"

"Ask me about it. A lot of people have relatives like this."

"Really? Not as bad as Dirk, though?"

"Depends. Depends on how you look at it."

"Go on."

"It's all on the female side in my family. I've got one chubby cousin who's always trying to diet but whenever she does, she goes off the rails, ends up ripping off all her clothes and riding her bicycle around town. We call her Lady Godiva."

It was my turn to laugh. "Nudity's okay."

"Glad you think so."

"No, really, it is."

"I also had a great-aunt who was a WREN driver during the war. Whenever she flipped, she went out and stole the vehicle of her choice. Rang the fire bell so that she could steal the fire truck. I don't know. That's just my family. I could tell you about some other folks I know."

"I feel better. Thanks, Sam."

"Good. I'm glad I could serve up the family nuts for some purpose."

I said, "And I'm sorry for phoning you so late. You're probably going out."

"You, too."

"I've just come in."

"So early on a Saturday night?" There was a sweet twist in Sam's voice.

"Well, you're working on a Saturday night."

"Hazards of the profession. My…clients…keep losing their copy of my work schedule. I'm not actually on call. I just wanted to keep you up to date, let you know the latest." His voice became serious. "I know it's hard for you at times, having a brother like Dirk. These folks take a toll on their families."

"Thank you for saying that. People don't realize. You're the first person I've ever met…well, I haven't actually met you, have I… It feels as though I have," I said.

"Yeah, it does. You were saying?"

"You're the first in that profession to tell me about your family skeletons. A lot of the other people who have worked on Dirk's case haven't had a clue. Okay, they may have come from slightly messed-up families and were working to put the universe right, but they couldn't make the leap. What made you choose social work, if you don't mind my asking?"

Sam laughed, "Social work kind of happened to me by accident. You could say I rebounded into it. It's a long story. Maybe I'll tell it to you sometime."

"I'd like to hear it." Anna was poking my shoulder and looming over me. "Oh, sorry, I've gotta go. My roommate wants the phone."

Anna was glaring and making gestures to let me know that she was waiting for an important phone call.

Sam said, "I'll let you know if we make any progress, and you let me know if Dirk shows up. And Lucy?"

"Yes?"

"Don't let the rubber chickens get you down."

"Bye, Sam. Thanks." I hung up.

Anna was wearing an ice-white evening dress, cut down to her coccyx at the back, cut to her navel at the front, slit to her hip at the side, and accented by a very heavy collar of what looked like real gold. Her pale blond hair fell sleekly down her back. She wore no makeup. She didn't need to. Nobody was going to be looking at her face for long.

I wanted to cry. Never in a million years could I wear a dress like that. A white dress. I'd look like Moby Dick on the high seas. With one difference. I'd have absolutely no danger of being harpooned.

The next morning, Sunday, it rained, a biting spring rain that slapped the branches and pavement and bounced back six inches. It made me feel that the world had always been wet, that the sun shining was a hallucination. Anna wasn't home so I drank my morning coffee without its usual lacing of envy. I listened to Ella Fitzgerald and Joe Pass on the stereo. But my world felt tilted, out of balance. No morning-after-the-day-after phone calls from Paul. And I had to go and see Connie again this morning. I'd promised Reebee and Jeremy's ashes that I'd make an effort.

I got out my big black umbrella and took the three bus rides down to the Commercial Drive area. It continued to pelt and I cursed Connie for making me come out in such weather and wasting part of my free day.

I stopped at a supermarket and bought a quart of milk, some lettuce and tomatoes, some oranges and bananas, and a small steak. In the middle of the aisle, I paused and said, "Connie, you bag," out loud to the meat section. I never bought steak for myself so why should Connie get it? I had to keep reminding myself that the steak was not really going to Connie but to the child in her womb. Connie was just a nine-month underwater taxi ride for the baby, an obstacle to be gotten past.

When I arrived at the house, all the curtains were drawn. I rang the doorbell and waited. Five minutes must have passed so I rang it again, this time leaning on it. I tried the door but it was locked. I leaned on the bell some more. I didn't want to leave until I'd seen her. She had no friends in Vancouver. Jeremy had told me she had no friends, that she hadn't any from her past life in Las Vegas either. No one ever wrote or phoned from the States and she never talked about people she might miss. He'd told me she had no family. He'd said she had a general mistrust of the human race. All of which made me wonder over and over why he had bothered with her.

I leaned on the bell again. Then I walked back down the front steps and looked up at the house. A corner of curtain flickered in one of the upstairs windows. I went back to the front door and this time knocked hard.

"Connie, open up," I said to the empty hallway beyond the glass door. "It's Lucy. Jeremy wanted it this way so it's going to be this way. I'm not leaving, so you better just come down and unlock the door." Still nothing. It occurred to me that she might not be home, but for some reason, a prickling at the back of my neck, I was sure she was.

"Lookit, Connie, I don't like this any better than you do. It's wet out here and I'm freezing but it was Jeremy's idea so I'm going to stand right here until you come out of your cave."

By this time I was yelling. A man's voice shouted from the house next door, "It's Sunday morning, goddammit, shut the hell up and let me sleep." It was noon but I guess it still qualified as morning for some.

"Listen, Connie, open that door. That's my cousin…I mean my aunt or uncle you're carrying around inside you…or maybe it's my second cousin, or my second cousin once removed, or…well Jeremy's kid. Oh, hell. Just open up, will you?"

She appeared, a dark blob at the end of the hallway, lumbering toward the front door. She opened it, gave me her deadpan stare, and asked, "What do you want?"

"To see that you and the baby are okay."

"Why don't you just go away and leave me alone. I just want to be left alone."

"Jeremy told me to insist."

"Well, Jeremy's dead. Doesn't have much say in the matter, does he?" Connie shuffled toward the living room and I followed her.

Inside the house, I felt faint. Under the cigarette smell, there was still the smell of Jeremy's life. I hadn't noticed it the last time. I held my breath and clenched my teeth, afraid I might start wailing like a Sicilian widow. Anything not to let the lingering odor in.

There was the animal smell of someone else's lair. That composite that makes up their private scent. The carpets they tread, the furniture they sprawl on, the air freshener they use to cover other smells, the food they cook, the parties they throw, the leathery, limey aftershave they wear, the damp musty wooden smell of the house that surrounds them. The scent of my adolescence.

Connie found a packet of cigarettes, shook one out and lit it. She was wearing a sloppy pink sweatsuit that really accentuated her green complexion nicely. Her cheekbones were high and looked even more pronounced now. She was losing weight, the little she had going to her bulging middle. Her strange blue eyes were more sunken than ever. And her hair fashion statement that day was black roots and greasy tangles. She smelled of smoke and biscuit-y sweat.

"What are you going to have for lunch?" I asked in my best Spanish Inquisition tone.

"Whadyou care?"

"I just told you. I'm here to see that you and the baby are doing all right. Okay, I'm lying. More the baby than you."

She stared at me again with that hard, expressionless, unreadable face. It was impossible to tell if she hated me or just thought of me as insignificant dust.

"I'm getting a cramp in my arm. I've got to put these groceries down." I marched into the big kitchen. It was a squalid scene. No chance of catching Jeremy's scent there.

She had crept up behind me. "The maid quit and good help is so hard to find," she said in her husky monotone.

The sink was piled with dirty dishes. Overflowing garbage bags filled the corner where the bin used to be. A dynasty of flies was breeding and ballroom dancing. I imagined that nobody had lifted a finger in that kitchen since well before Jeremy had died. I turned around to look at Connie but she was on her way down the hall to the bathroom. I heard loud retching and the toilet flush.

I got to work. It upset me that Jeremy's kitchen had reached such a state. It had never been pretty; it was an awful shade of yellow with gray arborite counters, and old, but he had always kept it with military neatness. Being a single dad had taught him how.

I carried garbage bags out to the side of the house. I washed, dried and put away dishes. I cleaned the floor and the appliances. By then it was midafternoon. I cooked the steak, tossed the salad, put it all on a plate and carried it up to Connie.

She had the TV on loud in the big upstairs bedroom. A rerun of *The Beachcombers.* I didn't bother knocking. She gave me another of her stares, but I put the plate down on the bedside table and said, "I want to see you take a bite of that meat."

She shook her head.

"If you don't, I'll call an ambulance and tell them how sick you are, how you can't keep food down, have them come and get you because yours is a pregnancy at risk. We might even talk about drugs." Her face went chalk white. "Then your neighbors will get all nosy and be bugging you every five minutes. I bet you don't even have B.C. medical insurance."

"Don't you have somewhere else to go? Go be a pain in the ass to someone else. Leave me alone."

"Not eating is affecting the welfare of the baby. If you don't put some food in your mouth, I'll call social services and report you for prenatal abuse and neglect. Unborn children have rights these days or didn't you know. I have friends in high places at social services." It was not the sort of thing to be boasting about but it was out of my mouth before I realized it.

Connie picked up the fork and stared at the plate.

"I already cut it for you."

She took a mouthful and chewed slowly, glaring at me as if I'd forced her to eat one of her relatives in a cannibalistic ceremony. Then she put down the fork and rolled over on her side with her back to me.

I stood there, helpless, staring at the back of her and wanting to give her a good hard kick. "Have it your own way, Connie. I'm going."

I don't know what I expected. Compassionate sainthood was not a role that suited me at all. I stomped down the stairs feeling the way I'd felt on the playground, age ten, when other kids excluded me because I was short and had carrot-red hair.

When I got home, I was on the phone to Reebee, telling her about it.

Her voice sounded a little stern. "You mustn't give up. Just keep at it, Lucy. Sometimes there are moments in life that we just have to work past." Now she was sounding like my mother. "I'll be very disappointed if you give up on Connie. There's more than just your pride at stake."

Then I phoned Sky, who said, "Connie? Tell her to go suck rocks," and that made me feel much better.

8

For Easter Sunday, Jacques put on a suit jacket and some nice slacks. The startling effect of seeing him dressed up was softened by his Bart Simpson T-shirt. I'd never seen him in anything but his lumberjack uniform. I was outfitted for the occasion in military khaki pants and the kind of mud-green thermal long-sleeved undershirt favored by South American terrorists hiding out in mountain stations. I thought it was magnanimous of me to be going to Cedar Narrows at all, where I would be a sitting duck if Dirk showed up. My mother had told me on the phone to stop being so silly.

Did I mention that my mother is the kind of person who hums serenely as she passes four cars in a row on the outside? Who thinks the crater of an active volcano is a fun place for a picnic?

When we got close to my parents' street, I didn't tell Jacques which house it was but directed him to a parking place nearby.

"You don't mind walking a bit, do you, Jacques?"

"No, not at all."

"There's something else I haven't told you about my family."

"I know your brother's a Froot Loop if that's what you mean."

"No, it's not that."

"Lemme see. You told me that your father's one of those big-time Dunking and Damning Christians."

"No, it's not that. It's something that'll be evident in a few seconds."

"So which house is it?"

"Keep walking. We're nearly there."

"We're nearly… Oh, hey, wow. It's not this house, is it?" He grinned at me.

"Afraid so."

"I've died and gone to heaven. Cool. Little people's heaven. Get a load of this. Wow." Jacques stood there grinning, gazing at the front yard of my parents' house. He ran a hand through his hair, something he always did when he was amazed or impressed.

"It's my mother's doing. And I should warn you. She's very sensitive about it. It's her biggest weak spot. Next to the fact that I'm not breeding according to her schedule. Let's go inside."

"No. Not yet. I want to stand here and take it all in. Jeez, they're all here. Sneezy, Sleepy, Doc, Grumpy… Truly amazing." He stood back and let out a long whistle. "Hey, there's something missing down there." He pointed to the empty pedestal between a pink flamingo and red-and-white polka-dotted toadstool with a plaster leprechaun seated on it.

"Winky. My mother's favorite garden gnome. It's a long

story. I find it's better not to bring it up. My mother gets worked up about it."

As we started up the path my mother was at the open doorway to greet us.

"Lucy." She clapped her hands together. She was wearing a large apron with a print of turkeys all over it.

"Hi, Mom. You've got the wrong apron on."

"Have I?" She looked down. "Oh, dear. Yes, I guess I have. I couldn't find the one with the bunnies."

"This is Jacques," I said.

"Hello, Jacques. It's so nice to meet one of Lucy's friends. She never brings anybody around anymore. Now, when she was little it was different. Do you remember that nice boy you used to play doctor with, Lucy? What was his name? Little Francis or little James…"

"Mo-ther," I hissed between clenched teeth.

Jacques leapt in, "I was just admiring your front garden, Mrs. Madison. I must say, that's some very fine statuary you have."

My mother beamed. "Do you think so, Jacques? It's so kind of you to say so. I've been collecting for years. I was hoping to have started on the backyard by now but what with one thing and another…"

"I hate to interrupt the garden party but it's not that warm out here. I'm going inside." I pushed past my mother and went into the house. It was quiet inside. Too quiet, in fact.

Every Easter my father greeted guests by playing recordings of the local church's most recent rendering of the *Messiah*. The choir generally sounded like a chorus of demented mice, and the alto soloist had a vibrato you could drive a Mack truck through, but after years of it, I looked forward to the tradition.

I walked through the living room to the den, back through

the kitchen and dining room. Empty. No music. No father. I went down into the basement and into his workshop. Fatherless.

My mother was still chatting with Jacques on the front porch. As I approached, I could hear her say, "Of course you two are taking every precaution?"

"Every precaution available, Mrs. Madison, and in a variety of colors."

"Call me June. Well, I'm glad you're both careful. Not that we want to be careful forever now, do we?"

"Oh, no, certainly not. Not forever."

"Otherwise how would the planet get populated."

"How indeed." Jacques was smooth. Very smooth.

"A little accident wouldn't be a bad thing. I can't wait forever and Lucy knows it."

"Mother," I barked. "Where's Dad?"

"Oh, your father. I meant to talk to you about that. I'm not sure if he's going to be…look, there's your cousin now with Michael and the kids. Yoohooo…"

Car doors slammed and there was the sound of children shrieking and bawling. It was my cousin Cherry and her brood. The second youngest boy escaped her grasp, raced up the steps to me, and whacked me across the ankles with a plastic sword. I gasped with pain. The youngest brother followed suit and whumped me in the stomach with his fist while Cherry and Michael looked on smiling, as if to say, "Our little darlings."

But Jacques grabbed them both by their jackets and suspended them in midair. "Tell Auntie Lucy you're sorry and that you won't ever do it again."

He held the miniature mobsters there until apologies trickled out of them like coins out of Scroogey pockets. Cherry and Michael looked on, dismayed, wanting to protest but not quite able to find the words. Jacques had a special kind of authority that you didn't question. And the fact that he was taller than everyone else helped.

I smiled at them all. "I need a drink," I said, and limped inside.

My father was abstemious, but my mother snuck her daily two gin and tonics before my father got home from school. She always had something to serve guests. In the dining room, I found bottles of everything set out on a silver tray and a bucket of ice cubes nearby. Before anyone could see me, I unscrewed the top of some London Dry and took a big swig straight from the bottle.

As I was slugging back gin, Jeremy's ghost assaulted me again. He wafted past, reminding me of other Easters when even Connie had come out to Cedar Narrows on the back of the Harley, and Jeremy told his irreverent stories, while my father fumed and my mother pursed her lips.

I also had an unexpected twinge of guilt, a flash of the greasy, sulking, bulging, puking, grieving Connie, alone at Easter.

I didn't like her. I didn't know her that well, and I didn't want to know her, but I had to concede that she probably wasn't such a gold digger after all, or she wouldn't have decided to stay and have a miserable time alone in that house. We were both tied to Jeremy, and for that reason, I couldn't get her out of my mind. In that moment, with the void left by Jeremy yawning up in front of me, I could feel Connie's solitude, and the way it must have been compounded by all those hormones. Her child would never know what a great father it had, and that thought made something catch in my throat.

More voices came up the front steps. Two couples had arrived. They were friends of my parents and were all on the church vestry together. They lived for gossip, the dirtier the better.

Everyone came inside and Michael started pouring the drinks officially. Each time I tried to ask my mother where my father was, my mother let herself be interrupted by one of the children, or one of her friends, or my cousin Cherry, who was helping in the kitchen, the very portrait of domesticity. My mother was clearly avoiding the subject.

Jacques stayed in the living room and talked computer futures, leaving Michael slack-jawed and admiring in a cloud of cyber-dust. Jacques used *we* a lot and threw melting glances my way. I let myself be melted and fell deeper and deeper into the gin bottle. I wondered how I was going to repay him for his award-winning performance.

When we sat down at the table, my father's place was still conspicuously empty. In the past, it had been my father who delivered an endless prayer over the meal, while Jeremy would whisper something brief and to the point like, "Rub-a-dub-dub, Thanks for the Grub, Go-o God," so that only I could hear.

In the past, it had been on my insistence that Jeremy had joined us for Christmas and Easter meals. I told my parents I wouldn't come if they didn't invite him. So they had invited him, getting Connie into the bargain, and she had always sat there silently, like Jeremy's shadow. Still, it wouldn't have been much of a family dinner without a few of the family's black sheep.

My mother had laid on a huge spread. There were phyllo pastry and feta cheese fingers, smoked salmon and dill tartlets, numerous garlicky dips and dippers, and for the main dishes, roast lamb, glazed ham, chicken pot pie and every kind of vegetable…there was an exaggerated amount of food.

My mother looked at the table and said, "There is rather

a lot, isn't there?" Everyone dug in. It was strange to realize that I had no appetite. I played with some asparagus tips, pushing them in circles around my plate. I was irritated that no one was explaining my father's absence.

Just before dessert, we heard the crash of glass breaking somewhere upstairs. I jumped up and ran up the stairs. Jacques, who seemed to know all the right moves, came behind me. I opened all the bedroom doors. On the floor of my old room was a rock with a piece of paper wrapped around it with an elastic band. I undid it and read the note.

"YOU'RE DEAD MEAT, LITTLE SISTER."

I started to tremble and Jacques put an arm around me. He frowned as he read the note. "Jeez, that brother of yours. What a big-time butthead. He can't be far away. I'll go after him." I could hear Jacques race out of the house, get into his car and drive down the street.

"Mother," I yelled. "Call the police."

"Why ever would you want to do that?"

"Where are the emergency numbers? Where do you keep them?"

"Just calm down. We don't want to go airing our little tiffs to strangers."

"This is not a little tiff."

It always happened this way. I got more and more agitated until it seemed as though I were the one who should be carted away to the Padded Palace of the Stars. "Oh, forget it," I grumbled, and stomped back to the silver tray to pour myself another drink.

A half hour later, Jacques came back alone, looking apologetic.

I took him by the arm. "Don't worry about it. He's eluded everyone, including the Vancouver police. Nobody can touch him."

My mother said, "Oh really, Lucille. You do overreact so. If only I'd known he was out there, I could have made him come in, change into some decent clothes, sit down at the table and eat a little lamb and roast potatoes. Roast potatoes can work wonders."

I just glanced heavenward. Jacques gave me a sympathetic smile.

After coffee had been served, and the children were getting high on Easter chocolate, my mother dragged me into the den, insisting that Jacques come, too. I thought, finally she'll tell me where Dad is. But instead, she took a wad of letters from the desk and said, "I've had more of them."

"'Them,' Mom?"

She mouthed the word *Winky*.

I restrained myself from screaming and forced myself into game mode. "You better show Jacques. He has some valuable connections. He might be able to help."

"Well, Jacques, it all started in the fall. Every year it's something new. Being a principal's wife has its price, I'm afraid. Teenagers! The senior high grads are the worst. You offer them an education and what do they do with it? This was the first letter from the kidnappers." She handed Jacques the piece of paper and a Polaroid. I could see him squint, then realize what he was looking at. He tried to suppress a smile.

Winky, my mother's largest garden gnome, disappeared back in October. In his place, the kidnappers had left a note which said, "Dear Mummy Madison, I've gone to see the world. Don't worry about me. I promise to wear an undershirt and eat all my greens. Love, Winky."

Next came a note and snapshot of Winky wearing a Busby hat, perched in front of Buckingham Palace. "Dear Mummy Madison, Been to see the Queen. Fish and chips are delicious.

Going to see the Crown Jewels then it's off to the theater. We've got tickets for Cats. Ta Ra, your Winky."

The second picture and note came from Paris. Winky wearing a beret and pencil-thin moustache and standing next to a plaster Madonna in front of the Eiffel Tower. "C'est magnifique, n'est-ce pas? Breakfast at Maxime's, a stroll through Montparnasse, Notre Dame de Gras, et l'amour. What else is Paris for?"

More notes came from Venice (Winky in a gondola), from Rome (Winky at the Colosseum), from Madrid (Winky at the bullfights) and from Sarajevo (Winky as a Red Cross volunteer).

My mother looked on it as an abduction. I tried to console her. "He'll be back when he's weary of travel."

"You're as bad as them," she snapped.

Jacques, on the other hand, clucked and tut-tutted along with her and used all the right words. Dreadful. Inhuman. Deplorable. Insensitive. Criminal.

My mother gazed up into Jacques's eyes. "Aren't you just adorable. You'll stay for supper, won't you?"

I blasted her. "Enough. Enough Winky. Where the hell is my father?"

My mother shook her head and sighed heavily. "I'm afraid your father is busy having a little midlife crisis."

"Midlife? He's fifty-six. It's an over-the-hill crisis."

"I don't think it makes much difference. The day before yesterday he bought himself a motorcycle. What is the name now? A Barley Richardson?"

"Harley Davidson," said Jacques.

"That's it. Well, he got the whole outfit that went with it, the leather pants, jacket, the whole kit'n'caboodle, and went off Friday night, telling me not to wait up for him. I'll hold on for a couple more days then call that nice fellow down at the police station, the one who's always so helpful when Dirk…"

I said, "He's cracking. And I'll bet, I'll just bet it's over Jeremy. He must be feeling guilty. He misses Jeremy." I didn't know whether to laugh or cry. I only knew that along with my grandfather, I wanted my stick-in-the-mud father back, the one who made me have childhood nightmares about church steeples flying into the air and exploding.

"Yes, I suppose he does miss that old reprobate after all," said my mother. "But I am a little worried. He's not used to alcohol."

"He was drinking?" I squealed.

"I'm afraid he did smell rather beery just before he rode away on the Barley Richardson."

"We better go and look for him," said Jacques. "Any idea which direction he might have taken, Mrs. Madison?"

"Call me June."

"A direction, June?"

"He may have said something about old friends and some pool. Oh my, I hope he wasn't thinking of going swimming in that condition."

"The pool hall," I said. "C'mon, Jacques. Let's go find him. If you don't mind, that is."

"No problem," said Jacques, but I could see he wished he had Madeline to rush home to.

Then I remembered Connie. "Mom, can I have some leftovers?"

My mother's expression became instantly cheerful. "Why, of course you can. You know, even before you start planning, you should try to get plenty of folic acid into your diet. It's especially important right in the first few weeks. I saw it in an article. Now, where was it? *Ladies' Home Journal,* I think. Yes, folic acid." She gave Jacques another adoring look. I followed my mother into the kitchen and watched her make tin foil packets.

Jacques drove fast toward town. He hadn't made the dent in the gin bottle that I had and was calm, while I twisted Kleenexes and moaned about my family. I directed Jacques to Pete's Pool Hall, a joint of minor scuzziness, not far from Jeremy's launderette.

Pete's Pool Hall was noisy for an Easter Sunday and a lot of drinking and illegal substance abuse was going on.

I found my father right away. He was there in a corner, seated on the floor, his back propped against the wall and his legs in spread-eagle fashion. He was wearing his leather outfit, a bandana, and along with a three-day growth of beard, he had a shiny gold earring piercing his left lobe, which looked sore. One of his canine teeth was chipped (trying to open beer bottles, I found out later) and he was chain-smoking cigarettes, ripping off the filter before he stuck the ciggie in the new gap in his teeth. I heard somebody say "Tequila" and my father answer "Over here." There were yelps of approval and calls of "Way ta go, Stu." My father's name is Stuart.

I don't know if my father saw me, but if he did, he pretended not to know me. I didn't try to get any closer. It was too scary.

Snake, who was shooting pool in a quiet corner, put down his cue when he saw me and came right over. He nodded in the direction of my father. "Bit of a mind-bender, eh?"

"He's gone nuts, Snake," I said.

"Naw. Stu's just doing a little catching up. He missed out on all the fun when he became a Holy Roller."

"Well, if the school board catches up with him, he might be missing out on even more of the fun. The fun of his monthly paycheck."

"Shit, Luce, I never took you for such a conservative."

"I'm just trying to put myself in his shoes."

"Sure you are. It's understandable. But I wouldn't have a hissy fit over it, if I were you."

"But just look at him, Snake." I pointed toward him and made frantic little motions with my hands.

My father's tall, like Jeremy was, and I would have said the getup almost suited him, if I didn't know that it was my father under all that animal skin. How was such an anally retentive neat-freak going to look at himself in the mirror when he finally decided to come to his senses?

Snake picked up where my thoughts left off. "He's over twenty-one, Luce. He's entitled to break out. Hell, he should have done it long ago. Cut him some slack. When he's properly screwed, he can grab some shut-eye on my couch. I'll see he doesn't get into any trouble."

On the way home, I got Jacques to stop outside Connie's house. I couldn't face her in person again so I set the leftovers on the old wooden porch chair, rang the bell several times, then ran away.

When Jacques dropped me off outside my apartment, he said, "Hey, Luce, if you're ever thinking of propagating and need some cross-pollination, keep me in mind. We've got your mother's seal of approval, after all."

I gave Jacques a nice kiss on the lips and tried to push the image of Madeline out of my head. My unborn children and I didn't want just the stud material. We wanted the package it was wrapped in, too.

I fell into a restless sleep full of dreams. Jacques was in them. We were kissing. In the background were hundreds of plaster gnomes, cement frogs and lawn jockeys. Some of the gnomes looked suspiciously like Madeline and I became convinced that she was spying on us. I kept whirling around to try to catch her at it but saw nothing but gnomes being their little plaster selves. Jacques held me more tightly and told me that I was just paranoid, that Madeline was away and had a heavy schedule. First, she would be in London, then Paris, then Sarajevo. I relaxed. We were just on the verge of cross-pollinating when noises woke me up.

There was a strange staccato sound at my window. A relentless tapping. The April wind was blowing hard and whined through the tree branches. I finally got out of bed to look. Through the curtain I could see a dark figure in the alley below. I ducked down quickly, thinking it might be

Dirk. But the tapping went on. No bricks or notes, just a light shower of something that sounded like pebbles.

I eased my way up and peeked again. When my eyes adjusted, I could see Paul Bleeker standing below my window, showing off the whiteness of his teeth. He had a plastic bag in his hand. He reached in, took a handful of something and hurled it at my window. I stuck my head out just in time to get a faceful of uncooked rice.

Rice!!!

Rice???

Was I supposed to read something more into this?

When he saw me, he starting laughing, or rather, snicker-snackering.

"You're awake," he yelled, and curtains flickered in at least three windows of nearby buildings.

"I am now. What time is it?"

"Four o'clock. Come out with me, Lucy. Come out with me right now. We're going to see some action."

Oh goody, I thought, he'll take me to one of those all-night eardrum-battering grunge clubs and we'll drink under-the-table plonk and maybe dance a little, then go and get some Chinese take-out and go back to his place and have a truly romantic time licking each other's fingers. What a great way to spend Easter Monday.

"Coming," I said, and hurried into my swishy black above-the-knee velour dress that clung to my body but hid most of the pudge at the same time. I yanked on skimpy black leather granny boots and my denim jacket and I was ready.

He was there at the front door, waiting. He grabbed my hand and said, "C'mon. Run."

I started toward his van but he pulled me in the other direction. "Not that way," he barked.

"Where are we running to then?" A gale force wind was

blowing and the temperature was around four degrees Celsius. I looked forward to the shelter of a vehicle and then some hot smoky nightclub.

"We're going to watch the storm. C'mon. Run."

Where did he find the energy? I pretended I was someone I wasn't, and forced myself to think "Athlete," think "Olympic track star." I was just barely able to keep up. We ran all the way to the sea wall at Stanley Park. When we got there, it took the last of my strength to pretend that I wasn't having an asthma attack.

Okay. I am not the kind of girl who works out. If I get on a bicycle, I expect it to take me from A to B, slowly, not to remain stationary in a row along with a whole lot of other sweaty, tortured, straining (but not flabby!) faux cyclists pedalling so fast their feet are a blur. For what? To be able to sit around the health club lounge drinking wheat germ and soya yuckshakes and look toned?

I'm willing to take a brisk walk somewhere as long as there's a reward at the end of it: a chocolate eclair, a baklava dripping with honey. Otherwise, forget it!

As for jogging, well, I'm against that, too. It's unhealthy. I tried it once with Sky. We decided to jog barefoot in the sand at the water's edge along Spanish Banks. It was a beautiful summer's evening. The apricot sun sat low in the sky, and the wharves were swarming with families setting their crab traps in the sunset and preparing lanterns for the darkness that would follow. The beach thrummed in that last light, as if the sand and logs and waves and mountains were all sighing with satisfaction.

We both felt really good that evening. It was going to be a whole new leaf, a new chapter for the two of us. We were about to become paragons of fitness. I would be the fantastically spry, slim, boundlessly energetic Lucy Madison. I would run every day, rain or shine, until I was a taut fast running machine, ready to go professional, perhaps run in the New York Marathon.

We tied our shoes around our necks and set our goal in the distance. Sky sproinged along like a baby gazelle, but I left footprints so deep that children's mothers were warning them to stay away from them in case they fell in and hurt themselves. Then I went a little too hard into some soft wet sand and fell flat on my face, spraining my ankle in the process. Sky turned to see what had happened to me and had a full-frontal collision with a very chunky, very dangerous-looking woman. At least we think it was a woman. We medicated our injuries with ice-cold margaritas, nachos, guacamole, sour cream and salsa.

Fortunately, Paul wasn't looking at me as I gasped for air and clutched the place in my side where a stitch had developed. He was standing on top of the sea wall, with his hands outstretched toward the swirling clouds, the jagged dangerous sea, the whitecaps, the frothing waves bashing the rocks.

"Bloody marvelous," he yelled. "Look at those tones. Those grays. That lead. That steel. That dove. That silver. That charcoal. Those blacks. That obsidian. That raven. That jet."

I could barely see a thing. My night vision is poor and with the wind whipping my hair into my face and the first lashings of rain coming at me, it was all I could do to stay standing.

Yes, Paul was just being an Englishman entranced by our West Coast weather. Inner London doesn't have big sea storms. He went on and on about the grays, the subtle tones of darkness, the chiaroscuro of the hours before dawn. And then he turned around, leapt from the wall, and pressed me up against some barnacle-covered rocks. He kissed me hard for a few seconds then pulled me to the ground.

The rain was coming harder now and the beach was wet and slimy. There was nothing between me and the beach with its pebbly sand and rocks but my poor little velour dress. A few gritty shiftings, clutchings and miscellaneous movements and he had my tights around my knees. Part of me wanted to protest. Another part of me was hovering above my body and saying, "Aren't I wild and reckless, and such a daring woman having sex on the beach during a storm with the famous artist Paul Bleeker. I'll have something to tell my grandchildren…if I ever have children, that is."

Our romantic encounter was all over in a few short minutes. My entire backside was drenched and my hair full of sand, seaweed and tiny desiccated crab carcasses. Paul managed to light his ritual Sobranie despite the wind and rain. As we walked back toward my apartment, he smoked and talked about how these predawn hours were the real hours, the time for creation, for gathering energy from other sleepers' dreams. He was completely oblivious to the rain that was trickling in rivulets off his hair and beard, and down his leather jacket.

When we reached my door, Paul gave me a long gentle kiss, smiled, said, "Go on then," and ushered me through the front door. I expected to see him behind me. He would come inside to the warmth and make up for the chilly encounter. But when I got to my door and turned around he was gone. I ran back to the main entrance and scanned the rainy street, but he had vanished.

Wet, cold and disappointed, I went inside, stripped off my soggy clothes and stood under the hot shower. It took a lot of water to get all the sticky sand off my skin and out of my hair. When I crawled into bed, the touch of the icy sheets sent me into fits of shivering. I refluffed my duvet, slid farther under the covers and lay there trembling until the first light of day edged through my window and a feverish sleep engulfed me.

I dreamt I was paddling around the ocean in a beautifully painted boat. It was like a gondola but had been painted with Aztec designs in bright colors. I noticed the water around the gondola was murky and dark and seemed to be rising. My boat was badly caulked and had started to leak. I was slowly sinking. The harder I bailed, the faster the water rose. On nearby rocks, a chorus of slender slimy mermaids taunted me. They alternated between being glistening and ethereal, and grotesque and fishy. Their voices grew louder until they were invading everything, blasting, ringing. It was a strangely familiar sound…like a telephone. I forced myself awake and stumbled out of bed to pick up the receiver.

"Hello?" I rasped.

"Hello? I'd like to speak to Lucy Madison, please."

"This is Lucy," I growled.

"It is? Gosh, you sound completely different. It's Sam. Sam Trelawny."

I perked up. "Hi, Sam. How're things? You're working on Easter Monday?"

"My clients don't take holidays unfortunately, which is why I'm calling. There's been a breakthrough with Dirk."

"Really?" I rasped.

"Are you okay? Your voice sounds strange," said Sam.

"I think I'm getting a cold or flu or something."

"Try some mulled wine. You put some oranges, cloves, cinnamon and honey on to boil in a little water, and when it's hot, add the wine."

I was tempted to ask him if he'd come over and make it for me. And maybe sit on the edge of my bed and feed it to me with a teaspoon. "I'd do it but I'm out of wine. My roommate's a Viking. She and one of her oarsmen drank it all. They were thirsty after a night of pillage and plunder."

"Plunder. Ha ha. I've never heard it called that. Hot lemon and honey's good, too," said Sam.

"Uh-huh," I croaked.

"Let me tell you about Dirk." Sam's tone was serious.

"Okay. If you must."

"It seems he was working the area around Broadway and 22nd, pestering women, mostly university students waiting for the bus. Apparently, he was telling everybody that he was looking for a six-foot-tall woman with brains to cast in his film…this is just what the storekeepers in the area have reported to the police. Anyway, the upshot of it all is that he broke a store window in the area. He's been arrested. Now, they've taken him out to the Forensic unit at Riverview."

"The Forensic?"

"I know, I know. Unfortunately, because of his size, they're a little intimidated by him. He was quite verbal when they were taking him away, although to be fair, he didn't put up any physical resistance. He kept shouting, 'A horse, a horse, my kingdom for a horse…' and 'what fools these mortals be…' The police officers weren't too sure what to think, but I guess he's a little frightening, with his height and physique. Dirk's a tall guy, I gather."

"He's six foot four." There was no doubt about it. Dirk was a member of a rare brotherhood. Emphasis on hood.

"Tall enough. He crossed the line by damaging private property, so officially, he's been booked as a criminal. He'll probably be in the Forensic until they have time to assess the situation. I'm going to try and get out there to see him in the next couple of days."

"That would be good." I felt weary. All that wasted manic energy.

"And you should go and see him, too, Lucy."

"Do I have to?"

I could almost hear Sam smiling. "Support from family is really helpful, Lucy, even though it might not seem like it to you. The Forensic isn't a very nice place. It's full of rapists and murderers."

"Are you trying to put a guilt trip on me, Sam?"

"Maybe just a tiny one. Strangely enough, the family members that the mentally ill individual often picks on the most are the ones whose forgiveness they really want."

"Tell me about it."

Sam went on, "I'll try to get out there on Wednesday. Maybe we can meet up. The visiting hours are just around dinnertime."

Now this was an incentive to go.

"Okay, I'll try to go, too."

"Good girl. Oh, by the way. Here's something you might be interested in. It's a support group for family and friends of manic depressives."

"Uh-huh." I could just imagine what a bundle of fun that would be.

"You're probably thinking, oh terrific, a bunch of un-happy people sitting around bitching about their depressed and crazy relatives."

"Yeah, more or less."

"Well, it's not quite like that. FOBIA has made great strides."

"Phobia?"

"Yeah, that's the name of the group. Friends of Bi-polar Individuals Alliance. Check it out. Here's the phone num-ber. They're having their next meeting Friday night at this address in Kerrisdale."

I took down the phone number and Kerrisdale address. Humor him, I told myself, he has a nice voice.

I spent the rest of the day shifting in and out of sleep. My whole body ached and my head pounded. I got up to take some aspirin and passed Anna in the hallway. She was semi-naked, on her way into the living room for another bout of the contortionist movements she called yoga. She radiated good health. I was too sick even to envy her. I crawled back into bed and hoped for death to come quickly.

On Tuesday morning, I called Nadine at home. "Dadine, it's be, Lucy. I can't cub id today. I have a terrible cold. You'll have to do without be."

"Absolutely not, Lucy. You get yourself down here and fast. Paul called me last night. We'll be discussing the preparations for his show. If you stand me up, you'll be queueing along with all the other deadbeats at the Canada Employment Centre faster than you can say Lucy Madison, former gallery assistant."

"Thanks, Dadine, you're a real Bensch."

"You're welcome, I'm sure. Now get your disproportionate ass down to the gallery and open up. I'll be along at ten."

I didn't let it get to me.

I took the bus to work. I'd taken an extra packet of superstrength cold formula and everyone drifting past me looked very beautiful and gracious and slightly hazy. I floated into the gallery, sat down at my desk and woke up when Nadine banged on it an hour later.

"Sorry, Dadine, I bust have dropped off. I'b sure dobody cabe id. They would have woken be."

She huffed and handed me a hundred-dollar bill. "Go out and get some food. A large mixed tray from Schultz's, all the different savories, and some spinach pies, some cream horns and Napoleon bars from Irene's and some cakes from Mozart's."

"Bozart's? Bozart's biles away," I protested.

"All the more reason to get going. Paul's going to be here soon, so hustle it."

Once, I had thought it was wonderful the way she always feted the artists, but now I understood it for the subterfuge that it was.

I made the rounds in a taxi using up some of Nadine's cash, so in Schultz's Deli, I talked them into opening an account and letting me charge it. I'd deny knowing anything about it when the bill arrived.

When I got back to the gallery, Paul was there. He was standing a little too close to Nadine, who was sitting on top of my desk and about to knock Jeremy's ashes onto the floor. I could barely hear what Paul was saying and just caught the words "…essential that the cooling systems keep it under five degrees."

What was he talking about?

He saw me and flashed a smile. It lasted approximately as long as a hummingbird's wingbeat. I smiled back, unable to rid my face of the idiot grin once it was in place.

The superstrength cold formula was doing a marvelous job, but, despite the drugs, I could feel a huge sneeze coming on. I ran for the washroom. One sneeze stretched out into a sneezing fit that nearly broke a rib. When it finally subsided, I stood in front of the mirror, staring at my shiny red nose and the little patch of chapped skin that was developing just below it on my upper lip.

Paul appeared behind me. He whirled me around and began to grope my backside. "I enjoyed our little outing. I wanna get close to you," he crooned.

Was it my imagination or the cold formula? I stared at him. He was swimming blurrily before my eyes and turning into that gorgeous ex-Wet, Marti Pellow. I felt all warm and drowsy at the thought of having Marti all to myself.

"Will you sing 'Love is Everywhere' for be, Barti? Or 'Angel Eyes'?"

"Love is what? Sorry? What are you going on about?" But it was too late. He'd already turned back into Paul Bleeker.

"I...dever bind."

"Sorry, didn't catch what you just said. You all right, Lucy? Your eyes look a little odd."

"I'b fide, just fide. What were you saying?"

"I had a nice time out in the wild night."

"Be too."

"We must do it again soon."

"Yes, we bust."

He planted a long kiss on my mouth and started to grope some more. I wasn't in the mood for sex on a damp bathroom countertop. And what was worse, I couldn't breathe through my nose. I had to push him away before I either suffocated or dripped onto his leather jacket.

"Dadine's cubbing," I lied, and ran into a cubicle to grab more scratchy toilet paper and hide for a while. As much as I wanted Paul to know more about me, I wanted to spare him intimate knowledge of my mucus. I pulled another packet of cold formula from my jeans pocket, ripped it open and licked the dry powder off a wetted finger.

I don't know how long I was in the cubicle. I must have dozed off again. It was clear that I wasn't missed or I would have heard Nadine barking for me. I came out and stared at myself in the mirror. It was only then that I realized my blouse was buttoned two buttons off-center. I thought about fixing it but that would have required a major effort and my fingers didn't work too well. And in my antihistamine stupor, it struck me as very chic to be mis-buttoned. So I left it the way it was and went back to my desk. Nadine was in her office with Paul. The door was closed and there were low murmurings then short silences.

I tried not to let it bother me. There were often such silences when Nadine talked money with the artists.

I surfed the Net for a while, looking for more information on Paul. One magazine article, with a rather shady sexy picture of him, talked about his role in the avant-garde anti-art movement. Another article, in a backhanded complimentary way, called him a trash artist. Another art review carried the title: Paul Bleeker, The Edible Man. If only it were true, I thought. I never seemed to get more than just a nibble.

Bangings and shufflings came from the office and then there was a crescendo of voices. I quickly flicked up the document I always kept handy for such occasions—a very boring inventory. It was a false alarm. The door stayed shut.

I got really self-indulgent and did a Net search on Marti Pellow. I read all about how he had been addicted to heroin for years and no one had known. I didn't care if he wanted to smoke kitchen tile sweepings or mainline peanut butter, just as long as he was okay again, as long as he was still alive and healthy and singing. But it did make me think hard about Connie.

I did another search on heroin addiction and found out that there had been a suit filed in the Province of British Columbia against doctors and nurses who carried on in their jobs thanks to maintenance doses of the drug. Whew! Connie was starting to look like Miss Average Reformed Smack Head. At least I hoped she was reformed.

I checked the e-mails. There was one from Sky, sent just

five minutes earlier. It read:"Lucy, very urgent.You absolutely have to get the afternoon off. Meet me at Retro at one. Don't be late.Very, very interesting dynamite mission."

10

I banged on Nadine's door, holding a sneeze at bay until she opened. Then I let it fly. She grimaced and checked her Armani jacket.

"Really, Dadine," I rasped, "I'b sick. Let be go hobe."

She waved me away and smoothed her jacket, carefully checking it once more. "Go, go, leave. Get out of my sight. You've done more than enough damage for one day."

Paul winked and blew me a kiss over Nadine's shoulder.

I raced down to the Retro Metro. It was on Pender not far from the gallery. When I opened the door to the boutique, Sky was hanging up a man's tuxedo. The garment was circa 1920. She caressed the fabric as if there were a man inside the suit. Sky has a passion for fabrics and textures, indeed, for all beautiful things. Her world is entirely about the prickly heat of a good wool blend, the heady silence of velvet, the brittle rustle of silk along the skin.

She hadn't seen me. She moved on to an ivory crepe de chine dinner dress, bringing it for a second to her cheek, and letting its odor, probably ancient Chanel N°5 and mothballs, transport her to that imaginary time and place.

She turned around and saw me, then banged her hands together. "You got my message. Yay. Great. We're going out. I'm so glad you could get away. I figured there was no way The Mummy would let you out to play."

Sky always referred to Nadine as The Mummy. She had said after meeting her the first time, "That woman was embalmed a few centuries ago and then passed off on an unsuspecting public as a living being. She doesn't fool me though."

Squashing another sneeze, I said, "Dadine doesn't know I'b playing. Besides, I had a good excuse. But you have to supply the tiszues on this expedition. I've rud out."

"You're sick." Sky looked dismayed.

"Paul Bleeker's fault."

She shook her head in puzzlement.

"Something is happening. Has fidally happened. This is a souvedir."

"Oh." Her face brightened. "Oh, I get it. I think. Good. I think it's good, isn't it?"

"Yeah, I think so. I hope so. Of course, there's always roob for improvement."

"Tell me about it," agreed Sky.

"We'll talk about this over a drink. Whed I'b better."

"Okay. Listen. We've got to hurry. Max is here from Seattle. He's collecting us outside in two minutes. I've got to lock up."

I was disappointed to hear our adventure would involve

Max. It was something I would just have to learn to accept if I wanted Sky's company.

Mr. Punctuality incarnate, Max pulled up in his van a minute later. We drove toward Southwest Marine Drive where it was considered shabby form to own a house with fewer than twenty-five rooms. Max and Sky held hands in the front whenever he wasn't playing with the gearshift. His paw slid occasionally onto her thigh where he would have stroked off all her skin if she hadn't been wearing pants.

Sky turned to me and asked, "Does the name Bella Montgomery mean anything to you?"

Sky was surprised to know that it did. I could recall *The Rage of Venus* and *Frostbite*. Amazing silent films. Bella Montgomery had been a silent movie star, very famous during the early part of the twentieth century.

"Bingo," said Sky. "Well, guess whose house we're going to now? Or more to the point, guess who kicked the bucket?"

"Sky," Max feigned shock. "Respect for the dead. Pulleeeease."

"Really?" I said. "I didn't dow she lived id Vadcouver."

"Nobody knew," said Sky.

"She bust have been…how old?"

"It's more complicated than that. She died a while ago, but because she left it all to her parrot…"

I groaned. "I think I've heard this story before."

"I know. I know. Anyway, there were all these solicitors sitting around waiting for the bloody bird to pop off, and the house sitting there rotting," said Sky. "So one of these solicitors happens to be a friend of Max's…."

Max turned and grinned at me and continued, "Bella Montgomery was another Louise Brooks, the Hollywood version, because Brooks defected to Europe. She was cute and

sexy like Brooks. They were all a bit chubby in those days. It
was the look, like Marlene Dietrich in *The Blue Angel*.

"Montgomery used to call up the most exclusive clothing stores in any town she happened to be passing through,
have them kick everyone else out of the store, put a heater
in the dressing room, then she'd buy the place out. Most of
the stuff she never wore more than once, if that. The auc-
tioneers know doodly squat about what they're dealing with
here. They were going to throw a lot of the things away, the
clothes anyway, so John called me. If she had been a forties
or fifties star it might have been different, but silent films got
a bit of a bad rap. Nobody remembers them, and most that
still do are gaga by now."

"Max does his homework," said Sky.

As I was listening to Max speak, there was something
about him—his mannerisms, his tone of voice—that bothered me, but I couldn't quite put my finger on it. I bore him
out. The Bella Montgomery business had my curiosity
piqued.

I'd been forced to sit through days and days of a silent film
festival with Frank. He was there for the big serious ones,
Metropolis, Intolerance, Potemkin, Napoleon. Secretly, I had been
there for Chaplin and Lloyd but the Bella Montgomery films
had been a discovery.

Max stopped the car in front of some very imposing stone
gates. He reached into the glove compartment and took out
a cluster of old metal. "I have the keys," he announced, preen-
ing. He climbed out, unlocked the gate, got back in and drove
us through, got out again and locked the gate, then drove the
rest of the way along a driveway of cracked asphalt to the
porte-cochere of the five-story mansion. The surrounding
garden was a tangle of monkey-puzzle trees, palms, rhodo-
dendrons, lilacs, yews and topiary box hedges run amok.

"Come and see the grounds," said Max. He started toward the other side of the house, which faced the river. We followed him.

"It's like the Great Gatsby's house," I said.

"Gone to seed," added Sky.

"They ran rum here during prohibition," said Max. "Anybody running rum had to have waterfront property."

We passed a huge glassed-in conservatory overrun with ivy. At the front of the house was an empty swimming pool and a rolling lawn that extended down to the waterfront. Max stared at the mounds of dead leaves at the bottom of the pool. "Let's go inside," he said.

We went back around to the front door and Max sorted through keys until he found the right one, inserted it, and pushed open the door. There was a whiff of dust and unused rooms, furniture polish and stale air. White sheets covered everything in each of the vast rooms. Max started up the wide staircase and we followed him for two flights. He took us through the master bedroom. Sky and I peeked under the dust sheets. It was a dream of Art Deco modern, mahogany and cream leather upholstery in smooth unadorned lines.

Max went through another door and held up his hands. "The dressing room."

It was more than a room. It was a small warehouse. Rows of dress racks and garment bags occupied the walls, while shelves, going up to the ceiling, were crowded with shoeboxes, hat boxes and glove boxes. Lingerie and boxes of silk stockings, ten pairs to the box, all as if bought yesterday, filled numerous drawers.

Sky's eyes were as wide as saucers as she carefully opened each drawer and box and gently touched the contents. "Look at the workmanship in these," she said, examining a pair of gray kid gloves. "This wash-'n'-wear society has a lot to answer for."

Max was unzipping garment bags systematically. I could almost see him toting up the figures in his head. Sky did the same. I watched her. There were crepe day dresses, satin, velvet and lace evening dresses in a rainbow of colors. There were suits with skirts, with trousers, riding jodhpurs, costumes for fancy dress balls. It was a staggering haul.

Sky went up to Max and whispered something in his ear. They both looked inside a garment bag then glanced over at me. Max unhooked the bag and brought it over. He looked me up and down until I was blushing then held up the garment. It was a cocktail dress, scarlet water silk, late fifties or early sixties, scoop neck at the front, back cut in a low V, drop waist and gently flaring skirt to below the knee, tight three-quarter sleeves. A large bow decorated the back like a discreet bustle. It was gorgeous.

"Try it on," said Max. Sky was nodding like crazy behind him.

"What? Here?"

"I won't look," said Max.

"You go away. Get out of here," said Sky, pushing him out of the room. Sky had a midnight-blue lace creation in her hand. "It's just a damn good thing that Bella Montgomery was so short."

Sky and I ripped off our clothes and gingerly pulled on the dresses. There was no doubt about it. Bella Montgomery was the woman for us. Sky swam a little in hers but it was nothing that a simple alteration couldn't fix.

But the red dress!

The red dress fitted me like a second skin.

"It's yours. Take it. Take advantage of Max while he's in a generous mood. It may not last."

"Really?"

Sky called him back into the room.

He came back in and stared at me. "It's you. It's fabulous. You must take it."

"Thank you, Bax." I looked over at Sky who mimed relief, mopping her brow.

"All you need are the shoes," he said.

"What kind of shoes, do you think?" I asked.

Sky said, "I think those cool sparkly shoes Dorothy had on her way back from Oz."

"Red shoes?"

Max exclaimed, "High-heeled red shoes. With pointy toes. Preferably in the same satin as the dress."

"Where will I ever wear this?"

"Well now, you'll just have to invent a life to go with the dress, won't you," said Sky.

It wasn't that I had no life. I had a "sort of" life. Just like I had a "sort of" salary, a "sort of" family and a "sort of" lover.

On that last point, I decided to take the initiative the next day. Thanks to the cold formula and some mulled wine that same night, I was feeling a lot better. And there was something about being in contact with the possessions of Bella Montgomery (whose life, I learned from Max, had been a long string of scandalous affairs right to the end) that made me feel alive, dangerous and wild. The next day, I was perky at work. I even sold a couple of the horrid phalli, and when lunchtime came around, I was ready for action.

It was shortly after noon when I rang Paul Bleeker's buzzer. Ten seconds passed. He popped his head out of one of the upper windows, looked down and said, "Lucy, it's you. Marvelous. Come up."

When I reached the door to his studio, tantalizing food smells and quite a lot of smoke were filling the hallway.

"You're cooking," I said.

"Breakfast." He did look quite tousled and scruffy, as if he'd just woken up.

"Bacon?" I was hopeful.

He nodded. "There was bacon but I finished it. I'm making bacon fat toast. Want a slice?"

We moved toward the row of stainless-steel fridges. One wasn't a fridge at all but a door that slid sideways to reveal a cooking unit. There was also a drop-leaf table and some folding chairs. He gallantly unfolded one for me.

In a large frying pan, a slab of white bread was sizzling and burning in smoking fat. Paul quickly rescued it and slapped it onto a plate.

I love bacon, but bread fried in bacon fat is taking the whole concept a bit too far. Okay. If I were a farmer and had to get up at four on a winter's morning in Saskatchewan to till the fields with oxen and a handheld plough, maybe I could justify eating that kind of pure cholesterol. It reminded me of university cafeteria meals—the heart attack specials.

I was polite. "No, you go ahead. I've already eaten." My stomach growled in protest.

"You should have come sooner," he said through mouthfuls.

"This is my lunch break."

"So it is." He put his plate down on the table and gave me a bacony kiss. "I'm so glad you've come."

I wanted to say, well actually I haven't, not with you, but I'd really like to sometime, if it isn't too much trouble.

The kissing carried on, took us from the folding chair directly to the bread crumbs on top of the table. Paul yanked open the snaps of my denim shirt, undid my zipper and skillfully got my jeans down around my knees. There was a short pause, a rustle, the sound of foil tearing, another pause, and he was in me. I could hear the plate clatter rhythmically somewhere too close to my head.

It was over even before the bacon fat had congealed. He pulled away, picked up his plate and finished off the toast with gusto. I shook crumbs off myself. There was nothing I could do about the greasy patch in my hair though.

He lit up his Sobranie, looked at his watch and said, "You still have some time left to your lunch hour, don't you, luv? Come sit over here. Without your clothes, mind. I'd like to do a few more sketches."

I did what he asked, mostly some simple poses on the shrink's couch. I figured as long as a girl was being immortalized, a lot of shortcomings could be excused.

I had to take three buses to get to Riverview. The psychiatric hospital was set in rolling hills and green fields. Everywhere, things were beginning to take on color with the first negligible warmth of spring. Trees were in blossom. Black-and-white cows grazed and gazed around them with beautiful stupid eyes. It was surreal and it was all wrong. When you knew what was waiting for you, it made the landscape seem like a lie, like a cosmetic used to hide a raging black plague.

When the bus dropped me off at the institution, I sat on a bench and watched a woman wandering around in front of the building. She was across the road, wearing pajamas and a dressing gown, batting imaginary parasites off her body, and giving God a good talking to. She shook her fist at the sky whenever her hands weren't employed in hitting herself.

At the designated pickup point, a small group of people waited for visiting hours to start at the Forensic. They too were going to visit their nearest and dearest—their beloved arsonists, rapists and axe murderers. We all sat in tense silence and watched the sun go down, golden rays striking the fields and trees, making it all seem like a fabled place. My stomach was in knots. I'd been through this before with Dirk. It would be too early to reason with him. He would be obnoxious and irrational before any treatment could take effect and that could take months.

Nobody looked anybody else in the eye. Nobody wanted to ask, "What did your loved one do?" We snuck furtive peeks at each other then quickly looked away. A dark green minibus finally pulled up and a driver got out and told us he would take us to the Forensic. We all got in and he drove us down a tree-lined avenue before stopping in front of an unimpressive cement block building. Numerous keys were turned in locks. We were told what we could and couldn't bring with us.

The visiting area had a few long tables, matching wooden chairs, and smoke permeating the air. I pulled out a couple of packs of Rothman's I'd brought for Dirk. I knew from past experience that, in these places, cigarettes were negotiable currency. Even if you weren't a smoker when you went in, you'd be a chain smoker by the time you were out.

The male patients trickled in and sat across from their visitors. A current of whispers and laments began to flow: the excuses, the promises, the apologies and rationales.

I waited for five minutes but there was no sign of Dirk.

One of the locked doors opened up and a very tall, thin, beautiful redheaded woman with a briefcase appeared. She had the kind of looks I would have had if God hadn't been such a joker. She spoke to one of the guards, glanced at me, then came over.

"You're here to see Dirk Madison?"

"Yes. And you are…?"

"Are you a friend or relative?"

"Relative. And you are…?"

"What relation are you exactly?"

"Sister. Who are you?"

"I'm Dirk's caseworker."

I got panicky. "What about Sam? Where's Sam Trelawny? He was supposed to be here."

She smirked and said, "Sam Trelawny," drawing out his name, tasting each syllable.

"Yes. I thought he was supposed to be Dirk's caseworker."

"Normally he would be. I'm replacing him." She saw my expression and added, "Not permanently. Just when he can't make it. My name is Francesca St. Claire de la Roche."

"I'm Lucy Madison." I presented my business card. Intentionally pretentious and misleading. Nothing on it but my name and Rogues' Gallery with the address and phone number.

She looked down her nose at me, took the card and read it, extended a long thin hand and gave me a limp nonhandshake.

I gave her fingers a good hard squeeze. "Is there something wrong? Is Sam okay? We had agreed to meet here today."

She laughed, a fluttery, twittery feminine laugh and said, "He had unavoidable personal business to attend to." It sounded like she wanted to be his unavoidable personal business.

"What's happened to Dirk? I've been waiting here—"

"There's been a bit of a problem," she snapped.

My heart skipped a beat. I pictured Dirk strapped down to a bed, a doctor hovering over him with electrodes in his hands and saying, "Oops, perhaps we overdid the voltage a bit. Musta fried the bastard."

"Oh yes? What kind of a problem? Where is he?" My voice was getting louder and edgier.

Francesca St. Claire de la La-Di-Da opened her briefcase, took out a file folder and consulted something inside it. "He was brought in on Monday evening and subdued…"

"Subdued?" I yelled. "How was he subdued?"

"Tranquilizers."

"Probably enough for an elephant," I grumbled.

"Your brother is not a small person." Her tone implied, "And neither are you."

"Okay, so where is he now that you people have got him completely zonked out, brainless and drooling?"

"It couldn't be avoided. He had to be neutralized." Francesca St. Claire de la Hoity Toity's voice was getting very harsh.

I made my fist into a pistol and pointed it at her. "Good one. Neutralized. I like that. Where the hell is he?"

"He escaped this morning."

"Escaped? ESCAPED!" My tiny nervous giggle erupted into hysterical laughter that went on until my ribs ached and everybody in the visiting area was staring. A guard touched his holster and started to move toward me. I calmed down and said, "Just how did he do that?"

"He walked off the premises."

"Just like that?"

"So I gather. There were some witnesses, although not terribly coherent ones. He was wearing clinic clothing, pajamas…"

"Terrific."

Several hours and another three bus rides later I arrived back at my apartment. Anna was on her way out. She looked stunning in blue leggings and a slinky blue silk shirt.

"Have a date?" I asked.

She squirmed a little, and flicked back her long blond hair. "None of my business?" I said.

"Ya." Her voice was icy. She put on her coat and left.

I went straight to the fridge. There were some Viking delicacies and some hard-boiled eggs. I put everything on a plate and plopped myself in front of the TV to watch the late movie.

An old pop song was playing in my mind but the words were a little scrambled—something about if you couldn't be with the one you loved, to love the food you were with.

My mother's voice was breathy and calm. "Yes, dear, I've been keeping up to date on Dirk. If he pops by, I'll have him come in and sit down for a nice nourishing meal."

I groaned inwardly and asked, "What about Dad?"

"I'm sure your father will be just fine."

"Motheeeer. What do you mean 'will be'?"

"Your father just has to sort it out for himself."

I could hear loud schmaltzy music in the background. "Mother. Aren't you even a little worried?"

"Of course I am, dear. But everything in its just proportion. Worrying isn't going to make him come home sooner."

"Come home sooner? You mean he hasn't come home yet?" I could hear ice cubes clinking in a glass and women's voices in the background.

"Well. He's been showing up at school to take care of paperwork, and that's something positive. And apparently your father's now a huge hit with all the students, what with all the leather and the scruffy hair. It must be his new costume. He came back to shower and change his underclothes, but frankly, after one quick look, I told him to take all the time he needed, and to come back when he was decent."

"Mommmm."

"Oh, don't be so dramatic, Lucille."

"Don't you care about him just a bit?"

"Of course I do. But after thirty-six years of marriage, I'm entitled to a little holiday from him, don't you think?"

"But he's…but you're…"

"Your father's not the easiest man in the world to live with, you know. Or have you forgotten?"

I hadn't forgotten. After a long silence, I sighed, "Whatever you say, Mom. Talk to you later."

"Lucy, dear. Don't forget Cherry and Michael's anniversary dinner Saturday night. You will bring that lovely boy Jacques, won't you?"

Arrrghhh.

I said goodbye and hung up. I could picture her without my father. My mother was already an exaggerated type; big and buxom with brassy country singer hair and a country singer's fashion sense. She also had a tendency to pee herself whenever she laughed hard. She would be flouncing around the house in all her favorite fashion items, namely the clothes my father wouldn't let her wear in public. She'd be like an exotic, oversized, slightly incontinent bird. I could picture her, inviting all her friends over to drink gin, eat bonbons, watch the soaps and choose upholstery fabrics. Her idea of paradise.

It was red alert. An invitation to Cherry and Michael's thirteenth anniversary dinner party was to be heeded at all costs. Not showing up would mean lectures from my mother about my lack of altruism, my crummy sense of family feeling, and not recognizing a possible ally, maybe not necessarily now, but when, for example, boxes and boxes of baby clothes and gewgaws might be required. Cherry's kept everything, my mother would add, in case the happy day should ever arrive for me. Gag. But it did get me thinking.

Jacques, still minus Madeline, was nowhere to be found. I had seventy-two hours to become attached again.

Parker's Funeral Home was a sedate white imitation Spanish hacienda.

I rang the buzzer and waited for a very long time. The door was finally opened by an unshaven balding man in a ripped sweatshirt and faded blue jeans with holes torn in strategic places. His face lit up when he saw me. "Miss Piggy!"

"Leo. Let me in. I've been standing out here forever."

"Come in, come in. Don't just stand there looking porky." Leo ushered the way and let me pass in front of him. "I've got to say, Lucy, you used to be such a buffalo butt, but from behind you're not nearly so porky as you used to be. What is this? Are we living on anorexic avenue or what?"

"It's the life I've been leading, Leo. There hasn't been a lot of time for eating. More to the point, how's your life?"

"Oh you know. We're such nitpickers. We're never satisfied."

"You mean, you're never satisfied."

Leo held his hand to his brow melodramatically. "It's hard being a Matzah-Mafia hoe-moe-secks-yu-al boy wonder."

"Did I interrupt you?" I asked.

"Concertus interruptus. Just as well. I was working on the Rach Two again."

"Not the Rach Two?" I made the appropriate sign of the cross for warding off vampires. It was also helpful in the case of pianists who were about to play Rachmaninov's Second Piano Concerto.

"It's a bitch, that piece. I don't know what made me accept. I guess I'm just a slut for glory and tendonitis. Gotta concert in a couple of weeks out in Mission."

I followed Leo through the casket-viewing rooms. He said, "You should have seen the ruckus in here yesterday. There was a big-time Catholic corpse. Open coffin job. All these people wailing and keening and trying to throw themselves on top of the stiff." He rolled his eyes. "And oh, Lucy, they've just got some gorgeous new caskets in. They're ebony wood with red satin lining. Red. Very decadent. If you ever plan to off yourself young, let me know and I'll get you a special deal. You'd look very striking in red satin."

"That's thoughtful of you, Leo."

"I know, but young, mind you. A fat, wrinkled old bag lying in red satin just wouldn't have the same effect. Mind you, they do have some fantastic embalming techniques these days. There's almost nothing you can't do with a stiff to make it more glamorous than it was in life. You get famous first, sell a few paintings, then end it all and we'll do you up like Evita, okay?"

"Sure. It's the sell-a-few-paintings part that I'm having trouble with. But I'll let you know."

Leo worked for the Parker family. It was his job to answer the night calls, open the door, and play the Wurlitzer at the odd funeral if he happened to be available. In exchange, he got to live in the funeral home's little apartment that came furnished with a grand piano. He could wake the dead if he wanted. The Parker family took care of all other aspects of the business.

We'd known each other in high school but become better friends when we both showed up in Vancouver at all the same clubs and university parties. One of our favorite sources of entertainment back in those days had been to sign up for viewing luxury apartments under the names of Mr. and Mrs. Archibald Spockwittle. As Mr. Spockwittle, the prospective buyer of a condo, Leo was merciless. He would kick walls, bang doors, rattle windows, open cupboards and shriek, "I've had Christmas turkeys that were wrapped in more durable materials."

When we were in his living room, he poured us a couple of double scotches on the rocks.

I didn't hesitate. I put it right to him. "Leo, I need you."

"That's what they all say. But then, when they have me, it's a different story."

"I need Mr. Archibald Spockwittle's straight cousin. Just for a night? I need a partner and I need him pronto. For Saturday night. You've got to be my macho hunk man-of-the-moment. My cousin Cherry is staging a big anniversary dinner."

"Saturday night? Saturday night? That's the big night. The gopher bashing night. The big schtuping night. Are you crazy? Are you completely out of your tiny mind? Do you think I have nothing better to do on a Saturday night than hang around with some old fag hag from my lurid, checkered past?" Leo was leaping over the threadbare furniture with his glass in hand, screaming this at the walls.

"Why, Leo? You have something better to do? Or someone better to do?" I knew Leo. Next to playing music, his favorite thing in the world was pretending to be straight.

He collapsed into an armchair and smiled a Leo smile. "No. Saturday will be just fine. Casual or black tie?"

Alone again on a Friday night.

I decided to give FOBIA a try. I had e-mailed Paul with the thinly disguised excuse of gallery business but he hadn't answered.

I had also tried reaching Sam Trelawny at two different numbers. I wanted to be sure he knew the latest on Dirk. All I reached were answering machines.

The address given for the FOBIA meeting was an old school building no longer being used as a school. There were several notices on the door announcing different meetings: Alcoholics Anonymous, Ceramic Garden Statuary (something for my mother?), Male Drumming Chorus (something for my father?), Beginner's Acupuncture (ouch!), Tai Chi and FOBIA.

I went into the building and walked along the corridor, looking for the right room number. When I finally found it, I realized the FOBIA meeting wasn't being held in a classroom at all, but in the auditorium. Too many friends of the depressed and neurotic to be contained in one small classroom? As I opened the auditorium door, there was the squeal of a microphone, the scraping sounds of a bow on a fiddle, and loud yahoos. The lights were flashing and a dance ball in the center of the room shot glittery mirrored reflections onto the walls, ceiling and floor.

Up on the stage, two guitarists and a fiddler played while a short man in a cowboy hat and horn-rimmed glasses crowed into a mike;

"Pick yer partner, do-si-do— Hook to your right and

away you go— Shimmy to yer left, and shine on through—
Twirl yer girl and skip to ma lou."

The auditorium was packed. There were a couple of hundred moms and dads and quite a few younger people, too.
Some were dressed in spangly cowboy and cowgirl outfits,
others in less fancy blue jeans and work shirts. But everybody,
and I mean EVERYBODY, except for me, was square-dancing.

When the number was over, a buxom, gray-haired woman
in frilly gingham stood panting against the wall. I grabbed
the opportunity and touched her arm. "Excuse me, I'm looking for the FOBIA meeting."

She lowered her rhinestone-rimmed cat's-eye glasses and
grinned at me. "You got it, honey."

"But everybody's square-dancing."

"Heh, heh, heh. Confusing, isn't it?"

"Sure is."

"Are you the friend of a bi-polar individual, dear?"

"I'm the sister of one."

"Regular or rapid cycler, dear?"

"Rapid cycler."

"You have my sympathy. It's rough going, honey, I know.
My husband's one of them, too. Got a couple of manic
cousins as well on my side. Miracle my kids are okay. Welcome to the meeting. I'm Mavis." She shook my hand firmly.

"I'm Lucy. So you're saying this is the meeting?"

"It's the FOBIA social, dear. We do it once every so often.
See, we were holding the regular meetings here, down the
hall in one of the classrooms, and one night, oh, about two
years ago, the square-dancing class knocked on our door and
said they were short of people to make up a decent quadrille.
Since then we been doing this every couple of months.
Helps keep our spirits up. C'mon, they're starting a butter-

fly waltz. No wallflowers allowed here." She was pulling me toward the center.

"But I can't… I don't…"

"Nothing to it. Just follow the music."

After quite a bit of stepping on other people's feet and getting stepped on, I actually started getting the hang of it, and, I hate to confess, enjoying it. I happened to be wearing blue jeans and my denim shirt, so I didn't feel too out of place clotheswise.

I reeled, shuffled, shined, hooked, flared, quarter-checked, twirled under, twirled over and hootenannied for a good hour and a half.

Then the lights went down, plunging the room into darkness except for the moving flecks from the dance ball. There was laughter and suggestive hooting. The man calling the dances starting singing, "Your Cheatin' Heart." People were doing a strange kind of quarter-time slow dance with partners changing every ten seconds. I had gone through five middle-aged paunchy men who smelled of denture-adhesive and sweat, when I was slow-danced into the arms of a tall man with a hard stomach, broad shoulders and the scent of cinnamon and wood fires permeating his shirt.

He twirled me twice, pressing me into his chest and caressing my hair for a second. My hormones went berserk. I barely had a chance to glimpse his face as he spun away. Were his eyes green or gray? Was his hair sandy-red and long, or blond and tied in a ponytail? I couldn't tell. There was just a vague impression of him. I was grabbed again and twirled into another pair of geriatric arms. I craned my neck to see if I could spot my previous partner, but it was impossible in the glittering darkness, and sea of spinning Merls and Mavises.

★ ★ ★

The phone rang at nine o'clock on Saturday morning.

Sky's hysterical voice said, "Lucy. Can you come over? I'm at the shop."

"Sky, what is it? You okay?"

"I don't know."

"You don't know?"

"No."

"Is there a man involved by any chance? And are his initials Max Kinghorn?"

"I guess so."

"What's he done? What's that creep Max done?"

"He's not a creep."

"If you say so. What's he done?"

"Nothing. I don't know if he's done anything or not."

"You're not making sense. I'll be down as soon as I can."

I threw my clothes on and hurried to the Retro Metro. Nadine had given me the day off but I was expected to work the next day, Sunday.

Sky, who is not a crier, was behind the front counter, pacing. Her mascara had run all over the place and she had raccoon eyes.

"Sky. You don't look too good."

"I look awful. Just call a spade a spade, will you?"

"Okay, you look like you've been dragged backward through a cat's rectum and then slung onto a heap of…"

"I know. I know."

"What's he done?"

"It's just a feeling."

"What's your feeling then?"

"He's got somebody else."

"Oh."

"Oh what?" Sky was looking frantic.

"Well…" I played for time.

"Well what?"

I let the axe fall. "It was never really to exclude. The fact that he could have somebody else. I mean, you know, the gay lifestyle and all that. Not hung up like women. They can go out and bonk each other in parks and back alleys and washrooms and steambaths whenever they feel like it and not give it a second guilty thought or wonder if they're up the spout with no way out. Of course, I'm talking about sex with condoms. I mean, nobody would be so stupid as to make that scene without about a million condoms on their person…"

Sky stood absolutely still, her face expressionless. Then she spoke. "You are such a fucking cliché, Madison."

"I know. I know. I'm just telling you what I think. How did you come to your conclusion about Max?"

"I phoned him at home," she said.

"So?"

"His regular phone, not his cell. The number he didn't give me. Unlisted. I got it through a friend of mine who works in Public Health in Seattle and they have ways of getting numbers, so I got it."

"Did somebody else answer? A lisping man's voice, for example? A man bent on interior decorating at all costs?"

"Jeez, Lucy, no. Max answered. No. It was his tone. He wasn't mad or anything. He sounded scared that I'd found that number and called him there. He begged me not to use it again. I asked him if he was upset, and he said no, but that I was to do as I was told."

"Hmmm."

"I know you don't like him, Lucy."

I said, "It's not that I don't like him."

"Oh c'mon. It was written all over your face when you met him."

"He doesn't have to appeal to me. He has to appeal to you. As for me, well, there's just something that isn't right there and I can't even put my finger on it."

"Let's go and find out," said Sky.

"What?"

"Let's check it out. Let's drive down to Seattle and—"

"Wait a minute, Sky. Whoa. You are reaching new heights in masochism here."

"I know. When are you free?"

"Are you sure you want to do this?"

"I'll borrow Reebee's car...."

"Wait a minute. I value my life."

"She's had it overhauled."

I raised an eyebrow.

"Really. No lie. She even paid money to have it done. None of her buddies knew how to fix a 1965 Valiant."

"I just think you're letting yourself in for a big disappointment."

"But Lucy, I love him."

"Sky!" I thought her tongue might turn black, shrivel up and drop out of her head. I realized then that in all the time I'd known her, she'd never once confessed to being in love.

That evening, Leo and I stood on the doorstep of Cherry and Michael's Shaunessy house.

"How do I look?" Leo was swank in a gray corduroy suit and store-bought tan. He'd been toasting himself under his sunlamp and looked prosperous, like someone who had a house in the Bahamas. I was wearing my black velour dress salvaged from the night on the beach with Paul.

The front door was opened to us by the Ecuadorian maid. Leo looked her up and down then said to her under his breath, "Honey, if you ever want to start a revolution, I know just who we have to put you in touch with. He's the sweet-est man from El Salvador…"

I dug him hard in the ribs with my elbow. "Leo."

"Well, you can't expect these poor Latins to carry on the role of oppressed subservience forever, can you?" The maid smiled wryly for a second, then looked oblivious.

Cherry appeared at that moment, dressed in something made of a bronze silk knit and slinky enough to show off every nub of her backbone and her flat, flat stomach despite three pregnancies. Her raven-black hair was in place, as usual.

"Lucy. You're here. Lucy and…" Her expression took a lit-tle tumble. "Have we met?"

"This is Leo," I said.

She offered her hand and Leo leapt in and did a European thing, kissing her on both cheeks and saying "Enchanté."

Cherry was clearly flustered. "I'm Charlotte-Mary."

The big fake. Nobody ever called her Charlotte-Mary. You couldn't say it all without choking on it.

She regained her composure. "My, Lucy. Aren't you…ac-tive? We were expecting you to bring Jacques."

"I just love the whole business of being single. Not tied down to anybody. It's so nice to have variety in life." I grinned. Leo was doing the can't-keep-hands-off routine. I gazed into his eyes and whispered, "Not here, darling."

"But we have so little time together." He laid the sexual urgency on thick.

"Leo's flying out tonight," I said to Cherry. "He has to con-duct some opera in New York in a few days. What did you say it was, Leo darling?"

We had decided to slightly expand Leo's career for Cherry's sake.

He looked appropriately world-weary as he spoke. "Wagner. *Lohengrin*. I don't mind a few phoney swans. But last year it was the whole *Ring* nightmare. Tons of dry ice and cast-iron tits."

Leo had just gone up about ten notches in Cherry's estimation. When it came to industrial-strength snobbery and collecting famous people, she had all the right genes. "Really?" She grabbed him by the elbow. "You must tell me all about it. I have a full subscription to the West Coast Opera Company."

"You do? You have my deepest sympathies," muttered Leo as Cherry led him away.

My mother was already fluttering around in the kitchen, one of Cherry's aprons protecting her cleavage-flaunting flame-colored chiffon dress.

"Hi, Mom. Where's Cherry's demon brood?"

"I do wish you wouldn't call them that, Lucy. It's just asking for trouble."

Something small and greenish-brown wriggled on a plate. My mother bopped it with a wooden spoon. All movement ceased.

"Okay. Her little Attila the Hun clones then." I went over and eyed what was on the platter. They looked like slugs.

"Really and truly, Lucille. I gather they're spending the night at a neighbor's down the road."

"Shouldn't we check down the road then for smoke or the arrival of the bomb squad?" My mother shook her head. "Any news on Dad?" I asked her.

"Your father's still on the loose, I'm afraid." She didn't seem very upset about it. In fact, she appeared to be thriving as never before. "Now where's that charming Jacques?"

"I didn't come with Jacques. I came with Leo."

"Do I know him?"

"No."

"You really must try to hang on to your man. You lost Frank and…"

"Frank needed to be lost."

"I thought he was very nice. Very intellectual."

"Forget about Frank, Mom. I want to know about Dad."

"Oh, he's around. He pops in to clean up and catch up on family business. We're still friends, of course."

"STILL FRIENDS?" Did I catch the whiff of separation?

"But I think if he were to become a grandfather, it might just help him get his feet back on the ground."

I fled into the other room and the drinks table where Michael was pouring.

"Triple gin tonic, please, Michael."

"Hi, Lucy. How's it going?"

"Just fine. You can put a little more gin in that."

He handed me my drink. "I think I'll join you." He raised his glass and said, "Here's to…I don't know what. What should we toast to?"

"Success. Any way you want it," I said.

"Cheers. You here alone?"

"No. I'm here with Leo."

"Oh. Do I know him?"

"No."

Cherry swept in just then and stood beside Michael, looking glowing. They were as much like a portrait of the happy couple as was possible at that moment, Cherry yanking Michael closer and telepathically commanding him to smile.

It was a buffet dinner, and it began with everyone awkwardly balancing plates of peculiar little fried and slimy hors d'oeuvres, snails, frogs' legs and other amphibious creatures' body parts, then progressed to larger animals. Ostrich. Buffalo. Reindeer.

"It must be mad cow hysteria," whispered Leo.

★ ★ ★

Halfway through dinner, I approached Cherry and said, "My mother tells me you've been keeping a lot of baby clothes. I'm very interested in laying my hands on some."

"Really?" Cherry looked at me as though I'd just sprouted wings, then a smug expression swept across her face. "Is it you we're talking about? If I may be so bold?"

I just stared at her. She would read into it whatever she wanted.

"Yes," she said, "looking at you now, I can see that you're starting to show, aren't you? Well then. This is definitely news. Might we know who the father is?"

I played along. "It's impossible to say. I've lost count of all the men in my life. Several have offered to take responsibility though." In my dream life!

She blanched before saying cautiously, "I've got all sorts of things in the attic."

"So Mom was saying. Let's talk about it later. After all, this is yours and Michael's evening."

When we got to the desserts, there was a lot of clinking of glasses and speech-making about thoroughbred race-horses that were only good for the short run and Clydesdales and plough-horses that were good for a lifetime. It seemed that Cherry was being compared to a plough-horse, which didn't sit well with her at all.

After all the anniversary toasting, Cherry said, "I think Lucy has an announcement to make."

"No, I don't," I snapped.

"I think you do," said Cherry.

"Okay. I'll make an announcement. I'm happy to announce that I am maintaining the status quo of single un-fettered womanhood."

Cherry frowned.

I escaped to the kitchen. I was in the pantry rooting around for some soda crackers to settle my stomach when a hand grabbed one of my buttocks.

"Leo."

"Don't think so."

But the voice was very familiar.

I2

I craned my neck. "Michael."

"You're looking very sexy these days, Lucy. I like a woman with a shape to her, and a little something up top to hold on to." His hands had migrated north and were carrying out an extensive exploration of my breasts.

"It's awfully hot in here…MUST…GET…AIR…" I pried myself out of his clutches and ran out the back door, down the steps to the garden and to the swimming pool area. I kept out of sight, lurking for a while behind the shrubbery, pretending to make an inspection of the bulbs at the side of the house. If I waited long enough, Michael would be too drunk to remember anything. On the other hand, he might be even more aggressive. I went back around to the pool area and tried the door to the little pavilion where the changing rooms were. It was open, so I went inside.

I must have been there for a half hour when Cherry appeared. She towered over me. She clamped her hands onto her hips and spat out her words. "They're going to find out sooner or later. It's ridiculous…it's so childish to think that hiding out here in the garden will help. These things can't be kept secret. I know the hormones make you do strange things but you really should grow up. Being a parent is a big responsibility."

"Jesus, Cherry. Lighten up. I'm not pregnant. I was just pulling your leg. Hasn't Mom told you about Connie?"

"Connie?" Cherry was a cousin on my mother's side. It was unusual that any tidbit of gossip ever escaped that particular network.

"Jeremy's girlfriend."

"That…person…Jeremy brought back from the States? I know Connie. Why? Your mother didn't say anything about her." Cherry's mouth tightened with a superior air.

I had just assumed my mother knew. If she didn't know before, she would know before the evening was out.

"We're going to have a new aunt or uncle," I said.

"We're what?"

"Connie's pregnant." In a sucky tone, I said, "It means my father's going to have a half brother or sister and we're going to have an uncle."

"That's absolutely disgusting."

Poor Cherry. She couldn't stand the unconventional unless it was in art or fiction. When it showed up in real life, it terrified her. I felt a tiny little tingle of power, knowing her perfect husband was a perfect lech. I felt a little sorry for her, too, for the first time in my life.

"I just wanted some baby things for Connie. She's been having a hard time. The nausea hasn't gone away and with Jeremy's death and everything…"

Guilt. The gift that goes on giving.

Cherry scrunched up her eyebrows and smoothed a non-existent wrinkle from her dress. After a long pause she said huffily, "Oh all right, we can take a look at the things a little later. They're boys' clothes though."

"She hasn't mentioned the sex. I'm not sure she's even been to a doctor."

"How grossly irresponsible."

"Give her a break. She doesn't have your…advantages."

"I find that people generally get what they deserve in life," said Cherry, very sure of herself.

I lowered my voice to a near-whisper. "Well, Cherry, maybe you've got what you deserve and don't even know it yet."

"What did you just say? I didn't catch that."

"Oh nothing."

That night I left with a cardboard box full of sleepers, booties, bibs, sweaters, undershirts, burp cloths and more.

In the taxi, Leo kept putting his finger in his throat and making very exaggerated gagging noises. "You're not becoming one of those broody women that are always goo-goo-ing and gaw-gawing and drooling and slobbering over other people's reproductive efforts. God, before we know it, you'll be knitting for other people's little pissers, too. There'll be the ubiquitous clicking of needles wherever we go. Then I suppose when you are old and barren and childless, and you've been dumped by numerous men, you'll just give up completely and let your mustache and chin hairs grow long."

"My leg and armpit hair, too, Leo. At that point, I might as well throw in the towel."

"Well, I must tell you, there's one advantage with age, the chin hairs turn white and you don't notice them so much."

"Thanks, Leo. Your comments are awfully consoling."

"Your two eyebrows will revert to one, then you'll invite all the stray cats into your one-room apartment, and there'll be a terrible smell of cat piss and all the neighbors will complain and you'll feed your kitties people-food, and knit little booties and coats for them and talk to them as though they were your children."

"There might be worse things in life," I replied. Although I couldn't think of a single one.

It was another Sunday morning at the gallery. I imagined Nadine curled up in her bed with one of her many sex slaves, or some other person who shall remain nameless.

I was forced to sit there at my desk, propping up my hungover head, suppressing yawns. The world went by and people stared in through the big plate-glass window from time to time, as if I were a fish in a tank. I didn't feel like one of the pretty ones though, the angel fish, or even a goldfish. I felt like one of those black bulgy-eyed Victorian curiosities that suck up stones then spit them back out onto the surface of the fishtank.

I called Reebee. She said, "You read my mind. I was just thinking of you and your Connie problem. I had some herbal preparations for aggravated morning sickness made up. They won't harm the child but I should probably come so I can make sure the instructions on how to take them are understood."

"A baby shower," I said.

"A baby shower?" asked Reebee.

"I know. It's a hopelessly fifties idea but I just couldn't think of anything better so I thought I'd pretend that Connie was normal and that everything was all right. I put together a few baby things and I figured if there were other people there we could call it a party, a baby shower and she wouldn't kick me out of the house so quickly."

"When did she ever kick you out of the house?"

"Well, never. Actually."

"Then she probably wants you to be there. She needs the company, whether she knows it or not. I think a shower is an excellent idea. I'm sure I can scrounge up the odd thing."

"It's a good excuse to stuff our faces with gooey sweet desserts."

"A cheesecake. Some carob brownies. A carrot cake. That way we can say it's a bit nutritional. Must think of health. When are you going to spring it on her?"

"I'll let you know."

"Lucy, another question. Your painting? How's it going?"

"What painting?"

"I see."

I phoned Connie that morning. She picked up after twelve rings and was her usual sullen self. I told her I needed to see her and that I would be over on Monday night around seven, if she was home, that was.

"Where am I going in this condition? Yeah, I'll be here," she droned.

I was flipping through catalogues from other galleries when a shadow fell across my desk. I looked up. Pressed against the window was Dirk. Six-feet-four inches of rapid-cycling manic depression with a long beard and mud-stained Chlorpromazine Cloisters pajamas. I shrieked, ran into Nadine's empty office and locked the door. Then I called both of Sam Trelawny's numbers. I had taken to carrying them next to my skin for just such an emergency.

I got Sam right away at the second number.

"He's here," I blurted.

"Wait a minute. Who's where? Who's speaking please?"

"Lucy. Lucy. It's Lucy Madison. He's here. Dirk's here. He's outside and about to come in. Send help. Send in the Marines. Send somebody."

"Lucy. Calm down. You'd find the Canadian Marines a bit of a disappointment, I think. Tell me where you are."

"Rogues' Gallery." I gave him the address.

"Okay, Lucy, now you hang up. I'll call the police and the team, and then call you back. Give me the number you're calling from."

Five minutes later, sirens screamed up in front of the gallery. I unlocked the door and peeked out. Of course there was no chance that Dirk would still be there. But on my desk was a note scrawled on a stick'em note with one of my pens. "YOU'RE HAMBURGER," it said.

I let the two officers in, then began to rant and rave at the ceiling and the gods in general. The two cops stared at each other hopelessly. Then I started on them, "You two. Go out there and get him. He can't be far away. How far can he have gone in five minutes? He's a wanted felon. He's a fugitive. Don't just stand there like lumps of dough."

I was so ineffective that they couldn't even be bothered to take offense. The two of them shrugged. The police department had spared sending me their best and brightest that morning. It took the two officers a long time to get a statement from me, the dotting of i's and the crossing of t's presenting all sorts of problems. When they'd gone, the phone rang.

It was Sam again. "Are you okay, Lucy? I'm really sorry to tell you this, but the team isn't available right at this moment. They have a hostage-taking situation in the West End. Some very upset man holding his wife and kids at gunpoint. The usual scenario. Man was just fired from his job. Went off his medication a few months ago. I'm really sorry."

"That's okay. It's useless anyway," I said through my

tears, "they're never going to get Dirk and if they do get him, they won't be able to keep him."

"You're crying," he said.

"It's nothing. I'm a crier."

"That's good. It means you let it go. You release your feelings." His voice ran over me like a gentle hand.

"If you say so. But I wish I didn't."

"It must seem to you that we're all pretty incompetent."

"Well…"

"Well, we are. We're letting you down. I'm the first to admit it. But Dirk really is calling for help. I know it doesn't look that way but he's going to come to earth and the landing will be hard… Lucy, are you there?"

Paul Bleeker had just come in. I quickly dried my eyes and tried to look collected. He sat on the edge of my desk and grinned at me.

"I'm here. Listen, Sam, I have to go."

"Okay. Remember, Lucy, he's wanted and we're going to get him."

"Sure. Bye."

Paul took the receiver out of my hand, hung it up and said, "Lucy, I came around to your place yesterday evening but you weren't there."

And to think I could have spent my Saturday night with Paul instead of my family.

"I was out," I said.

He bent over and kissed me. Then he pulled me up out of my chair, put his arm around my waist and led me to the back of the gallery, where he began to open doors.

"What are we doing?" I asked. Pre-exhibit preparations I hoped. I couldn't wait to see how he had immortalized me.

"What do you think we're doing?" he said.

He led me into the storage cupboard. It was filled with

old crates, boxes, pedestals and room dividers. He lunged at me and I tumbled onto a heap of filthy old dustcovers and rugs.

The fact that I was wearing a skirt made him gleeful. "I just love this kind of clothing," he said, lowering himself on top of me and not even bothering to unbutton my blouse. "So easy to ravish you." As usual, the ravishing took approximately three minutes and I was covered from head to toe with dust when I finally stood up and brushed myself off. Once out of the storeroom and back in the gallery, he lit up his Sobranie. I tried not to let it get to me, but I have to admit, I was starting to feel a little used.

"No smoking in here, Paul." At first I whispered it and then when he appeared not to have heard, I barked it.

"Good lord, listen to little Miss Propriety. Nadine's never complained."

"Well, the day that we have to call the fire department because the place has burned to the ground and the insurance won't cover it because someone was smoking and they find that cute little gold tip, believe me, she'll be complaining."

Paul looked around for an ashtray, saw Jeremy's urn and began to make a move.

"I think we've been through all this before, Paul. This is my grandfather and I will personally cut the marrons glacés off anybody who tries to butt their cigarette out in his remains."

He looked slightly startled then smiled. "Yeah, all right. Try to come round to the studio when you have a moment. I wouldn't mind doing a few last-minute adjustments. It's not absolutely essential but it could be helpful. Do try to make it round. See you, luv," he said, and headed for the street.

★ ★ ★

Reebee came to pick me up on Monday evening. I'd talked Sky into coming, too. The back seat of Reebee's car was full of baby things. A high chair, a small cot, a basinette. We also had lots of food.

Connie opened the door, took one look at all of us, shook her head, turned around and went inside. She motioned with one hand for us to come in and we followed her to the smoky living room. The house looked undisturbed. Neither messed-up nor cleaned-up. As though no one had been living there.

Her face was caving in. She was so thin, a stick figure with a bulge. She scrutinized us and lit up a cigarette.

"How's it going, Connie?" I asked.

"How do you think it's going? Life's a fucking bed of roses, isn't it?"

Reebee suddenly became stern and matronly, her eyes were like twin storms. "Sky. Lucy. Go take a walk around the block. I want to be alone with this woman."

Sky rolled her eyes and said, "Voodoo. C'mon."

Reebee continued, "In about an hour you can bring in the things from the car, okay? Now disappear, both of you."

"Jeez," said Sky. "When she acts like a mother she can be such a Nazi." This seemed to please Sky somehow.

We walked around the block slowly. It was well into April and spring was beginning to make itself felt. The early buds on the trees made a lacy backdrop and the air was a little warmer and sweet with the scent of the first daffodils and new grass. Sky raved about Max and I raved about Paul and the two of us decided we would drive to Seattle that Wednesday, my day off, and spy on Max.

An hour later, we lugged all the baby things up the front steps and into the house.

In the living room, the windows were open, Connie's cigarette was out, and she had a mug of something in her hand. She sipped slowly. Sky and I looked at each other. Reebee was in major mother mode and started ordering us around: put these things there, those things here, unwrap the baby clothes, show Connie those little sleepers, go get a plate from the kitchen, cut the cheesecake, pour the fruit juice.

"Heil, heil, heil," said Sky.

Connie had a strange expression on her face. Like something really brutal had been exorcised, like there was a light coming on. The poison was starting to ease out of her. She sipped and then said to Reebee, "You know, this is making me feel better already. This is the first time in months I haven't wanted to woof all my cookies immediately. I was giving up on ever feeling normal again."

"I know. I understand," said Reebee.

Reebee fussed over Connie, cutting her little pieces of cake and pushing them toward her. "Here try this. See if you can keep it down. You don't have to worry about feeling terrible. Being pregnant can be the weirdest sensation on this earth. There you are, with this stranger, this alien creature, inhabiting your body, squirming around, sitting on your ovaries till you're screaming in pain, pushing on your windpipe and stomach and basically making your life hell…"

"Mother!" Sky stared at Reebee, appalled.

Reebee laughed. "One's children have the most outrageous expectations. Oh, don't get so worked up about it, Sky. You weren't an abandoned child. All those strange non-maternal feelings sort themselves out with time. But there are moments when you don't think it's natural at all."

Connie was smiling slightly. She ate as if testing each bite, as if it all might come back up in a second. It didn't and she looked almost happy as she sat there munching. I guess it was the Banging Your Head Against the Brick Wall Syndrome. It feels so good when it stops.

On our way out, Connie stopped me at the door. Her tone was confidential. "I forgot to tell you. Your father came around here the day after Easter."

"My father?"

"Yeah. The whole thing was really freaky. He was pissed out of his mind. He banged on my door in the middle of the night and said he wanted to see the house. He was in a pretty bad way. I let him in. I figured an old Jesus freak like him wouldn't hurt anybody, but when I saw the way he was dressed I almost had second thoughts. He kinda stumbled from room to room touching pieces of furniture and stuff I guess he remembered from his childhood. You know Jeremy kept everything the way it was when his first woman ran off on him? You didn't? Well, that's why this place is filled with this fuckin' awful furniture. I guess I'm used to it. Then he asked if he could see his old room. Had the room in the attic, right? So I let him go up. I guess he was just homesick, missing Jeremy. He passed out on the bed. Good thing he wasn't sick 'cause I couldn't have handled it. Would have set me off bad-style. The next day I gave him the leftovers you left. It was you, wasn't it? Yeah. It was pretty weird 'cause Stu and I have never gotten along."

I wanted to ask, Who have you ever gotten along with, Connie, apart from Jeremy? Though I suppose that would have been unfair. I was grateful she had put my father up for the night.

She added, grudgingly, "Uh…thanks for the…all this stuff…you know…for the…"

"Don't worry about it. 'Night, Connie." I walked to the car, expecting hell to freeze over any minute.

★ ★ ★

Nadine called me later that night. "Wear your oldest clothes tomorrow, Lucy. We're taking down the temporary exhibit."

Translation: I, Lucy Madison, lonely art drudge and white slave would be taking down and putting away the party of pee-pees while Nadine gave orders and ate bonbons to keep up her strength. I was relieved to hear it though. Sitting alone hour after hour in the gallery, I was starting to grow attached to all those willies, giving them names and personality traits and having little fantasies about them. What else could I do? Quick-Draw-McGraw Bleeker had only given me very brief glimpses of his pizzle. And for all I knew, it was as imposing as a puckered parsnip.

I dreamed the penises were all assembled in a chorus line. They'd grown legs and were adorned with colorful ribbons, fishnet stockings and high-heeled women's shoes. The music started up and they danced and did high-kicks and romped their way through a rendition of "Hey Big Spender" in funny little squeaky voices. Just as they were getting to the climax, a tidal wave swept in and washed them away.

I was awoken by loud gurglings. I sat up in bed, heart pounding hard. More sloshing sounds followed. They were coming from the bathroom.

I staggered out of bed and down the hallway to the open bathroom door. Anna was at it again. Possessed by the cleaning demon, she was furiously attacking the toilet bowl with my long-handled back-scrubbing brush. I shuddered. She'd probably been using it like that for ages and I'd been merrily scouring my skin with it.

She hadn't seen me. She put down the brush, picked up

my loofa, liberally doused it with Mr. Clean and started in on the bathtub tiles. I didn't let it get to me. I couldn't afford to. They say serving time for homicide in women's prison can be pretty tough.

And anyway, the one thing you can count on in life is change. Change had to come. It just had to.

The next day I got to the gallery early. I spent most of the day packaging up the penises and preparing them to be shipped off to their owners. In the afternoon, Nadine sent me out to La Tazza to get doughnuts, two dozen of them.

Nelly the Grape said, "You guys sure eat a lot of pastries. Gallery people must have a big sweet tooth. Artists, too. One of your artist guys keeps coming round here for chocolates. Kinda cute." She smiled a purple lip gloss smile. Nelly had huge white teeth and a sixties back-combed flip-curl hairdo.

I carried the doughnuts back to the gallery and set them down on Nadine's desk. Then I returned to the last of the packaging. I had only been in the storeroom for fifteen minutes, but when I came back out there were only three doughnuts left. Nadine didn't even bother to look embarrassed. She said, "Three greasy doughnuts is far more calories than you need in one afternoon."

Just before six o'clock, ten air-conditioning units arrived. I shivered. The gallery was already chilly without help. What medium had Paul chosen? Ice?

13

Wednesday morning, Sky pulled up in front of my place in her mother's Valiant. On the dashboard were two double lattes and four chantilly cream-filled croissants. "Thought we needed some extra nourishment," she said.

"I was feeling a little faint now that you mention it. You sure this old heap is roadworthy?"

"Positive. Reebee got the works done. Really. You'll feel the difference as soon as we get going."

The radio played golden oldies and we sang along with Elvis, Jerry Lee, The Beatles, Aretha, The Mamas and Papas and The Rolling Stones at the top of our lungs for the whole way south. It was still morning when we reached downtown Seattle.

Sky parked the car and looked grim.

"What's your plan?" I asked, half expecting her to produce a shotgun or chain saw.

Sky held up a page torn from a Seattle phone book and a street map. "Directions," she said. "You wait here and make sure they don't tow away the car or steal the hubcaps." Then she got out of the car and stomped up the road. I watched her go in and out of three different stores. She was in the last one for fifteen minutes.

She came out and got back into the car. "I know where we need to go." She'd traced a route on the map. I was supposed to be the navigator, telling her when to turn.

After an hour of driving around, we ended up in a suburb of large homes and tree-lined streets.

"That's it there." Sky pointed at a white two-story fake colonial house with dark green shutters.

She parked a few houses away and we donned sunglasses and baseball caps and slumped down into our seats to wait. Sky opened the glove compartment and produced a big paper bag full of gourmet jelly beans. She said, "Try the eggnog-flavored ones. They're amazing." Sky kept the radio on low and we sat there in a mute near-slumber, only to break our stupor to make occasional comments about the neighbors.

It was around four in the afternoon when we finally got results. A van pulled into the driveway. Sky slumped even farther into her seat. "Oh fuck. That's Max's van. I can't look. Tell me what you see."

"Well. I see Max getting out…and an adolescent boy…a boyfriend do you think?"

"Omagod. Omagod."

I said, "No wait. There's a young girl, too. A ménage à trois, do you think?" I confess I wasn't too broken up by the idea of Max being a two-timing slime. I wanted Sky the way she'd been before him.

The boy and girl ran up the front steps and then the boy yelled back to Max, "Dad, I haven't got my key."

"Dad?" Sky nearly choked on her jelly bean. She sat bolt upright. "He called him Dad? Those? Are? His? Children?"

"It looks that way," I said.

"He's a goddamn father?"

"Maybe they're adopted."

"Sure."

"Maybe they're all acting, reciting from a script, and there're hidden cameras rolling somewhere nearby."

"Right. Oh fuck. Would you look at that? I can't believe it. He's wearing sweats and Adidas."

"I don't think that's a crime."

"Are you kidding? Max is always going on about the vanished days of sartorial splendor and how everyone looks like they're wearing pajamas when they're dressed in sweats. It's one of his pet peeves."

"Maybe he's one of a pair, an identical twin. This is the evil twin, or should he be the good one? I can't decide."

"It's just so awful. He's just so…so…so…"

"So what, Sky?"

"So average."

That was it. That was the thing that had been bugging me. Max hadn't set my gay radar going. He exuded heterosexual normality under all the finickiness.

Then Sky started to cry. Again.

All those times I'd seen her so furious and sharp, and I'd wondered if she ever cried. Now it seemed she was starting to make up for lost time. She was getting wet and gushy. Wet and gushy was my classic routine, not hers. I put an arm around her shoulder.

"Sky, it's going to be okay. Really, it is. You're going to look back on all this and laugh."

She nodded.

I rummaged in my purse and found a crumpled Kleenex. "It just looks used but it's clean really."

She blew her nose loudly. The tip of it was bright red. Now I understood why she avoided crying when possible.

I said, "This is the first time I've come up against the straight married guy playing gay so that he can be seduced into being straight. At least that's how it seems to me. I don't know what else to say."

Sky was already calm again. She looked resolute. "Well, I do. Let's go eat. I'm starving and if we sit here any longer I'll have a bad case of jelly bean mouth."

We drove around for another hour then picked a place called The Spectacular All American Restaurant because the prices were good and there was a huge choice. Sky ordered lasagna and I ordered a triple bacon cheeseburger with fries.

"That's it," she said. "I am through with men forever. I'm going to get my libido surgically removed."

"Isn't that a bit drastic? I've heard it's an outrageously expensive operation. Where is your libido anyway?"

"Under your Freudian slip, I imagine. I can tell you one thing. When I figure out how, I'm getting it removed and taking it back for a refund."

"They don't give you much for a used libido these days."

"But mine's obviously defective, or it wouldn't have let me get involved with Max in the first place."

"What are you going to do, Sky? You still have to work with him. He's your boss."

"I don't know, but one thing's for sure. These are not things to ponder on an empty stomach."

The waitress brought our orders. As soon as she'd set them down, she put a small bowler hat on her head and burst into the theme song from the musical "Cabaret."

She belted it out at top volume until Sky held up her hand

and said, "EXCUSE ME. Excuse me. Excuse me for just one second."

The girl stopped singing.

Sky whipped out a ten-dollar bill and waved it in front of her. "This will be your tip if you'll kindly piss off, unless we want food or drink. In which case, we'll snap our fingers in your direction. And tell the other waiters to stay out of our faces, too."

The girl was completely crestfallen. She crept away to inform the others.

How were we to know that all the waiters and waitresses were aspiring musical comedy performers? That the restaurant was famous for showcasing undiscovered talent?

Sky said, "I can't stand people in my face unless I invite them to be in my face. And I can't stand musical theater if it isn't in a theater."

We finished eating, paid the bill and got back in the car. We were on the road again by seven.

It was somewhere not far from the Canadian border, along a deserted stretch of highway, that the car began to sputter and die. Sky was able to pull over just in time.

"Shit," she said. "No goddamn gas left."

"Sky," I wailed. "Whad'you mean no gas?"

"I'm sorry. I got so caught up with being mad at Max the Dickhead Daddy that I just forgot to look at the gas gauge."

"You just forgot? I've got to get home. I've got a show to mount tomorrow. Paul's show. Paul Bleeker, the man I'm sleeping with. Well, technically not actually sleeping with but…"

"Listen. First, my advice: Do Not Panic. Take my phone and call The Mummy right now. Let her know the situation. If you leave it till the last minute it could be worse. Don't give her the chance to twist it around and use it against you later."

I made the call on Sky's cellular.

Nadine said, "Where have you been? I've been trying to get in touch with you all day. I wanted to tell you not to come in tomorrow. Paul has decided to change all the plans at the eleventh hour. He's having the show set up by his own handlers. He's very particular about not revealing anything to anybody until the very last minute."

"His own handlers?" I tried hard to imagine what they might look like.

"You'll be on duty for the opening. Friday night, you have to stop by at Schultz's at about six and make sure the trays of food are ready. Make sure they get the order right. They've been getting sloppy lately. Tell them we won't use them again if they don't get it right. The trays are to be delivered by seven. The champagne will be delivered earlier. Your share of the work will be during and afterward. You're pouring, cleaning up and doing the closing. And I want the place spotless. Is that clear?"

"Clear as the ice water that runs through your veins, Nadine."

"Maybe you're not aware of it but you're expendable, Lucy."

I pressed the phone's off button.

Change had to come soon. It just had to.

Sky and I wasted several hours waiting for the guys from AAA to come with enough gas to get us to an all-night gas station. At the border, the customs officials were sure we were hiding something and all but dismantled the car, coming up with some earrings Reebee had lost the year before and a few handfuls of jelly beans.

All Thursday, I practiced getting dressed for Paul's opening. I tried on nearly everything in my closet twice. I put makeup on and took it off until my face hurt. I took a three-hour bath, running more hot water whenever it got cold.

Sky still had my red dress at the Retro Metro. I toyed with the idea of wearing it to the opening, but something stopped me. I wasn't quite ready. It felt wrong. A red dress like that could be worn when you had nothing left to hide, when you just didn't care what the world thought. It wasn't fashionable but it was beautiful. It would be my day when I wore it, a day that belonged entirely to me. It wasn't the kind of dress you wore when you had to clean up afterward.

I opted for my usual cop-out artsy-fartsy dark look: hair up, black flats, black leotard and leggings covered by big black baggy silk shirt to hide bulges. Sort of like Audrey Hepburn in *Sabrina* when she cooks eggs for Humphrey Bogart. Well…okay. Add fifty pounds or so.

I don't know what made me call Sam. Maybe it was because Friday was such torture. The whole empty day stretching before me, nothing to do but worry about Paul Bleeker until evening. I thought I would get an answering machine and be able to listen to Sam's message voice. But he picked up and I had to invent something.

"It's me, Lucy Madison."

"Lucy. Are you okay? Are you being threatened? Is Dirk there?"

"No, no. This is uh…an unofficial call. I…er…uh…wanted to tell you…I mean I forgot to mention last time we talked on the phone, I went to the FOBIA meeting. It was great. I got a bit of a shock though at first. All that square-dancing."

"I thought you might get a kick out of it. Band was okay, wasn't it?"

"You were there?"

"Popped in for a few minutes," said Sam.

I jumped in with, "Listen, um, there's going to be a big show opening tonight in the gallery where I work. Lots of free food and champagne. It's an important artist. His name's Paul Bleeker."

"I've heard of him."

"Really? You have?"

"Yep."

"I just thought, um, you might like…"

"Sure. If I get freed up in time I might take a run down there. Rogues' Gallery. In Gastown. Right?"

"You have a good memory."

"One of the people in the office was mentioning it yesterday. She's something of an art buff, too."

I stiffened to hear Sam say "She" then said, "It kicks off just before eight. I hope you can make it."

"I'll do my best," said Sam, "Thanks for letting me know. Bye, Lucy."

"Bye, Sam."

By the time I left the apartment and started toward Schultz's on Friday evening, I was a bundle of nerves. First of all, none of my friends would be there. Sky was at home, and she was going to have to have her telephone receiver surgically removed from her ear because she'd been stuck to it, talking things over with Max, since her return from Seattle.

I tried phoning Jacques's place, hoping he would come and give me moral support, but nobody was home and I had no idea where he was.

And Leo had a gig that night.

I wasn't sure what to expect. Knowing I would somehow be part of Paul Bleeker's exhibit made it worse. At first, I had thought it would be wonderful. I had planned to stand next to the portrait he'd done of me and look svelte, wait for people to notice the resemblance, then bask in the glory of being a famous artist's model.

I realized I was dreaming again. Svelte was out the window. So was standing around. Nadine wanted me to serve as a kind of mobile human trash can, ready to grab empty glasses, scrunched napkins, paper plates, the minute they were dropped or abandoned.

When I got to Schultz's, I ordered a cup of their good old-fashioned percolator coffee and checked the trays they'd prepared. They looked wonderful. And as usual, I was starving. On the excuse of having to approve the merchandise, I popped a prawn square into my mouth and declared it fantastic—like sex on tiny crackers. I told them to send the food on.

From there I walked to the gallery. There was a full moon that night. The air was warm, well…warm for Canada, salt-swept and heavy with pollen. I was brimming with a sense of expectation, a premonition of things to come, but of things with no name or shape. I was looking up at the sky, at the beginnings of the luminous moon making its way up and across, and wasn't looking where I was putting my feet. I nearly tripped over a homeless man lounging on a warm air vent. He stared up at me with weepy hound-dog eyes. In that moment, it was as though I had become him and he had become me. For a split second, we were inseparable, sharing the human chain, both of us as strong as its weakest link.

Then he sank back down onto his air vent and closed his eyes.

The vague sense of hope plummeted and turned into misery.

What was I doing, nearly thirty years old, alone, unaccompanied, solo, conspicuously single—walking along in this city that wasn't my city, and not even getting the walking right, but tripping over derelict human beings in the street—on my way to an exhibit of somebody else's art—not even my own art? Why did Jeremy have to abandon me? How had I ended up in this situation?

This was not part of the master plan. Where had it all gone wrong?

When was my life going to feel like it was really mine and not a spectator sport? When was I going to look in the mirror and say, Yes, I know you. You're Lucy Madison. You're that girl who knows what she wants and goes out and gets it. Welcome back. Everybody's missed you. Your chubby, wimpy shadow here has been standing in for you but doing a terrible job. Everybody's been waiting for your return.

When was it going to feel more like Christmas and less like PMS?

Or were my expectations too high?

Then I thought, Omagod. I'm just like Dirk. I'm insane and don't even realize it.

I walked a little faster.

Outside the gallery, a fair-sized group of people had started to gather. The windows were obscured by heavy black velvet drapes and it was impossible to see in. I tried the door but it was locked. I used my key and slipped inside.

The temperature was just above freezing. As well as being chilly, it was pitch-black in the gallery. There was a strange, sickly-sweet smell, but my nose was still a bit stuffed up and I couldn't quite place it.

I was in a maze of black drapery. Black curtains created a spiraling corridor, like a snail's shell, in which more black curtains divided areas off into cubicles. At the center of each cubicle was a tall object hidden by a silk black cover sheet. Sculptures, I suspected. There were single overhead spotlights for each object but they hadn't been turned on. Suspended above each object was a video screen.

I tried to find my way out of the spiral, battling with the curtains. I finally gave up, got down on my hands and knees, lifted the bottom of one of the curtains and crawled out near Nadine's office. The door was slightly ajar and I could hear voices inside. I went in without knocking.

There was a small crowd in there. Nadine, The Mortician, Mae West and Onassis all drank champagne from crystal glasses. They were dressed in either fur coats or camel hair. Why hadn't anybody told me to bring my own dead animal to wear? It was freezing in there.

I took a closer look at the four hairy men lurking in the corner and recognized Paul Bleeker's cronies. Even they had the sense to be wearing heavy sweaters.

"About time," said Nadine when she saw me. "Go and see that there's enough loo paper, would you, Lucy? And give the toilet bowls a quick scrub while you're there. And be fast about it. The trays have arrived. They're all by the tables. You checked them on your way over, I hope, to see they didn't forget anything. The staff there has been getting sloppy lately…"

"They didn't forget anything. The order was complete."

She noticed the way I looked at Paul's friends. They didn't recognize me.

"These are Paul's handlers," she said. "They have years of experience with his work."

Sure, I thought.

Years of sitting around with brains fried on who-knows-what and discussing whether toe-jam or belly-button lint was the better medium. They didn't seem too worried about Nadine's demoting them from the East Sheen Group of Artists to gallery lackeys. They looked so stoned that remembering their own names would probably have presented a problem.

"We open the doors in twenty minutes," said Nadine, checking her watch. "As soon as we open, you're to get over by the food tables and pour champagne. They're in the circular space at the center of the spiral. When you've got the tables organized, I want you to patrol for garbage, anything that gets dropped. Oh yes, and discourage smokers."

"It's pitch dark in there, Nadine. How am I supposed to pour in the dark?"

"There will be some indirect lighting. The sculptures will be spotlit and there should be light from the videos. In the meantime, use this." She opened her desk drawer and handed me a tiny penlight flashlight.

"And where's Paul?"

"Paul? Ha ha ha." She laughed as though she had him tucked away in her pocket or purse. "He'll be making an appearance soon, I shouldn't wonder. Now hurry up and do those loos. We're letting people in soon."

I shuffled away to the storeroom to get rolls of toilet paper, rubber gloves, sponges and cleansers. Just as well I hadn't worn the red dress.

I quickly scoured the bathrooms, inspected myself in the mirror, then went to look for the tables. It was strange, like being in a stage production, groping around in the dark to take my place before the curtain went up. I turned on the flashlight, squinted and stumbled around until I found the tables.

They were there at the center of the spiral, in a big circular space. There were several large tubs containing crushed ice and bottles of champagne. On one of the tables were rows of glass champagne flutes as opposed to the plastic cups we usually brought out for openings. There were also china plates and linen napkins. I rearranged the trays, then grabbed a couple of artichoke hors d'oeuvres and stuffed them in my mouth. I had to keep rubbing my hands together and hugging myself to stay warm. My teeth began to chatter. My leotard wasn't nearly heavy enough.

I uncorked a bottle of Brut, poured myself two glasses, and clinked them together, toasting in silence to my faltering sanity and a better future. Then I downed them both.

The lights came on. I could hear the woosh of the cover sheets being pulled off the sculptures. I was miffed. It was the first time I had ever been excluded from an exhibit's preparations. The videos started automatically, creating flashes that gave a strobe-light effect. Through all that fabric, I could hear the muffled sounds of Nadine opening the front door and letting in the public. Little by little, wooly voices seeped through the curtains. Snatches of conversation reached me then drifted away.

I continued to pour champagne until most of the glasses were filled. Over the next half hour, there were sounds of awe and appreciation, and then a few people trickled into the center and began to drink champagne. Through the drapes I could hear The Mortician commenting, "Interesting choice of medium. Witty. Very definitely enhanced by the projections. Good Lord. Is that who I think it is? Do I recognize…?" And then his voice wafted away and disappeared.

Another slightly familiar woman's voice came into earshot but I couldn't place it. I strained to hear more.

"…at a party…quite interesting…the forefront of the modern art scene in Britain…very sweet really…a little party up in West Vancouver…"

I knew that voice. It was Francesca de la Hoity Toity, Sam's colleague from the Forensic.

And then I heard the other voice.

"They're funny…not bad…but perishable…has he thought about longevity? I mean, hell, Leonardo's stuff didn't last and now we're all sorry. I'd worry about mice. Or people with a bad case of the munchies."

Sam's voice.

He was here.

Here with Francesca St. Claire de la Roche.

I had to see what he looked like.

I fought my way through the people who were now crowding and blocking the corridor. It was frustrating. I could make out Sam's voice somewhere in the maze, but not the words, and whenever I tried to get closer to where I thought he was, the voice disappeared. There was too much confusion.

Then it occurred to me. I was rushing past all Paul's work without taking anything in. I hadn't seen myself immortalized. I hadn't looked at the show.

I peered into one of the cubicles. At the center was a life-sized white sculpture of a nude woman. It was stylized, angular and definitely not me. Square shoulders, impossibly long legs. Above the sculpture, a TV screen projected a naked woman, moving, posing, moving again, all slightly out of focus.

The video disturbed me. It was done so that if you really wanted to, you could recognize the model.

I moved on to the next sculpture. It was dark brown, a tall woman, but this time with spidery limbs. The video above it seemed to be another out-of-focus woman posing, moving, posing. She was so thin her ribs stuck out.

The next sculpture was light brown, a tall, slender, flat-chested woman. The video above, again blurred images, corresponded.

And that sweet smell. I moved closer to the sculpture. It was…what was it anyway? I touched it. It was smooth. I held my finger against it. The surface beneath melted slightly and left a small dent.

I licked my finger.

Chocolate.

His sculptures were made of chocolate. Some portrayed female nudes in a prone position, stretched out on their backs, others resting on their sides. Some looked as though they were about to fly, others just languishing. Some of the sculptures were white chocolate with a slight tint. One was deep brownish purple. And above each was an image of a blurry naked woman moving on a screen.

My impatience was growing. And then, about three quarters of the way through the spiral, I stumbled onto myself.

14

I stared for a long time. At first, it was in disbelief and then with the thudding heaviness of certainty. There was no mistake. It was like one of those dreams where you're in front of the class at school, or on a stage with millions of people in the audience, or walking down a crowded street. You look down and realize you're naked and weigh three million tons.

Not that I think being naked is a bad thing. On the contrary, naked is wonderful. But it's best when you know it's happening or you planned it to happen and you know what its consequences are going to be.

Paul Bleeker had taken all my most noticeable problem zones and exaggerated them wildly. The blobby sculpted Lucy Madison was reclining on her side, enormous thighs tapering down to dainty little feet. Huge globes for breasts with a pink tinge at the nipple. Pink tinged the knees, elbows, and cheeks. I looked like a cross between the Easter Bunny and Elmer Fudd.

As for the video, although he'd kept the images out of focus, there was no doubt it was me. I was just a little fuzzy at the edges. Like the ace pornographer he was turning out to be, he must have had the camera very cunningly hidden.

My eyes were blurry with tears as I hurried back to the champagne. Quite a large group had gathered. They ate and drank and warbled praise for the show. I watched the people milling and chattering. Then I saw the sheaf of white-blond hair gleaming above the other heads. It was Anna, my roommate. Of all people. I hadn't mentioned the show to her. I didn't think she was interested in art. I felt an affinity to her just then. I needed to see a friendly face and roommates can be good in those bad moments. I mean, we'd shared so many things, things you could almost call intimate, like boxes of Tampax, dish soap, Glug and bathtub rings. I would like to have talked to her in that moment, but she turned away before I could catch her eye.

Francesca was there, too, standing alone, off to one side, tasting the caviar. No prospective Sam-types stood nearby, though.

It was another surprise to see Nelly the Grape, the girl from La Tazza, sipping champagne and schmoozing. She was even more purple than usual.

I'd had enough. I grabbed a full bottle and headed for the bathrooms. There was only one remedy. I locked myself into a cubicle and began to drown my sorrows in a whole delicious bottle of Brut. I was down to the bottom part of the label and on the verge of hiccups when I heard voices approach, the door open, and two sets of footsteps stop in front of my cubicle. I yanked my feet up onto the toilet seat.

A voice whispered, "Oh, Sam, you should. I could make

us dinner, then we could take a swim in the pool. There's a Jacuzzi, too. You need to relax. I know you've been under a lot of pressure lately with the Jennifer business."

Sam!

And who the Bojangles was Jennifer?

I was dying to peek through the crack and see what Sam looked like but couldn't risk discovery. I held my breath and squeezed back the hiccups.

There was the flick of a lighter and a blue curl of smoke rose into the air.

"Francesca. You think you should? I don't know that they'd appreciate you smoking," said Sam.

"That's why we're in here. It's just like school, isn't it?" She laughed her fluttery laugh. I could picture Francesca as a girl, at some elite private school, taking bites out of each and every forbidden fruit.

"Francesca. What are you doing?" Sam's voice was soft and teasing.

There was more fluttery laughter, then the dry shoosh of hands on fabric and the wet slurpy sound of lips on lips.

"How was that?" asked Francesca.

"Um, you've caught me…the champagne must have… uh…I mean, I'm a little surprised…um…uh…what about Gordon?"

"Gordon and I have an understanding."

"Look. Let's get out of this place. I'm freezing and I need to get some air."

"Whatever you say."

They were gone, and with them my stupid slim hope that Sam might be available. I could be fairly sure that he wasn't a hunchback with bad acne scars and two long hairs vainly covering some bald spot. He was kissable in Francesca's books, and women like Francesca could have anyone they wanted. I didn't know who Gordon was but it sounded as though she wasn't letting monogamy get in her way. I couldn't compete with her. I chug-a-lugged the rest of the champagne and sat there in a maudlin haze, wishing Jeremy were alive, wishing for a Sam…I mean…a man…of my own.

I staggered out of the bathroom and back to the tables. Paul had arrived. His voice filtered through the curtains. He was holding court. All the disciples and adoring fans surrounding him had stopped chattering.

He spoke. "The corridor represents the female void, the darkness is the sense of terror and emptiness on entering it, or penetrating it, as it were. The video images are intended as brief moments of light, that which tempts us in flesh and the female form. Females as constellations, beautiful and alluring at a distance, but close up, one discovers that this is no star but a planet, surrounded by noxious unbreathable gasses and temperatures unfit for human habitation. The female is portrayed here as a paradox, nature's lure, a biological trick designed to have us believe that she is an entity of light, when really she is a creature of a darkness so total that you should fear for your life. All a trap to ensure the race's procreation."

"What about the chocolate?" asked a voice.

"Heh heh heh," snicker-snacked Paul. "It seemed the perfect medium. Women and chocolate. They're inseparable."

On that point, there was no faulting him. Following the other line of reasoning, all that babble about light and dark, Paul, the misogynist creep was the occupant of a warehouse that he'd taken all sorts of pains to paint black, and so by his own definition, had built himself a made-to-measure female void. That was my interpretation anyway. Paul Bleeker had created a monumental womb for himself and crawled inside it.

Why hadn't I seen right away that he was a first-class weirdo?

I knew his mother's death must have affected him, perhaps even traumatized him a little, but I had no idea that he was thinking such dark thoughts about women all that time that he was pretending to be so charming and understanding. No wonder sex with him always happened like an air raid.

On automatic pilot, I wandered through the area, pouring champagne and picking up whatever was dropped. Humiliation buzzed through me, making me blind and deaf to everything and everyone.

When the crowd had finally left, Nadine gave me her mile-long list of closing-up instructions. Then she left, arm in arm with Paul, who blatantly ignored me.

I stumbled out of the spiral and into the dark storeroom. It was warm compared to the rest of the gallery. I plopped myself down onto the pile of old coverings, pulled a couple of sheets over myself and sank into a drunken sleep.

I dreamed the chocolate women. There was a battalion of them, and in the way that dreams try to tell you things you've overlooked in your waking life, I knew those women were familiar.

They were also gothic, horrifying. Rags and bits of gauzy bandage hung and fluttered from their torsos and limbs as they moved toward me like zombies, like the living dead, their sickly-sweet aroma filling me with nausea.

I could see myself at the back of the group, moving with them, as big as a circus Fat Woman, lumbering along and falling behind as usual. The only difference was that I was fresh and undamaged in my fat way, no bandages hung off my body. I had to take this as a good omen, that I was at least alive.

Paul appeared out of nowhere. At first his eyes seemed normal, black and flashing, but then his pupils began to glow bloodred. He was touching the chocolate women, unbandaging them, licking them all over, chewing bits of face and limb.

I understood in a flash. It was a question of eat or be eaten.

I sat bolt upright. It was impossible to tell what time it was. I staggered to my feet and back out into the freezing gallery. I stumbled from one cubicle to another, scrutinizing the sculptures. How had I missed it? As well as I knew artists and what it meant to be their "model," I had chosen not to see the obvious.

The Other Women.

Recognizing Nadine wasn't hard. She was the spidery one, all elbows and ribs. Naturally, I'd expected her to be one of Paul's models. She had more than one tick. She had a megalomaniacal habit of forcing artists to involve her in their work whenever they were going to have a show in her gallery. But it still made me furious.

I broke the big toe off the chocolate Nadine's foot. It was a full two inches of dark chocolate that in real life had seen more Ferragamo shoe leather than was decent.

And Anna the Viking. He must have been sloshing and pillaging with her behind my back since the day he met her—that evening when she had been doing yoga in the front room, her buns in the air, and I had been running around collecting my things. I took both of her white chocolate index fingers.

Francesca St. Claire de la Roche was the one that stuck in my craw the most. Because she was beautiful and could have whoever she wanted. She was the biggest surprise. How had she infiltrated my social circle so quickly? All that pale milk chocolate, I took her thumbs, her ring finger and both big toes.

Nelly the Grape from La Tazza was among them, too, dark chocolate with a purplish tinge. I took both of her middle fingers.

Of the rest of them, those of Paul's chocolate lovers that I'd never met, I took one digit each. I found some clean tissue paper in the storage room, wrapped all the appendages neatly and stuffed them into my purse.

Then I went on a final random binge, breaking off little bits here and there and popping them into my mouth. My face shivered with too much sweetness.

When I'd had enough, I emptied the contents of my desk into a plastic bag, grabbed Jeremy's ashes and left the gallery, oblivious to where I was going.

I stood in front of the launderette. I'd walked for most of the night and ended up in Jeremy's neighborhood. Unable to face Anna back at my apartment, I'd wandered, still blurry from all the champagne but buzzing with chocolate-powered energy. I blended in with the bag ladies and threadbare night people. I should have been terrified but I wasn't. I was too angry, striding in a fury past the central knot of cement and glass high-rises, toward East Hastings and Chinatown. I'd clutched my bags in one hand and my little brass urn with Jeremy's ashes in the other, holding it out in front of me as if it were a talisman for warding off evil spirits.

I felt seasick with Jeremy gone, his life, my safe island, had vanished, the magic had fallen into the sea like Atlantis, and left me to swim or drown.

It was seven in the morning. The venetian blinds had been lowered on the inside. The launderette seemed as dead as its owner. There was a card on the front door that announced in large sloppy handwritten letters: Closed Until Further Notice.

I still had the emergency set of launderette keys that Jeremy had given me years back. I unlocked the door and went inside. At the far end was a little utility room with a two-way mirror and a big lost-and-found box. I unlocked the door, went inside the little room, turned on the light and locked myself in. I pulled a few towels and some sweatshirts out of the lost-and-found, improvised a bed and lay down. The smell was delicious. Laundry soap, Borax, bleach and fabric softener.

I dreamt I was walking with Jeremy. The landscape shifted constantly. We were visiting places where we'd spent parts of my childhood. We walked through a forest. The trees, huge Douglas firs, were bending toward us, eavesdropping and sighing. He said, "It's okay, Lucy, honey, it's okay to look at these places again with me. It's okay to think you're always gonna come back to them. But if you do things right, it doesn't matter if you do come back to them or not."

"How can you say that?" I screamed the words and hit his chest with my fists. He just looked at me, softly, unresisting. We had come to the ocean, a sparkling cove. There was a little dock, and the slurp slurp of dinghies rocking against it. The water was a rich sapphire blue, ruffled by wind.

Jeremy said, "The way that water looks out there on the ocean, that was our time when you were a kid jumping out of boats, swimming all summer. It belongs to that time. You won't remember it any better than that."

"I will. I will," I protested.

"Don't get attached to it. Let it go."

"What are you telling me?"

We had moved on and were standing in a vast sunlit field.

It smelled of damp hay and late summer sun. His hair was whiter and longer than I had ever seen it. His feet were not quite touching the ground. "My house, all the stuff in it. Don't get worked up over it. Try to forget it."

"You don't know what you're saying," I sobbed. "You're crazy. You've completely lost your mind."

"You see, you've gotta let me go because my leaving is your permission to fly. Lucy, the past is weighing you down."

"Crazy, crazy, you're crazy."

"Your memories of me will be a drag unless you know how to use them. And the way to use them is to let them go. I'll be part of you, count on that."

"You can't fool me. I know this is a dream and that your voice is really my voice. I've been through a little therapy, too, you know."

"Therapy shmerapy," he said.

"I'm not afraid."

"It's only natural to be afraid. You're supposed to be afraid. It's part of the game. Hold my hand." I took his hand. We began to lift off the ground and glide over the field. I could hear the ocean roaring in the distance. The sun was shining but the moon and stars were glimmering in a darker sky as well. We glided toward that part of the sky.

Jeremy's hair was growing longer and gleaming silver. We glided higher and I could feel the terror of falling growing in me.

"Don't let me go," I cried.

"I'm with you. I'll always be with you. Don't look back. And don't look for me. It'll just slow you down."

"But I'm in pain," I cried, "my world is gone. You died and took my world with you."

"Connie," he said, and I could feel my hand slipping out of his.

"No," I yelled.

His voice became distant. "Lucy, Lucy, Lucy…"

I opened my eyes. Looming above me were shining stainless-steel spokes. It was a wheelchair. Sitting in it was a bulky bearded grizzly bear of a middle-aged man.

He was leaning over the edge of his chair and shaking me with one hand, saying my name. "Lucy. Lucy. Chrissake, Lucy, wake up."

I sat up and stared around me in a daze, unable to get my bearings.

"Bob."

Bob smiled and said, "I gotta tell you, Lucy. Thought somebody was gonna call the police with all the screamin' you were doin' back here. I could hear you through my apartment wall. What the hell you doin' here anyway? How the hell did you get in?"

"I missed Jeremy. I've still got the keys. When I was a kid, I used to curl up on the washing and go to sleep."

Bob laughed—it sounded like tires on gravel—then said, "Think we all miss Jeremy, Kiddo. C'mon, get up. Let's go to my place. You look…" He scratched his head. "I was gonna say you don't look so good but it ain't true. You always look good to me, Lucy Madison."

"Thanks, Bob."

"Yer welcome. C'mon. You turn sideways, you gonna disappear. Jeez, you're lookin' kinda thin. I mean, you look great. I'm just not used to seein' you lookin' so thin. How much you lost anyway?"

"I don't know."

Bob wheeled ahead of me out the front door of the launderette, around to the back, and into his entrance. He maneuvered the two steps expertly. I followed him into the apartment.

His living room was a shrine to technology. He had all the latest toys, computer, minicam, stereo, flat-screen television with DVD and quadrophonic sound.

"Siddown. What can I get ya? Coffee? A beer? A joint?" He disappeared into the kitchen.

Bob had his own little cultivation of pot plants flourishing in the spare room under lights. He'd once told me that he needed all that marijuana because it made him sleep. When he went to sleep stoned, he dreamed more, and that was important because in his dreams he was always walking or running on his own legs, just as he was before the accident.

"How about food? Want something to eat? Don't want you to faint on me or anything. You're skin and bones. Got some whole wheat bread and some…" I heard the sounds of rummaging in a fridge "…tuna. Really good. Had it at lunch today. Still fresh. Put in a little onion and celery and mayo…"

"You mean it's after lunch?"

Bob wheeled out of the kitchen and stared at me. "Sure is. Half past three."

"I've lost more than half a day."

"You been up to something you can't talk about?"

"No, not really. It's my job. I think I quit. I mean I have quit. I just haven't told my boss."

"Happens."

"But I didn't call in sick or anything."

"Where you been working lately?"

I went into the long saga of Nadine and Rogues' Gallery but I left out Paul Bleeker and the chocolate digits. "Bob. I've gotta go. Can I ask you a favor?"

"Shoot."

"First, I need to know what's going to happen to the launderette? Now that Jeremy's gone, I mean."

"Nothin'. Not as long as I'm here. But out of respect for Jeremy, eh, I thought it should stay closed for a bit. And as the revenue goes to Connie, I wanted her to feel the squeeze. Trouble is, she don't feel nothin'. Call me a mean bastard if ya like."

"Then I really have to ask you this favor."

"Shoot again."

"Can I stay here tonight? I don't want to go back to my apartment."

"You can stay here in my spare room."

"No. I meant the launderette. I just want to be around the old familiar places and smells a little longer. I can't exactly sniff around his house with Connie living in it."

"Jeez, it's kinda an uncomfortable way ta hang out."

"I just want another couple of nights."

"Whatever. No skin off my nose. Connie's the boss but she hasn't ever been interested in the launderette. Wouldn't set foot inside it right from the start. Figures she's too good for some things."

"I wanted to ask you about Connie. Have you seen her or talked to her lately?"

"I expected to hear from her after the funeral. Ain't heard nothing. We ain't really been on speakin' terms for over a year. And she only lives two blocks from here. Go figure. The last time we talked, or maybe I should say, snarled at each other, was just before Jeremy started gettin' bad. We agree to disagree. Lemme put it this way. We hate each other's guts so we just stay out of each other's way. All launderette business goes through an estate manager."

"You know she's pregnant?"

"Hell, what?"

"I figure four or five months, maybe more. It's hard to tell because she hasn't been eating."

Bob spoke as though he had a bug stuck in his throat. "I just can't picture Connie as a mother. Whose is it?"

"That's a little unfair, Bob. It's Jeremy's."

"Yeah, I know. Just gotta digest it."

"What is it about her?" I said, more to myself than to Bob.

"Can't tell you. Just know she gives me the vibes."

"I better go, Bob. I've got myself in a bit of trouble."

"You too…" He stared at my stomach.

"Not that kind of trouble."

"Oh. Good. I mean, I hope it's good. Unless you were planning…"

"No. I'm not planning anything. I'm not even attached."

"Hey, you wanna get attached?"

"Maybe some day."

"You could always marry me. If you don't mind marrying a cripple." Bob looked down at his useless legs.

"If I ever get in the mood to marry, I'll definitely keep you in mind."

Bob sent me off with a tuna sandwich wrapped in foil and the promise to have dinner with him later to put some flesh on my bones. I caught a bus back to Gastown and arrived at the gallery just before five o'clock. All hell had broken loose.

Paul Bleeker was inside Nadine's office, tugging at his hair and puffing furiously on a Sobranie. I could tell he'd been at it for a while. The place was filled with smoke.

"WHERE HAVE YOU BEEN?" screeched Nadine. Her mouth was open so wide and for so long that if I'd been a dentist, I could have done an estimate.

"DO YOU KNOW ANYTHING ABOUT THIS?" she shrieked, then stomped up to her own chocolate image and pointed at the missing toe.

"Oh heavens." I put my hand to my mouth in mock horror. "Vandalism. I hope his pieces are insured," I said.

"You were the last one out of here last night."

I could feel a blush rising but forced myself to stay calm. "So?"

"You must have seen something."

"Didn't see a thing."

"Well, you can't have been cleaning up because the place was a dump this morning."

"That's because I quit," I said.

"YOU WHAT?"

"I quit. Just before the cleaning up. And I want this month's salary for all the days I worked and my separation pay."

"You can't quit."

"Why not?"

"First of all, you'll never find another job. Certainly not a gallery job because I'll put the word out and nobody will hire you."

"All those threats about me being expendable and now you don't want me to quit. Why is that? Is it because nobody else would take the same crap? Like I said, I quit. Write me a cheque. I'm in a hurry."

Nadine glared at me. The shoulder strap on my purse felt as though it were cutting into my shoulder, getting heavier and bigger by the minute, begging to be searched for evidence of the chocolate crimes.

Nadine scrutinized me. "You did it."

Paul Bleeker came out of Nadine's office. Nadine said to him, "She did it." He joined her in glaring at me.

"What did I do, Nadine?" My voice was sugary, angelic.

"You damaged the sculptures."

"Why would I do an infantile thing like that?" In fact, I *was* wondering myself how I could have been so infantile.

Betsy Burke

"Jealousy, I shouldn't wonder. His sculpture of you isn't exactly flattering. Perhaps you did it out of spite."

For once, I had everybody's full attention.

Something in me cracked. I brought up the unmentionable. "I think it's more likely that you did it, Nadine. Who else? You can't resist stuffing anything edible into your mouth. Because you're starving. It doesn't ever really stay in your system, does it? I don't know why you don't just dump all your food directly down the toilet. It's where it all ends up anyway. Regurgitated. You've never fooled me. All that flushing and running water. Those bite marks on your hands. All I can say is, it's a pity that so much food has gone to waste. With all the hungry people in the world and one bulemic old bag hogging it all to herself."

Nadine had turned ash white and stayed frozen to the spot.

"You can mail me my cheque, Nadine."

The deadly silence was a great cue for an exit, so I took it.

15

Bob made Mexican food for dinner, tortillas, refried beans, guacamole, salsa. It was fantastic. All washed down with a few cervesas.

We got onto the subject of Jeremy pretty quickly. "Tell me everything you remember about him," I said.

Bob sat back. "Well, lemme see. Whenever there was shit goin' down between band members, if it looked like there was gonna be some bad stuff bustin' out, he was the one everyone called on to settle it. He had a way of makin' people feel stupid for wasting their time over fightin'. He kept telling us life was too short, there was too much good shit out there to be enjoyed. He was always sayin', 'Don't worry over the small stuff.'"

Bob's voice became almost a whisper. "There was that time a little after my accident when I'd been out of the coma for almost a year. Hell, about fourteen years ago. Can't believe it's been that long. You know, at first, you're glad to be alive and then it hits you that you ain't got no legs and you ain't never gonna have no legs again. Well, I started drinkin' my lunch, my breakfast, too, while we're at it, and it was Jeremy kept shovelin' me up off the carpet. You knew my lady was killed in the accident, too, eh?"

"Yeah, I knew, Bob."

"Well, I was feelin' pretty guilty about that as well, I can tell ya. So, yeah, Jeremy kept scrapin' me up and pokin' at my misery. Kinda like a can opener pokin' at a can a worms, eh? Jeremy kept telling me, 'You can't just go and make up your mind about life. It doesn't work that way. You don't know what the surprises are gonna be.' He had to do a lot of talkin' 'cause I was plannin' on a forty-proof one-way ticket outa here. Anyway, he just kept pokin' an' pokin' until it got to me so bad that I just started to howl and rave at him. Like an animal, man. An' he kept sayin', 'That the best you can do?' Until I'd howled it all outa me. Then he gave me this place an' management of the launderette. Just to show me surprises could happen. Anyway. He really helped me. I'm a goddam wonder. You know I been in the Olympics with my chair?"

"No, I didn't." There seemed to be little that Bob couldn't do with his chair and his two strong arms.

"Yeah. Got myself a bronze. Play a little basketball, too. It woulda been shitty of me to let him down. Jeremy gave me this line, it seemed like a line at the time, that he was gettin' too old to be bothered with it all, wanted to think about other things. That was years ago. Maybe he was sicker than we knew. You're his granddaughter. You probably heard all this before."

"Some of it passed me by, Bob. Jeremy had secrets. There's some stuff we'll never know."

"Like?"

"Like why he chose Connie."

"I'm with you on that one."

It was after midnight when Bob offered me an air mattress and a sleeping bag for the utility room. His expression told me he thought I was coloring outside the lines, but then his biker days had made him used to crazy people. People who fell asleep any old place, under bridges, in abandoned warehouses, on top of grand pianos and billiard tables.

"Listen, you change your mind, Lucy, I got this nice comfortable spare room."

"It's okay, Bob. Really. Not to hurt your feelings, but that would be Bob's smell, not Jeremy's."

"I get yer point. Uh, listen, Lucy. It's my turn to ask you a favor."

"Sure. If I can help."

"Well, I figured since the place was closed, and you were gonna be here anyway…"

"Yeah?"

"I'd really like to go visit my brother in Kelowna. I haven't had a break from this place in years. My brother usually comes here but it's not the same. Know what they say. Change is as good as a rest."

"Sure, Bob. No problem."

"Great. I'll go tomorrow morning. You don't mind keeping an eye on the launderette then? My apartment, too?"

"Not at all. How long are you going to be gone?"

"A couple of weeks anyway."

"Isn't it a long time to keep the launderette closed?"

"Maybe. I just want to get outa here for a bit. Listen, I'll give you my spare keys. The main thing is that my dope plants get a little water. You won't forget, eh?"

* * *

I set up camp. A few lights were always left on in the launderette and enough light seeped into the utility room that I
wasn't in total darkness.

I lay there, taking in the familiar odor of old lost laundry
and trying to remember something I'd forgotten. It was so
big that I had no business forgetting it but I just couldn't remember what it was. I got up and went out into the main
part of the launderette.

It was an immense space, ugly and utilitarian, and much
of it wasn't used at all. Up to about nose height, cheap wood
paneling lined the walls. The washers and dryers were a cross
between a sickly yellow and avocado color. There were hard
wooden benches for people to sit on while waiting for their
clothes to dry. Some ancient, dog-eared magazines lay in a
pile. Anything the customers felt generous enough to leave.

Above the wood paneling were vast expanses of stale off-
white wall, badly in need of a paint job.

That's when I remembered.

I was thinking of how the place would look with a new
paint job, picturing the painters scrambling up the scaffolding, the rollers and wide brushes slapping paint across the surfaces, bringing the space back to life.

I started to see colors. Why couldn't they paint the walls
an interesting color? Cerulean blue. Emerald green. Hot rose.
Sunflower yellow. Then in my mind, the painters started
using all the colors together. They went wild using bold
brush strokes, creating bright abstracts.

Painting.

It was time for me to start painting again. All that running
around for Nadine, mooning after Paul Bleeker, had been
keeping me from my own work. The walls were there in front
of me, bare and inviting, begging to be filled.

I went back into the utility room and lay back down on the air mattress. I started to think about Frida Kahlo and Diego Rivera. Diego was the real wall man, the mural man, but it was Frida's art, that colorful surrealism, that fascinated me.

Frida.

How could I be such a fool? I had perfectly good arms and legs and yet I'd found a million ways to sabotage myself, to put off the work. Whereas Frida, who'd been crippled by a bus accident at eighteen, and had a handrail run through her back and uterus, had still managed to paint through her pain.

I lay there for ages, deciding what I would do, until I finally drifted off to sleep. That night was filled with Frida's birds, flowers and vines, her dogs and monkeys.

The next day I called my mother from Bob's place. In a moment of simpiness, my unknown future yawning a little too widely before me, I wanted to be a child again. I had to let her know that I couldn't be reached at my apartment. I even toyed with the idea of going back to Cedar Narrows for a few days, but when I heard her voice, I realized it would be self-defeating.

My mother said, "Lucy. Just who I've been looking for. I want you to come to the movies with us tonight. It's in town at the Ridge. My treat. We'll meet you there. It starts at eight but there's bound to be a line-up, so get there as soon as you can."

"What's the movie?" I asked.

"It's a surprise," she said. Coming from my mother's mouth, these words were an omen.

In the afternoon I went back to my apartment. Anna wasn't there. I left a post-dated cheque for the rent then

packed a sports bag full of clothes. I went into my storage
locker and found art supplies, several huge plastic jars of
acrylic paint, still not dried out after all these months, and
brushes. I put them in another sports bag. Before I set off toward the launderette, I called Sky.

"Where have you been?" she asked. "I've been trying to
get in touch with you all day."

I told her.

"Listen," she said. "Meet me at the Ridge Theatre tonight."

"I'm meeting my mother there tonight."

Sky laughed. "Really? She's going, too? That's hilarious."

"Why? What's playing?"

Sky was on the verge of telling me, then said, "No, I won't
give it away. It's a surprise. I'm not going to tell you because
you might not come if I do. Be there at seven-thirty. There's
sure to be a crowd."

At seven-thirty, I was walking toward the Ridge Theatre.
The line-up was quite long and at least half of it was made
up of nuns. That had me worried. What were they making
me see? The unedited version of *The Song of Bernadette?* I finally got close enough to the cinema's marquee to read the
lettering.

Sing-a-long-a Sound of Music.

Whoa!

Before I could sneak away, I heard Sky's voice behind me.
I wheeled around, saw her and started to laugh. She was wearing a little girl's white dress with a blue satin sash. Standing
next to her was Max, wrapped from head to toe in brown
paper and tied up with string, a round cut-out hole framing
his face.

"Nobody told me it was fancy dress," I said. I was wearing my safe sloppy jeans outfit.

"It's a big event," said Sky. She was excited and doing nothing to hide it.

Max went ahead and got the tickets. While we stood around watching the crowd gather, I gave Sky all my latest news. All except for the chocolate theft. I was feeling slightly ashamed of myself. Sky was thrilled to hear that I'd finally quit working for Nadine.

In the crowd, there were plenty of drunk nuns with heavy five o'clock shadows and bass voices. Quite a few people were dressed in dirndls and kerchiefs clearly made of curtain material. There were also raindrops on roses, represented by a group of men in white leotards well-doused in silver glitter. They left sparkly trails wherever they went.

Max came back with the tickets and three little kits. Each contained a head scarf, a packet of cough drops in case our throats got sore from all the singing, and foam rubber nun finger puppets, which we were supposed to wave in the air in time to the music.

It was then that the Harley Davidson pulled up with my father and mother. My father squeezed the bike into a parking space between two cars and climbed off, my mother following. He was dressed in Tyrolean hiking gear, the outfit of Captain Von Trapp as he, Maria and the little Von Trapps make their escape over the Alps. My mother was the Mother Superior, her habit yanked up around her knees and a motorcycle helmet over her wimple. What could I say? At least my parents were together.

My father looked more robust than usual. "Lucy, how's life?"

"It's okay, Dad. More to the point, how's your life?"

"Great. Just great. Praise the Lord." Back to his old self. Almost. His ear was still pierced and he'd kept the three-day growth of beard but his chipped tooth had been fixed.

My mother came over and whispered to me, "We're on a date. He hasn't actually come home yet."

This would have depressed me if the mood hadn't been growing crazier as the movie crowd gathered. A few Nazi officers arrived. People even dressed as schnitzel with noodles, long white strands dragging behind them, bread crumbs rubber-cemented to their bodies.

My father, mother, Sky, Max and I all sat together in one row. The music started up and everybody belted forth the first lines. We sang our way through all of it. I was a bit disturbed at how well I knew the words. But then I had an excuse. When I was a small child, my mother used to park me in front of all her favorite musicals on videotape. When one was over, she'd wind it back and start again. I was a victim of big-time brainwashing. My mother had forced me to endure *Brigadoon, The King and I, The Music Man, Guys and Dolls, South Pacific, My Fair Lady* and *Pajama Game*. These were her favorites but there were many, many others. I was a walking encyclopedia of silly songs.

The atmosphere grew increasingly giddy. By the time we had reached the big party scene there was nothing left for me to do but open my purse.

I held out a bunch of digits and elbowed Sky, "Care for a chocolate?"

She accepted a couple of milk chocolate thumbs, then passed the rest on down the row. My mother clapped her hands together and said, "Oh, goody. Choccies."

The Heinous Chocolate Crime evidence taken care of, I sat back to enjoy Maria falling to pieces for love of that delicious and slightly diabolical navy captain.

I knew what I had to do. If they didn't like it, the damage would be easy to repair. I found a tall aluminum ladder in the back of the launderette's utility room. On top of its hinges, I placed a large piece of plywood to form a table. Then I brought out my economy-size plastic jars of acrylic paint. I'd closed them tightly and sealed them with tape, but one of the light blues had gone moldy anyway. It didn't matter. I had enough white to create lighter shades. The jar of gel was still fresh, unopened. Gel was indispensable for wall work. It stopped the colors from dribbling.

I started in the far back corner. First I washed the surface from nose-level to ceiling with a sponge and soap to get off any grease. Then I rinsed the area. I decided to work blind, without a plan. The whole thing had been boiling away in me on its own, organizing itself. Certain images were already in place.

I began to work. It took me over. I couldn't have stopped myself if I'd wanted to. I suppose it also had something to do with the fact that I couldn't help looking on the place as partially mine. When we're small children, all places that belong to family members also belong to us. What a horrible shock it is to grow up and learn the truth.

For four days, I worked, only stopping to take naps and squirrel-amount food breaks. I nourished myself on Bob's leftovers, tap water and trail mix from a health-food store down the street. I got cups of terrible coffee from the local 7-Eleven.

I covered the whole back wall of the launderette and began to move into the area where the machines were. It came when I spattered a couple of washers with a shocking fuchsia-pink shade of paint. The big idea. The scary idea. The great idea.

I banged on Connie's door. I was wearing an old pair of loose pants and shirt that were covered with at least a decade of paint spatters. Paint was in my hair, on my shoes, on my face and hands. As usual, Connie was hiding inside, and it took ages for her to come to the door. As soon as she opened, I asked, "Can I come in?" She stood aside and I barged past her.

"Can I just say something?" she droned.

"What?"

"You look worse than I do."

I stared at her. Then I caught a glimpse of myself in the hall mirror. I started to laugh. "You know, you're right." We both started to laugh and I almost went into shock. I'd never heard her laugh before. It was a raucous sound, like a couple of crows murdering each other.

"I've gotta talk to you, Connie. It's life or death. More for me than for you. But it could be important for you, too…I mean it could be…"

"Would you just quit babbling and get to the point?"

I told her what I'd done on the wall of the launderette. She didn't look happy but she didn't say anything. She found a cigarette and stuck it in her mouth. I waited but she didn't light it, just let it sit there on her lip.

"Let me tell you my plan," I said.

"Just wait a minute." She lumbered over to the armchair and sat down. She looked fatter, healthier. "Yeah, okay."

I expounded for twenty minutes then asked, "What do you think?"

16

Connie stared at me in her deadpan way for a long time then said, "I dunno. It's harebrain. And whose money you planning to use?"

"You could take out a loan on the house. Jeremy told me he was debt-free."

"Forget it."

"It's a good plan. Don't junk it before you've thought about it."

"Naw."

"You haven't thought about it."

"Listen. I don't really give a shit what you do to the walls. They couldn't be worse than they are. And I haven't talked to a lawyer yet about finding a loophole in the arrangements. I'd really like to sell the launderette. It's not exactly big business."

"You can't sell it. There's Bob."

"Yeah. Right. Bob." She gave me one of her slitty-eyed stares and took a drag of the unlit cigarette. "Listen. I'm going away for a while."

"You're what?"

I didn't want to hear this. I was getting used to the idea of having Connie as a permanent arch-nemesis.

"Your friend Reebee's idea. She's been comin' around, talkin' to me, makin' me eat. We been talking really a lot. About the past and stuff. She thinks I should take this road trip with her, down the coast and on to Arizona, maybe New Mexico, too."

"Reebee's crazy to think you should take a trip now. And her car's an old beater. You can't take a road trip with her. Not in your condition."

"She's been doing an okay job of lookin' after me. I wanna go. I wanna get outa here, away from Jeremy's stuff. It's depressing. Maybe you could do me a favor. Stay here and water the plants while I'm gone."

She raised her eyebrow in the direction of one two-inch high cactus plant.

"You're being funny?" I couldn't believe it.

"Yeah. And if any thieves break in, make sure they take the valuables, all of them."

"You serious? You're really going to go with Reebee?" I said.

"Deadly serious."

"I think it's a stupid idea. A road trip when you're pregnant. You don't know what could happen."

"It's my life. I can fuck it up any old way I want."

"Yeah. I guess that's true. I have to tell you, I wouldn't mind staying here. I still need to be around Jeremy's world a little longer."

She stared at me. Her face was so inscrutable she could have been a hundred years old, a wise woman or a zombie.

That was the thing about Connie. You just didn't know what was lurking in there. She caressed her stomach and said very softly, "You gotta remember one thing, Lucy."

"What's that?"

"He's dead. He's gone. He's dust," said Connie. "It's useless to hang on." In that moment she looked stressed to the point of desperation. Her eyes may even have been glistening a little but it was hard to tell because she immediately looked away then down at her stomach again.

"Yeah, maybe you do need to get out of here," I said. "But first, come and see the damage. If you feel like walking."

"I'm supposed to move more. Reebee's been on my case. She made me go to the gynecologist and she got on my case, too. Everybody's on my case."

"That's what happens when there's a baby involved. Just wait till it's born if you think they're on your case now."

Connie took another half hour to change into some street clothes. They must have been donated by Reebee. The influence was clear. The clothes were nice, but they were shrubby earth mother clothes, dusty dark greens and tans, not Connie's usual style at all.

She dragged along beside me, puffing for air, and squinting in the bright light of day. When we got to the launderette, I unlocked the door.

"So you have the keys, eh? When did he give them to you?" Her voice was edged with bitterness.

I said, "Years ago. Before he met you. Just in case his or Bob's were lost. Bob said you didn't want to have anything to do with launderette business."

Connie seemed almost to be pushing something away physically. "I don't care. It doesn't matter."

We went inside the launderette and down to the back. I turned on the lights.

Connie stood and examined my work for a few minutes then said, "Hey, that one there is me." One of the figures was a depiction of her with a huge stomach. Inside the stomach, a fat baby of undetermined gender peered around curiously. I'd painted Connie with tree roots curling out of her feet and into the ground and her hair curling wildly upward and transforming into leaves.

"And that's Jeremy," she said. "What's he doing? Flying? And that's his Harley. Shit."

I nodded. I'd painted Jeremy flying with long silver hair and beard almost as he'd been in my dream except that I'd added angel's wings. His bike was flying along beside him with its own set of angel's wings.

"That's Bob. Hey, that's funny considering he's a cripple." Bob was shown the way he liked to dream of himself—running on his own legs. Flowers, birds, fish and vines wove around the figures. Some of the figures were underwater and quite content to be there, like my parents, for instance, in their *Sing-along-a Sound of Music* costumes.

There were open windows and doorways looking onto dream vistas that reminded me of Jeremy: the arbutus trees outside his cabin up the coast, his little boat in the bay of azure ripples, beach fires under a starry night sky, opal-white winter mountains.

"It's not bad. I sorta like it," said Connie, reaching into her pocket and taking out a cigarette. Again, she put it in her mouth but didn't light it. "I gotta say though, you got one warped imagination."

I was there when Reebee came in the Valiant to get Connie. I helped carry suitcases out to the car. Reebee knew as soon as she saw me that I thought it was a dumb idea.

"You've got to stop worrying so much, Lucy," Reebee said.

"I'm a good driver. The universe is on my side. So just go and paint and let us do what we have to do. I'll see what you've produced when we get back."

"When will that be?" I asked sulkily.

"It'll be when it'll be. When it's right."

"Terrific. Try not to have the baby in the back of the car, Connie."

"I would never let that happen," said Reebee. "I had the upholstery redone."

"Just get back here before it's born, would you? I'd really hate to miss out," I said.

"Yeah, sure," said Connie. But she didn't sound convincing.

They were strange, those days in the spring, finally alone, circumstances finally conspiring to let me paint.

I felt as though I were a figure in one of my dreams, my movements liquid and slow. I woke up when I wanted to, took my time over coffee. I wallowed quite a bit in the misery brought on by remembering Jeremy, but I couldn't help myself. If I didn't get it out then, it would get me later when I least expected it. In a crowd. On a bus. At a job interview.

I wasn't ready for anything more than the present in this strange slow-motion speed.

I revelled in that private limbo of wandering down to the launderette and painting for hours, for as long as I liked with no interruptions.

Sometimes I wandered around the streets, going nowhere in particular, just wandering and thinking. I'd see the back of a man that looked like Paul Bleeker. I'd quicken my pace to catch up, thinking he'd changed his mind and come down to this neighborhood to find me, that he'd searched everywhere and was finally here. Then I'd realize how stupid this was and slow my pace just short of stopping the stranger in front of me and making a fool of myself.

In the long empty hours, I listened to Bob's CD collection and made lists and sketches of my big idea. I did a few chores, cleaned both Connie's and Bob's kitchen cupboards and fridges. I mowed Jeremy's lawn and pulled out weeds. I accepted some seeds and cuttings, along with condolences, offered to me by the elderly woman who shared Jeremy's back fence. Her garden was fantastic.

Apartment gardening in the West End was limited. Back at the apartment, there were just my house plants and no balcony to put them on. My weeping fig was probably dead by now since it was allergic to Anna. I also had some pots of chives and sage and rosemary on the windowsill overlooking Didi and Gogo's Dumpster.

I should have been happier without Nadine to hound me. There was all the time in the world for painting. The chance to dig my hands into the real earth had finally come.

But the thing I really felt was the loneliness.

It kidnapped me, like a spaceship from a distant galaxy, and carried me off to a dark, freezing planet where no one spoke my language.

It was May and I'd been at Jeremy's and the launderette for almost two weeks. Neither Connie nor Bob had returned and I'd had no word from either of them. The mural was growing up onto the ceiling. I'd cadged some ancient rusty scaffolding from a painting and construction business nearby, banking on their friendship with Jeremy, with the promise to let them have it back the minute they needed it. I was going to give Diego Rivera a run for his money.

As I was working up there, doing a good imitation of Quasi Modo, there was a violent banging on the launderette's front door. I scrambled down, opened the venetian blind and looked out. A young woman stood outside holding on to the hands of two small children. Beside her was an old super-market shopping cart stuffed to the brim with balled-up clothes, towels and bed sheets. She pointed to the Closed sign and held out her hands in exasperation, then she shouted through the door, "When are you opening up? I've got to do my laundry."

I signalled for her to wait, then went to get the keys. I un-locked the door and let her in. She pushed the kids in front of her then dragged in the shopping cart.

"About time," she said. "Where am I supposed to go to do the washing? There's only so much stuff you can wash by hand in the bathtub. There's nowhere else for miles around here. Last week, my upstairs neighbor said I could use his washer and dryer. Yeah, right, in my dreams. He's got one of those little apartment gadgets. Kinda small. With my kids that means about fifty million loads. Anyway, I went up there to do some washing and, man, how could I have been so stu-pid? Nothing in life is free, eh? He expected me to be 'nice' to him in return. So I just told him straight out, 'Look, Buddy, I've had it up to here with guys like you.' I always had to put up with that crap with the friends of THEIR FA-THER…his friends were always trying it on."

She pointed to her children who were chasing each other in circles and clambering over the benches. "THEIR FA-THER plays in a band, eh? Musicians. THEIR FATHER's a bass player. And the bass isn't the only thing he's play-ing…nope. The field. That's what he's playing. The whole sta-dium. Oh, wow. What's that?" She was looking toward the scaffolding.

"I'm doing a little renovating," I said.

"You doing that painting?"

"Yes."

"You're an artist."

"I don't know…well I guess…"

What was I saying? It was time to…how was it Reebee always put it? Throw out the net and leap? Something like that. "Yes, I'm an artist," I said.

"I don't know any artists. I know lots of musicians. Too many, if you want the truth. Just hope my kids don't think they want to be musicians, too." She turned abruptly and yelled at the children, "Get down off there." They were swinging from the bottom of the scaffolding. Both children, a girl of around four and a boy of about two, were beautiful, with curly blond hair and huge, dark-lashed blue eyes. The mother was thin, brunette and harassed, twenty-two going on forty. Whoever he was, THEIR FATHER must have been a looker.

She gestured toward the machines. "So can I…?"

"Sure," I said. "Just let me turn everything on." I went to throw the switches in the utility room.

When I came back she was already stuffing sheets into one of the washers and setting her coins out in little piles. "So you're an artist, eh? Cool. My name's Rita by the way."

"Lucy."

"That's so cool. I can't do any of those artistic things. I can't draw, I can't sing…or anyway, THEIR FATHER was always telling me to be quiet…whenever I started singing he would tell me to shut up because I was attracting all the other sick dogs in the neighborhood. Now, I don't think that's a very nice thing to say to a person, do you?"

I shook my head.

"Well, neither do I. He was always telling me stuff. That I didn't know how to do this, I didn't know how to do that, while he sat there with his unplugged bass, plucking

away…he never lifted a finger to help with the kids, didn't
do a damn thing except fool with that guitar… It's funny.
When I first met him I was such a groupie. I just wanted
to follow him everywhere. And I did. I loved to listen to
the band. They gave me goose bumps all over. But when
he was off the stage, what did he do? Nothing. He just
planted himself on that couch and twiddled away with his
fingers…it always looks like they're playing with themselves when they do that…fiddling and diddling while he
would tell me all the things I was so lousy at. Like it was
some really long boring song. I guess I just kind of got sick
of it. Figured, go tell some other chick all the things that
are wrong with her. I've had enough. There's only so much
a person can take. But you know something? Just between
you and me, Lucy?"

"What, Rita?"

"I really miss the bastard."

After that, I kept the launderette open. I was surprised
to see how many single mothers came in during the day.
I figured that nowadays most people had washers and dryers of their own. But I was wrong. A lot of the mothers
lived in cramped apartments with their children. The apartment blocks usually had a laundry room in the basement
with coin-operated machines but none of the women
wanted to use them. They didn't like going down there.
The laundry rooms were spidery dismal concrete holes.
There was always one oddball hovering around, that
strange guy who lived on the fourth floor, the one who
swung his cat around by its tail. The kind of guy who
looked even more like a serial killer under the cold fluorescent basement lights.

In the evenings, there was a steady trickle of working people, guys and girls in jogging or cycling gear or blue jeans, all discreetly checking each other out over the rinse cycles.

I went on working. I was a curiosity, a sideshow freak, and people gathered round to watch me paint. My mural gave them something to talk about.

I phoned Sky.

"Meet me at Evvie's," she said.

"You got news?"

"I need someone to bitch to. And I haven't seen you in ages. How are you doing down there in shabbyland?"

"It's not shabbyland. It's a vital multi-ethnic urban and residential hub," I protested.

"I prefer a brand-new steel and glass high-rise. The East End is full of cockroaches."

"It is not. It has color."

"Okay. So the cockroaches are colorful. Listen, I would have come and visited you before now but I don't know. It gets me down, that part of town. It's not exactly what you'd call upscale."

"It's not supposed to be. But it might be one day. You need to hear my plan."

"And you need to hear my news. About Max."

"Oh, God."

"You'll laugh, Madison. Really you will. This is one I bet you haven't heard."

"Go on, Sky. Tell me."

"Not over the phone."

"Okay. Evvie's at nine o'clock."

17

I sat in our booth at the back and ordered a pot of tea. Five minutes later, Sky arrived. She looked great in a leather miniskirt, calf-high lace-up boots, patterned black stockings, black leather jacket with studs and white chiffon T-shirt underneath.

"You're wasting away," she said when she saw me.

"Really?"

"You look almost THIN. Whatever it is you're doing, stop now. You don't want to get a chicken neck. People who lose weight too fast get chicken necks."

"I haven't had time to even think about my lard. I've been painting."

"And about time, too. I'm really hungry. What should I order?"

"The shrimp melt. Then I can have a bite of it."

Sky slid into the booth and started playing the silent piano on the edge of the table. It was one of the things she did when she was bursting with news. "Then you have to order something I want a bite of."

"Okay. How about the bacon and tomato sandwich with fries and coleslaw?"

"Cholesterol? What's that? Go for it."

We ordered and then Sky leaned forward, dropped her voice to a whisper, and got ready to give me her news.

It was always a good idea to have a confidential approach. I don't know why it was, but even in a city as large as Vancouver, somebody we both knew, some terminally nosy, backbiting acquaintance, always happened to be sitting invisibly nearby when we were dishing the dirt at top volume.

"So tell me all about Max," I said.

"You won't believe this."

"No, I probably won't but tell me anyway."

"Those were his kids we saw down in Seattle."

"Uh-huh."

"And he does have a wife."

"Big surprise."

"But."

"But?"

"He and his wife have been living separate lives for ages."

"Oh, sure," I said. "That's what they all say."

"It's not what you think. It's his kids' fault."

"That he's an indoor-outdoor, hotel–motel man?"

"I'll get to that. He and his wife were going to break up but their kids threatened them," said Sky.

"What do you mean? How? I'm not following you."

"They didn't want the family to break up. They didn't want their parents to separate so they made it impossible for them."

"How?"

"They threatened to accuse them of anything…holding

Satanic rituals…psychological abuse…physical abuse…starvation."

"The little buggers. The starvation one wouldn't have held water. They looked pretty chunky and healthy to me."

"They are. But they're fixated with keeping their parents together. Max and Irene…that's his wife…know their kids well enough to believe they'd actually go ahead and do what they're threatening. Too bad there aren't any parent abuse groups around. I don't know of any, do you?"

"No. Gee. That's kind of rough." I was sincere. It was always interesting to hear about the prisons and torture chambers other families could create for themselves. "So what about the uh…"

"The gay part?" asked Sky.

"Yeah."

"Well, now, that's another story. You see, quite a few years ago, Max had been in the sportswear business."

"I thought you said he hated sportswear, that he was broken up over the demise of sartorial splendor."

"He is. He really does think people look like giant babies in pajamas when they wear sweats or track suits, so it's been pretty hard for him. The sportswear store was his father's and basically he was forced to go into the family business. Then his father died and Max's sense of duty along with him. He'd been wanting to get into the nostalgia line for a long time. It's a history thing with him. He just happens to have a really good instinct for antiques, antique anything, furnishings, clothes. Anyway, he'd had his eye on a small group of stores in Seattle that were doing okay, a little more than breaking even. He knew the owner wanted to sell. Trouble is, the guy is so YMCA you get pink flamingos in front of your eyes just talking to him on the phone. Not just gay, but militantly so. He does a female impersonator thing in a club in Seattle, goes by the name of Elvira. He absolutely refused to do business with anybody straight. So Max figured the only way he was going to get what he wanted was by being something that he wasn't. He figured he would set out and court Elvira, put on the dog, as it were."

"Only the dog had to be a poodle with a diamond collar and leash."

"Rottweiler it wasn't."

"So it's all been an act."

Sky nodded.

My sandwich arrived. I took a huge bite. I had to keep up my strength if I wanted to hear the rest of the story.

Sky said, "I would have told you all this before. You miss things when you stay down there in Scuzzville. I tried to get in touch with you, find a number for you, but your Amazon roommate just kept saying 'don't know, don't know.'"

"It's in the book, the Yellow Pages, under coin wash. Madison's Coin Wash. And it is not a scuzzy part of town. It has…character."

"Whatever you say. Back to Max. The thing is, Max's kids don't know anything about their other lives. Irene has someone else, too. They just told the kids that they'd grown apart, which is the truth."

"What does his wife, Irene, think of all of this?" I asked.

"She couldn't care less. As long as the money's coming in. They've got their obnoxious kids to support, after all. What does a teenager need more than a parent who's a walking wallet?"

"Nothing."

"Right. So anyway, what does Max discover as he's hanging out in all these gay clubs and bars?"

"Don't know."

"That women are falling all over him because they think he's gay."

I gave Sky a snarky smile. "What about his macho dignity?"

She said, "Screw dignity. He couldn't get laid until he jumped the tracks. So yeah. I know what you're thinking and yes, he had a few other women before me, but women. Not men. Anyway, then came the day they were ready to break the news to their kids, that they were planning on separating definitively, and what happens? The nasty overgrown rug rats retaliate. So Max and Irene just went on sneaking around behind their backs and then Max met me. It's easier for him because he has the excuse of being away on business. It's harder for Irene. Someone has to be there for the kids so it's usually her. She has a new man, but as far as the kids are concerned, he's a colleague of their mom's who's always dropping around, an editor. Irene works at home. She's a children's book illustrator. I guess she sees the guy during the day when they're at school. But he works, too, so that leaves lunch hour."

"Why is it that when you find someone you like there's always another kind of problem?"

"Max and I are luckier. The only people who know him up here are the nostalgia connections that Elvira put him on to, and believe me, some of them haven't seen the light of day in years. Die-hard clubbers and vampires. Come out of their coffins and caves only after midnight. So Max's life has been a little weird. And whenever he's back in Seattle, those kids of his are terrible. They control Max's and Irene's every movement, getting their friends to help spy on them to make sure there's no extracurricular nooky going on. Can you imagine a life like that?"

"Er. No."

I thought my life was complicated. Somebody needed to open up university-level courses dealing with these kinds of situations. Extramarital Chaos 101. Rotten Teenage Children 200.

"So that means that you and Max are…?"

"Back together? Yeah. Pretty much."

"Handcuffs, whips and all?"

"Wouldn't you like to know," Sky gloated.

I sighed. While Sky's private life was moving ahead, I was right back to square one, mentally lining up my sexual disasters like toy soldiers and then knocking them down over and over.

"There's something I want to show you. "Sky had a devious look on her face. She reached into her purse, brought out a folded piece of newspaper and slid it across the table to me. "Unfold it."

It was from the arts section of the daily newspaper. The article was about the vandalism performed on the works of the well-known British artist Paul Bleeker. I couldn't help blushing as I read it.

"That night at the movies," said Sky. "Those little goodies you offered wouldn't have anything to do with this, would they?"

She knew most of it. She might as well know the last detail. I nodded slowly.

She shoved a fist up into the air and said, "Yes!" then laughed. "He was crazy not to recognize the real Lucy Madison, artist and W-O-M-A-N. You did the right thing. Anybody who's stupid enough to use chocolate as a medium is just asking for gangs of premenstrual women to attack and destroy his work the first chance they get. Just look on Paul Bleeker as an in-betweenie."

Emphasis on weenie.

I said, "I don't know what hit me. Insanity, I guess. It just seemed like the thing to do at the time. Now I've got something to tell you."

I started to talk. All about the launderette and my big idea. I went on and on describing my plan in detail. Sky sat very still and listened, an intense expression on her face. Then I said, "Of course there's one big problem with the idea."

"What's that?" asked Sky.

"I haven't a cent to finance this baby."

"You haven't been paying much attention to what my mother tells you. Leap and the net will be there. This is a really great idea. I love it. And there's somebody else I bet would love it, too. Might even want to put some money into it."

"Who's that?"

"Max."

I groaned.

"You underestimate him. He's a great businessman and he's not afraid to take risks."

"I've got a problem with it."

"Yeah, I know you do."

"I'll bet he doesn't have any liquid assets either."

"He has more than you'd think. There's money in muck as my grandfather used to say. Max and I are glorified ragpickers if you stop to think about it. Vintage stuff really is a gold mine."

"I don't know, Sky. I really have to think about it."

"You think about it then," said Sky, "while I run the idea by him."

"No. Not yet. Don't tell anybody. You and Connie are the only people I've talked to about it and quite frankly there's one thing I'd really like to do."

"What's that?"

"Leave men out of it."

Sky nodded and smiled her wise-woman smile.

"I suppose you could have a point. Listen. There's another thing. They're inaugurating a new club tomorrow night and Max and I are invited. Max knows the owner. You have to come."

"Try to stop me."

"Come round to the shop first and we'll put together an outfit for you. For the new you. Listen, there's something else."

"What?" I asked.

"Guess who I saw in the Oakridge Mall."

"I dunno. Who?"

"Candace Sharp."

"No! Back for a visit, I hope."

"Nope. She's back to stay." Sky shook her head.

Candace had been a good friend of ours in the university art department years. Of all the students in painting class, she was the one I thought had the makings of a truly great painter. Her work was figurative and colorful, a little like mine, except that it was more scathing. It had real guts.

I said to Sky, "I hope you're kidding. Her idea was to stay in New York until she'd broken into the art scene big-time, and not come back here until she did. Not even for a visit, she said. I had a couple of postcards from her. It sounded like she was doing okay. Oh, let me see…the last one was about two years ago."

"Yeah, well, she's back. And it gets worse."

"How?"

"She's grown her hair and she's wearing it up in a bun."

"Omagod."

"A very tight bun. Max was with me when we bumped into her. She's working in a store in the mall. Max calls her Miss Bun-too-tight. You know, when it's so tight it gives you squinty eyes?"

Our Candace. Who'd signed her paintings "Hard Candy."

Who, when she wasn't shaving her head, had colored her electroshock hairstyles all shades of the rainbow. The Candy who'd made body-piercing into high art.

"What store?" I asked.

"Get this. It's a lingerie store for the…what do they call it? The full-figured woman. You know the one? It has the name of that Italian artist who always does big people."

"Boito's Beauties," I said.

"That's the one. Yeah. A coy way to say fat women, eh? She's working in there. A humble little employee. You remember when she was at school she used to manage that record store? No management for her these days. Now, she's got the tight bun and she's wearing glasses on an old lady chain. Calf-length skirts, support hose and sensible shoes. Really, really scary."

"Did you talk to her? What did she say?"

Sky looked solemn. "I asked her about New York but she didn't want to talk about it. Then I asked her about her painting and you know what she said? I mean, you know, a painter can paint anywhere. Right?"

"Right. What did she say?"

"That it was in the past and she didn't want to talk about that, either."

"Oh, Jeez. I hope she didn't get religion, too."

"I didn't ask her," said Sky. "It was all so spooky."

I wanted to cry. "But she's so talented."

"I know," said Sky. "So I invited her to the club opening, too."

"Is she going to come?"

"She said she would. She said she wanted to see you."

"Good. I want to see her, too."

It was half past nine when I banged on the Retro Metro door. It was nearly the end of May and the last rays of sun beat golden bronze against high-rise windows turning the city into a sequined giant.

Sky emerged from the back, opened the door and waved me in. She was wearing a man's tuxedo.

"Sky? Something else going on that I don't know about?"

"No." She tugged at her lapels. "The suit was Max's idea. C'mon, we're a martini ahead of you."

I followed her into the back room. Max was seated in front of a mirror. He turned to me and grinned, brandishing a mascara brush. One half of his face was made up in a vampiresque way. "Hi, Lucy." He wasn't the least bit flustered.

"Hi…er…Max. I'm assuming it's you, Max?"

"It's him," said Sky.

Max wore tight metallic gold jeans and over those, a set of leather chaps. His top was a see-through net shirt that revealed a tattoo of Freddie Mercury on his stomach and a pierced navel. He'd shaved his mustache for the occasion and was wearing a gold stud earring with a little chain that crossed his cheek and was linked to a ring through one side of his nose.

Was it time to start worrying about Sky all over again? Or was there something wrong with me? Had I been living inside my own head for so long that I'd failed to notice that every man now had lots of weird little items in his closet? I was sliding into the quicksand of insecurity again.

Then Max whipped off the ear stud and chain and said to me in a very Alpha male voice, "They're fakes. So's the Freddie Mercury. It's one of those stencil jobs. The things we have to do to get ahead in business. Don't believe for a minute the clothes make the man. I just love a good facade, don't you? I've got to see some people tonight. Clinch a deal. After that, I can put the fetish gear away for a while." He sighed, then brusquely adjusted his chaps.

He made it sound like a put-on, but I couldn't help feeling that everyone was getting dressed up but me. That everyone was getting a little kinky in the corners and possibly having a good time. For all I knew my father was dressing up as the Mother Superior and my mother as Captain Von Trapp at that very moment.

"Drink?" Max held out the martini shaker.

"Yes, please." He poured it out and minced masterfully over to hand me the glass.

"What are we going to do to her?" Sky asked Max.

"Oh well, something a little twenties bordello, I think. Or maybe we should try her in a zoot suit, the Janet Jackson pimp look. Don't know."

It didn't matter. Whatever I wore was going to look conservative next to Max and Sky.

I threw back the martini and said, "Do your worst."

After an hour of trying on and taking off, I ended up in an original Mary Quant minidress in black and white eye-popping geometrics. I had matching white patent leather go-go boots, a poor-boy cap and lime green fishnet stockings.

"You look truly groovy, Lucy," said Max. "You should know that the girl who once wore this outfit bought it in Carnaby Street at the end of the sixties and, as she is no longer a girl but one fat mama of an over-the-hill housewife, only fit to cover her poundage in wash-'n'-wear leisure wear, I talked her into letting me take this treasure off her hands along with quite a few trunk loads of other fantastically hip, cool and groovy stuff."

Sky and I stared at Max and then grimaced at each other.

He sighed. "Oh, I know. You're just babies. You had to be there. Those were the years."

The club was called Anastasia's and was located downtown near the stadium.

Standing outside the old brick building, I imagined it was going to be yet another club just like all the other ones, with a lot of slick surfaces, flashing lights and plushy couches. How wrong I was.

Beyond the coat-check area was a maze of rooms decorated like the palace interiors of royal despots just before the start of the Bolshevik Revolution. The shooter bar and main dance floor areas were done in gold, teal blue and Chinese lacquer red, reflecting the colors of St. Basil's in Red Square. Huge twisting gold columns topped with lions reached up to a lit mandala ceiling. It was like some Byzantine dream, or nightmare, depending on your point of view. In the background was a mix of Borodin's Polovtsian Dances with a hip-hop beat. In one anteroom, tea was served from a samovar and a woman with a heavy accent read fortunes in the tea leaves. Another room was oriental rugs from ceiling to floor and huge cushions tossed everywhere, no tables or chairs. Still another room was like an oasis, a tiled fountain tinkling at its center and plants everywhere. In yet another room, men in costume were performing Cossack dances.

We pushed our way through the people with Max in the lead. He said, "Come on, I'll introduce you to the owner." We followed him into the most intimate room, which was made up of booths divided by carved wooden screens, like those in a harem. What a shock it was to see Max shake hands with Onassis, Nadine's Greek friend. Except that I found out that night that he wasn't Greek. And his name was Nikolai. Nadine always called him Nick.

He invited us to sit down and have a few peppered vodkas. It turned out Nick and Max had met when Nick went looking for pre-revolution Russian memorabilia. Nick's maternal grandparents had been Russian nobility, on the run from the Bolsheviks. They'd fled first to Paris and then to

London where Nick's parents had met. His father had been part Turkish and part Russian, while his mother had been all Russian and intent on preserving what she could of a vague and useless nobility handed down to her by her parents. They both hated the cold and headed south to a remote Greek island where parts of Nick's childhood had been spent. But his mother had done her best to fill Nick's head with her dreams, and Anastasia's was the realization of a child's fantasy, a weird mix of his parents' worlds. It made me think.

I got up to go to the bathroom. It was an orgy of imitation black and gold marble and bronze fixtures. I spent far longer than was necessary in there. On my way back, a familiar voice stopped me in my tracks. Paul Bleeker was holding court in the seraglio room. I stayed hidden behind the partition. I could feel my heart trying to pound its way out of my chest.

"…well, of course, the so-called vandalism in the show was intentional. Much like Yoko Ono's piece in which the audience snip away with a pair of scissors at the dress she's wearing until she's virtually naked on-stage, my pieces were designed to tempt. It was inevitable that there would be someone who was unable to resist the temptation and it was precisely this weakness that I aimed to exploit. The pieces are being documented as they are gradually being eaten away. Analogous to woman, and her devastation through the ravages of time, is that all that remains of her original beauty is a collection of old photographs…the Chocolate Women really has been a fantastic success so far…"

Thanks to Lucy Madison and her weakness, I wanted to add.

Arrrghh.

Nadine, Felicity and the Mortician were there, too, hanging off his words. I could hear their snuffles and snorts. It was one big happy family. I suddenly had the urge to leave. I retreated back to the coat-check area where the pay phones were located and called Sky's cell.

"Sky."

"Who is this?"

"It's me, Lucy."

"Lucy?" She lowered her voice. "What are you doing? Where have you got to?"

"Paul Bleeker's here in the club with Nadine and her henchmen. They're in the room next to yours."

"Oh for Christ's sake, Lucy. You're not ditching us, are you? I want you to stay."

"So do I. But I just can't face him and Nadine tonight. Create a diversion. How brave do you feel?"

"You know me. I'm a natural-born shit disturber. Max and I might just wander over and say a sloppy hello. Max will do anything when he's dressed up."

"Thanks. You're a true friend."

"I know," said Sky, and hung up.

I left the club and waited in the shadows out on the street. Several minutes later, Paul and Nadine burst through the doorway, patting the wet spots on their clothes and complaining about how hard it was to get stains out of silk and suede. I slipped back inside and joined Sky and Max on the dance floor.

Everything went smoothly for another hour. We were all dancing and drinking and having a pretty good time when the ripple started. A wave of tension began to run through the club, a sense of something dangerous happening, moving through the crowd, like a shark streaking through a shallow bay full of swimmers.

Then I saw it.

Dressed in a sackcloth robe with a rope at the waist, sporting long greasy hair and a beard, my brother Dirk was doing a perfect impersonation of Rasputin. It was enough for him to just stand at the center of the room, expand his chest and leer to impress his audience.

I grabbed Sky's arm and pulled her along with me into the bathrooms. I should have been keeping my eye on Dirk, to be sure he didn't slip away, but I preferred to hide. His gaze had shifted my way. I knew it too well. The whites of his eyes were showing all round. He was capable of anything in that state. In that state, he had humiliated me publicly quite a number of times. It was smarter to stay out of his way.

I was practically under the bathroom sinks as I dialed Sam's numbers. I knew them by heart now. No one was home at either of the numbers so I left a message. I gave him the address of the launderette and told him that I couldn't be reached by phone at the moment.

Okay. I confess. It was a ploy. I wanted to see Sam in person. I wanted to see if he found our phone conversations interesting, too, and was tempted to check me out.

We were only in the bathrooms for a few minutes because Sky convinced me that we should go back and keep an eye on Dirk. Of course, when we came out again, he was gone. And then it occurred to me that Candace hadn't shown up either.

The next day I went down to Boito's Beauties myself. I paused in the doorway and peeked in. Sure enough, Hard Candy had now become demure and boring Candace Miss Bun-too-tight. She was putting away bras. And these weren't normal bras, but rigging that could have moved a sailboat in a high wind—we're talking spinnakers here. She looked up from her folding and froze.

I came out of hiding. "Candy. How the hell are you?"

"Hi, Lucy." Her voice was completely flat, devoid of emotion.

"Sky told me she bumped into you. Why didn't you let us know you were back in town?"

"I haven't been back that long."

She was strange, shifty. She was definitely trying to avoid my eyes.

I started to babble, just to fill the unbearable silence. "When I stopped getting your postcards, I wondered if something had happened. I did Net searches trying to find news of you in New York. I tried to find addresses for you, phone numbers, but you just disappeared. I even phoned your parents but they hadn't heard from you for a while. They were a little frantic. I figured you'd gone even farther, maybe you'd gone to Paris. You used to talk about Paris a lot, if I remember correctly."

She looked away from me.

I babbled on. "So I even did some Net searches for Paris but my French really stinks so I didn't get very far…we missed you…we missed getting your news…Candy, what's up?"

She stared down at the counter and went on folding.

I persisted. "Remember me? Lucy Madison? We used to be able to talk about things. I was really looking forward to seeing you at the new club the other night. When you didn't show, I wondered if something had happened to you."

Candy seemed to have vacated the body that was wearing all those middle-aged clothes. Her voice seemed to come from a distance. "I shouldn't have said I would go. I didn't want to hurt Sky's feelings."

"Sky's feelings are made of rubber most of the time. Besides, the truth works pretty well with her. So how was New York?"

"It was fine." The dull emptiness of her tone frightened me.

"Where are you living now?"

"I'm…uh…living at my parents' place."

"Your *parents'*?"

Back in university days, Candy had always insisted that her mother was Lady Macbeth and her father was Benito Mussolini. They were the last people she would have stayed with. It had to be serious.

"Do they let you out of your cage for coffee in this place?" I asked. There was another woman working in the store, a bit of a Boito herself. I looked in her direction and whispered, "Can't *she* hold the fort for a bit?"

Candy hesitated, sighed, then said, "Yeah, I guess so." Then she added in a voice that sounded like the old Candy, "They can hardly fire me. It's my mother's store."

We got our coffees and sat down in the Food Fair area. I couldn't just come out and say, "What's with the schoolmarm clothes and the Stepford Wives stare?" so I prattled about everything that had happened since Candy had been away. But it was my account of my adventures with Paul Bleeker that cracked her open. She'd been in my class, too, when he'd been a guest lecturer. She could appreciate the dynamic.

I continued to probe. "So what about you? Any interesting men in your life?"

Candy stared at me with an absolutely blank face. Then she started to talk in a flat, dead voice. "When I first got to New York, I met a lot of people. I went to a lot of parties. It was a pretty wild time. I was staying with some friends and I painted a lot but didn't eat much. When I wasn't painting, I was partying, trying to make connections. There were a lot of drugs around. Then I met this gallery owner, an important gallery, and we started seeing a lot of each other. He promised me a show. I kept pushing for it and he kept telling me it was going to happen but it never did. He kept telling me that I needed to push the envelope, that I had to keep working till the breakthrough came. He showed everybody else's work but mine. I didn't understand this at all. I thought I was a good enough painter to exhibit."

"You're a great painter," I said.

"Well, I kept working, kept producing. I hardly ever slept. And then he dumped me. Just like that. He found another girl artist to sleep with. I lost it, Lucy. Not just a little. I really lost it. I did some weird things. I guess it was the drugs, too. My roommates had a dog. I put mascara on the dog's eye-lashes. I went for a swim in the ocean at Christmas. Some-body called my parents and they came and got me. I've been HERE, Lucy. I've been in Riverview for the last six months. When I came out I made a deal with my parents. No more artsy-fartsy stuff. Their words."

"But Candy, you can't. You're the best painter I know."

"I'm scared. I'm scared I'll go crazy again."

"But you said yourself, it was the drugs."

"Maybe. I don't know."

"What about your work, your paintings? What about all the stuff you did while you were in New York?"

"As far as I know, it's still there where I left it. Listen, Lucy. I want to forget about all that. It belongs to the past. I'm in neutral now. I'm doing okay with Prozac. I'm doing okay. Really I am."

And I'm the Queen of England, I wanted to say.

Two days later, Sky came down to the launderette for a long visit. She wanted to hang out, to see the painting I'd done and talk about my idea. The mural had grown. A distinct Paradise, Inferno and Purgatory were emerging. There were starry skies populated with unlikely angels. There were oceans with murky floors along which crawled primeval slimy creatures. One of the creatures bore a surprising resemblance to Paul Bleeker. There was an earthly zone of fields and forests and oceans that hosted me and my friends. I left an empty space for a Sam figure but still had no idea what it would look like.

Sky paced back and forth in front of the painted walls. "This is definitely one of your finer works. I really think you should talk to Max about your plan." I eased down off the scaffolding and sat on one of the benches. She came over and sat down beside me. A clutch of black-clad widows chattered and lamented in Italian in the other corner of the launderette.

"C'mon," I said, "Let's go into the back room."

I'd made myself a kind of informal office-workshop-napping place in the utility room. I'd moved a table, chairs and a lamp into it as well as a mattress I'd found in Jeremy's attic but I'd stopped sleeping there at night and moved into my father's old room in Jeremy's house.

Sky sank into the armchair and went on, "The sooner you put this plan into action, the sooner you'll be able to get rid of the present clientele." She rolled her eyeballs in the direction of the women on the other side of the mirror.

"Look out, Sky, they'll put a curse on you. You should know better than I do that the customer is always right, bag ladies, Bagwans and scuzz-buckets included."

"Yeah…unfortunately. Really, Lucy. Talk to Max. I know you don't want men involved in this thing but sexist discrimination can backfire in your face."

"Well, I suppose he is kind of a borderline case, having to

temporarily explore his anima, empathize with people of other sexualities, if only for business purposes. Still, I'd like it better if he was a woman."

"You could regard him as an honorary female. A sort of half-baked ambassador to the oasis of females," said Sky.

"Implying that the land of males is a desert? That seems awfully grim," I said. "I'll think about it."

We wasted time well into the afternoon, gossiping about everyone we knew. I filled her in on my meeting with Candace, and she agreed with me. We'd work on it. We wouldn't leave Candy alone. We wouldn't let her decline into a blob of Prozac jelly.

All our plotting made us very hungry. Sky phoned to order some Chinese food. When it came, we sat in the back room over egg rolls, mushroom chow mein, almond chicken and deep-fried prawns, and went on discussing my big project in detail.

Sky had her eye on the two-way mirror the whole time, studying the "clientele." It was around six-thirty in the evening when she abruptly stopped chewing and grabbed my arm. "Get a load of this clown."

I followed her gaze. A man had just come in. His movements were painfully slow. He had propped the door open with a cardboard box full of laundry and was carting other similar cardboard boxes into the launderette. There must have been nearly a dozen of them. Once he had all his boxes lined up in front of the machines, he began to dig around in his pants pockets. And I have to say, they were the ugliest plaid pants I'd ever seen. The plaid was in vibrant orange, yellow and brown. There was a tear in one knee, a brown paint stain drooling across the other leg, a torn back pocket that flapped, and the pant legs were just short enough so that every so often, his mismatched gym socks showed. The top half of him wasn't much better. He had one of those hooded sweatshirts with the kangaroo pouch and over that, a fluorescent green windbreaker. The hood was pulled up over hair that was either very wet or very greasy. I couldn't tell. He had a scruffy reddish-blond week's growth of beard and wore classic nerd glasses, black tortoiseshell with a bit of white surgical tape holding them together at the bridge of the nose and at one of the sides.

When he finally managed to dig all the coins out of his pockets, he held them for a second then fumbled them. They burst across the floor and rolled in all directions. He dropped down onto his knees and started to gather them up.

"This guy's a real prize," said Sky.

"Quite the classy dresser," I said.

"What do you think he has in all those boxes?"

"I don't know. Nobody has that many clothes."

"Nobody. Not even Max."

He'd managed to scoop up all his coins and was arranging them in little piles along the top of a washer. He began to pull things out of boxes and stuff them into the machines. We watched him, hypnotized by how slow and awkward he was. It was taking him forever to put his loads in. And the things were blotched and stained so badly, I figured this was a guy who regularly ate lasagna with his feet. I gave up and looked away, shaking my head.

Twenty minutes later, I remembered I still had to contact Sam, tell him about Dirk's Russian phase.

"Can I borrow your cell again for just a minute?" I asked Sky.

"I think it's time you thought about getting your own phone."

I just grinned at her.

"Go on then, Madison. Take it." She handed it to me.

"I've got to get in touch with Dirk's caseworker. Let him know the latest." I punched out one of Sam's numbers.

"Omagod," said Sky. She leapt up and moved closer to the two-way mirror. "I have to stop that guy."

"He still hasn't finished putting in his loads?"

Sky was already running out into the main area toward the geeky man. He was dropping a red towel into the machine where a second before he had been stuffing some very grotty whites. Sky moved closer to him, looked around her with a strange expression on her face then pulled back a little. I could see her telling him something but couldn't make out the words. He nodded and smiled then pulled the red towel out and put it back in one of the boxes. He had narrowly avoided having a very rosy future.

I sat back in the armchair to concentrate on my call. The phone had rung six times when a voice said, "Sam Trelawny here."

"Is that the real Sam Trelawny or is this a recording?"

"It's the real me. Who's this?" His voice sounded strange, thick and slurry.

"Lucy Madison."

"Hi, Lucy Madison. I've been trying to get in touch with you."

I turned back toward the two-way mirror to see a strange sight: Sky standing behind the man's back, jumping up and down, grimacing at me through the mirror and pointing at him; and the man looking toward my murals and talking on a cell phone.

"I left a message for you," I said.

"I got it. You left the address of a launderette."

"That's right."

"Well, I'm there. I mean here. In the launderette. Where are you?"

As I watched the man, I realized his mouth was in perfect synchronization with Sam's half of the phone conversation.

"I'm not sure," I said, "but I think I'm here in front of you." I walked out of the utility room, still talking. I approached the man. He stared at me, then at his phone.

"Sam Trelawny?" I asked. He nodded.

"Lucy Madison?" he asked. I nodded in turn.

There was an overpowering smell of rotting cabbage, old diapers, fish on the turn, overflowing ashtrays and alcohol. It was coming from Sam.

18

"Nice to meet you at last, Lucy." He reached out his hand to shake mine then changed his mind and yanked it back quickly. "No, better not," he mumbled.

The smell coming from him was quite pungent. It probably would have rubbed off on me. And he was definitely drunk. A good strong vodka whiff mingled in with all the other disgusting smells. Some of it must have spilled on his clothes. He reeked like a big-time rubbie.

But despite the booze, his speech was still relatively under control. He said, "When I got your message, I thought Lucy Madison—launderette. I'll kill two birds with one stone. This place is off-beat. Is that your work?" He pointed toward the murals, leaned a little too far and swayed dangerously.

"Yes."

"Yes, I figured it must be since you seem to be wearing a whole lot of your art materials."

"My what?"

"Your art materials. Your work." He pointed at me, smiling. "All that paint on your clothes."

For a second, when I'd realized it was Sam the Voice there in person, I'd had the knee-jerk instinct to worry about the way I looked. I was no prize either. My face was smudged with paint, my hair bundled up in an old scarf, bits flying out at the sides. I was wearing my baggy painting grubbies and a pair of old paint-splotched runners with holes in the toes. I'd been living in these clothes for weeks. Self-consciously, I'd yanked the scarf from my head and tried to smooth my hair down.

"Don't get me wrong," he said, looking back at the murals. "I like it. It's weird. It's punchy and yet lyrical…listen, I better get on with it. I've got a ton of washing to do."

Given the way he looked, it was silly for me to worry about my appearance. He was a certified slob. It was hard to imagine why Francesca St. Claire de la Roche would want to smooch with this malodorous individual. And he was ineffectual, too. The whole thing had started at the beginning of March and now it was the end of May and he still hadn't rounded up Dirk for an interview. He'd never even seen him.

"About my brother Dirk…" I said.

"I have his file right here." He went over to the bench, undid his briefcase and a sheaf of papers flew out of his hand and across the floor. They were stained with coffee and other unidentifiable foodstuffs.

I huffed with exasperation. He was down on all fours again gathering the file.

"Sorry about this," he muttered, "I'm a little distracted today. Really sorry."

"Are you people ever going to apprehend Dirk?"

"Yes." His tone was sharp and for a second he looked almost scary. "But these things sometimes take time. You just have to have faith. We'll get him."

I filled him in on Dirk's Russian gig but he seemed to be only half listening.

"I'm telling you again, Lucy. We'll get him."

Hollow words from a useless government employee.

"You've been saying this for weeks." My voice was loud and hard.

"But you also have to remember that he's not our only case and definitely not the worst one," he snapped, "so just calm down, will you?"

Without another word, I walked away, regretting the fact that the launderette didn't have the kinds of doors you could slam.

Everything happened at once. There was a message from Bob on his answering machine to say he would be back at the end of the week and he hoped his pot plants were still alive.

Reebee got in touch with Sky to say that she and Connie were alive and well and that they were in Oregon. They were planning to be back in Vancouver in the next couple of days.

I put all my sketches and estimates and drafts together in a large file folder and got ready to face Connie.

Sky and I sat on the front steps of Jeremy's house inhaling the evening air and watching the light disappear, the palest of blue dusks above a white haze of cherry, plum and apple blossoms. The streets flowed with people, glad to welcome the warmth. A new sidewalk café had opened around the corner and was crowded. Scents of coffee, pastry and cut grass wafted down to us.

The Valiant pulled up. Reebee got out first, looked up at me and waved. Connie was still just a shadow in the front seat.

Reebee yelled up to Sky and me, "Get down here, you two, and help me with these suitcases."

The door on the passenger side opened and the bulky shadow struggled forward then straightened up slowly.

"Well, holy futhermucker, Batman," said Sky. "Is that her?"

I didn't recognize her either. "Connie, is that you?" I called out.

I heard her barking laugh then the monotone, "Yeah, it's me." She started toward the front steps.

It was a different person. The blond hair had all been shorn off and in its place was very short black hair. With her pronounced cheekbones and tanned skin, she looked better than ever, but what she was, undeniably, and magnificently, was native. This was accentuated by the clothes and jewelry, big dangling earrings and a heavy necklace of turquoise and silver. She wore a full-length coarse-weave cotton dress in subtle stripes of dark blue and dark rose with an embroidered panel across the yoke. She looked regal.

When she was up close, I had to stare at her irises. "You used to have blue eyes."

"Contacts," said Connie, "you know, those cheap colored ones." Her real irises were nearly black. "Reebee was stuck on this thing about making me get in touch with my roots."

I said, "I didn't know you had…ah…I didn't know your roots were…ah…"

"Yeah. I got native roots…Paleface."

I said, "It suits you…Pocahontas."

Connie laughed and clutched her belly. "Let's go inside. I gotta sit. This brat's doing acrobatics again. I see the house didn't burn down. Too bad. Garden looks nice, too."

Connie went inside while Sky and I helped Reebee lug the suitcases up the steps and into the house.

"Reebee," said Sky, "I'd like to know what you barter with. You always come back with twice the stuff you left with and I know you don't have any money."

"Money is an abstract concept, Sky," said Reebee.

"Uh-huh." Sky turned to me. "I tell you, Madison, my mother has horseshoes up her butt because nobody takes a trip with as little money as she does, and survives."

"What makes you think I don't have money?" Reebee said, then winked at me.

"We passed through Vegas," said Connie. "Your mother won a pile."

"She what?" squealed Sky.

"Yeah. First she was black up to the elbows with playin' the slot machines. She won enough there to go on to the bigger stakes. A little blackjack. A little roulette. I've never seen anyone with luck like hers."

"It's the law of attraction," said Reebee. "All you have to do is send out positive energy and the universe will send it back to you."

"Yeah, right," said Sky. "More like the law of premature senility. She should team up with your father, Madison."

Reebee went into the kitchen to make tea and unpack the exotic foods she'd brought back with her. Sky and I hung around in the living room where Connie had plopped herself into the armchair. We tried not to stare but couldn't help ourselves. It was embarrassing. Connie had been transformed into the new fascinating kid on the block. We wanted to hear how it had happened but we wanted her to volunteer the information.

But instead, she just sat in the armchair and looked all around her impatiently, scrutinizing the dingy beige walls, the splintery, worn-down floorboards and threadbare carpet covering them, the textured plaster on the ceiling, the fifties teak furniture. Then she said, "I really gotta do something about this place."

From the kitchen, we heard Reebee call out, "Feng shui. That's what you need."

Finally Sky said, "Tell us about the trip, Connie. Every detail. My mother tends to edit out all the bad bits."

"I will when we've got some food in front of us."

It had grown dark in the room but rather than turn on lights, Reebee produced beeswax and scented candles they'd picked up on the trip. She set them all over the room and lit them. The atmosphere became magic.

I had a sense that Reebee was orchestrating something. She went back into the kitchen, and we could hear her crashing around. Every so often she came in and checked on us, like a schoolteacher checking on her class of delinquent girls. Then she called us to come and help her.

We brought plates and bowls into the living room and set them down on the large coffee table. She insisted we sit on the floor to eat. The food was shrubby, super organic, no doubt procured from a withered ancient medicine woman who did something ghoulish with snakes. Among the unidentifiable roots and fruits, there was wild rice, some strange-looking mushrooms, wild asparagus, cayenne peppers, special honeys and some good straightforward California Chablis for the un-pregnant among us.

At first, Sky and I were a bit worried about tempting Connie, that if she got the whiff of alcohol, she'd be cranking poppy juice into her veins the following week. But Connie said to go ahead, just not to breathe on her as the smell of alcohol made her sick.

"Go on, Connie," said Reebee, "tell them about your trip."

"We took the coast road for a bit. That was nothing special."

"Now, Connie, we talked about attitude," Reebee scolded.

"Okay, I admit, the Olympic Mountains impressed me, there was still snow on them. The park in Washington with all those big uh…" She looked at Reebee who nodded, urging. "Those conifers. Although I prefer sclerophyllous vegetation myself."

Sky and I exchanged glances.

"Do-it-yourself vocabulary enhancement program," said Connie. "Don't want my brat to be the class idiot like I was."

"I think we can safely say you had your reasons," Reebee said softly.

Connie snorted. "Yeah…what was I talking about?"

"Conifers. Washington. The Park. The big trees," said Reebee.

"Yeah, it was okay. But Oregon was the place that really got to me." I heard a slight tremor in her voice, another thing I'd never heard before.

"When we got to those stretches of incredible beach, those sand dunes, I felt so excited. I'd forgotten what they were like. I was born in Oregon." Her voice was strange and distant, as if she didn't believe it, or was talking about someone else. She stared at me. "You didn't know that, did you, Lucy?"

"We don't know anything about you, except that you were with Jeremy. And he never told us anything."

"He knew quite a bit of it but he didn't know it all. I didn't tell him all of it. But it really didn't matter. He must have guessed at most of it. He was good at seeing into people. That's why I let him talk me into coming up here with him. God, if I'd known he was in the Laundromat business…he just looked inside me that first time and I knew I didn't have to hide from him."

"I'm not really following you, Connie," I said.

Sky was sitting to one side, looking through Jeremy's old

record collection. Jeremy's tastes, eclectic, going against all ap-
pearances. Sky pulled out a tattered Etta James album and put
the record on the old Phillips player.

Connie listened for a few seconds and then said, "Jeremy
thought that Etta James was a singer with balls. He loved
her... Yeah, where was I? Oregon. All that talking Reebee
made me do when I first met her. She got me going on about
Oregon, stuff I thought I'd forgotten forever. She figured it
was important to go down there, to remember." She looked
over at Reebee. "Do I talk about the bad part first or the good
part?"

"Whatever comes more easily."

"You have to know that I was raised by my grandmother.
She was a Cowichan Indian, born in Canada, but went to
the States later when she married. He was a white. American. A cowboy. Died before I was born. Anyway, when I was
a kid she was always talking about her people. She missed
them a lot but didn't want to go back there. Figured she'd
fall into a kind of life that wouldn't be good for anybody.

"We lived in a trailer park near the beach somewhere outside of Florence, Oregon. She left the reserves because she
couldn't stand what drink was doing to everyone, what it did
to my parents. They were both breeds. My grandmother
didn't touch alcohol, you see, and she needed to be as far away
from it as she could get. So we lived near the beach. I can remember she was always getting on at me for tracking sand
into the trailer. She was a cook. She'd been raised in a residential school in Canada and they'd taught her to cook. She
cooked in a diner along the highway outside of Florence.
Used to bring home any leftovers she could sneak out of
there.

"The only time she let me down, apart from dying, was
when she used to leave me with the neighbors once a month

and disappear to go to see a fight, a boxing match. She didn't want me to go with her, see them mashing each other's heads in. It was the only way she could deal with the crazy feeling that she got when she saw what was happening to her people…our people, I guess, on the reserves.

"The thing I can remember really well is those sand dunes where we lived, and dancing around them in bare feet. I thought I was going to be a dancer." Her barking laugh interrupted. "Now you've gotta picture this. When we got down to those dunes Reebee told me to go ahead and do it, to take off my shoes and dance and try to get the uh…sensation back. So there I was, with this belly, dancing. If anybody saw me…"

"I'm sure those people thought it was delightful," said Reebee.

"I surprised myself. Didn't figure I'd be able to move still."

"Just how much time do you have left anyway, Connie?" I had to ask.

"Two months or so they think, give or take a week. I figure it'll come when it wants to come."

"Know the sex?"

"Naw, don't want to be…biased. Not that I hate men or anything. But sometimes I just can't like them. As a race, I mean."

"The hand that rocks the cradle, though…" said Sky.

"I dunno," said Connie, "because you gotta understand, when my grandmother died, I was only ten. My life ended the day she died. Until then, I might have thought women ruled the world. She was a sweet kind woman who let me run free. When I think about her, all I want to do is go out and buy a hit and get stoned and brainless. My parents died a long time ago. Killed when I was one. Car crash. They were both pissed out of their skulls.

"After my grandmother's pathetic little funeral, they put me in a foster home in Portland. I thought it was going to be okay until the day that Rudy, that was my foster father, took me down to see his dry cleaning business. Norma, my foster mother, was too harassed to figure things out. Or maybe she knew, because she treated me in a funny way, like she was sorry about something, making up for something. They only had one kid of their own but Carl was already a teenager. He was a real creepy quiet guy, auto mechanic. Never saw much of him. He was always out tinkering with cars. I'm pretty sure he was scared shitless of Rudy. I heard that Rudy used to beat on him whenever he got the chance, so Carl just avoided him.

"Rudy used to shove me into the bathroom in the back of the dry cleaning place, lock the door and do what he wanted with me. He told me if I ratted on him, he'd torch the business and blame it on me, they'd put me in reform school. Said he could use the insurance money. When I started getting my periods I got pregnant right away. He figured it out, must have been keeping track. Took me to a clinic and got me an abortion. On my fourteenth birthday, I decided to run away. The funny thing was, everybody must have been walking around with sixth and seventh senses because I talked my foster brother, Carl, into giving me a ride all the way to Vegas. He even gave me fifty dollars to see me on my way. He didn't have to do it, but he must have known all along what a shit Rudy had been with me.

"Yeah. Sometimes, I think about him, Rudy I mean, really late at night when I can't sleep…and I hope something really awful has happened to him, like he's crippled and slobbering in a wheelchair, and has home help that sticks it to him every which way. That would drive him nuts because he was a cheap bastard, too. To have him robbed blind in front of his

own eyes and not be able to do anything about that. Yeah,
I'd like that."

"Sending out those kind of negative vibrations are only
going to bring them back to you twofold," said Reebee.

"I know, I know. You keep telling me, but you gotta let
me have a few little harmless revenge fantasies."

Reebee shook her head hopelessly.

"Reebee's got these weird ideas. We been experimenting
with all this positive vibe crap. She made me wish for things,
like, stop feeling like an insignificant piece of dog poop and
feel like somebody people might respect. She says you have
to imagine you're already there, respected, what it feels like,
what you look like, how other people treat you.

"I was imagining all this ridiculous stuff and we pulled up
into a pueblo in New Mexico and no shit, it was like coming home. I started getting all these feelings, about who I was,
or could be, and being with brothers and sisters, native people, tribes, in that amazing place…it was mind-blowing."

Reebee just smiled and nodded.

"Anyways," Connie went on, "back to the past. After the
Rudy stuff, I got to Vegas and it wasn't too difficult to stay
alive turning little tricks here and there. The other girls put
me onto the drugs. I needed to earn enough money to have
my drugs. I tell you, when I smoked heroin for the first time
it was like…whoa baby, where have you been all my life? It
melts you away, you see. No pain, no worries. I never shot it.
I can't stand needles and I didn't want track marks all over
my skin, it's not pretty. So there I was, just needing to make
enough money so that I could have my drugs, that's all I
wanted…you think that's how it is until you find out it's
never enough. Never enough money, never enough drugs.

"I got in a bad way one night, got to thinking about my
grandmother, the parents I never had and stuff, I guess I

overdid it. Jeremy told me I was curled up in a ball by the side of the road going out of town, said it made him sick the way other people just passed me by. He got me in a taxi only I don't remember any of it. I woke up in a hospital room and asked him why he didn't just let me die, it all would have been easier, and he said it was because he'd been a thorn in people's sides all his life and he wasn't going to stop being one now, besides I looked like someone he'd once known—and I told him, hell she musta been a cheap half-dead bottle-blond junkie, too, by the sounds of it. I guess that would be your grandmother, eh, Lucy?"

"God, I guess so. I never thought about it much because Jeremy never talked about it. About her, I mean."

Sky said, "Gee, Madison, not everyone has the child-abandoning biker-chick genes that you do."

"Thanks, Sky, for reminding me."

"Think nothing of it."

Connie went on, "Jeremy never let her go. It wasn't what he said about her, it was all he didn't say. And all this awful furniture that he refused to get rid of."

Reebee said, "If we wipe out the painful memories, sometimes it doesn't leave much. For some people, it's like cancelling an entire life. Jeremy found a way to live with it, to keep it alive. On the other hand, cancer is a very telling disease."

"I don't know what Jeremy was trying to prove when he got involved with me. I figure maybe he wanted to do something before he died, maybe he knew back then that he was sick. I figure he wanted to do, you know, a good deed, like, save someone. I figured he wanted to be Jesus Christ for a day."

As we were sitting around the lemon cake, Reebee said, "Now go on, Connie, say it."

Connie stared at Reebee. The silence was explosive. Then she looked back at me with those new black eyes, and said, "Er, Lucy, I want to know if you would…"

"Go on, ask her," said Reebee.

19

"I want to know if you would stay here with me."

"Stay here?"

"Keep me company until the baby's born and I can get something else figured out."

"I…uh…I don't know, Connie."

I was beginning to long for my apartment again.

"It would be a kind of a job. I mean, you don't have one at the moment, do you?"

"A job? You mean one of those things with a wage attached?"

"Yeah. Now, listen. This is the way I figure it. I don't want to be here alone. Not with a baby. You're the kid's family, too, aren't you? We can talk about your project. Reebee thinks I should go for it." There was a pleading tone in Connie's voice. Wonders would never cease.

"What do *you* think about it, Connie? Forget about me.

Do *you* want to do it? Because if *you* don't want to do it we might as well not bother." My body started to tingle with the possibility of realizing my plan.

"It's kind of a crazy idea but I've been thinking about it a lot. It could work. And you can stay where you been staying, in the attic, in your dad's old room. The house is big. We won't get in each other's way. And you're going to need to be close to the launderette, aren't you? So we can get working on your project."

"You mean I can do it?"

"No, I mean we'll do it together. I gotta start doin' something so that the kid doesn't think I'm just a couch potato. It's gotta see that women are doin' it for themselves. Jeremy put a little cash aside. It's not a lot but it's a start. We can use that." She spoke directly, not in her usual evasive way, or in that dark defensive tone of someone who's just waiting for the next horrible thing to happen to them.

Reebee and Sky brought covers and pillows into the living room so we could stretch out and be comfortable. The talk turned to my project. We got very excited. Sky played the silent piano on the coffee table.

Every so often one of us would ask Connie if she wasn't exhausted, but she would just shake her head.

Then Connie asked us, "What would you do if this house was yours? What would you do to fix it up?" and it opened up a whole new can of worms. It was a shock to see that the sky was no longer a royal blue-black but a lighter blue shot with gold. Without realizing it, we had talked until dawn.

The others gave in to fatigue and all straggled up to find a bed somewhere in the house. Sky went up to an empty bedroom on the third floor and Reebee got the other spare room next to Connie's.

I ran outside and over to the launderette to open it up for

the day, throw the switches, check for forgotten laundry, fill up the detergent, softener and bleach dispensers. When I'd finished, I went back to the house and climbed the extra flights of stairs to my father's old room.

It was after noon when I woke up. The others were still sleeping. I got dressed quickly and ran out to the store to buy coffee, pancake mix, bacon, eggs, orange juice and maple syrup.

I began to prepare breakfast. The kitchen was filled with sunlight and delicious smells. When I couldn't stand being alone any longer, I forced the others to wake up with Van Morrison at top volume.

Connie was the first one down. It was still a shock to see her new appearance. She looked pleased, sat down and dug right in hungrily. Finally, she held up her fork and said, "I know Reebee's way of eating is healthier, but I really love this greasy stuff. It reminds me of my granny's cooking."

Sky was the next to come down. She had her usual three cups of coffee then started in on the toast. I was going to go up and wake Reebee but then Connie said, "She did all the driving and the tour guiding for our trip. She's probably exhausted. You know, she always seems so energetic and super-human, but she wipes herself out sometimes. She really needs a break. Let's just let her sleep."

When Reebee finally came down she scolded me for my unhealthy breakfast choices but couldn't resist joining us in the food orgy when it came to the crunch. She kept saying, "So much for my body being a temple. Right now it's a garbage dump. I shouldn't be doing this but it's so good."

I was sopping up some maple syrup with a bit of pancake when I remembered.

"Bob," I said.

Connie stopped chewing and gave me one of her dead stares. She sighed.

I said, "He must be back by now. He'll be insulted if I don't go and see him right away."

"Bob hates me," said Connie, almost cheerfully, as if it didn't matter an iota.

"Bob's vision of the world at large is a little limited," said Sky. "For him there are bikers, ex-bikers who are crippled and non-bikers."

Connie added, "And people who came between him and Jeremy."

I said, "I think you're all underestimating him. You can tell a lot about a person by checking out their favorite Web sites."

Everyone stared at me.

"He told me I could use his computer," I protested.

"Like which Web sites?" said Sky.

"Creative composting."

"Don't have to think too far on that one. That would be for his pot plants," said Sky.

"All right," I said, "he's an Amazon.com user and likes science fiction and self-help books."

"No kidding," said Sky. "Favorite titles?"

"All sorts of stuff on loss and grief management."

Reebee asked, "That would be the girlfriend who died in the accident?"

I nodded. "Maybe. Her or Jeremy. Anyway, I better get over there and see him. You want to come, too, Connie?"

She poked her chest with her finger. "Me? What do you want me to come for? He hates my guts. I already told you."

Reebee had that disapproving expression. "Now, Connie, we talked about these things, didn't we?"

"Oh Christ," she moaned. But she stood up and got ready

to come out with me. I was a bit worried. We needed Bob. Or maybe it was just me that needed Bob. He was a fixture, an institution. I couldn't picture the launderette without him.

We left Reebee and Sky to clean up the kitchen then walked the couple of blocks to the launderette. I couldn't stop thinking about Connie's life story. She must have had a bit of a shock when she found out where Jeremy's income came from. It was a short leap from coin washing to dry cleaning.

We went round to the back of the building and rang the buzzer.

Bob's voice blurted out through the speaker. "Yeah, who is it?"

"Lucy, Bob. Can we come in?"

"We? Who's with you?" Bob was constantly on guard for the narcotics squad.

"Not the cops if that's what you want to know."

"Yeah, okay, c'mon in."

The door clicked open and we went into the vestibule. The inner door opened slowly. Bob rolled into sight. When he saw us he looked straight past me.

"Who's your friend…? Jesus. Is that Connie?"

"Hi, Bob," she said, "Are you gonna let us in? The kid's doing somersaults and I gotta sit down fast. Unless maybe ya want me to give birth here in the hallway."

"Yeah, yeah, c'mon in." Bob swiveled out of the way and let us pass. When we were inside he gestured to a big armchair. Connie's new look was having the same effect on him that it had had on Sky and me. Bob wasn't at all sure what to make of the new Connie. He kept sneaking glances at her and under his beard, he was blushing.

He cleared his throat a little nervously and asked, "You guys want something, coffee, tea, a joint? No, sorry, forget I said that. Don't want to get the kid stoned before it's even seen daylight, eh?"

It was easy to tell what he was thinking. That Connie had arrived to give him the axe, to tell him that she'd found a loophole in the arrangements and he was about to be out on his ear.

"How was your visit to your brother's, Bob?" I asked, hoping to lighten the mood a little.

"It was okay. Listen, let's cut the formalities, eh? What are you here for?" This was directed at Connie and the tone was definitely hostile.

But Connie beat him to it. She smiled, a little sadly I thought, and said, "I know we haven't gotten on too well in the past, Bob, but I'm here to make you a proposition." Bob raised his eyebrows. "I'm not touching your arrangement with Jeremy. This apartment, the management of the launderette, those'll be yours as long as you feel like doin' it. The thing is…Lucy's had some ideas."

"Have you been around to the launderette yet, Bob?" I asked.

"Hell, no. I just got back last night. I had a long drive. Figured I'd open it up tomorrow. Why?"

"I opened it a little after you left. There were people who needed to do their washing and had nowhere else to go. Not always long hours. Enough so that some of those single mothers could do their laundry. It gave me some ideas."

"You need to hear these ideas, Bob, because we need your help."

"I gotta get my hearin' checked," said Bob. "Was that Connie Pete askin' me for help or am I hearin' funny?"

Connie nodded.

"Then I wanna hear ya say please."

"Please," said Connie, a little stiffly.

"Well, I'll be damned." Bob raked his salt-and-pepper hair with a big meaty hand. "So what are these ideas, Lucy?"

I talked and talked and when I'd finished, Bob said, "It all sounds a little airy-fairy to me. Don't know what Jeremy would make of it."

"He'd like it," said Connie. "He would have wanted to do something with the place. He couldn't admit he didn't have the energy for it anymore. That would have been like giving up."

"I just wanna know one thing," said Bob. "You figure this scheme will get some hot babes comin' round?"

Connie and I looked at each other, looked at Bob, and grinned.

Sky called me at Connie's the next evening. "Listen, Madison. You've got to call that Trelawny guy. He's phoned me every half hour for the whole day trying to get in touch with you. I guess his home phone stored my cell number. Call him. It'll make his day. I've never heard anybody so eager. Jeeez."

"I'll do it right away."

"If only to tell him to stop bugging me."

"Right. It may be about Dirk. There may have been another incident."

"Maybe. And listen, Lucy, if he asks you out, tell him you have a horrible disease. You want to stay away from any man who drinks half a bottle of vodka for breakfast and is offering you a plaid fashion experience."

We hung up and I punched out Sam Trelawny's home number.

A tired "Hello?" answered at the other end.

My voice was crisp. "This is Lucy Madison."

"Oh…uh…Lucy. Listen. I'm a little embarrassed. We did not get off on the right foot the other day."

"No." My voice was so cool his ear was sure to freeze.

"Listen. I think I should explain…my…er…state that day."

"You were pissed out of your tree. If I'd lit a match, the fumes alone would have been enough to torch the place."

"I admit…I was a little intoxicated. I don't usually do that. If it makes you feel any better, I was as sick as a dog the next day."

"Sure."

"I was quite stewed. Is that what you want to hear me say? Reasonably close to blotto. Okay?"

"Yes, you were."

"The thing is…I was out of my head. I'd been skunked."

"Sorry?"

"I was skunked. In a manner of speaking. My ex-wife Jennifer broke into the house and filled it with garbage. I don't know how she did it. She must have used at least two truckloads. It was everywhere when I came home that day. In all the drawers and cupboards. She didn't miss a corner. I had to borrow some clothes from my neighbor, and they were things he leaves in the garage for dirty jobs. I didn't really get a chance to explain. It's been such a heavy time at work and then to come home to all that garbage…I just lost it."

"You mean those plaid pants aren't part of your regular wardrobe?"

"Shit. Was I wearing plaid pants?"

"You were."

"I would never consciously put on a pair of plaid pants."

"Well, you did that day. And they came through loud and clear. I could hear the bagpipes coming over the hills for miles."

Sam let out a little chuckle and said, "Jeez, I guess they'd be okay if I was attending the annual Robbie Burns banquet."

"The what?"

"It's a Scottish thing. My grandparents' kind of thing. It involves a lot of haggis and scotch drinking and…never mind…so I was saying. None of this would have happened if I hadn't…" There was a silence.

"If you hadn't what, Sam?"

"I'm getting off the track."

"So your ex-wife really has it in for you, eh?"

"I'm afraid it's all a little blurry. Jennifer skunked my desk and my filing cabinets as well…absolutely everything."

"That's an awful thing to do to a person," I said. I was genuinely shocked. And it was nice to have a justification for his outfit. Reebee was wrong. Young women aren't much more sophisticated. We still fall for nice clothes and hair.

Sam said, "I had to wash everything. Everything I didn't throw away. Curtains, sofa and chair covers… Most of it was new. She'd taken all the other stuff with her when she moved out so I'd gone and bought…" He made a sound of disgust.

"Hell hath no fury like a woman scorned." I said this with authority, considering myself something of an expert in the scorned woman department.

Sam said quietly, "It's funny what money does to some people."

I decided to be diplomatic. "It's a good thing my friend Sky was there that day, watching you. Your future was a garment away from being entirely pink."

Sam laughed and a shiver went down my spine. Oh, that voice. There was something about it. I regretted not having hung around and helped him sort his coloreds from his whites that day.

You get to know a few things about a person by sorting through their laundry. For example, whether they have nice taste in home furnishings, whether they wear briefs or boxer shorts. I recalled that Sam's bathroom towels were red and black and very new. A lot of the other things, under the stains, had been quite tasteful.

I added, "She must have used big-time Italian restaurant refuse. There were some pretty messy tomato-y stains in there."

"Sure," said Sam, "A mafioso restaurant. She must have a contract out on me. Going to trash whatever she can of my life…" The words were severe but his tone was light. He really did have a wonderful voice. It was so persuasive, so intelligent, so delicious. Too bad it was trapped inside that dubious body. Maybe it was only a tiny little image problem, just a temporary thing. Maybe he was telling the truth and only had occasional lapses into plaid pants and greasy hair. Maybe it was the company he was keeping on the job. Maybe he was trying too hard to blend in with the manic depressives.

I said, "Now listen, Sam. I know more about stains than a lot of people, having to remove paint from everything. And what I don't know my friend Sky does. She works in a used clothing boutique. You wouldn't believe how creative people can be when it comes to leaving their mark on expensive clothing, and in the most conspicuous places. And listen, what we don't know, our friend Mr. Yee at the Busy Bee Cleaners does. The man is a genius with spot remover. Sky already owes him her first- and second-born children for all the items he's rescued for the boutique. Don't despair yet."

"Yeah, well, listen…I better go. This place is still in a terrible state. I'll be cleaning up for the next month. Just wanted to set things straight and let you know that we're still on the lookout for Dirk. He's a devious one, isn't he?"

Truer words were never spoken.

20

Early Sunday morning, not more than forty-eight hours after Connie had said please to Bob, there was a knock at her front door.

Connie was already awake and downstairs by then. She was only sleeping a couple of hours at a time but was so energetic it gave me the creeps. I could hear her at night, restless, thumping about, skittering around. She'd begun to make plans for the house, taking inventory of all the things she was going to tear out or throw out. Only the day before, she had gone into a small room at the end of the hallway on the second floor, a room that had been used to store junk, and emptied it out, excited to find that behind the junk was a small gabled window with a window seat. With her bare hands, she'd begun to tear off the wallpaper—a stained and faded pattern of roses and cupids.

"This is going to be the kid's room," she announced, "and

I'm going to paint it white and strip down the floor." Most of the house had floorboards that could have been beautiful, but were badly in need of sanding and varnishing.

She said, "A kid needs a room their own size. A little kid needs a little room. When my grandmother died and they put me in temporary care, the dorm we slept in was so big I felt like a tiny insect. I can't have my kid feeling like an insect."

Later, I'd mentioned to Bob that I didn't think Connie should be pushing herself. Or working with paints and varnishes.

So that was why, on Sunday morning, the gang started coming.

Connie was already lumbering around the kitchen, making herself a mammoth breakfast. There was the knock at the door. Connie looked up, surprised, and I said I would go and see who it was. Through the bevelled glass, I could make out Snake, Brewbelly and two more gang members I didn't know well. I opened the door.

Snake grinned. His gold front tooth glinted. "Hiya, Luce."

"Hey, Snake. Brew. You guys are up early. C'mon in."

We all went into the kitchen. It was a big kitchen, but it seemed full. These guys took up more space than other people.

They all said hello to Connie, a little shyly, as if they were apologizing for something.

Then Snake said, "Hear ya finally fixin' the launderette up. Jeremy said he wanted to do somethin' to it, but I guess he just ran outa steam." Snake pulled something out of his pocket. It was a stack of color cards, the samples I'd given to Bob. It hadn't occurred to me that a guy like Snake, a guy with an auto body shop, might be just the person I needed.

He said, "Think we can give you a hand with this. Done a lotta time with pink, eh? Used to get a few of them Mary

Kay Cosmetics babes with them pink Cadillacs. Kinda slacked off in that area. Babies' ear, I called it, that color. Okay. Bob's given me the rundown. Figure if we start with yer babies' ear—I still got some old tins a that lyin' around—we add a splash of yer carmine rose, and yer dark cherry, a splash of cadmium yellow, that's how we get yer flamingo, eh? Now fer the black. Ya got about twenty kindsa that. I like yer anthracite. Got a little purple undertone. Gives it a gleam. Then ya want them few little bits a red to be deep an' clear an' go right to yer heart, eh? Like a hooker's lips. Yeah. No problem. We got the paint and spray guns out in the truck. Can start right now if ya like?"

The other gang members nodded.

For two weeks they kept coming. The men brought muscle and equipment, the women, coming in posses, young and old biker chicks, with things for Connie, the baby and the house. In those two weeks in June, while the Closed for Renovations sign was up on the launderette door, both the interior of the house and the launderette were practically gutted, repainted, refloored and rewired. New light fixtures and wheelchair accessible bathrooms were our biggest expense at the launderette, but they were important. The bathrooms were regulation and the lights were needed to create mood and show off art. The biggest, messiest jobs were done.

In the meantime, Bob chased down permits.

In the early days, just after his accident and before his long soused phase, he'd been a one-man campaign for wheelchair access. Anywhere the way was blocked, Bob had been there, either chained and padlocked to some railing, or just basically harassing everyone in the vicinity. At city hall and in government offices, he'd made a few enemies and a lot of friends, and when votes had been needed from a part of the population that cared more about helical gears and chrome than politics, Bob had been useful PR for the local candidates.

The permits came through right on schedule, at the end of the second week, no questions asked. I wondered what Bob had said to his high-powered connections. What promises or threats he'd made.

The launderette was taking shape. It now had a new floor of black-and-white diamond tiles punctuated with a tiny bloodred diamond tile every six feet. The walls, wherever my mural wasn't wreaking havoc, were ice white. Although they were a couple of years old, the machines looked brand-new with their fresh coats of auto paint, in rows of alternating pink flamingo and black. One scarlet machine gleamed at the center of each of the rows, like a prize, a jackpot. There were twenty-four washers and dryers in all. We were able to limp along, keeping the launderette section open and closing off the other areas as we fixed things up.

In the weeks that followed, it was Max who found us, first the couches, and then the rest of the furnishings. He got the couches from a club that went bankrupt almost as soon as it opened. They were used, but in excellent condition. Black Naugahyde. Real man-eaters. The kind you sink into and never want to rise from again. We put some of them in the reading corner and others, we used for mothers' seating surrounding the children's play area. Needless to say, again it was Max who found the toys and furniture for that space. Children's play equipment had to be regulation, and it wasn't easy to find secondhand. He also found us the tables, chairs and the espresso machine and cash register on lease for the coffee bar area.

I was beginning to see what Sky saw in him.

Max was very enthusiastic and energetic. He popped in

and out every two days to check on progress. Sky was even more ecstatic about the launderette because it kept Max in town and thus close to her.

We turned the utility room into an office, with dusty-rose wall-to-wall carpet, a hidden bar, black couches, a decent desk and black walls (Paul Bleeker had his own womb, why couldn't I?). Jeremy's ashes were installed on the desk so that I could talk to them whenever I felt like it. I invited Connie to talk to them, too, but she said it wasn't her style. I put a few fresh flowers next to the urn. It was like a proper little shrine.

And Sky gave me a gift—a red cell phone of my own.

I used the red phone to call Jacques.

"Lucy. I've been thinking about you."

"I've been thinking about you, too," I lied. "I need to ask you a big favor, Jacques. A paying favor."

"Oh, okay. Shoot."

"I need a couple of computers. It's okay if they're used, but they should look like new and have enough memory for Net surfing and some of the basic stuff. Then I need someone expert to install them. Cable, I figure. Jacques, I'm a complete techno-idiot, so you'll have to help me out on this one."

"Be my pleasure, Lucy," he said, "but there's something I want you to do for me."

"What's that?"

"Let me take you to lunch. And leave that Nadine Thorpe at home. She's a really scary customer."

"I don't work for Nadine anymore."

"You don't?"

"Starting yesterday, I'm sort of the manager of a business."

"Right on. What kind of business?"

"Er…a Laundromat."

"You mean like those places to wash 'n' dry your clothes?"

"Yeah, sort of."

"I didn't think those kind of places needed much managing. That's funny."

"I know. It sounds funny, but you have to see it. When you see it for yourself, you'll know how serious I am."

"Just tell me where and when, and I'll be there."

I told him how to get to the launderette and we agreed on a day when he could come and see. Then I asked, "How's Madeline?"

Jacques' voice became gloomy. "She's in Los Angeles with a new show."

And probably having quite a romp without you, I wanted to say.

I hadn't been back to my apartment in weeks. I'd phoned Anna several times to ask if there was any mail and to let her know that I was still alive and hadn't gone into a convent. Neither had she, by the sounds of it. Whenever I called, she had that breathless irritated voice, the voice you have when someone is slightly squashing your windpipe. The phone had a long cord. She must have moved it into her bedroom.

I was feeling nostalgic about my apartment, remembering my elation over it in the early days when I'd just moved in, when I first got my job at the gallery, before Frank, before crow's feet, before I'd figured out that aliens inhabited Nadine's body. Now the interest in Nadine was purely scientific, in the same way that an anthropologist finds a lost tribe of pygmy cannibals fascinating.

I remembered the sense of excitement in that first year in my own place, that mix of freedom and fear. That sense of getting closer to where I wanted to be. I was finally living in the heart of the city. To me, that cluster of high-rises was a miniature Manhattan.

Maybe I was just being maudlin, but I missed those days. I missed the parties with the friends I'd made at university, the fencing matches with uncooked spaghetti, and everyone dancing in the empty apartment, then sprawling out on the floor as the evening wore on—I couldn't afford furniture yet. Boozy philosophizing lasted until four in the morning, with everybody sleeping over right on the spot where they'd sat all night.

I missed all the meeting places, drinks at the Sylvia, and brunch with Sky on Robson Street or Granville Island. I missed the hive of activity of all those buildings, especially in the summer. I missed those floors of people flowing out into the warm streets. I missed the crowded walks through Stanley Park and along the sea wall, the popcorn vendors' machines glittering in the hot dusk, the freighters out on the glassy blue horizon, and the carnival atmosphere in general.

I took the three bus rides to my apartment. Apart from the Anna factor, I was looking forward to the day when I could move back in again full-time. As I walked down the main hallway, the manageress, whose doorway faced mine on the opposite side of the hall, stuck her head out.

"Hi, Lucy. Haven't seen you in ages."

"Hi, Sue. I've been living somewhere else."

"Listen. There's been a problem with your apartment. I mean, there still is a problem."

"What kind of problem?"

"I think I'll just show you myself. Follow me."

Sue and I went downstairs into the basement and the locker area. She pointed to the ceiling.

"Look at that. What you see there is directly under your apartment," she said.

There was a massive water stain on the ceiling and under it, in the locker area, I could see that the floor was damp and there had been water damage to the contents of several lockers. Against one wall was a pile of discarded soggy cardboard boxes. My locker had been drenched as well, and because Anna hadn't mentioned it to me, nobody had bothered trying to salvage the contents. My paintings would be soaked if not ruined.

"Oh Jesus," I said. "What happened?"

"Well, your roommate tried to make me think that a pipe had burst in the bathroom, but the damage was in the wrong area for the bathroom. I mean, these apartments are all the same, right? I'm not so stupid that I don't know the layout by now. The damage started in one of the bedrooms."

"Shit. Anna's waterbed."

"Yeah, right, she was supposed to have the safety frame, eh? The one that keeps the water from leaking everywhere," said Sue.

"She does. I mean I thought she did."

Sue shook her head.

"She didn't?"

"No," said Sue.

"I'm really sorry. She lied to me. It's been a bonkfest since she moved in. High tide, stormy seas, if you know what I mean."

"Yeah, I get your drift. But I gotta tell you, the hardwood floors in that room are now history. They're driftwood. Listen, Lucy, you've been a good tenant. And I'm really going to miss those parties you used to throw. I loved them. But the owner's really ticked off over this. I'm afraid I'm gonna have to give you your notice. Your name's the one on the contract, which means you're the legally responsible one and the one I've got to kick out. You're gonna lose your damage deposit, too. It's a real bummer but there it is."

"Shit. Double shit."

"I know. It sucks."

"I didn't have anything to do with it though."

"I know. I tried explaining it to the owner. That it wasn't your fault, that you weren't even here when it happened. But he's a lawyer, a real old fart in a pinstripe suit, starchy shirt and tie. When it comes to the regulations, he's a stickler."

I turned away. I didn't want Sue to see the tears welling up in my eyes.

With my back to Sue, I said, "Listen, I better stay down here and sort through my locker. It looks like everything got soaked."

"I'm really sorry, Lucy. I hope you won't hold it against me. It's my job."

"It's okay, Sue. I'd never hold it against you. It's Anna I want to kill."

"Yeah. Well. Okay. I'll leave you to it. And I'm really sorry."

Maybe serving time for homicide would be worth it after all.

First, I sorted through my paintings. The pieces I had done using the *carta intelata* technique were ruined, because the base was paper which was then glued to a stretched canvas. For the most part, they'd disintegrated. Some of the wooden stretchers had warped, but those pieces that had been done in acrylic or oil could be remounted. The pieces in tempera were only fit for the garbage pile. Most of my sketches were destroyed, soggy and blurred. Only a few drawings were salvageable. And I added to the damage by blubbering all over my ruined belongings.

When I'd finally collected myself, I marched upstairs to my apartment and let myself in quietly. I stood at the entrance, my ears pricked like a hunting hound, listening for my prey.

At first it seemed as though the apartment might be empty but then I heard slight rustling sounds and little moans. I advanced down the hallway. The sounds were coming from my bedroom. MY BEDROOM. I flung the door open.

Anna was underneath. Paul Bleeker was on top. Just where he liked to be. Anna raised her head and stared at me, barely changing her expression. Paul Bleeker crawled off her and stood up, then grabbed his jeans to cover himself.

I forced myself to play the urbane woman of the world, someone who found the whole situation ludicrous.

I said, "Please, you two, don't stop on my account. I'm a person who believes one should finish what they start." I began to root through my drawers, taking out my clothes like an efficient secretary and neatly placing them in a suitcase.

Paul stood there for a second then said, "Er…listen, Lucy. I've…been meaning to call you." He was scrambling to get into his jeans. Anna sat there in my bed with my favorite teal blue bedsheet pulled around her, looking haughty.

"I'll bet you have. And as for you Anna…" I reached into my purse, "this is this month's rent check. But as I'm no longer allowed to live here, I think I just won't bother giving it to you. You can have the outstanding bills, too. The place is all yours. I'll be back for my furniture in a couple of days. Oh, by the way, you'll have to come up with another damage deposit when they put the place in your name. Wash the sheets, would you?"

Her face turned hard and pouty. Very unattractive.

I turned my back on them, closed my bedroom door behind me, grabbed the pile of mail on the hall table and left.

As I was riding the bus back toward the East End, I opened the first of the letters. It was from a downtown legal office, informing me that a copy of Jeremy's will was waiting for me if I wished to pick it up. The letter went on to say that a copy had not been sent to the above address as they were not certain it was the right one and had been unable to reach me by telephone. I pulled the cord and leapt off the bus before it left the downtown area.

I didn't have to walk far to get back to their law offices. They were on Georgia, on the twenty-second floor of a twenty-three floor high-rise. The lobby of the building was very plush, cream wall-to-wall carpet, brass elevators, cream and pink marble hallways. I rode up to the twenty-second floor and stepped directly into the lobby of the legal offices. They took up the whole floor and the pervading odor was one of big money. It looked as though Jeremy, when it came to his estate, wanted to do things right.

I went up to the secretary and handed her the letter. "I received this in the mail. I'm here for my copy of Jeremy Madison's will."

"Just one moment," said the secretary. She picked up the phone and pushed a button. "The Madison girl's here, Doug. I thought you'd like to know. Yes, I will." She looked up at me and said, "The third door to your right, Miss Madison." She reminded me of the guidance counselor at high school just before she was about to inform me that my life was a total disaster.

The door was open. Behind a huge mahogany desk sat a quite handsome middle-aged man with silver hair and bright eyes. He looked familiar but I couldn't place him. He stood up as soon as he saw me and I instantly regretted that again, I was dressed in blue jeans. "Lucy Madison. Very nice to meet you indeed." He gave me one of those firm handshakes, first the one hand, and then the other on top of that until you feel all your bones melting. It wasn't a come-on from a man twice my age. I was sure that this guy had the kind of expansive personality that treated everyone, women, men, dogs, in exactly the same way. "I'm Doug, Jeremy's lawyer." No formalities for this man. He indicated a chair in front of the desk. "Have a seat." He sat back down and scrutinized me. "Jeremy's granddaughter. He told me quite a bit about you."

"He did?"

"Yes indeed. He was very proud of you. Said you were a fine painter."

"He did?"

"He certainly did. Care for a cup of coffee?"

"Uh...I..."

"Some mint tea maybe? The coffee's sometimes a little like battery acid. An herbal tea. That's what I usually have."

"No. A coffee would be fine."

"What do you take?"

"A little milk, please."

He picked up the phone and talked to a secretary, then went on, "So tell me, how's the pregnancy progressing?"

"Excuse me?"

"Jeremy's young lady. Connie Pete."

"Oh. She's fine. The baby's fine."

"Boy or girl?" he asked.

"Connie doesn't want to know."

"Fair enough. Jeremy wasn't particular either way. He did have a few concerns that the young lady would be isolated though. Few friends."

"He talked about that?"

"There weren't many things we didn't talk about."

"I'm living at Connie's...well...what was Jeremy's house, now. She asked me to. We're opening a business together."

"That's wonderful news. Jeremy would be pleased. What sort of business, if you don't mind my asking?"

I launched into my saga of the launderette and at the end

I gave Doug one of the flyers announcing the big opening. Doug nodded and accepted it, smiling appreciatively as I talked. Then I became bolder. "I've seen you somewhere before…"

"Jeremy's funeral." He chuckled. "Although burying the motorcycle was a little unusual. It took a bit of work to get permission for that."

That was where I'd seen him. He'd been one of the suits standing back from the group of bikers.

Doug became serious. "Jeremy had great courage. I know because a few years ago we were both facing the same problem more or less. You see, we met at the cancer clinic. A man gets a very different view of things when he thinks he might be cheated out of his life. Things went better for me than they did for him. I came out with a clean slate while Jeremy's situation was black. But he handled it bravely. He made plans for the future. He wanted to have some kind of guarantee even when he wouldn't be around. I'll confess, I'm being a lot nosier than I usually am with clients. I made a promise to your grandfather that I'd check on you, and on Connie, too, from time to time. You'll see when you read the will, that he was thinking ahead." He handed me an envelope containing several pages.

"Should I read it now?" I asked.

"No reason why not."

I began to read. The will was as I might have expected except for two details. A trust fund, with a principal sum of seventy-five thousand dollars, had been set up for the baby, who would have access to it on his or her eighteenth birthday. The other detail regarded me. It read; "To my granddaughter Lucy Margaret Madison, I leave the contents of the southwest basement room of my house."

★ ★ ★

I hurried home. First I told Connie what had happened with Anna and the apartment. Her expression perked up. "But you're staying here. I don't see the problem."

But I was still sulking over my drenched paintings. "This is a temporary situation. It's just that I'm used to having my own space."

"But you had to put up with a roommate. You didn't have your own space. Not anymore."

At times Connie could be so irritatingly accurate. "I know. It's just that...oh, I don't know."

"What are you getting so worked up about? You're staying here."

"I need to have a studio space."

"You can make a space here. I'm glad you're here. There's way too much room anyway."

I didn't say anything.

Connie's mouth drooped. "Listen, Lucy, I know I'm not the easiest person in the world. If it's me you can say so. I can take it."

I wanted to speak but the words wouldn't come.

There was a long cool silence.

Connie persisted. "Listen. I know I can be really shitty and I know I been acting like a real drag...sometimes I just can't help myself...it's like I'm possessed. I know what I should be doing and saying but something stronger than me won't let me do it...and I'm really...uh...sorry. But I'm asking you again. I don't just want you to stay. I want you to feel like this is your home. It doesn't have to be forever, but we might as well try to enjoy ourselves here and now. It would have made Jeremy glad."

She'd hit me in my weak spot. I nodded feebly. Then I said, "Connie, have you seen a copy of the will?"

"No. Jeremy told me how things would be."

"How long has it been since you checked your mail?"

"Oh, God, a while I guess, now that you mention it."

We both got up and went to the hall table where letters and junk mail were heaped up. Connie began to sort, then held up one envelope and said, "This must be it." She went into the living room, sat down, tore it open and read, then started to grin at me, bursting to say something else.

"What?" I asked. "WHAT? You're obviously dying to tell me something."

"It's amazing. It's what Reebee calls…uh…synchronicity. I've really got to show you this." She struggled up out of the armchair and plodded toward the kitchen and the basement door.

"You haven't been going up and down these stairs, have you?" I snapped.

She just went on grinning.

"Connnieeee. How many times do I have to tell you? You're supposed to be taking it easy."

"Yeah, right."

We headed down the stairs into the basement.

She said, "I was trying to clean up a bit down here. I wanna make a rec room, so when my kid's bigger, this can be a playroom, too. A wreck room. Get it? Anyway, I found these." She maneuvered her way through the clutter and pulled a huge tarpaulin off a stack in the corner. It appeared to be canvasses. Paintings. I moved in to take a closer look.

21

"These are...mine," I whispered.

Some of the pieces were things that had gone missing in university art shows. Others were paintings I'd done especially for Jeremy—for Christmases and birthdays. There were over thirty canvasses.

Connie said, "These must be what Jeremy meant in the will. I gotta confess something to you. Jeremy figured you were going to be a famous painter one day. I was more than a little jealous, eh? The way he was always going on and on about it. I didn't know he had all these down here but he did say something about you not trusting your talent. Maybe he thought you'd do something stupid."

"Stupid how?"

"I dunno. Selling art to the wrong people. Selling your paintings before it's the right time to sell them. Or just giving them away."

I was overwhelmed. Jeremy's spirit was watching over me.

★ ★ ★

It didn't take long to get the rec room organized. I happened to mention it casually to Bob, and the guys were on the doorstep within the week. The room got some jade-green indoor-outdoor carpeting, some knotty pine wood panelling and some electric heat. The guys also helped me move my possessions out of the West End apartment. We put most of my living room furniture down in the rec room. It now had a very cozy atmosphere. Reebee added a beanbag chair she'd found at a Salvation Army store.

"What we gotta do," said Connie, "is sit down here and do something you do in a rec room like have a party or watch videos, then see how many spiders, you know those big ones that you always catch out of the corner of your eye, see how many of them stomp across the floor during the evening. That's the trouble with basement rooms, eh? Big ugly spiders."

So when the room was finished, we decided to give it a trial run. Sky and Reebee came over, with Sky waving a video box. "I got popcorn, nacho chips, orange juice, Diet Coke and the *Bridget Jones's Diary* video."

"Bridget Jones?" asked Connie. "Who's she?"

"She's a fictional character, from a novel called *Bridget Jones's Diary,*" said Sky.

"I don't read novels," said Connie.

I tried not to take this as the statement of a Philistine but of a person who perhaps preferred action to words.

"Maybe you'll start," said Reebee.

When the film was over, we all agreed that we would have fallen like fools for the hot but dastardly Daniel Cleaver, and ignored the morally correct and uptight Mark Darcy.

"Why are we women so self-destructive?" I asked.

"Because one minute of something wicked you want badly enough might just be worth all the trouble," said Sky.

"If you don't mind paying for it for the rest of your life," said Reebee, fatefully.

We all gawked at her, then Sky said, "Motherrrr. How could you?"

"I'm joking," squealed Reebee.

"Anybody notice any big ugly spiders?" ventured Connie.

I was at the launderette when I remembered the unopened mail in my purse. I retreated to the new office to look through it. There were no bills. I'd been unusually responsible and taken care of them earlier in the month, and after my visit to Anna, I'd immediately called and canceled my phone and hydro accounts.

I was sitting at my desk in the new office, facing Jeremy's ashes, when I picked up the first letter. It was in Dirk's handwriting, a looping wild scrawl. Each envelope contained one dirty piece of paper. The first one read: I'LL GET YOU WHILE YOU'RE SLEEPING; the second said: YOU'RE A NOTHING; another said; LET ME HELP YOU WRITE YOUR OBITUARY; yet another said: HOW WOULD YOU LIKE TO BE HANDCUFFED TO A MOVING TRAIN?

The last one was ridiculous. Laughable. There were hardly any trains still running in Canada. He'd say or do anything to get to me.

I could remember occasions, in university days, when I'd come home to find Dirk lounging on my couch, having found a way into my place without a set of keys. My refrigerator would be empty, my bathroom a filthy boggy mire, my CDs ruined from being left on top of the radiator, all my possessions searched through, and my letters and diary read. This was so that in some opportune moment, Dirk could tease me with a detail of my private life, chanting it, calling it out for the whole world to hear.

Once, when this happened, I walked out of my apartment in the direction of the nearest police station to make a formal complaint, and Dirk followed me. He grabbed me from behind, dragging me back along the street by the hair, and all those passersby, those average men on the street, not lifting a finger…it was my first really big disillusionment with mankind.

I'd taken my case to Jeremy that time. Dirk was his grandson, after all. I'd thought at best, Jeremy might have some wisdom to impart and at worst, he could put him in his place. It wasn't really my style to run squealing to my grandfather, but that time I'd been scared.

Jeremy wasn't someone to waste time or words. He sicced the gang on Dirk. They tracked Dirk down at his favorite coffee bar on Davie Street, called in their reserves and approached his table. In a knot of leather and steel and hair and grizzle they menaced him. Jeremy told him, "You lay one finger on Lucy, Dirk, and you'll have my buddies to deal with." It worked for a while. Dirk stayed away.

Generally, Dirk's brand of violence was mostly psychological, and mostly involved words alone. Deep down he knew how much he would be risking if he depended heavily on physical violence. But, it is worth noting that whenever he did manage to get a girlfriend, he usually ended up ruining things by slugging the poor girl of the moment. I know this because the ex-girlfriends, in their stunned confusion, always confided this detail to me, as if I could make a difference. As if I were my brother's keeper.

It was early evening when I used my red cell phone to call Sam's numbers. I didn't want him to hear my voice shaking so I waited a long time. I consulted with Jeremy's ashes until I felt calm enough to talk to a living human being.

I didn't reach Sam at either number so I called his office. Francesca answered. I told her who I was and why I was calling and I have to say she was unusually sympathetic and cooperative. I couldn't help but be suspicious.

"Dirk's sister. Yes. I've been looking over his case. You've had more threats?"

"I think these should be added to his file. They're concrete evidence. In his handwriting."

"Yes, of course. Sam's out on another case. But it's a FOBIA night. You might be able to reach him there later. He likes to pop in and touch base with the families."

I had my doubts. I wasn't really up for another night of square-dancing. And the FOBIA nights were dry events. The rigid regulations prohibiting alcohol just made me thirstier than ever for a real drink. But I did want Sam to have those letters for Dirk's file. I wanted to thrust them into his hot little hand. I wanted him to realize that I was being harassed.

Okay. As harassment went, it was as slow and innocuous as nasty notes. But it was working. It was eroding my life. Just when enough time had passed that I'd forgotten Dirk again, he'd reappear like a debilitating condition. Like malaria. Like psoriasis.

So I pulled out my reliable jeans ensemble and headed for Kerrisdale and the old school building. When I approached the gym I was surprised there was no fiddle music. It was very quiet in there. I opened the door cautiously and peeked in. The room was dark except for flickering candles here and there and a spotlight up on the stage.

The space was organized like a club, with groups of people clustered at little round tables with red tablecloths. At the center of each table was a red glass containing a lit candle. It was a little hokey but I could see what they were aiming at; the sixties coffeehouse effect.

Up on the stage, a young woman with long black hair was getting hyper and emotional. It took me a minute to realize that she was acting. It was Tennessee Williams, one of Blanche Dubois's scenes. The girl played subtly deranged quite well, with just the right degree of weirdness. When she had finished and everyone was applauding, I crept along the back of the auditorium looking for a familiar face. I spotted Mavis, from the last meeting, and snuck over to her table. I drew up a chair and whispered into her ear. "Hi, Mavis. Remember me?"

"Oh hi. Sure, dear. You're Lucy. Brother a rapid cycler. If I remember correctly."

"That's right. What's going on here? I was expecting square-dancing."

She whispered, "We're having a little change of pace, dear. This is talent night. We find we can get some of our bi-po-lars involved. You know, a lot of them have talents you wouldn't imagine."

Dirk certainly had talents she wouldn't have imagined. Like wool-pulling. For years he had been getting one big free lunch from the government in the form of a pension. That was a talent.

Mavis went on, "Now your rapid cycler wouldn't happen to have some little specialty we could put up on that stage, would he, Lucy?"

"Well, he did train as an actor but..."

"Bingo. There you are right there. We just gotta get him up there and emoting his little heart out. Usually does them a world of good."

There was a commotion up on the stage as they set up for the next number. Loudspeakers, some kind of sound box and a video screen were rolled onto the stage.

"This is going to be fun," said Mavis. "This is the part I'm really looking forward to. Now my hubby's going to sing 'In the Ghetto.' Know that old Elvis song? Yep. He's got a real pretty bass voice on him. And we managed to get a few of our kids from social services in on the show to kind of flesh things out. It's karaoke because a band was a little too complicated but it sounds real good just the same."

I was curious. I pulled in a little closer to Mavis's table.

Mavis's hubby sang first and it wasn't bad except that he didn't have the right look. He was string-bean skinny and as bald as a bowling ball. But if you closed your eyes it could almost be Elvis. There was lots of applause.

The next singer was a very nervous woman with manic-depressive hair and fingers that never stopped twitching. I should explain: it's hair that's flattened at the back from hours of lying in bed and counting the little dots in the ceiling during the depressive phases. Dirk had been through a few flat hair phases himself. In a thin nasal soprano, she sang that old Gloria Gaynor hit, "I Will Survive." I wondered if she would.

I was looking away when the next person walked on stage. The music started up in the semidarkness. It was familiar, so familiar that a little shudder ran along my spine. In a near-perfect Marti Pellow imitation, the singer launched into "Love Is All Around." The lights finally came up on him. I squinted into the brightness. The man was tall with reddish-gold hair that came to his shoulders. He wore a denim shirt and jeans and if I hadn't known better, I would have said it was the man I'd square-danced with at the last FOBIA meeting.

I said, "Mavis, do you know who that is singing?"

"That's one of ours from social services. That young Trelawny fellow. Very nice kid. Smart, too. Always available for an emergency. And doesn't he have the prettiest voice on him?"

Sam.

And could he ever sing, goddammit.

I was in trouble. A little tiny part of me would now be trying to find a way to get him to croon for me. It was humiliating being a slave to sound but there was a thirteen-year-old groupie in me that just refused to die. When the voice was right, only serious social conditioning kept me from climbing up onto the stage, laying myself at the singer's feet and clutching onto his ankles so that he couldn't get away from me.

My eyes were glued to Sam right to the end of the song. The applause was frenzied. He was quite a favorite with the FOBIA crowd.

I remembered what I was there for. I said a hurried goodbye to Mavis and ran toward what I thought would be the right door to take me to the backstage area.

I was in an empty equipment room and although there was no equipment, the walls were still permeated with that old familiar odor of juvenile feet, chalk dust and rubber. I raced through an abandoned locker room and came out into a dark hallway. At the far end was Sam. His hand was on the door's push bar, but he'd paused, as though he'd forgotten something.

"Sam?" I called down the hallway. He looked up at me.

"Who is that?"

"It's Lucy Madison."

"Lucy." He looked startled, not quite pleased.

"They told me at your office that I'd find you here."

By then I had closed the gap between us. Sam's look had improved considerably. He wasn't the same person I'd seen that day in the launderette. Although he still had a beard it was trimmed a bit. His clothes looked good on him. This was the Sam who'd twirled me round on square-dance night. I was sure of it now. I moved in a little closer to find out if he had that other smell of cinnamon and wood fires. That scent was gone though and in its place was the neutral safe smell of soap and some kind of musky men's cologne.

"What is it, Lucy? I'm really sorry but I'm in a bit of a hurry. Walk out to my car with me. I've got a group home to look in on."

"I wanted you to have these for Dirk's file. They might be concrete evidence. You know, for the police." I'd put all the letters in a big envelope along with a separate sheet of paper with my new address and cell phone number.

"What's in here?" he asked as I handed him the envelope.

"Threatening letters."

Sam ran a hand over his forehead and through his hair. He looked exasperated. "Yes, okay. I'll look at all this later, shall I? It's just that I'm in a bit of a hurry. In fact, I'm already late. I like to touch base with the FOBIA people but there's only so much a person can do in a day." We'd already reached his car, a blue Hyundai with a shattered rear window, a dent in the passenger's door and one windshield wiper askew.

"I'll be in touch about this, Lucy." He had already slid into the driver's seat and turned on the ignition.

"By the way," I said, "I liked your..."

But the last word, "singing," was cut off as Sam called out, "Sorry, Lucy, really gotta go. I'll be in touch," and roared out of the parking lot.

I felt dismal. Why was it that whenever we met in person, we always managed to disappoint each other?

I called Leo.

"Miss Piggy! How lovely to hear from your porkiness."

"Hi, Leo. How's it going? How was the Rach Two?"

"I survived. My left hand cramped a little in the last movement, but apart from that, I was divine. I was fabulous. Martha Argerich, eat your heart out. What are you doing right now?"

"I've got loads to do but I wouldn't mind taking a break. I've got to ask your advice about something," I said.

"Let's be hearty types for an afternoon and take your pork chops and wrinkles for a walk."

"Where?"

"Well, it's spring. Let's go somewhere we can see the sap run."

"The sap? Anybody I know?" I asked.

"I hope not," said Leo. "Unless you've started hanging out at the YMCA and not telling me about it."

"No, Leo. I'm afraid the sex change operation didn't take."

"Good. What would I do without at least one pouchy-faced porcine fag hag in my life?"

"You flatter me, Leo."

Leo and I met in the afternoon and walked around the sea wall in Stanley Park. Well, I walked while Leo gawked and leered at all the gay men jogging, zooming past and flinging their sweat at us. But Leo seemed to have his eye out for someone in particular.

It was a beautiful May day. The sun glistened off the ocean. Seagulls screeched and careened across the clear sky. The park was crazy with new growth. But I was anxious, impatient. At the launderette, things had come to a standstill. I wanted everything turned on at once, so until all the components were ready, nothing could happen. The espresso machine was empty and waiting to express, the jukebox was unplugged and silent, the computers were purchased and waiting in Jacques's office for the go-ahead from me, and the walls were painted and waiting for the art to be hung. Before anything could happen, before everything could be turned on, it had to be perfect.

"Leo, we need a piano and someone to play from time to time."

"Uh-huh?"

"And someone to send aspiring musicians my way. Someone like you. Someone who knows lots of young promising talent that wouldn't mind the exposure but wouldn't have to be paid a lot."

"What are you up to, Lucy?"

"We're opening up this business."

"We? Who's we?"

"Me and Jeremy's old girlfriend, Connie."

"Connie? But you hate Connie."

"No. I don't. Maybe I thought I hated Connie. I didn't really know her. I don't think she really knew herself when it comes down to it. She's okay. Anyway, it's sort of a launderette cum art gallery cum coffee-bar cum cyber-joint cum music venue."

"Buff. Very buff."

"Thank you."

"I'm talking about that man, that GOD who just ran past."

"Leo. You're not listening to me."

"Yes, of course I am. I have symphonic hearing. I could listen to you and forty other lardy wenches trashing your best friends simultaneously and tell you what each and every one of you said."

"Good. Okay. In this launderette, there's a small space that would be good for live music. Small ensembles. Jazz or classical. So I figure we need a piano."

"What did you have in mind? A Steinway baby perhaps?"

"Not a very good piano but one that sounds okay."

"An old upright grand," said Leo. "You can lease one for next to nothing and they're playable."

"You think?"

"Sure. I'll come with you and try it out for sound. All you have to do is pay."

"Good. Good. Okay. So now tell me about this guy you're hoping to accidentally bump into out here, Leo. I haven't seen you behave like such a dork for quite a long time."

"Well…" said Leo, rolling his eyes melodramatically.

I groaned. "I know that expression. He's straight, right?"

"Well…" Leo repeated.

"And married, right?"

"Only a little married," whined Leo.

"Like being a little pregnant, eh?" And I thought I was a glutton for punishment.

22

It was getting close. The official opening of the launderette was almost upon us. Connie and I sat in the rec room eating popcorn and playing channel roulette, but neither of us could pay attention to the TV. We were too excited.

"Okay," said Connie. She was wearing tortoise-rimmed glasses that made her look very serious and efficient. When she wasn't shifting uncomfortably, or clasping the place where the baby just kicked her, she was ticking things off a list with a pencil. "We've got Hit and Run Kitchen set up for the sandwiches, croissants, cakes and cookies. I think we should forget about salads."

"Why?" I asked.

"Just too much limp lettuce left over at the end of the day. If we do some decent vegetarian sandwiches, that oughta be enough. Okay. We do Italian Espresso coffee orders with Marini Food Imports. Milk delivery each morning for the cappuccinos and lattes. The cable guys are coming tomorrow to put in the lines for the computers and your friend Jacques is bringing them and he's going to do the fiddly stuff…"

"Programming."

"The programming. Tomorrow morning, right?"

I nodded.

"Then we got the cartoon tapes and TV set with video for the kids'…"

"Educational TV…nonstop. So we don't have to go and change tapes all the time."

"Educational TV…for the kids' corner. Then we got the art. Listen, you've gotta get that stuff hung. What about your friend? Cindy?"

"Candy. I'm still working on her. She's a special case. And listen, I'm going to ask her if she wants to work the espresso bar. She's smart. She managed a record store. Right now she's working for her mother and that can't be good for anyone."

I'd been doing my best with Candy, going round to Boito's Beauties and pestering her, trying to remind her of who she'd been, the artist she'd been, to reassure her that she had friends whenever she felt scared. I'd assured her that if we saw her pulling out her mascara brush and looking at a dog whimsically, or tearing off her clothes and heading for the ocean, that we'd stop her. She was still afraid of everything but had mentioned she missed painting.

I said, "She may not be in on the first show but one of these days there may be something."

"Okay," said Connie. "Bob is technical manager. That what we're calling him? Officially?"

"Yeah. Any mechanical or electrical problems are his. And he has lots more to worry about now."

"Listen, we gotta look carefully at revenues here."

"I know it's not going to be big money…."

"Well, *I've* had a few ideas," said Connie.

"Shoot."

"Okay, you've got your washer and dryer revenues, your very inflated soap, bleach and softener revenues, your coffee bar, your jukebox, your Internet time. And now how about tapes? You get any half-decent musicians in there you could tape the evenings. But it's gotta be a free platform. We can't afford to pay musicians but we can pass a hat. Now the paintings and drawings are going to be for sale, so the launderette gets a commission. I figure thirty percent, and maybe we can put together little books of the artwork whenever there's a new show. That could be down the line a bit when we can afford it. Keep reminding everyone it's local. It's happening here and now. It's original. You could get people who write to come and read their stuff. Poems and stuff…"

"Hey, Connie, slow down."

"We'll make it work, Lucy. It's gonna work. We'll make ourselves proud. But there's one more thing."

"What's that?"

"The old name's gotta go."

I felt a little twinge of sadness. "You don't want Madison's Coin Wash? But it's a way to remember Jeremy."

"Who's forgetting him? It's just not catchy enough. It's sort of sad and run-down, like a name from the depression years. I had a better name in mind."

"What?"

"Lucy's Launderette. In pink neon writing with a red heart in the middle, like the decor. The launderette was your idea."

"No, I don't think…"

Connie cut me off. "Yes. It's my place and I've decided and I'm not going to change my mind. It sounds good. And you're his granddaughter so it's still kinda in the family. It's gotta ring to it. Lucy's Launderette."

Jacques arrived the next morning with two computers. When he saw the launderette he said, "Awesome. This is an amazing place you got here. If I'd known it was going to be like this, I wouldn't have brought you these hunks of junk." He pointed to the computers.

"They look brand-new to me. What's wrong with them?"

"They're about two generations old. A generation lasts about six months. Maybe less these days. But I guess they'll do for the basics."

I let Jacques get to work and began hanging my paintings. I didn't bother to ask him about Madeline. I didn't want to depress either of us so early in the day.

Just before noon, Connie showed up. She was walking like a duck now with the weight of her belly. She stood behind me while I adjusted my canvasses. "Your stuff's growing on me, Paleface," she said.

Jacques looked up from what he was doing, saw Connie and leapt to his feet. "Can I offer you a chair, ma'am?"

"She's not ma'am, Jacques. She's Connie, my boss, the owner of this place."

Jacques was staring at her in the most peculiar way. He rushed forward with a chair and said, "Connie, please sit down. I'm getting swollen ankles just looking at you."

Connie accepted the chair.

When lunchtime came around, Jacques stretched and said, "All finished. Now I'm taking you to lunch. And I think Connie and her little passenger should come, too."

★ ★ ★

It was two o'clock in the afternoon when my cell phone beeped at me with my first real caller. I didn't count all the times Sky had phoned me from the next room just to try it out. I had great expectations now, but they were dashed when I heard the voice.

"Mom."

"Lucy. Brush your hair and put on some makeup. Oh yes, and do put on a bra. You're going out." I never went braless these days, but she seemed to think I was still an adolescent trying to sneak out of the house with too much black eyeliner and too little clothing.

"Mom. What's the problem?" I'd rarely heard such anxiety in her voice.

"I'm coming to get you. I'm just finishing my coffee now, then I'll have a quick visit to the bathroom then I'm getting into the car, that should be in about five minutes, which would get me into town and to Connie's house within about forty-five minutes, so be ready and waiting on the doorstep."

"Where are we going? Mom? Mom…?" But she'd already hung up.

She was punctual. Forty-five minutes later, I was on the doorstep, wearing a flowing, flowery summer dress. It was another warm, cloudless July day. I toyed with the idea that we might be going somewhere fun, somewhere I'd want to be seen looking nice. Sometimes my mother got urges to take me shopping, to buy me something "decent" and I usually humored her. She was good for those neutral all-purpose items of clothing, plain black slacks, sweaters, that sort of thing. And she was a great believer in support garments, ever willing to buy me new bras.

My mother's Toyota pulled up. She flapped her hand for me to get in. Before the passenger door was even shut she was speeding out into the road. It was going to be one of her white-knuckle specials.

"What's this all about, Mom? And slow down, would you? You just cut that guy off."

"He was creeping along like a snail. You'll see where we're going when we get there."

"You can tell me now. I'm over twenty-one. I'm considered an adult by most people."

"Horse-frocky. When you're married with children of your own, you'll have a better idea of what it means to be an adult. What it means to be responsible. A concept that seems to have escaped a few people."

"Where are we going? Can you tell me that much? Because we're certainly going in the wrong direction for anything fun and townlike."

"I suppose I can. We're going to the airport."

"The airport? Who's leaving?"

I could picture it, my father with his possessions in a little red-and-white biker kerchief, off to see the world he'd missed seeing because he was so young when his career as a stick-in-the-mud started. Where do over-the-hill, rebel sticks-in-the-mud go when they cut loose? Marakesh? Upper Volta?

"Motherrrr. Is this about Dad?"

"Your father? Heavens no. He'll be fine when he comes back down to earth."

"You mean he still hasn't… Oh, Mom." I wished it had been about Dad. It was unsettling to think that my father was still a bible-thumping biker, at large. Why couldn't it be some boring parentlike reaction to a crisis of my father's. No such luck.

"The question you should ask," said my mother, "is who's arriving."

"Who's arriving then?"

"Wait and see."

"Couldn't you meet them alone?"

"I might not be able to manage it." The way my mother's jaw was clenched would have been appropriate for in-laws, but she'd never had a mother-in-law and Jeremy was gone. Was it one of her own relatives from back East? Her mother? My maternal grandmother from Hell?

When my mother was a young woman just married, she announced that she was pregnant with her first child. That was Dirk. Her mother grimaced and said, "Oh my God, how awful," and that was that. I often wondered if Dirk, lying there as a mere squiggle of a fetus, had heard her comment through the walls of my mother's uterus and let it get to him, deciding right then and there to be mentally ill, out of protest.

My mother had escaped westward to university, but every so often, her mother flew in from the East and pounced.

"It's not Granny Clara, is it?" I ventured.

"Oh no. Spare us. You'll see in good time."

There was nothing left to do but let myself be hurtled along as if I were a passenger on the space shuttle. I had to close my eyes a few times to avoid scaring myself. It wasn't so much that my mother was a bad driver. It was simply that she moved in another time dimension, one where everyone else drove far too slowly for her tastes.

When we reached the airport, she cut another man off and zoomed into a parking space.

"Hurry up," she snapped. "We've got to be there before 3:25. Ridiculous rules. Some union thing makes them open and close at the strangest times."

"The flights are always late getting in. And then there's waiting around for the baggage. Don't worry. You can usually add an hour to the time." But my mother hadn't heard me.

She was already rushing into the main part of the building. When I caught up to her she was consulting with someone at an information desk.

"Downstairs," she ordered. I followed obediently.

We were lost in carpeted corridors. "The passengers don't come through here," I said. "We're going the wrong way."

"No, we're not," snapped my mother. "We don't want passenger arrivals."

"We don't?"

"No."

My mother was determined to keep me guessing. "Okay. Whatever it is, is it international or domestic?"

"International."

"Oooo. Intriguing."

"Here we are," my mother announced. We were in some kind of freight deposit. "Yoo hoo. Anybody home?"

A uniformed man rounded a corner. "Can I help you?"

My mother handed him something furtively, a slip of paper or a ticket.

"Okey doke," said the man, and disappeared again. He returned carrying a huge oblong parcel wrapped in well-traveled brown paper. "It's heavy. Better if the two of you carry it."

My mother and I each took an end.

"Okay, Mom, I give up. What's in here?"

"Let's take it upstairs, get ourselves a coffee, then open it up and have a look." My mother was nearly peeing herself with anticipation but refused, as usual, to give away her surprise.

I sighed. We hauled the parcel up an escalator, lugged it through the airport's main lobby, hobbled with it over to the cappuccino bar and sat it on a chair.

"Okay," I said, grabbing a loose bit of paper. "Let's rip her open."

My mother slapped my hand. "Not so fast, Lucille. First, the coffees." I sighed again and went up to the counter. "A part-skimmed double latte for me and the cocoa mocha with whipped cream for my mother." The guy behind the counter looked at my mother with something akin to admiration then started making the coffees. I waited there, gazing beyond him, looking into the milling airport crowd, looking but not really seeing. Until something caught my eye.

It was Sam Trelawny. He had his arm around a very pretty brunette woman. She was caressing his face. I squinted hard to focus better. She seemed to be crying. Then she pulled his face into hers and there was a long kiss. I felt a pang of envy and longing. It was starting to look as though a lot of other women weren't put off by the occasional lapses into plaid either.

I paid for the coffees and went back to the table. My mother, hardly able to contain herself, had started to tear away at the parcel's brown paper. I gave her a hand. There was a carton underneath, with words printed all over it in a strange script that looked like Greek.

"Go on, Mom. If you don't hurry up and open it, I will."

My mother tore off the flap at one end of the oblong and peered down into the carton. She let out a little whimpering "Ohhh."

I went over and took a look. "Jeeezus. Really, Motherrrr."

"Those criminals sent me another letter with the claim ticket. Does he look all right to you?" she asked. "I think they've done something to him. I think he's been tampered with. Poor Winky."

I'm the only person I know whose mother makes more fuss over a missing garden gnome than she does over the rest of her family.

She yanked him up out of the box so that his head and

shoulders were visible. "They've done something to him. He's not the same as he was before he left."

"It's only natural, Mom. He's been on the grand tour of Europe. He's bound to be more worldly than before."

"You're as bad as them," she said.

Winky did look a little brighter, a little snappier. His wink was more impertinent than it had been before his trip. Somebody had given him a fresh coat of paint.

"Hi, Lucy," said a man's voice.

I looked up to see Sam staring at us. He'd managed to lose the brunette.

"Hello, Sam. Mom, this is Sam Trelawny, Dirk's caseworker. Sam, do you know my mother?"

"Lovely to meet you, Sam," said my mother, oozing cheerfulness.

"Mrs. Madison." Sam shook her hand.

"Call me June."

"June," said Sam.

I added, "And this is another important member of our family, Winky, our long-lost garden gnome. He was kidnapped back in October, although if you ask me, it's a case of the Patty Hearst Syndrome. I think he wanted to be kidnapped. He's been partway around the world, seen all sorts of things, hasn't he, Mom? I'm really quite jealous. The kidnappers have finally let him come home."

Sam smiled and nodded, then said, "I'll be in touch with you about Dirk. We're trying to get a new court order but it may not be easy. Anyway, hang in there. I've gotta go. I'm late for a meeting. Nice to have made your acquaintance, Mrs. Madison. You, too, Winky," he said to the plaster statue. Then with a little bow of his head, he turned and walked toward the exit.

"What an interesting young man. Really, Lucy," said my

mother, "what would it cost you to try flirting a little *harder?* To take some initiative? To ask him to our house for dinner? Now you've gone and scared him off with your silly sarcasm."

That night I dreamed about Sam. He was interrogating Winky, who was propped up on a metal chair under one of those glaring lamps police detectives use when they want to extort a confession. Sam went on and on, saying things like, "Keeping silent won't help you. We know you did it. You sent those threatening letters to Lucy, didn't you? Didn't think we'd catch up to you in Europe, did you? But you're back now. You're going to have to answer for your behavior."

Meanwhile, Dirk was there behind Sam. He was making unnaturally high leaps into the air, like a ballerina, and making faces at Sam's back. And worse, he was wearing my red dress. I could see that he'd ripped it in a few places and I was furious. I tried screaming at Sam, "He's there behind you, Dirk's there behind you. Turn around." But Sam didn't hear me. It was as though there were a soundproof glass wall between us, because I kept trying to run toward him. I wanted to grab him and make him look, but I kept coming up against a barrier. My feet seemed to be stuck in molasses. I turned back to Dirk and screamed, "Take off my red dress, take it off this minute or I'll…"

"What?" said Dirk, taunting me. "You'll what?"

I roared like an animal in the dream but the sound that woke me up was a strangled croak. My face was wet with tears. I lay there in the dark, in a very bad mood.

23

Two days before the big opening, Candy called me. "When do I start?"

"You mean you'll take the job?"

"I really have to tell you, I don't know the first thing about making cappuccinos."

"Anybody can do it. I'm sure anybody can do it." I was talking through my hat. Put to the test, I wasn't sure that I could do it myself.

Then Candy whispered, "I've been painting."

"How? Where? Not at your parents' place."

"God, no. Remember David Yee?"

"From our painting class?"

"Yeah."

"Sure I remember him. He was good. I remember his scary series. Scary cats, scary flowers, scary people. They were funny."

"Yeah, well. We had a little thing when we were at school."

"You did? I didn't know that."

"You weren't supposed to. I was going out with that cowboy idiot from the poli-sci department and he was jealous. Anyway, the thing with David was more of an accident than a thing but he seems to think there was some meaning to it. And hell, it's nice to be lusted after by someone. I'd forgotten. Turns out he's working in his cousins' fast-food place there in the mall, the Chinese food place. Just to make a little extra cash. He's got this run-down studio in Chinatown where he lives and works and said I could work there whenever I felt like it. So that's what I've been doing. We take leftovers, chow mein and egg rolls and stuff back to his place after we get off our shifts and we go and paint."

"And you don't feel like you're going crazy, do you?"

"No."

"And even if you did, you'd tell your friends, wouldn't you. Talking about things always helps, and we'd work it out somehow. Not wanting to go crazy is half the battle, I figure."

"I've been slapping together these paintings really fast. All these ideas were just sitting there, waiting to be put on canvas. Do you still want some stuff of mine for your place?"

"Do I? I sure as hell do. Tell me where to go and I'll send Bob with the van. Are you going to come and help mount it? We haven't got much time. Just two days."

"Maybe. What about David?" said Candy.

"How do you mean?"

"Have you got room for some of David's paintings?"

"The space is huge. It's an idea. You've gotta be there for the Grand Opening, too, Candy. Real work wouldn't start until the next morning but you want to be in on the kick-off."

"If I can get away. My parents think I've been using my spare time to go work out in the gym."

"They can hardly deny you exercise, can they?"

"Exactly."

David's most recent work was a perfect fit for our first exhibit. The pieces had the simplicity and color of Matisse but were much funnier. And Candy's new work! Candy's new work was a series, depicting very large women climbing into and bursting out of fancy lingerie. Working in Boito's Beauties had had its uses after all.

We had plastered the area with posters announcing the Grand Opening of Lucy's Launderette, hired kids to distribute flyers, and taken out an ad in the main daily paper. We'd sent out invitations to all of Jeremy's biker friends. There was a footnote to remind everyone that formal attire was requested. Max's idea. I thought it was pushing things a bit too far but he pointed out that a few tuxedos would look great against the pinks and reds and blacks. He said I'd want to make it as extravagant as possible so that I'd really have something to remember. Prophetic words.

The neon Lucy's Launderette sign was installed. We also put up a black-and-white striped awning so that people could sit out on the sidewalk. It was mid-July and the weather was perfect.

We were ready. Food was arranged with Hit and Run Kitchen, who were going to be our regular suppliers for the espresso bar, and Leo called to tell me not to worry about music on the night of the opening, that he would take care of everything. The bikers said they would supply the champagne, that it was the least they could do, and finally, Sky brought over my red dress.

She was carrying a shoe box as well. "Okay, this is what we're going to do." She opened the box to reveal a pair of white vintage high heels, pointed toes, classic late fifties, early sixties. Then she pulled a little bottle out of her purse. "Shoe dye," she said. "If we hurry they'll be dry for tonight. Try 'em on. Make sure they fit." The fit was usually guaranteed since Sky and I had the same shoe size. I tried them on. They were almost comfortable.

Sky shook the little bottle of dye. "Hell of a hard color to find. The reds were all too orange or too pink. This is true ruby red. Just like Dorothy's magic shoes. Careful not to bang your heels together or you might end up going straight to Kansas."

The Grand Opening was scheduled for 8:00 p.m. At six, Leo, dressed in a black leather tuxedo, arrived in a taxi. He had brought keyboards, speakers, synthesizers, a laptop computer, a turntable, cables and mikes. He was a one-man band. It was a side of him I'd never seen before. He started setting up in the corner allotted to musical groups, then said to me, "Just keep funnelling booze to me and I'll be your entertainment center. I adore being the only star in my galaxy."

Bob wheeled into the launderette, very elegant in a rented tux. His wheelchair was festooned with red jewel helium balloons.

"Nice threads, Bob. I'm sure the babes won't be able to leave you alone."

Bob grinned. "Yeah, well, gotta give 'er a shot, eh? I may be a legless gimp but I'm still one hot dude."

I moved through the launderette, checking things for the last time. The girls from Hit and Run Kitchen had delivered the food. There was sushi for cowards (crab and smoked salmon filling instead of raw fish). There were piquant samosas, tiny spinach pies and Cornish pasties. There were

Italian crostini with tomato, basil and garlic, porcini mushrooms, pickled artichoke hearts, fried polenta with chicken livers and spicy olives. There were Swedish meatballs, asparagus rolls, little cucumber-and-cream-cheese sandwiches with the crusts cut off and chicken wings grilled in garlic, soya sauce and honey. The bottles of champagne sat in tubs of ice behind the espresso bar. I'd opted for plastic wineglasses and plates.

At the front end of the vast wall where the paintings were exhibited, a large printed notice had been put up:

"The works of Candace Sharp, David Yee and Lucy Madison are for sale. Interested parties should contact Connie Pete."

Connie's phone number and our new e-mail address were given in smaller print at the bottom of the notice. There had been quite a lot of arguing over the pricing of our paintings. In the end, Connie had said, "Leave it in my hands. You artists won't be any good at getting a price for your work. I can tell. You'll be so flattered that anyone could be interested that you'll be ready to give them away. If there's one thing I know about, it's how to recognize want. When people want something bad enough, they'll pay for it." Maybe she had a point. Somebody had to have a cutthroat approach to the art business.

Electronic squeaks and squawks came from Leo's corner. He was testing his equipment. I opened a bottle of champagne, grabbed two plastic glasses and went over to him.

"Have some liquid courage," I said.

"You can't possibly be scared, Miss Piggy." Leo knocked back the first glass and poured himself another.

"Can't I? Well, I am. What if no one comes? What if they all hate it or think it's stupid?"

Leo gave a snorting laugh. "Oh, stop fussing. You're being an old woman. And behaving like an old woman gets to be a habit. You do it over and over and suddenly you ARE an old woman."

"You're such a comfort, Leo."

"Now go home and get dressed. You can't attend your own Grand Opening dressed in the greasy newspaper liners from the bottom of your garbage pail." He pointed at my painting clothes. I was still wearing them most of the time now that I didn't have to play a role or answer to some ogre of a boss.

I went home to get ready. Connie was in the kitchen, snacking. She was going through a phase in which it didn't matter what she ate as long as there was a big blob of crunchy peanut butter smeared on top of it. She said it was a question of contrasts, the crunchy and the smooth, the oily and the watery, the salty and the sour. I came in just as she was spreading some on a peach.

"Ooo yuck, Connie. You better get off that stuff. It'll stick to the roof of your mouth and you'll have a speech impediment for the rest of the evening. And there's some much nicer food over at the launderette."

Connie looked wistfully at the economy-size jar of Skippy. "I suppose I could always bring this over with me."

"Don't you dare. I'm going upstairs to get ready. What about you? We open in half an hour."

"Don't worry. I'll be ready," she said.

I went up to my room. The red dress was hanging in its plastic and the shoes were ever so slightly tacky, but dry enough if I didn't, as Sky had said, bang my heels together. Sky convinced me that I had to wear the vintage natural-colored sheer silk stockings, like the women in the movies, and she'd given me one of the boxes (ten pairs!) that had be-

longed to Bella Montgomery. I had to get a garter belt for
the occasion and because the only one I could find was
black, I had to get the rest of the underwear in black lace.
Panty hose hadn't even been invented when they made those
stockings. I was so nervous about ruining them that I put on
a pair of wooly mittens to pull them on. I stepped into the
red dress, reached around and zipped myself up. It was slightly
looser than it had been the first time I'd tried it. Now it hung
beautifully. I even had shoulder blades to show off in the low-
cut V-shaped back. I slid my feet into the shoes and stood in
front of the mirror. Lucy Madison, the old Lucy Madison,
was on her way back.

I went downstairs and along to Connie's bedroom and
knocked on the door. "You nearly ready in there?" I asked.

"C'mon in," came Connie's voice. I opened the door.

"Wow," I said.

"Double wow," she replied.

"Where did you get that amazing vest?" Connie was wearing an ankle-length root-beer-colored crushed velvet dress
that fell like a tent. She had flat-heeled brown suede ankle
boots and a suede vest embroidered with myriad little colored beads in designs of flowers.

"Um…your friend Jacques brought it over."

"My what? You mean Jacques? Madeline's Jacques…
brought that over for you? He GAVE it to you?"

Connie looked a bit embarrassed. "Well, you know he does
computer stuff all over the place, eh? He told me he was
down at the Anthropology Museum and a friend of his works
there, and he said they get all this native stuff, people donate
it or they dig it up, and they got so much of it that some never
goes on display. Anyway, this guy was showing Jacques some
of the stuff they've got rotting away there and what does
Jacques go and do but talk the guy into giving this to him.

Said he knew someone who'd put it to good use. It had a little rip in the back but I was able to fix it."

"Jacques? My Jacques?"

Connie nodded.

"Not even my Jacques. He's Madeline's, I mean he's really hers. She's got him wrapped around her little finger and God help anyone who tries to pry him off."

"I didn't know that. I mean, I barely know the guy. But he seemed so set on giving me this thing I figured I would hurt his feelings if I said no. He's nice, I mean, really nice. His grandmother was a native from the Queen Charlottes. We kind of got talking about our grandmothers, you know…it was really neat to be able to talk about it, I mean the stuff you don't tell anybody. And it's weird, he keeps going on and on about the baby and wanting to feel it move in my stomach," said Connie.

I just stood there gaping. I was remembering back to university days. Someone, just a voice with no face by now, had once told me that Madeline had had two abortions without bothering to consult Jacques, and that he'd been quite upset both times.

Connie broke into my thoughts. "Listen. You know the guy better than I do. You can tell me if I'm stepping on any toes and I'll get out of the way."

"No. It's just taking a minute to sink in. Maybe he's finally going to be cured of Madeline." The thought cheered me up no end, as did the idea of having Jacques around more often. "Go ahead, Connie, step on all the toes you like. Life is short."

"And that is a great dress," she said. "You look so sophisticated. You're missing something though." She went to her dresser and opened the top drawer. "Jeremy gave me these a few Christmases ago. They're kind of neat but I didn't realize it at the time. I didn't think they were my style. But now I can see they have possibilities. They're red amber, antiques. Jeremy found them in some old pawn shop." It was a string of large beads the color of blood and a pair of matching earrings. Perfect fifties jewelry. "You have to wear them. They'll go great with the dress. Put your hair up though. Then you can see the earrings better."

I did as I was told and I have to say, the effect was very glamorous.

"Well," said Connie, "let's go and get this thing on the road."

The neon sign was lit and the awning down. I felt something swelling up and brimming over in me. Connie caught my eye and said, "It's a great feeling, isn't it." But I was so excited I couldn't answer.

She laughed her scraping laugh and slammed me on the back. "C'mon. It'll be fine."

We went through the open doors and into a small crowd of people. Leo was playing laid-back jazz improvisations. Sky rushed up to me. She was wearing her midnight-blue body-hugging Bella Montgomery dress. Max was pouring champagne and being responsible for the buffet, looking very suave in his tuxedo. Quite a few of the bikers and biker chicks were there, squirming and twitching in their formal clothes. A few people wandered in off the street. The party atmosphere crescendoed.

Candace arrived with David Yee. She was wearing a black long-sleeved dress that went down to her ankles, but at least her hair was down and she'd left the bifocals at home. I hadn't seen David in about seven years. He'd filled out. Where at university he had seemed quite boyish, now he looked like a man, and quite a good-looking man at that. I got the feeling from the way he looked at Candace, that she could have been bald and fifty pounds overweight, and he wouldn't have cared. He appeared to worship her. I went up and whispered in her ear, "Nice work, Candy. You're not doing badly for a mentally challenged person. Have you noticed the way he looks at you?" I made eyes in David's direction.

"We're just friends," said Candace.

"Yeah, right."

"No, really."

"Well, if he has it his way, you won't be for much longer. You lucky bitch."

"You think so?" She turned and looked over to the buffet, where David was receiving two glasses of champagne from Max. She shrugged and went over to join him.

Connie had said hello to everyone she had to say hello to and gone to sit on one of the couches.

It shocked me to think that there really wasn't anything for me to do except hobnob and have a good time. There were volunteers and friends doing all the dirty jobs now.

Jacques arrived still *sans* Madeline. He was wearing a black jacket and a T-shirt printed with the drawing of a dress shirt and bow tie. "Like it?" he asked me.

"Very chic," I said. He took off the jacket and showed me the back, which was printed with drawings of penguins. Then he grinned at me shyly and headed straight over to where Connie was sitting. And that's where they remained for the next hour. Talking, talking, talking.

My mother was the next to arrive. She was wearing her flamingo chiffon number and had misplaced my father again. I rushed up to her. "Where's Dad? The invitation was for the both of you."

"Your father's still orbiting around in outer space. Now he

thinks he has a mission bringing the Lord to the Hells Angels." My mother sighed.

I sighed, too. "Well, just as long as he doesn't get himself too badly beaten up."

"That remains to be seen," said my mother. "Now direct me to the champagne. I'm absolutely parched." She swooped over to where Max was pouring, grabbed a glass and picked up a conversation they'd been having the night of *Sing-a-long-a Sound of Music,* about a secret source of garden ornaments that only Max and a few curb-jockey collectors knew about.

Reebee arrived with a friend, a man dressed in the saffron robes of a Tibetan Buddhist, but who spoke with a very upper-crust British accent. She came up to me and gave me a big hug. She was wearing a scant peacock silk dress. Lots of amazingly youthful skin was showing. She had managed to maintain the tan she'd picked up on her trip south with Connie. She said, "Didn't I tell you, Lucy? This is just the beginning. You wait and see. Once it all starts to roll there's no stopping it. Fantastic dress." Her faith in Positive Thinking was positively unnerving.

When the Mortician arrived I ran to get a big drink. I'd invited him against my better judgment. But even a negative review from him had its benefits. People were always curious to see the corpse.

Leo's fingers were moving faster on the keyboard and he'd slipped into a catchy rhythmic bass. I could see people jiggling their feet and knees in time without even realizing it. The launderette started to pulsate.

When regular launderette customers showed up with laundry to do, I made sure they got champagne. Some were a little surprised to find so many people, but I told them it was part of the launderette's new look, that that was the idea, to party through their wash and rinse cycles, and all the way through to the fluff dry.

Over in Leo's corner, the music was shifting back and forth between techno-pop and classic rock 'n' roll, and people were starting to dance. I kept one eye on the Mortician as he paced back and forth in front of the paintings and made notes.

Finally, I stood back a little, taking in the colors, the paintings, the scent of food, the glowing lights, the elegantly dressed crowd. Then it hit me. We'd done it. We'd created Lucy's Launderette and it was perfect. I had an irresistible urge to share it all with Jeremy. I wove my way through the crowd to my new office. I unlocked the door and slipped inside.

"I wish you were here, Jeremy," I said to the little urn. "I wish so much that you were here. I think you'd like the way it's turned out. I mean, it's perfect. It really is."

Of course, the thing about perfection is that it just can't last.

I turned to look at my creation through the two-way mirror. My brother Dirk had made his entrance.

24

At first, Dirk wasn't noticed. He stood absolutely still in the doorway doing something odd with his eyes and face—it looked like isometric exercises. But then those people nearest to him did a double take and stepped back to clear a space for him. He was wearing his Our Man in Havana suit. It was very grimy. He also wore a red-and-white polka-dot bow tie. And he had a clean-shaven face. He resembled an overweight PeeWee Herman after a couple of weeks of binge drinking and sleeping in ditches. I barely breathed as I watched his next move.

He went over to the buffet, reached across the counter and snatched a full open bottle of champagne out of Max's hand. I have to say Max reacted well. He made a little gesture as if to say, "Be my guest." Dirk grabbed fistfuls of food and stuffed them into his already lurid pockets then began to chug-a-lug the champagne from the bottle. After that, the crowd was watching him, en masse.

I got out my cell phone and dialed the first of Sam's numbers. Locked inside my office with the two-way mirror, I wasn't as frantic as I would have been with Dirk in the same room.

The phone rang twice before a voice said, "Sam Trelawny here."

"I can't believe it. I got you the first time."

"Lucy!" he said.

"Listen, Sam. This may be it. Our big chance. Dirk is here at the launderette. It's the Grand Opening, you see, and wouldn't you know he'd have to come along just in time to wreck it."

"Okay, Lucy. Don't do anything. Don't scare him off. Just try to keep him there any way you can. I'll call the emergency unit and the police and I'll be at the launderette in about ten minutes. I'm in my car right now, so it just depends on traffic. We won't let you down. I promise. If I have to personally drag the unit there by force."

"Thanks, Sam." I hung up. Dirk was starting in on the women now. He approached the tallest ones and gave them his terrible sick leer, all teeth bared like a dog's snarl. They seemed to be able to handle themselves because whatever they were saying back to him was enough to put him off. He began to make the rounds. He fiddled with one of the computers, sat down and surfed the Net for a couple of minutes. Then he stood up and stuffed a chicken wing into his mouth. He crunched on that for a while then swallowed it, bones and all. He walked over to one of Candy's paintings, a buxom blonde half in and half out of a red Merry Widow, and sniggered. He made a move as if to straighten the picture but shifted it so that it was left hanging crookedly. By now, he had a captive audience and Leo had stopped playing.

Dirk then walked around to the mural and stared for a long time, taking occasional swigs from the champagne bottle. He cocked his head to one side and took something large out of his pocket. I was close enough to see that it was an aerosol can. He was poised to spray.

I raced out of the office and toward him, screaming, "Don't you dare do anything to that wall, Dirk. If you touch that wall, I swear, I'm going to kill you." I managed to snatch the spray can out of his hand.

He mimicked me in a high squeaky voice. "I'm going to kill you. Oooo. I'm so scared." That was when he brought out the gun. It was a black revolver of some kind, a heavy square thing. He pointed it straight at me and said, "No, Lucy, I think it's me that's going to kill you." Then he waved it around the room at the other people and said, "And nobody else move." I heard a girl's whimper in the far corner. My mind was speeding, remembering similar past incidents.

My voice came out high and raspy. "What do you think you're doing, Dirk? What do you want anyway?"

Dirk mimicked me again. "What do you think you're doing, Dirk? Dirk? Dirk? What do you want anyway?"

At that point, my mother whooshed like a giant flamingo to my side. Sky came with her.

My mother said, "Would you just stop it, the two of you? If you must argue, kindly do it outside or someplace private. Now, Dirk, just stop being so silly. Go and get a plate for those samosas. We're not living in a barnyard, after all." As if we were still a couple of kids. We both ignored her.

Dirk's face was maniacal. "I want to PARTY PARTY PARTY. But I can't. And it's your fault. Because you're in on it with the Russians. My informants told me you're in on it,

Lucy. I know you ordered them to put those microphones in my teeth. You and the dentist thought you could screw me around. I saw the look on his face when he said he was putting in some fillings. I know a Russian spy when I see one. And now the goddamn Russians are after me. They've been tailing me for weeks. They've got bugs everywhere." He whipped another chicken wing out of his pocket and waved it frantically. "These are bugged, too."

Sam had arrived. He'd been standing there in the doorway, listening, and I hadn't noticed him. He broke the silence by taking out his cell phone and punching in a number. Then in a very loud voice, he spoke Russian into the phone, "Lutcha pozdna chem neekogda. Dosvedanya Tavaritch."

He put the phone away and approached Dirk. "Well, Mr. Madison. I've just spoken with my people in Moscow. They were absolutely categorical. They say the Russians don't want you. The KGB were interested in you for a while but that was some time ago, and what with all the shifts in government, it seems that they no longer want anything to do with you. They're releasing you to the Canadians. I'll take that if you don't mind."

He reached across and took the gun from Dirk, looked into its barrel, and shot a squirt of water toward the ceiling. It was only then that I saw how gorgeous Sam was that evening. His face was clean-shaven, his long sandy hair tied back, and he wore a very expensive, charcoal-gray Armani suit.

"You mean the Canadiens," said Dirk.

"Oh Christ," I said, "He's sliding into hockey star mode."

Sky shook her head. "His what?"

"Any minute now he's going to tell us he's the goalie for the Montreal Canadiens."

"Pain in the butt, your brother, isn't he?" said Sky.

Sam seemed to be having a conversation with Dirk. He had managed to get him sitting down in a corner, facing away from the door, so that when the special emergency unit and the police arrived a few minutes later, Dirk was handcuffed and led away with very little fuss. Except for my mother. She was doing a lot of fussing. Scolding the police and telling them that Dirk was a good boy and that the handcuffs were evil and certainly not necessary.

Through the big front window, I watched them escort Dirk into the squad car, and drive away. I turned back and faced the crowd. My expression would have driven them all away if Max hadn't gallantly said, "Please, everybody. Let's not let a little old arrest ruin the evening. Everybody. Quickly. Fill your glasses. We need to make a toast." There was a general clamoring for glasses.

"To Lucy's Launderette," said Max.

"To Lucy's Launderette," echoed the crowd.

We all drank and Leo began to play again. I was feeling shaky all over after my confrontation with Dirk. I headed for the office. I needed to have a few minutes in a private corner, to collect myself.

I was leaning against the bar, doing a pretty good job of holding back the floodwaters, when a voice came from behind me. "Lucy."

It was Sam. He came up to me and touched my shoulder. I fought the urge to burst into tears. Sam must have sensed my mood because he reached out and put his arms around me. A lone tear trickled down my cheek. "Allergies," I sniffed.

"I know those kinds of allergies well," he laughed, and pulled me closer. "It's okay to cry. These are tense situations. When it's over, you're so relieved you just want to collapse. I've seen it time and time again. But we can see the light at the end of the tunnel now. And you know, it's not too late.

They might change their minds. Maybe I can still fix something up with the Russians, trade Dirk to them for one of theirs."

I started to laugh. He took a handkerchief from one of his pockets and began, with slow gentle movements, to wipe the few tears from my face. He stopped and we stared at each other, both of us a little astonished but knowing what had to come next. And then his mouth was on mine and he was kissing me and I was kissing him back. His body was pressed close and it was deliciously hard and his woodsy spicy scent was back and starting to make my heart beat faster and then I kept remembering the brunette in the airport and Francesca de la Hoity Toity in the bathroom at Rogues' Gallery and I knew I should be pushing him away and was on the verge of doing it when a scream like that of an animal about to be slaughtered made us pull away from each other.

"What the hell was that? I better go and see what it was," I said.

Sam followed me out into the launderette.

A small group of people was clustered around Connie. She was half sitting, half lying on the edge of the couch where she'd been all evening. On the floor at her feet was a puddle of water.

Jacques had his hands in his pockets and was bouncing up and down on the balls of his feet. "Shit. It's coming, Lucy."

"It can't come. It's too early," I protested.

"If she says the baby's coming, it's coming. I offered to take her to the hospital but she says there's no time. Maybe I should call an ambulance, eh?" I'd never seen Jacques so nervous or excited.

Connie let out another agonized howl and then a series of short moans.

Sky said, "Isn't there supposed to be more warning than

this? I've always heard of women making the bed and doing the dishes after their water broke. And where's Reebee? She's supposed to be the big birthing fanatic and where is she when we need her? She knows what to do in these situations."

Max said, "Reebee slipped away just before Dirk's arrival. Her friend needed a ride back to his ashram."

"Better call the ambulance right away," I said.

"I'll do it," said Jacques.

But Connie wailed, "There isn't time. It's coming. I can feel the little bugger coming. Aaaiieeeeeeeeeeeeeeee."

"Let's move her into the back room," said Sam. "It's a little more private."

Connie read my thoughts and said in a strained, panting voice, "I'll ruin the new carpet."

"Don't worry about it," I said. "There are lots of old towels in the lost-and-found box. We can put them on the floor."

Max said, "I'm sure we can get some people to volunteer some cleaner newer towels."

"I feel sick. I feel like I'm going to throw up," said Connie.

Sam said, "Somebody go and get some ice for her to suck on. Can you walk?" he asked Connie.

"I guess if I have to," she said.

Sam took off his Armani jacket, put it over a chair and rolled up the sleeves of his white dress shirt. Then he said, "Okay, Connie, let's go," and helped her to her feet. He got her into the office and onto the couch there and towels were placed all around.

He whispered to me, "Help her to get comfortable, would you, Lucy?" I gave him an "Are you crazy?" kind of look.

He said, "As comfortable as possible under the circumstances." Then in a louder voice, "I know it sounds like a cliché, but could we get some boiling water here? Or something to disinfect with? For my hands?"

I gazed at Sam. He was looking more and more delicious with every minute that passed. "You've done this before I take it?"

"Well, it was part of my basic first aid training. But, yes. It has happened to me before. I need to clean my hands."

"How about alcohol?" asked Sky.

"What kind?"

Sky went over and opened the bar. "Let's see what we have here. There's a bottle of gin, a bottle of vodka and a bottle of Scotch."

"The vodka should do the trick. Lucy, you wash your hands, too. Another pair of hands never hurts."

Sky got the bottle and poured some vodka over his hands and then over mine.

"I don't wanna do this," screamed Connie. She had managed to crawl off the couch and was on all fours on the floor.

"That's okay, Connie," said Sam, "if you feel better pushing in a different position go ahead. But you do have to push."

Sky looked at Sam approvingly, looked at me and gave me a thumbs-up signal.

"I want it to go away," screamed Connie, and then, "Wherever you are, Jeremy, I hate you, you bastard." She pulled herself back onto the edge of the couch in a half-sitting position.

"Oh dear," I muttered.

"Never mind. It's the angry hormones. They're supposed to do that, make her so mad she just wants to get it out of her. All right, Connie," said Sam, his voice taking on a hard edge, "no more Mr. Nice Guy. Now push, goddammit. Wait for the contraction and push with it." Sam was crouched on the floor beneath Connie.

"Aaaiiieee," yelled Connie.

"That's it, I can see the top of the baby's head. Push. PUSH."

There were ten more minutes of big league screaming before the baby's head crowned.

"That's it. It's got black hair just in case you want to know, and not very much of it. One last big one," said Sam, "that's all you need."

Connie gave one huge terrible cry. Sam had the head of the baby and a second later, it was sliding out into his hands. "Lucy, come over here. Hold the baby. Here, use that towel. Don't move." He leaned forward over Connie and pressed on her stomach violently. There was another gush and Sam had blood all down the front of his shirt and on his pants and shoes. "The afterbirth," he said. "Lie down and relax, Connie. Now, Lucy, place the baby on Connie's stomach." I did as I was told.

Connie's expression was indescribable. Dazed? Tired? Exalted?

Jacques had been watching at a distance, lurking near the doorway in case he had to escape, silently hovering between fainting and fascination. "Is it a boy or a girl?" he asked in a tiny exhausted voice.

25

"It's a boy," I said.

An angry red jowly little face, like an old man's, with a few scraps of black hair and very black eyes, blinked at us all and then began to cry the strangled indignant cry of newborn babies.

"Isn't he beautiful?" said Connie.

We could hardly tell her the truth, that he looked like a cross between a marmoset monkey and Winston Churchill. We all echoed, "Beautiful. Just gorgeous."

Jacques reappeared again. "The ambulance is here."

"Perfect timing," said Sam, staring down at his ruined clothes.

Jacques ushered the paramedics into the office. They took over quickly, checking the baby and Connie. Connie was made to lie on the stretcher with the baby in her arms. They were bustled out through the eager crowd, out the front door and off to the hospital, choruses of "way ta go, Connie" following in their wake.

Sky snapped to life and said to Sam, "Take those clothes off right now. I'm very good with stains."

Sam stared at her wanly.

"Go on," she said.

"Yes, go on, Sam," I said. I went over to the lost-and-found box and began to burrow through it. "I'm sure we can find something for you to put on. Something in checks. Or a nice plaid maybe."

Sam gave me a wry look and began to unbutton his shirt reluctantly. I didn't hurry. When I finally came up with a slightly holey men's T-shirt and some baggy drawstring cotton pants, I was slow about handing them over. I was checking out every inch of his body. And it was a very firm body that was standing there in socks and briefs. Washboard stomach, muscular arms and legs, and broad chest covered with a pelt of golden hairs. He gave Sky his clothes and she rushed away to work her stain-removing magic.

Sam had just finished yanking the other clothes on when Max poked his head through the door. Max did a double take, smiled at the both of us and said, "There's a man asking for you, Lucy. Should I send him in?"

"A man? For me?"

"Look for yourself." Max indicated the two-way window. Pacing nearby was Jeremy's lawyer, Doug.

"Yeah, tell him to come in," I said. Doug appeared in the doorway, very elegant in a dark blue suit. I went up to him and shook his hand. "I'm glad to see you made it, Doug. So now you've seen the launderette."

"Congratulations, Lucy. Jeremy would be proud of you all. I'm sure of it." Then he looked beyond me and over to Sam.

"Sam," he said, his voice full of surprise.

"Hi, Dad."

"Dad?" I said. "Doug's your father?"

"Yup," said Sam.

"But he's Jeremy's lawyer."

Sam said, "It's right there on the letterhead. Take a look at it sometime. Hackett, Steel and Trelawny. He's the Douglas Trelawny."

No wonder he'd seemed familiar. It was Sam I was seeing in Douglas Trelawny, not the man who'd been at the funeral.

Doug said, "We missed you at the dinner tonight, son."

"Yeah, I know, Dad. I was on my way when I got a call from Lucy here."

"I imagined something of the sort must have happened. They were moving pretty slowly, only up to the appetizers when I left. Thought I'd just pop round here and see what this young lady has dreamt up. I was curious. I must say, I'm impressed."

"She's impressive, our Lucy Madison," said Sam.

And that little word of possession, *our,* only one step away from the word *my,* washed over my body like a warm glow, made all my extremities tingle, made me wonder what it would be like to be possessed by Sam Trelawny. If anybody had looked at me with infrared viewers in that moment, I would have blinded them.

Douglas Trelawny picked a bit of fluff off his suit and said, "Well, I better get back. You know those Foundation dinners. They may be endless but it doesn't look too good if you're not there for the speeches."

Sam smiled and nodded. "Bye, Dad."

"Drop round whenever you feel like it, Doug," I said.

"Nice to see you again, Lucy. We'll be expecting great things from Lucy's Launderette."

"I don't know about great. I'd be satisfied with good.

Thanks again for coming." Something tugged at my heart as I shook his hand again. I was looking for Jeremy in him. No doubt about it. And he must have known because he held my hand a little longer and gave it an extra squeeze.

When his father had gone, Sam stood up and said, "There wouldn't happen to be a little of that food left, would there? A few of those nibbly things I saw on the way in? I could eat a couple of head of cattle."

"So you're not a vegetarian, I take it." It was important to get these things established right away. The first thing on the human survival list is food. Sex comes after that and then comes more food and more sex. If I was going to consider Sam as potential boyfriend material, I had to know exactly what we'd be licking off each other's fingers.

"Not likely," said Sam, "A cow is beef to me, a nice juicy steak with legs."

"I'm sorry. Stupid me. You were on your way to a dinner when I called you…"

"The Foundation dinner. They're dull but there's usually lots of food. I was kind of counting on eating at least once today."

"The Foundation…" I said. Something was starting to click over in my mind.

"It's more my father's thing…" said Sam.

"Wait a minute." Once again, my one-track mind had kept me from seeing what was in front of me. "Trelawny," I said limply. "That wouldn't be the Trelawny Foundation, would it?"

The biggest donations in the city. Name at the top of every list of contributors. For the SPCA, the Symphony Orchestra, the Art Gallery, the Women's Shelter, the Hunger Project, Greenpeace, the Heart Foundation, the Cancer Foundation…the list went on and on. In these parts, it was a name like Rockefeller or Mellon or Carnegie.

Sam looked at the floor and then at me. It was a guilty look, as though I'd caught him at something.

"Oh dear," I said. "If you're…a Foundation Trelawny…of THE Trelawnys…I mean…then that means…that your family…is very…very…rich." The last word barely came out. There were no vowels left, just consonants.

"'Fraid so," said Sam.

It shouldn't have made a difference, his being one of the "Foundation" Trelawnys, but all of a sudden I was afraid. I'd never known anybody that came from old money, and piles of it. And I'd certainly never had a rich boyfriend. But then I looked at Sam in that holey T-shirt and ugly drawstring pants and it was easy to say, "C'mon, let's go find some food."

Max had sagely held back a platter of goodies. He was hiding it under the counter. He saw me coming, and spotted the way I was frowning at the picked-over trays sitting on the countertop. He pulled out his hoard.

"You're a genius, Max," I said.

"I know," he sighed.

We took a table in the corner. The crowd had finally started to thin out a bit and the atmosphere was relaxed. Leo had lapsed back into easy jazz.

Sam gobbled a few appetizers and then said, "So now tell me, Lucy, who is Connie exactly? It's nice to know whose baby you're helping to deliver."

I laughed. "Connie was my grandfather's girlfriend. This place is hers now. Jeremy, my grandfather, died a few months ago."

"So the baby is your uncle," he mused.

"Uh-huh."

"That's pretty interesting," he said.

"My grandfather had some kind of tumor. I figure he must have been pretty sick. He drove his Harley into a ravine."

"I'm sorry."

"So am I. I miss him so much. Did you know that your father met Jeremy in a cancer clinic a few years ago? That's how he became his lawyer." I was probing. "I'm assuming that your dad's okay now. He looks very fit."

"Yeah," said Sam, "he's had a clean slate for about seven years. Gave us all a pretty big scare for a while there. I was back East fooling around at the time."

"Fooling around?"

"I was trying to break into show biz, doing a bit of theater, singing with a band."

"Really?"

"Yeah. I was just playing. As I say, fooling around. It wasn't really for me," he said.

My hand was placed flat on the table. He started to trace around my fingers with one of his, then slid his hand over mine. I didn't change my attitude though. I wanted to hear the whole story, ugly bits and all.

"Why wasn't it for you?" I asked.

"Everybody's on an ego trip. Haven't you seen the way actors are always catching themselves in mirrors and checking themselves out. It's me, me, me all the time. Maybe my parents did a better job than I knew. I kept having the feeling that I was useless to society, that I ought to be doing something to help other people and not just thinking of myself all the time."

"That's very noble," I said.

"Yeah. I'm a noble sort of guy. Modest, too."

I laughed.

"Well, then, Dad announced that he had this tumor and the rug came out from under me. I was living with Jennifer, my girlfriend at the time. She suddenly got a bad case of Family Values and suggested we get married and move back West.

She knew I wanted to be closer to my father. I should have smelled a rat right away."

"Sorry?"

"Jennifer wasn't really the family type. I didn't find out till much later though."

"What was she interested in?"

"Money."

"Oh dear," I said.

"Yeah. I think she figured Dad would kick the bucket and there'd be something huge in it for her. A few of the Trelawny millions. Suddenly wanting to get married like that. When we moved back here, I made sure that life stayed pretty humble. You have to see the way my parents live to understand this. Conspicuous consumption was never really a theme in my family. The idea my father always promoted was that if you're lucky enough to have money then you try to do something useful with it. That's not to say we don't have fun from time to time.

"I went back to university to get the courses I needed for social work and Jennifer mooned around wondering when she was going to see some of the Trelawny loot. It was a big shock for her when my dad came through his treatment and survived." Sam laughed bitterly.

"So what you're telling me," I said, "is that you're a stingy SOB."

"Only when the person trying to pry open my wallet has no ethics."

"You're being awfully hard on poor Janet."

"Jennifer. She was a better actress than I took her for. She'll be able to mold herself to the next man and maybe he'll appreciate her more than I did. When I put her on the plane for Toronto, I felt like a thousand tons had been lifted."

"That day in the airport…I saw you kissing a beautiful brunette. Was that…?"

"Jennifer. I couldn't let her go with all those sour grapes. After she trashed the house, I made a deal with her, a cash deal. It was no skin off my nose. I have a few good investments. I just regret…"

"What do you regret?"

"That I've wasted so much time." He reached out and touched an escaped strand of my hair.

We stayed in that corner all night talking about our hopes. He asked me what I'd be painting next and that took us into new territory of art and music and books. He had slowly shifted around so that we were sitting close together side by side. He held my hand but that was all. Very innocent. I was so content I could have stayed like that forever.

My friends had come over to say goodbye one by one and I'd barely been aware of them. Bob was the last to leave and said he'd take care of things the following morning, that I didn't need to worry. The place was empty and it was starting to grow light when Sam stood up brusquely and said, "Listen, Lucy, I better get down to the police station and find out what they've done with Dirk. There's going to be a load of follow-up and paperwork and bureaucratic crap to deal with. I'll talk to you soon." He gave me a lingering kiss on the mouth, gathered up his ruined clothes, said, "I'll call you," and was gone.

The next day, Sky phoned me. "Have you seen the paper?"

"No. My eyes are too sore for reading. I didn't just drown my sorrows, I pickled them, too. It was those two enormous gin and tonics I drank as I watched the dawn. Alone, I should add."

"This isn't over that Sam guy, I hope?"

"He could have stayed longer."

"No, he couldn't, Lucy. He came when you called, he had your brother arrested, he delivered a baby, and he ruined an Armani suit. Well, almost ruined. I think I managed to salvage it. That's enough for one evening. What did you expect? That after all that, he was going to throw you down on the new carpet and have passionate, uncontrolled sex with you?"

I said, wistfully, "It would have finished off the evening nicely."

"Well, I know it's fun to be an obsessive compulsive but some people have other schedules. And what about all those other women you said he had. You don't want another Paul Bleeker, do you?"

"Paul Bleeker never kissed me like that. And those other women are accounted for. At least I think they are."

"Forget about all of them. You wanna know what the Mortician said about your show?"

"What?"

"Well, the title was 'Grandma Moses Goes Punk.' There were only a few lines in the night-life section."

"With all those notes he took?" I said.

"Who knows? To paraphrase, he said the show was puerile and apparently lacking in technique, though whether this was intentional he couldn't say. The show is curious enough to merit a quick visit, but not if you don't already happen to be in that part of town."

"Well," I said, "he hates everything and everyone. Coming from him, that's almost high praise. Usually he tells people not to bother at all."

"That's what I thought, too. Well, listen, I'll let you go. You've got a business to run."

And business was good. Candace was beginning to snap

back to her old self like the elastic girl I'd always thought she
was. After the first week, she managed the cappuccino bar
like she'd been born to it. Bob and I shared shifts with her.
Bob had a clever way of hauling himself on to a high stool
so that he could work all the machines.

They let Connie out of the hospital forty-eight hours
after they'd taken her in. There were never really any doubts
that if the baby was a boy, he'd be named Jeremy, so Jeremy
was the name she put on his birth certificate.

Connie and Little Jeremy took up residence in the launderette during the daytime. This thrilled the group of Italian
widows who came to do their laundry and criticize our cappuccinos. Those women could spot a baby carriage at twenty
miles and as soon as they spotted Little Jeremy's, they were
in the baby's face. Connie got a lot of advice on how to in-
sure his well-being, medieval advice involving hot peppers,
wild boars' tusks and holy water. When he wasn't feeding,
the baby slept in the pram in the back room. Connie napped
on the couch when he slept. She came to life for any problems or inquiries about paintings.

In the first week after the opening, Connie sold two pieces
of mine for much more than they were worth. It was hard
letting go of my paintings like that. My children. I was
tempted to hire a detective and find out where they'd been
taken, who their new parents were, how they were being
hung, how they were being treated. But Connie said I had
something to learn about success, that it sometimes comes
with a feeling of loss. I thought that was pretty funny coming from Connie, somebody who really didn't have a lot of
experience with success. But then I thought about it a bit
harder. Maybe we're all doing what we intend to do, and
sometimes, for a reason that's much bigger than us, or just

too difficult to comprehend, we choose to live what looks like the life of a loser. Maybe it's just a way of getting from point A to point B.

When Connie realized how many people were going to be there for the music evenings, she got agitated.

"They can't just sit there, listening. They've got to consume, consume, consume."

I said, "Whoa, Connie."

And she said, "Whoa, nothing. This is a business. We gotta run it like a business." So she added some fruit juices and Perrier water to the menu, and got the Hit and Run girls making more ambitious ready-to-eat food, pizza by the slice, foccaccias stuffed with brie and prosciutto, spinach pies and a dense vegetable minestrone soup.

The second big music night was two Saturdays following the opening. The group of musicians that Leo sent us came from the college where he occasionally taught piano. They were serious classical string students by day, but by night they liked to cut loose with their own mix of rocky bluegrass hip-hop. Very weird sound but a big hit with the evening crowd at the launderette.

Sky and Max came down that evening. At the musicians' halftime, I invited them both into the office for a drink. Sky was obsessed with the two-way mirror. She never took her eyes off it. She loved to spy on people. So of course, she was the first to spot Nadine with Paul Bleeker.

"My God, would you look who just slithered in? It's the woman with the Stretch 'n' Sew skin and her maintenance man." I looked to where she was pointing. Nadine was dressed in black. She planted herself in front of each painting and stared, her expression growing as black as her clothing. Paul was beside her. He'd lost weight and looked wasted. He kept wiping his nose with his sleeve and glancing behind him. "Just look at him. He's on a skiing weekend. The old coke nose is unmistakeable, a dead giveaway. Now, I know you don't like reading the paper, Lucy, but you'd learn all sorts of interesting things if you did."

"Like?"

"Well, it looks like your friend Paul is going to have to come up with a lot of hard cash. He's being investigated for tax evasion."

I said, "It's not as though he can sell a lot of his work. So many of his pieces were conceptual or comestible."

"Exactly," said Sky, very smugly. "And I imagine that's why he has to stay stuck to Nadine and her purse strings, and do her bidding."

What a chilling thought.

Sam didn't call. I'd been counting the days that had passed since the night of the opening. Seventeen. Seventeen days of staring at the launderette door and hoping he'd hurry up and darken it. Seventeen nights of being woken in the dark by a yowling infant and wondering who Sam was with in that moment. Lying there in the dark, my mind skidded out in all directions. Maybe I had it all wrong. Maybe he was a completely different kind of man from the one he appeared to be. Probably an octopus man, the kind that stares you solemnly in the eyes while his tentacles are clamping on to eight other women at the same time.

And then he reappeared. Three weeks after our last meeting. It was a slow lunchtime and he was in a hurry. There were no kisses and he didn't touch me once, but he smiled a lot and said, "Just wanted to see how you were doing." He stayed long enough to drink an espresso. Well, as you probably know, any self-respecting espresso drinker downs that little shot of caffeine in one gulp, and that's what he did. And then he was gone again. I had a terrible sensation of déjà vu.

But then he came in again two days later. He ordered a sandwich and a Perrier and said, "Can you sit down and keep me company, Lucy? I've got fifteen whole minutes." He spent the whole time giving me the rundown on Dirk and then as he was standing up to leave, he said, "I'll drop by again in a couple of days. I should have a little more time." He touched me on the cheek and hurried out.

As soon as he was gone, I called Sky. "I'm depressed," I whined.

"That Sam guy, right?"

"Right. He's probably gay. You know, one of those married gay guys, just afraid to come out of the closet."

"Naw," said Sky, "Listen. Max is in Seattle. You want me to come over tonight? I'll bring a couple of videos."

"And some of those Belgian chocolates," I said.

"I would have thought you might never want to taste chocolate again."

"I'm over that. I've got a new set of problems."

"What?"

"If Sam doesn't touch me again soon, I'm going to have to attack him."

But the rest of the summer passed like that. Sam's short but frequent visits, bringing gossip or news or some tidbit of trivia. He was becoming a familiar fixture. We traded books and CDs, he talked about some of his cases, I talked about paintings and new ideas. I resigned myself to the fact that Sam had changed his mind, that he was not interested in me, not in THAT way, at any rate.

We were becoming friends. Of a sort. Real friends would have gone somewhere, done things together. We never saw anything but the inside of the launderette. But I got used to it. Not having to worry about whether I'd shaved my legs or put on the right underwear. I could look forward to his noncommittal fly-by visits and be completely relaxed.

Whenever I thought about the fact that I had no boyfriend, painting consoled me. When I painted, there was no sense of lack or loss. It buoyed me up and kept me going. And helping to look after Little Jeremy took up the rest of the time.

Then one day in late September, in the afternoon, I was up on a chair refilling the soap machine when Candace came over and whispered, "He's been sitting there for the last ten minutes just staring at you." She jerked her head in the direction of the cappuccino bar. Sam was sitting there, leaning against the wall, blue-jeaned legs and cowboy boots stretched out, watching me. There was something different about him. He had a sleepy ruffled look. He took a long time standing up. He came over to me and said, "You free tonight, Lucy?"

I wanted to scream, "I've been free for the last sixty-five nights but who's counting?"

"Depends when," I said.

"Eight o'clock. I wondered if you might come to the Rain Room with me. For dinner."

I wanted to ask, "Where's the hitch?" but said, "I think I can manage it." My heart was racing. Only a couple of shopping hours left.

"I'll pick you up at seven-thirty. It's funny, I don't even know where you live." IT'S NOT FUNNY, I wanted to scream. But I gave him my address. As soon as he was gone, I called Sky.

"This is it, Sky, it's the big countdown. I've got a date, a real date with Sam Trelawny. The Rain Room. What the hell am I going to wear?"

"That's easy," said Sky, "your red dress, of course."

Sam sat across from me in the Rain Room. We had finished dining on crab cocktail, steak and lobster, rugola salad, asparagus, and wild rice and mushrooms. Half-finished dishes of strawberries and cream were in front of us. We sipped a chilled Sauterne.

Sam was casual chic, black dress jacket and pants, white shirt and no tie. He said, "I had to backpedal with you, Lucy."

"I didn't notice," I lied. "Painting takes up all my energy these days."

"Uh-huh. I finally got some holidays," he said, "I've been putting them off for months. Up till now, it's been all emergencies. I have two and a half more weeks left. Caught up on a lot of missed sleep the last couple of days."

"You look more rested," I said.

"Holding back can be a good thing," he said. "It makes the senses more acute." He reached across the table and took my hand. "I've got a friend who runs a seaplane between here and Victoria and I've got a booking at the Empress Hotel. There's just enough time to throw some things together and make the last flight. Will you come with me, Lucy?"

I nodded.

Sam shut the door, locked it and put the key on the bureau. It was a suite, a whole suite in the Empress Hotel, looking out onto the inner harbor. I went over to the window. Lights glittered across the water. From the sailboats below, I could hear the cowbell-like clanging of lines against masts. The wind was coming up.

Sam came and stood beside me at the window. "If it blows any harder, we may be stranded here."

His arms were around me.

I pulled away. "I'm not sure I'm ready for this."

"Oh, I wasn't touching YOU. I was admiring the fabric. I meant to tell you before, the night of the launderette's opening, that's a very pretty red dress. Now I just have to figure out how to get you out of it."

"I'm really not…"

"Not what?"

"Ready."

"Ready for what?" Sam faked innocence as he fingered the neckline of my dress.

"Another first time." My face felt hot.

He continued to move toward me and I continued to back away.

"We'll just forget about the first time and skip to the second then."

"Er…" I'd reached the wall and had nowhere to go. He rested his hands above me on the wall and pressed in close.

"Is there some problem?" he asked. "No. Don't tell me. I know. You're afraid all our children will look like your brother and think they're superheroes. Sorry. Low blow. Feel free to hit me if it makes you feel better."

I raised my hand to swat him. He caught it, turned it over and kissed its palm. He went on holding it for a minute then led me over to the couch.

"It's not that," I said, looking away and into the flames that leapt in the fireplace.

He didn't let go of my hand. "Okay, let me see. You already

have a child locked in your basement, fruit of a relationship with a famous politician?"

I shook my head.

"An alcoholic husband locked in your attic?"

"Nooooo."

"A girlfriend?"

"Not likely."

"You're under contract to a big studio and are only allowed to be seen with the star of their choice."

"That might be interesting."

"Go on. Who is he? Tell me about the other guy. There's always another guy lurking around somewhere. Just open up your emotional baggage and dump its contents all over me. I can take it." He assumed a Christ-like stance, arms outstretched.

"Well, it's just that…I'd really hate for something to start and then find out it was all a lot of hot air, a big nothing, that the initial potential wasn't…er…fulfilled. I mean I went through this already this year…and he was just such a disappointment."

"In what way exactly? I want details," Sam said. By then he had moved off the couch and was kneeling on one knee, looking up at me, green eyes, long sleek sandy hair and very predatory smile.

"Well, really, in every way, when I think about it, and especially in THAT way." I raised my eyebrows.

"Oh, THAT way," said Sam, slowly. "Well, I don't know about you, Lucy. But for me, it's like falling off a log when you're with the right person. Money-back guarantee if you're disappointed. Oh. And I should mention that I believe in a global approach," said Sam, taking off one of my shoes then the other and massaging first my feet then moving up my legs. "No stone should be left unturned. I think the most practical thing at this stage would be to caress every part of your body very, very slowly. What do you think, Miss Madison?"

I tried to think of something smart to say but all that came out was "Ahhh."

He stopped.

I came to my senses.

He moved back up on the couch beside me, leaned back and stared.

"What did you stop for? And don't look at me that way. It's unnerving," I said.

"What do you want me to do?" he asked earnestly.

"I want you to kiss me." I hate having to beg.

"Are you sure?"

I nodded. He leaned in slowly and pressed his lips against mine. A little after that I started losing all sense of time and all of our movements became liquid. There was an unzipping sound and his hands were on my shoulders, gently pulling the sleeves of my dress down.

"Oh God. Black lace… Do you know what black lace can do to a guy? Are you trying to drive me crazy, Lucy?"

"Maybe."

"Definitely."

"I wore it because I want to ask a little favor of you."

"Anything for a woman in black lace."

"It's a little unusual."

"I try not to limit myself…in any activity."

"That's a…ahhh…oh wow…that's an amazing…ahhh…a FANTASTIC thing you're…ahhhh…doing with your…oooo…hands…ahhh…I just want to ask you to…no, no don't stop doing it…ah…I just want to know…while you're doing that…could you sing?"

That was a couple of months ago. Lucy's Launderette is a going concern these days and the artwork is actually selling.

We've had a couple of write-ups in some small but important art journals and a gallery owner from Seattle sent me an e-mail last week asking me if I wanted to have a show there.

Sky and Max are planning a trip to Europe together. I'm absolutely green with envy. Neither of them want to live together. They've decided their relationship works better with clandestine overtones so they're maintaining the status quo.

Jacques has been hanging around our house a lot. He and Connie seem to be getting along pretty well. They can be together for hours without saying anything or exchanging a word and each seems to know what the other person is thinking. It's positively creepy. Oh, and Jacques is teaching Little Jeremy to wiggle his eyebrows up and down like Groucho Marx. He says it's an indispensable life skill.

My father has gone home to my mother, although sometimes he disappears mysteriously for a few days at a time. We figure he's out there on his Harley trying to bring God to the underbelly of Vancouver.

Sam has handed Dirk's case over to Francesca. He doesn't want to mix business with pleasure or have any conflicts of interest. And Francesca does seem very taken with Dirk's case, though not in an entirely professional way. Dirk isn't too bad-looking when he isn't rapid-cycling. But it still makes me giggle. Maybe we really do get what we deserve.

Although that's not the scariest part in all of this. Do you want to know what the really scary thing is? It's Sam's biggest defect, that is, his determination to make everyone get along. It's me and Sam, my mother and my father, Dirk and Francesca St. Claire de la Roche, all down at the FOBIA social doing the butterfly waltz. Now THAT is a scary sight.

Name & Address Withheld

Jane Sigaloff

Life couldn't be better for Lizzie Ford. Not only
does she have a great job doling out advice on the
radio, but now she has a new love interest *and* a
new best friend. Unfortunately she's about to learn
that they're husband and wife. Can this expert on
social etiquette keep the man, her friend *and* her
principles? Find out in *Name & Address Withheld,*
a bittersweet comedy of morals and manners.

RED
DRESS
I N K
TM

Visit us at www.reddressink.com